A DISTANT DAWN

'How can you still love him after what I've told you about him?'

'Even if that horrible story is true, and it seems strange that you waited this long to relate it, you still don't know all the facts, Jane. You can't; you weren't there.'

Exasperated, Jane gripped the rail and stared out across the rolling expanse of blue-grey sea. 'I waited this long to tell you because I'd given him my word I would never tell anyone. When I made that vow I still believed that blood was thicker than water and I owed him unquestioning loyalty. I've broken my word now because I care about you, Claudia. He'll destroy you; I know it.'

'You're wrong, so wrong. I don't care what happened in the past. That's over and done with. It's now, today, that counts.'

'Nobody ever escapes from the past. All of us are shaped by our history, and our past can come back to haunt us when we least expect it.'

**Also by the same author,
and available from NEL:**

Journeys of the Heart
Far Horizons

About the author

Katherine Sinclair is the pseudonym of Joan
Dial, who used to be president of the Romantic
Novelists Association in America. She was born
in Liverpool but now lives in California with her
husband.

A Distant Dawn

Katherine Sinclair

NEW ENGLISH LIBRARY
Hodder and Stoughton

Copyright © 1991 by Katherine Sinclair

First published in the USA in 1991 by Berkley Books

First published in Great Britain in 1991 by Judy Piatkus (Publishers) Ltd

New English Library paperback edition 1992

The right of Katherine Sinclair to be identified as the author of this work has been asserted by her in accordance with the Copyright, Designs and Patents Act 1988.

Printed and bound in Great Britain for Hodder and Stoughton Paperbacks, a division of Hodder and Stoughton Ltd., Mill Road, Dunton Green, Sevenoaks, Kent TN13 2YA (Editorial Office: 47 Bedford Square, London WC1B 3DP) by Clays Ltd., St Ives plc.

British Library C.I.P.

A CIP catalogue record for this title is available from the British Library

ISBN 0-450-57104-1

A Distant Dawn

❧ Prologue ❧

May 7, 1915

JANE WEATHERLY stepped out onto the promenade deck of the liner and paused, breathing the fresh tang of brine and sea-washed air. She blinked in the sunlight as her gaze searched among the strolling passengers.

She saw Claudia almost immediately, leaning on the polished rail, her platinum hair blowing in a mild breeze that also stirred the silken fur of the sable coat in which she huddled. Claudia always felt cold, even in warm sunshine.

Dreading the inevitable confrontation, Jane walked as quickly as the rolling deck would allow. Claudia looked up as she approached, a mixture of apology and defiance written on her lovely face.

Jane steeled herself to withstand any tearful pleading. A head taller and a stone heavier than her fragile friend, as well as being blessed with perfect health and far greater stamina, Jane was well aware that in the past Claudia had prevailed in an argument by the simple tactic of making her feel like a bully.

"Oh, dear," Claudia said miserably as Jane reached her side. "Must we discuss him now? I'm not feeling well."

"Look, Claudia—that smudge of green over there is the Irish coast. We're almost home. We have to settle this before we land."

Claudia turned drowning blue-violet eyes imploringly toward Jane. "Can't you try to understand? I love him more than life."

"How can you still love him after what I've told you about him?"

"Even if that horrible story is true, and it seems strange that you waited this long to relate it, you still don't know all the facts, Jane. You can't; you weren't there."

Exasperated, Jane gripped the rail and stared out across the rolling expanse of blue-gray sea. "I waited this long to tell you because I'd given him my word I would never tell anyone. When I made that vow I still believed that blood was thicker than water and I owed him unquestioning loyalty. I've broken my word now because I care about you, Claudia. He'll destroy you; I know it."

"You're wrong, so wrong. I don't care what happened in the past. That's over and done with. It's now, today, that counts."

"Nobody ever escapes from the past. All of us are shaped by our history, and our past can come back to haunt us when we least expect it."

Claudia placed a small, cool hand on Jane's arm. "Jane, if you're not on my side I don't know what I shall do. Please, let's not quarrel. I can't bear it. I need you to be my ally when Leith finds out I defied him and came home."

Jane's breath escaped in a long sigh. "We should have let him know we were sailing. He'll be furious when we simply arrive without any warning."

"I don't care," Claudia declared recklessly. "He robbed me of all these months when I could have been with my love."

"Come on, Claudia! Your 'love' didn't even bother to write to you for nearly nine months."

"But his wire explained why . . ."

"And you believe him? Oh, Lord, I wish I could talk some sense into you."

They were silent for a moment, aware of the sway of the deck, of the endless vista of the ocean and the murmurs of conversation as other passengers strolled by.

Claudia shivered suddenly and clutched her fur coat closer to her slender body. Her translucent complexion grew even paler than usual, and she bit down on her lower lip.

"What is it?" Jane asked at once. "Are you afraid to face Lord Marrick? I won't desert you, Claudia, I promise."

"No, it isn't that. I suddenly felt . . . Oh, God, I haven't experienced that particular feeling for years. She reached for me again . . . just now."

Jane felt a chill. "Your ghost mother? You haven't mentioned her for years." She spoke more brusquely than she intended, inwardly castigating herself for saying that the past could return to haunt the unwary. That remark had undoubtedly precipitated Claudia's relapse into her childhood fantasy.

Claudia seemed to have frozen in an attitude of utter terror, her lips parted as though to scream, her hands white-knuckled as they gripped the wooden rail of the ship. She was staring wide-eyed at the churning ocean.

Out of the corner of her eye Jane caught a slight movement on the sea's surface. A tiny wake, like a narrow ruffle of white lace rapidly unwinding from a spool, was heading directly toward the ship.

"Oh, my God," Jane muttered. She grabbed Claudia and flung her to the deck seconds before the torpedo struck the ship broadside and a deafening explosion rent the air.

They felt the ship lurch under them, sending them rolling away from the rail. As the liner shook from stem to stern with the impact, a second explosion, even stronger than the first, lifted the bow of the great ship out of the water.

Instantly the air was filled with smoke and the screams of the other passengers. Faintly above the din they heard one of the ship's officers shout, "Lifeboat stations!"

Everything amidships seemed to be disintegrating, shooting upward in a huge column of water, coal dust, and wreckage. Jane's arms were hooked firmly around Claudia's waist, and she hung on as they slid down the rapidly listing deck.

Deck planks and gratings crashed down around them, and Jane felt something strike her lower back. Two thoughts occurred to her simultaneously. First that she was lucky enough to be well padded where she was hit, and second that they were fortunately on the perimeter of that avalanche of debris.

Claudia gasped as they slammed into something hard in the smoky confusion, and Jane realized it was the starboard rail. A moment later they were engulfed in steam so thick it was difficult to breathe. The boilers have burst, Jane thought, stunned by the realization that many of the passengers and crew belowdecks were probably already dead.

She disentangled herself from Claudia's fur coat and asked, "Are you all right?"

But Claudia had fainted.

Quickly Jane loosened her friend's collar and, as best she could in the dense pall of steam and smoke, looked for signs of injury. She could not find any blood or broken bones or even a bump on her head.

Massaging Claudia's wrists, Jane was acutely aware of passing time, realizing that each second was precious. She needed to go to their stateroom and get their life jackets and valuables, but could not leave her unconscious friend. How would she ever find her again?

The ship tilted once more, and Jane wedged herself between Claudia and the rail to protect her from further battering. A male passenger materialized in the steam, staggering and looking haggard with fear.

"Sir . . ." Jane called. "Could you get me a life jacket? My friend is unconscious."

He raised his hands helplessly. "Sorry, I don't have one." He paused. "I wouldn't go below if I were you. You might not get back on deck. It's bedlam down there, and the water's rising fast. We're listing badly, and the ship is still moving forward because they can't shut down the engines, so they're having trouble lowering the lifeboats. They swing so far inward that even if the ship came to a complete halt they'd be difficult to launch. The few they've managed to put over the side are crowded to overflowing. I just saw one boat capsize and empty its passengers into the sea." As he lurched away Jane heard him mutter desperately, "I must find my wife and baby."

Jane massaged Claudia's wrists, patted her cheek, and willed her to come to her senses. Although they had not been given a lifeboat drill, Jane had carefully read the instructions left in their cabin and knew that in addition to twenty-two wooden lifeboats, the liner carried twenty-six collapsibles made of wood and canvas, which were stowed beneath the conventional boats. The lighter craft would surely be easier to launch. Perhaps she could get Claudia into one of those.

Claudia opened her eyes suddenly and said, "We've been torpedoed, haven't we? Oh, God, are we going to die?" She began to shake violently.

"Of course not. We're too young to die." Jane pulled herself to her feet and looked over the rail. To her horror she saw the sea rising rapidly toward her.

The starboard list was increasing so swiftly that she knew it was too late to try to get to a boat station. The crew couldn't possibly lower the boats on this side of the ship, and there was no way to clamber up the steeply sloping deck to the port side, even supposing that in the smoke and confusion they could somehow find space in a boat. Around them passengers stumbled about aimlessly, most in shock, many injured, unsure what to do, where to go.

Jane grabbed Claudia's shoulder. "Get up—quickly. We're going to have to jump."

"Into the sea? No, I can't! Jane, you know what a poor swimmer I am."

"We've got to, or we'll go down with the ship. We have to get as far away from her as we can. Take off your coat."

"Not my beautiful sable!"

Jane scrabbled along the rail, searching for a life belt, but could not find one. Other terrified passengers now crowded the rail, and the available life belts had already been claimed.

Looking down, Jane saw the sea rising inexorably toward them. She seized one sleeve of Claudia's coat, yanked it off her, and tossed it into the roiling water. "It would pull you under. Hold my hand and we'll jump together."

They felt the ship shudder in her death throes. Several passengers near them leapt into the water. The great liner now listed so severely that Jane knew any second the decision would be out of their hands, they would simply fall into the water. She grabbed Claudia's hand and jumped.

The shock of the cold water closing over her head took her breath away, but Jane broke the surface still clutching her friend's hand. Claudia coughed, spitting seawater, and her lips were already blue.

"Swim!" Jane ordered. "We've got to get as far away as we can." She released Claudia's hand and gave her a shove. Claudia began a rather feeble breaststroke, and Jane slowed her own strong sidestroke to keep pace with her.

Something flew through the air and splashed into the sea

beside them. Some sixth sense caused Jane to yell, "Duck!" as flying fragments hurtled from the ship all around them.

They dived beneath the surface again, going down as far as they could, and stayed until they needed to breathe. Breaking the surface again, Jane found herself surrounded by floating debris. To her dismay, there were also several bodies in the water. She looked around frantically for Claudia.

Her face bobbed into view over the top of a wave, eyes wide and terror-stricken.

"Keep going," Jane ordered. "We're still too close to the ship."

But Claudia stared in mesmerized horror at the sinking ship. People clinging desperately to anything that offered a handhold were falling from the decks into the sea as the stern reared up, the rudders and propeller lifting into the air just before the liner rolled onto her side. As two of the huge smokestacks hit the water, their gaping mouths sucked in those floating nearby, then, surprisingly, spewed them out again in a mixture of escaping air and sooty water. The liner's keel capsized one lifeboat, flinging its occupants into the sea. A funnel crashed down onto the survivors in another waterlogged boat.

"Don't look!" Jane cried, urgency sharpening her voice. "Swim!"

Fear propelled Claudia now, and she swam as fast as she could, but less than fifty yards from the ship Jane could see her friend was exhausted. She swam alongside her. "Turn over onto your back. I'll help you." Too weary to argue, Claudia did so.

Jane hooked her arm under Claudia's chin and kicked hard. Their progress seemed frighteningly slow, but Jane kept going until she was forced to pause and catch her breath. "Claudia, I need to rest. Tread water for a minute."

A jagged-edged board that might have been part of a lifeboat floated by, and Jane grabbed it. "Here, hold on to this."

"Oh, my God, Jane—look!"

The great ocean liner, pride of the Cunard transatlantic fleet, had almost disappeared. Her stern and four proud red and black funnels were already below the surface. As her bow began to sink, the waves lapped greedily at the name painted in gold letters on her hull: *Lusitania* . . . Liverpool.

There were some lifeboats in the water, pathetically few, and they were crammed with survivors, but more people were swimming or clinging to floating debris. Many women and children were in the water. One man swam slowly by, pushing a baby lying on an open life jacket.

Jane stared at the scene before her, angrier than she had ever been in her life. How could the Germans have done this to innocent civilians? To sink a passenger liner filled with women and children, without any warning . . . It's barbaric, inhuman.

"Jane . . ." Claudia's voice, hoarse with fear, broke into her thoughts. "I'm freezing. . . . I can't hold on."

"Put your arms around my neck. . . . No, get behind me. I'll keep you afloat. We'll be picked up soon, Claudia. Don't despair. At least it isn't dark; they'll be able to see us. There'll be rescue ships here soon, even if we can't get into a lifeboat. You've got to hold on until they come."

Her own feet were numb with cold, and she wished she'd thought to remove her shoes, but Jane pulled Claudia's arms around her neck and grabbed the board Claudia had been holding. She resolutely pumped her feet up and down to try to keep her circulation going.

How long would it really be before help came? Claudia was so frail, and the water seemed bitter cold. How long could she survive?

One lifeboat came within range, but it was already overloaded. Heads bobbing near them in the water abruptly went under and did not come up. The body of a young child drifted by.

When Claudia's arms began to slip from around her neck Jane grabbed her limp hands and held them. Claudia was now a deadweight, her head lolling on Jane's shoulder, and she worried that her friend might again lose consciousness. She kept up a steady barrage of reassuring chatter, but Claudia did not respond.

Jane began to feel disoriented, unsure how much time had passed. How long would it take for rescuers to arrive? Had there been time to radio an SOS? It had all happened so quickly, perhaps only twenty minutes had elapsed between the time the torpedo struck and the moment the ship sank. But the Irish coast was so close. Surely someone must be aware of the disaster. All that remained of the pride of the Cunard fleet was a glistening circle of white foam on the placid surface of the sea.

Jane's thoughts began to fragment and wander. She thought of her father and wished he had enough faith to believe that he'd be waiting for her in heaven. But did she seriously believe there was a heaven, and if there was, that she might aspire to such a state of grace?

If I'm drowning, isn't my life supposed to flash before my eyes? she asked herself, only half jokingly. She wondered vaguely if she would have done anything differently if she'd known she might die young.

Claudia's weight was dragging her down. It was becoming an unbearable strain to keep them both afloat since Jane had been forced to let go of the board in order to hold on to her friend.

Another, larger piece of debris drifted within range, and Jane let go of one of Claudia's hands to grab it. She managed to drape Claudia's limp body over the flotsam, which appeared to be a hatch cover. Steadying her with one hand, Jane held on with the other. She concentrated on keeping her feet moving and tried to imagine being warm and dry.

After a moment memories returned unbidden, one clearer than the rest. Misty pastel images drifted through her mind, of an afternoon ten months earlier when she and Claudia had sat on the lawn at Rathbourne Abbey and Claudia had confided she was in love with the last man on earth Jane wanted her friend to love.

❦ One ❧

THERE HAD NEVER been days more golden than those of the summer of 1914. Never were the flowers more fragrant or the sunlight more mellow. There was a special clarity to the air like that last piercing band of light that rims the earth just before night falls.

It was the summer that the Kingsley brothers were in love with Claudia Abelard and Claudia loved her guardian's chauffeur and Jane Weatherly loved all of them. And how could they have foreseen that a cataclysm was only a heartbeat away?

On a glorious afternoon in early June, Claudia and Jane sat on a grassy bank overlooking the south wing of Rathbourne Abbey, Claudia's guardian's estate. From where they sat they could see the tower and the parapet walk from which, in the fifteenth century, a lovesick nun had flung herself into the arms of her disconsolate lover in the garden far below, killing both of them.

Seeing Jane glance in the direction of the parapet walk, Claudia said, "Oh, really, Jane! I know you think I dramatize myself, but really! You don't seriously believe I might kill myself if I can't have him?"

"Of course not. I was just considering the disasters caused by human passions. And so should you. You can't possibly be serious about Royce. Apart from what Lord Marrick would do to you both if he found out, Royce isn't worthy of a second glance from you. He's a rogue and a rake, and no woman can tame him, not even you."

"You haven't a very high opinion of your own brother."

"I know him a lot better than you do, and I'm quite sure he hasn't even hinted at marriage."

"Not yet. But he will, I know he will. He's still doing battle with himself about our different stations in life."

"You do realize"—Jane twisted a stray lock of autumn brown hair into a knot as she spoke—"that the minute Lord Marrick finds out, Royce will lose his job."

Claudia cocked her head to one side in that particularly endearing way she had, seemingly oblivious of the effect of perfect features framed by shining platinum hair, or the way her brows arched in innocent surprise over violet-shadowed blue eyes when she was disturbed. "By the time Leith finds out about Royce and me, Royce will have popped the question. Leith can't possibly give him the sack for that. I mean, it's the highest compliment a man can pay a woman, isn't it?"

Jane stifled an exasperated sigh. "A chauffeur is not even supposed to view you as a woman, never mind see you alone. Lord Marrick would have Royce horsewhipped if he knew."

"But we love each other," Claudia responded indignantly. "And if Leith were to dismiss Royce, I wouldn't care. I'd be willing to starve in a garret with the man I love."

Jane groaned. "Oh, spare me the dramatics! You've never had a hunger pang in your entire life. Or lifted a finger to do anything for yourself. Lord, why did I ever suggest Royce for the chauffeur's job? Why did you two ever meet? Claudia, be honest, now. He hasn't proposed to you, has he?"

Claudia lowered her long golden eyelashes, and a faint blush crept over her translucent complexion. "He told me he loved me."

"That isn't a marriage proposal. Damn him, I'll skin him alive myself when I get my hands on him. Claudia, listen to me, please. He's playing with you, flirting; it doesn't mean anything to him. Don't take him seriously or you'll be hurt—" She broke off as hooves thundered across the turf toward them.

"Oh, no. It's Bran," Claudia murmured, shading her eyes to watch the rider's approach. "Or is it Roald? I can't tell them apart unless they're up close."

Jane's heart leapt into her throat as the rider reined in his mount in front of where they sat. She whispered, "It's Bran."

Branston Kingsley jumped to the ground, immaculate in light fawn riding breeches and a white shirt, his fair hair tousled from his ride. He managed to drag adoring green eyes away from Claudia long enough to acknowledge Jane's presence when Claudia said, "Hullo, Bran. You remember Jane Weatherly, don't you?"

He knitted his brow. "Weatherly? The name rings a bell."

Jane carefully turned her foot so that he could not see the hole in the sole of her shoe. She was acutely aware of the shine her serge skirt had acquired with long wear and of the fact that her blouse looked yellowish gray next to Claudia's rosebud-sprigged white afternoon gown.

Feeling out of place and awkward, Jane rose to the occasion, as she always did—and usually regretted later—by snapping, "You probably heard someone say, 'Have Weatherly bring the Bentley around' or 'Take our guest into the village, Weatherly' or, most likely 'Where the devil is that damned Weatherly?' "

Bran blinked, clearly taken aback by her tone. Giggling, Claudia explained, "Weatherly is our new chauffeur. You must have noticed him. Royce has enormously broad shoulders, and he's so handsome!"

Jane flashed her a warning glance, and Claudia finished, "Jane is Royce Weatherly's sister. Their father was Leith's stable master when I first came to the abbey. You must remember Jane and me playing together as children? Royce was quite a bit older, and he'd already run away to seek his fortune."

She sighed extravagantly, her lovely eyes misty. "He came back just a few months ago. . . ."

"Without a fortune, I take it?" Bran asked, obviously annoyed by Claudia's adoring tone and lengthy discussion of Royce. "I mean, since he's now Lord Marrick's chauffeur."

Jane said, "Claudia, can't you see that Mr. Kingsley has absolutely no interest in either Royce or me? I'm sure he came to invite you to a garden party or to watch him play polo or some equally earth-shattering event."

Bran turned to look at her, his expression showing he was now even more perplexed by her tone than he had been earlier. But then, how could he guess that she had thought about the fair-haired Kingsley twins almost constantly over the years, measuring every other male against their polished good looks?

He said, "Do I detect a trace of irritation—sarcasm even?"

"Better beware, Bran," Claudia said. "Jane's not only an

intellectual but also a radical. She believes the upper classes are parasites who should be eradicated from English society. She's frightfully clever, she's actually been attending Manchester University."

"Do shut up, Claudia. He really isn't interested."

"Oh, but I am. I saw very few women at Oxford while I was there."

"And those few were required to make themselves as inconspicuous as possible, were they not?" Jane flashed back. "They were there on sufferance, allowed to attend lectures but not really be a part of the university. Walk quickly across the quadrangle, but do not dare to sit on the grass! They would be allowed into the libraries only if accompanied by a Fellow of the College—in fact, most doors were closed to them. They were considered odd and perverted for desiring an education—a sort of cross between an exhibitionist and a mutant bent upon dishonoring her feminine destiny."

Both Bran and Claudia were staring at her in open-mouthed astonishment.

Jane stood up, brushing grass from her skirt. "I'd better go."

"Don't run off because of me," Bran said quickly. "I can certainly understand how you felt at university, but I can hardly be blamed for your treatment there. However, at least give me a chance to defend myself against the charge that as a member of the upper classes I am a parasite and should therefore be eradicated from English society."

"I'm not in the mood to fight the battle of the classes today," Jane answered shortly, angry because he didn't remember her. Throughout her early adolescence she had alternated between being in love with Bran and mad about Roald, peering through the hawthorne hedge when they came to the abbey to play polo or cricket, covertly watching their arrivals and departures for social events.

"In that case," Bran drawled, a smile plucking at the corner of his mouth, "allow me to congratulate you on your accomplishments and swear by all that's holy that I will never again demand to know where the devil Weatherly is."

"What did you want, Bran?" Claudia asked pointedly. "Jane and I were having a rather important discussion."

He avoided looking at Jane as he replied, "I came to ask if

you'd come to the regatta with us on Saturday. Roald and I will be in opposing shells."

Claudia smiled bewitchingly. "In that case, whom could I possibly cheer for?"

"For me, of course. There'll be a picnic on the riverbank and a victory party at our place afterward."

Jane reflected that it was typical of the Kingsley brothers to expect to be the first, the best, to excel in everything they did. They were endearingly matter-of-fact about it, and none of their friends resented their attitude, since one of them was always the winner in any competition, to the delight of the other.

"We did send you an invitation," Bran said to Claudia, "but you didn't respond."

"Oh, I meant to, Bran, I really did. But Jane arrived, and I forgot everything. . . . Jane, will you come, too? Then there'll be two of us to cheer them on."

Jane felt a flush stain her cheeks. "Claudia, please don't put Mr. Kingsley and me into such an impossible position!"

"We'd be delighted if you'd join us," Bran said at once. "And please, when you address me as Mr. Kingsley it sounds like a reprimand. I'd much prefer Bran."

"I'm not sure I'll still be here on Saturday," Jane said.

"Jane, please!" Claudia begged, and looking into her beseeching blue eyes, Jane couldn't refuse, despite the certain knowledge that none of her clothes were suitable for a regatta and picnic with the Kingsleys and their ilk, never mind a party at Willowford afterward.

"I'll think about it," she answered. "On one condition—that you two think about how your upper-crust family and friends are going to feel about my being there." She held up her hand as Claudia and Bran both began to protest. "No, let's be realistic about this. You two may believe it's all right to hobnob with the lower classes, but—"

The rest of her argument was drowned in a barrage of rebuttal from them, and Jane gave up. "Very well, be it on your own heads. Now you must excuse me, I really have to go and see my brother." She gave one last pleading look at Claudia. "Please think about what I said, and don't act hastily."

"I'll see you tomorrow," Claudia called after her.

* * *

Jane glared at her older brother, who was sprawled in the window seat of his cramped room above the garages, idly twanging the strings of a ukelele. "*You didn't tell her?*"

"Of course not. It's none of her business, Janey: Besides, I don't recall you saying you'd ever told her either. I mean, it's not something we want broadcast, is it?"

"Royce, for God's sake, she thinks you're getting ready to ask her to marry you."

He shrugged, regarding her with eyes the color of polished pewter. Someone had once said that she and Royce were like the two sides of a coin, that one was aware they were cast from the same mold, but searched in vain for similarities. Her own eyes, a softer gray, could emit sparks when she was angry, but never acquired Royce's steely coldness. His hair was a darker brown, his cheekbones more pronounced, his mouth, accented by a cleft chin, more sensual. Jane had always felt like a paler, less distinct copy of her older brother.

"Janey old girl, of course I want to marry her. Who wouldn't? She's beautiful, she's rich as Croesus, and she makes me feel like a king."

Jane stared at him incredulously. "Have you gone mad? She's Lord Marrick's ward, not some scullery maid you make wild promises to so you can have your way with her. Royce, you led her on, told her you loved her. Since every young blade in the county has told her that and then promptly proposed to her, she equates a declaration of love with a proposal of marriage. How could she know all you have on your mind is seduction? Do you have any idea what Lord Marrick will do to you if he finds out?"

"I'm tired of being at the beck and call of that arrogant swine." Royce tossed the ukelele down beside him on the faded plaid blanket draped over the window seat. "I'm ready to move on as soon as you go back to university."

"And do what? What will you live on? Royce, I'm not going back to university for the simple reason I've run out of money. That's what I came to tell you. You can't count on me for any more financial help, so please don't give up this job. Besides, Lord Marrick is abroad so much I can't believe he's that strict a taskmaster."

"If I stay on, it will be to court Claudia." He gave her a sidelong glance, a crafty smile spreading across his handsome features. How many times Jane had wished she'd been blessed with a feminine version of Royce's good looks. Her own features were even but, in her view, nondescript.

"Royce, she's my best friend. I won't let you hurt her, I'm warning you. You're not going to seduce her."

"Oh? And how are you going to prevent me?"

"I'll tell her about Edith."

For an instant his eyes narrowed to glittering slits; then he laughed. "Do you really think she'd believe you? Lord, I hardly believe the saga of poor tragic Edith myself. Besides, I'd simply deny it and tell Claudia it's your ploy to break us up. Listen, old girl, be reasonable. Maybe Marrick will let her marry me, and then we'll both be on easy street."

Jane recoiled from him. "I can't believe even you would sink this low. How can you marry Claudia? You're already married, or had you forgotten?"

The bell connecting Royce's room to the main house rang a shrill summons. He stood up, unhurried, and reached for his uniform jacket and chauffeur's peaked cap. "Ah, but Edith is hardly in a position to relate that little fact to Claudia or anyone else, is she?"

❧ Two ☙

ROYCE TOOK CLAUDIA into his arms and held her, cradling her head against his chest so that the moonlight slipped in through the slats of the summerhouse and turned her hair to spun silver. She sighed and clung to him.

"I do love you so, Royce, but I can't . . . I can't let you make love to me until we're married. Please don't ask me to."

He drew her down onto the bench and dropped to his knees

in front of her, his fingers playing with the buttons of her blouse. He could feel her heart beating beneath the thin silk.

"You don't love me, Claudia. You say you do, but you won't prove your love. You're such a child. Do you really need a piece of paper to give you permission to love me? Does a marriage license make one whit of difference in how we feel about each other?"

"No, Royce, but . . ."

"But that tyrant of a guardian of yours has filled your head with old-fashioned nonsense about waiting until the wedding night. I know. Don't put me through this torture, Claudia. I'm in agony, wanting you so much. Give me your hand. . . . Can you feel how much I want you? Can you feel my desire, my torment? God, if I don't get some relief soon . . ."

He pulled her long, slender fingers down to the bulge in his trousers, allowed them to touch him briefly, while his other hand deftly unfastened two buttons and slipped inside her blouse. He felt her tremble as he cupped her small breast, rubbing his thumb gently over the hardening nipple.

Before she could protest, his mouth covered hers and he parted her clenched teeth with his tongue. When he unbuttoned his trousers her fingers, cool and hot at the same time, stayed tremulously near.

"He's yours, Claudia," Royce whispered, licking her ear as he did so. "Only yours. Touch him, feel his passion. It's only for you."

"No, Royce, please. Not until we're married."

"Dearest one, I'd marry you in a minute if Lord Marrick would allow it, but you know he won't, at least not until you're of age. Do you want to wait that long? I don't. But there may be a way to persuade him to give us permission."

"How? Oh, Royce, how?"

His fingertip touched her lips, as though to seal them. "By becoming man and wife in the eyes of God, Claudia. By telling your guardian this, so that he knows we're bound together, no matter what he does or says."

"I love you so much, Royce."

She didn't resist as he laid her down on the hard bench, took off his jacket, and placed it under her head, then pulled up her skirt and petticoat. Her thighs were silken smooth as he slid her drawers down over her ankles, then slowly, her stockings. Her eyes were tightly shut, and the moonlight cast its ghostly pall on her lovely face.

He laid bare her breasts and buried his face in them, sucked on a nipple and felt her moan in terrified pleasure. Then he bent his head to prepare her to receive him, a skill that he had practiced to a fine art. Once a woman felt his hot breath in her secret place, she was his.

Claudia was already writhing, her hips moving in ancient rhythms. Her hands clutched him, wanting to bring him inside her even as she whispered her last pleas for him to stop.

Then he mounted her and drove past the resistance of her maidenhead, ignoring her stifled gasp of pain as he lost himself in his own pleasure. There would be time to attend to hers later.

"As you see," Lord Leith Marrick said to Karl Bruner, "my predecessors were careful to preserve the ground floor of the abbey in its original form. The nuns' quarters survive almost unaltered."

Bruner's piercingly blue eyes took in every detail as the two men strolled through the fifteenth-century cloister about which the nuns' rooms were clustered. "What became of the nuns?"

"King Henry the Eighth closed all the monastic buildings. Their vast estates were taken over by the Crown and later either sold at giveaway prices or handed out as rewards and payments to courtiers or government officials. Rathbourne Abbey was a convent that was sold to a courtier who moved in upstairs and left everything down here intact. He tore down the church, added a new courtyard and the tower you see at the end of the parapet walk. The result is that the abbey from the outside looks like a rambling country house, but then you enter the ground floor and are transported back to the fifteenth century."

"Quite magnificent," Bruner murmured.

"The early owners of the abbey were amateur architects, as were many country gentlemen of their time, and fortunately all adhered to the same Gothic style for their renovations, although they clearly had no real understanding of medieval Gothic, since the abbey today bears little resemblance to anything built in the Middle Ages."

"You have much to be proud of here, Lord Marrick, but more to the point, your home is perfect for our purpose. It is isolated, large, yet comfortable. I particularly like the fact that the living quarters are upstairs. One gets the feeling of being insulated from the world. He will appreciate that."

"How long does he wish to stay?"

"Not long. A week, perhaps."

"The payment of my old debt will be satisfied by this visit, I take it?"

"My dear Lord Marrick, you were never under any obligation."

Marrick resisted the urge to laugh aloud.

Bruner said, "I am somewhat concerned about the presence of your ward. If she were not so stunningly lovely it would be one thing, but he has an eye for beauty and the archduchess might be jealous."

Marrick looked at him sharply. "My dear fellow, and so might I, if the archduke casts any lascivious glances in the direction of my ward. Perhaps you are unaware that when Claudia reaches the age of consent she will become my wife."

Bruner managed to conceal his surprise at this announcement, although he was certain that the girl herself had no inkling of her guardian's intentions. She had been uncommunicative during dinner and had quickly excused herself when the meal ended. He'd seen the look in her eyes as she passed by his chair on her way out of the dining room. The sudden sparkle of anticipation in those enormous blue-violet eyes hinted that perhaps she was slipping away to meet a man.

Jane had taken a room at the Hunter's Arms, a Tudor-style inn halfway between Rathbourne Abbey and the village, declining Claudia's invitation to stay with her at the abbey.

"I'd rather not," Jane had told her. "Royce is your chauffeur and . . . well, I'd prefer to stay at the inn."

After her disturbing conversation with her brother, Jane returned to the inn, needing to be away from both Royce and Claudia in order to decide what to do. If, indeed, anything could be done to prevent what Jane knew would be a disaster.

At the rear of the inn a rose garden had been planted and cared for by the publican's young wife, whom Jane had known from her school days. She was in the rose garden the following morning when, unannounced and unexpected, Lord Leith Marrick arrived to see her.

She saw him coming along the flagged path toward her, and for an instant she was again a child of one of his servants, frozen to the spot in dread of being caught somewhere she was not supposed to be. Then she remembered he no longer had any authority over her.

Since she was alone in the garden, it was apparent that he was coming to see her, and the only possible reason had to be that he'd found out about Royce and would ask her to use her influence to persuade her brother to leave Claudia alone. Royce had no doubt already been given the sack. Jane squared her shoulders and waited for Marrick to reach her.

He'd changed little over the years. His hair was black, with no hint of brown, and he had the darkest eyes she'd ever seen. As a child she'd thought his features resembled a carving of a satyr she'd once seen adorning an early Victorian theater. But as he drew near she realized that his features were actually quite arresting, despite the coldly imperious expression he wore.

It occurred to her now that she'd always thought of him as a much older man than he actually was. Somehow during the time she'd been away at school she had caught up a little. He was now in his late thirties, she guessed, which meant that he had been a young man in his twenties when he took Claudia to be his ward. But such a stern and remote young man that he'd seemed older.

"If I might have a word with you, Miss Weatherly?"

The voice, low, resonant, brought back memories. The only other time the master of Rathbourne Abbey had spoken directly to her was at her father's funeral, and then she'd been too crazed with grief to understand or care about what he said.

She nodded and gestured toward a bench beside the path. The air was filled with the fragrance of the roses, and he paused to look at a bush of dark red blooms beside the bench.

"I've never seen such roses. I thought the rose garden at the abbey was lovely this year, but these are spectacular."

"Almost unreal," she murmured.

"Yes."

They sat down, one at either end of the bench, and she waited. If she was to be berated about her brother, she certainly wasn't going to precipitate it.

He said, "You and Claudia have been friends for a long time now, haven't you? I never told you how glad I was you took her under your wing when she first came to live at the abbey. I was sorry when your father died and you went away, but glad that you kept in touch. You were a steadying influence on her, you know."

Jane thought of Claudia's infatuation with Royce and remained silent.

"Miss Weatherly, I wonder if I might ask a favor of you. I've heard from Claudia that you are not going back to university, but intend to seek a position. I might be of some assistance to you in that regard later on, but wonder if you could be prevailed upon to spend a couple of extra weeks with Claudia."

"I'm not sure I understand . . ."

"I'm expecting some visitors at the abbey, and . . . well, it will be better if Claudia is not there while my guests are in residence. I shall send her away on holiday somewhere, and I would like you to accompany her."

Jane regarded him quizzically. "As a chaperon, you mean?"

He frowned slightly. "A rather archaic thought. No, I meant more as a companion. You two young ladies can choose any spot on earth you wish to visit."

He doesn't know about Royce, Jane thought, relieved. Perhaps there's still time to avert a catastrophe.

"I can't imagine anything more wonderful than spending a holiday with Claudia," she answered.

"Good. Then perhaps you'll join us for dinner tonight to make plans?" He rose to his feet. "About eight?"

"Thank you. I'll be there."

Marrick started down the pathway again, then stopped and turned back. "Why did you insist upon staying here at the inn?

It would have been much more convenient for you to stay at the abbey."

Jane gave him a cool stare. "Claudia invited me, but I declined. After all, my brother is your chauffeur."

Marrick raised an eyebrow. "I hadn't realized you were such a snob."

"Not a snob, Lord Marrick, simply one who had my station in life hammered into my head every day I lived in your stable master's cottage."

"Not by me. Certainly not by Claudia. Why punish her?"

His dark stare pinned her to the spot, and she cast about desperately for some appropriate remark, but could not think of one.

He added, "I'll send the car for you at five. That will give you time to talk over your plans with Claudia before dinner. Perhaps you'd like to bring your luggage with you." It seemed more a command than an invitation.

She stood in the garden for several minutes after he disappeared from view. His presence seemed to linger, mysterious and sinister as an unfamiliar shadow. Yet he had been, if not warm, at least polite and agreeable. His invitation to go away with Claudia was surely a godsend, since it solved several problems simultaneously. Why, then, did Jane suddenly shiver in the mellow sunlight, as though someone had walked over her grave?

❦ Three ❧

FROM THE FIRST, Jane had been drawn to the lonely little girl who was Lord Marrick's ward. Claudia had arrived at Rathbourne Abbey in the middle of an unexpected late-winter storm, with snow cloaking the abbey and icicles glistening on bare branches.

Jane thought she caught a glimpse of a pale face at a frost-crusted window once or twice, but several days went by before she actually met Claudia Abelard.

At ten years of age, Jane was intrigued that the stern master of Rathbourne Abbey had taken in a girl even younger than she. Not that Lord Marrick was in residence at the time. He was abroad somewhere.

He traveled to mysterious foreign destinations a great deal of the time, and some of the staff felt that even when he was present he was as remote and unapproachable as some distant god. A closed, secretive man, no one really knew him, and he seemed to be the last person on earth who would take in a homeless child.

"What's a ward?" Jane had asked her father.

"Someone his lordship will take care of like she was his own daughter, but she's really no relation. A Frenchie, probably, judging by her name. All very mysterious, I'd say. Sprung it on the staff as a complete surprise, he did, according to the housekeeper. Sent her a letter from Marseilles telling her that the girl and her governess would be arriving. Now, listen, Janey, you remember your station, and don't go hanging around the main house hoping to meet her. No ward of Lord Marrick is going to have anything to do with his stable master's daughter."

Jane bristled at the mention of her station in life, something she had accepted until Royce, who was then nineteen, became involved with a crowd of trade unionists who talked about the coming worker's revolution and how all men were born equal. Jane had idolized her older brother in those days and had imitated everything he did.

She had become more of a socialist than he was, to the dismay of their father. Albert Weatherly, a simple man who knew more about horses than about children, moved through life perpetually baffled by his offspring. John's wife had died within hours of Jane's birth.

Despite her curiosity about Claudia, Jane stayed well away from the abbey, mainly because she knew that if she didn't obey her father, her footprints in the snow would give her away.

She was concerned about a foal born too early in the season

and had been visiting the stables each morning before going to school to see if the frail creature had survived the night. On the third day after Claudia's arrival the mare that had given birth was suckling the foal, who was on his feet, to Jane's relief, and at first she didn't see the small figure crouched in the corner of the stall.

· Jane gave the sugar cubes she'd brought to the mare, stroked her nose encouragingly, and was about to pet the foal when a voice behind her said, "You shouldn't touch the baby. Animal mothers often reject their young if they're handled by humans."

Turning, Jane saw a diminutive girl who was as pale as a nun, lovelier than a rose, and shivering in a blouse and skirt meant for warmer climes. Her almost white blond hair fell in two neat plaits, secured by rosettes of black grosgrain ribbon, which matched a black armband that made its own somber statement.

"That sounds like something you read in a book," Jane said when she recovered from her surprise. "I've been touching this foal since the day he was born, and I happen to be the stable master's daughter, so I think I know a lot more about horses than you do."

Violet-blue eyes, large as saucers, widened still further. "You're rather rude, aren't you? I don't like your tone at all."

"And you're rather stupid, coming out of the house dressed like that. You'll get chilblains and then you'll be sorry. Here, take my muffler and gloves. I'll put my hands in my coat pockets."

"No, I couldn't possibly—"

Ignoring her, Jane removed her long woolen muffler and wrapped it around a goose-pimpled neck, then helped the girl pull her gloves over ice-cold fingers. "My name is Jane Weatherly. I expect yours is Claudia Abelard."

"You're very bossy, Jane Weatherly."

"And you're freezing, Claudia Abelard."

They glared at each other for a moment and then both burst out laughing.

"Well," Jane said at length, "now that we've settled that, perhaps you'll tell me why you're out here without a coat."

"I had to get out of that dreadful old house, and my

governess has locked up all my clothes except what I'm wearing."

"Why, for goodness' sake?"

"She thinks I'm going to run away."

"Are you?"

Claudia nodded vehemently. "First chance I get. Could you loan me some clothes and a horse?"

"You can't ride anywhere today. The ground is covered with frozen snow. Lord Marrick would have a fit if you rode his prized horses in such conditions. Besides, where would you go?"

"I don't know. Away from here. I hate it here."

"You've hardly given it a chance yet. Come on, let's go to our cottage and I'll make you some chocolate to warm you up."

She led the shivering Claudia back to the cottage and piled coal on the fire until it roared up the chimney. She wrapped a blanket around Claudia, heated some chocolate, and brought her a pair of well-worn slippers to replace her snow-caked shoes.

Claudia sipped the chocolate through chattering teeth and looked around enviously. The room was clean but cluttered. The chintz-covered armchairs were faded, the rug almost threadbare. Piles of magazines and books were stacked on the floor, dishes were piled in the sink, and on the scrubbed wood table were a couple of jars of homemade jam left there since breakfast.

"This is only a four-room cottage," Jane said defensively. "We don't have separate rooms for cooking and dining and sitting; we do it all in here."

"Oh, it's so cozy, so warm. How lucky you are! This is the first time I've felt warm since I came to your dreary country."

"Dreary! England isn't dreary," Jane exclaimed indignantly. "It's the greatest country on earth, and you should go down on your knees and give thanks that you've been privileged to come here."

"I was referring to your weather," Claudia responded with some spirit. "It's cold and damp and . . . dreary."

"Where have you been living that you avoided winter?"

"We divided our time between the south of France and the

Costa del Sol—that's Spain, the Mediterranean coast. Have you always lived here at the abbey?"

"No. We've been here two years. Before that my father was head groom on a smaller estate in Lancashire."

There was a sudden commotion outside, voices raised, the sound of a car engine. Jane went to the window and lifted a lace curtain. "Sounds like a hue and cry. I think you've been missed. I'll probably catch it for bringing you here."

"Could you show me how to get back to the main house without being seen?"

"We could go out the back door and through the stable yard. Come on."

Winter at last gave way to spring, and the two girls slipped away together whenever Jane was not at school or doing the cooking and housekeeping for her father. Claudia didn't mention running away again.

Royce had gone to London to look for work. If Claudia's acerbic governess, Miss Winthrace, or anyone else was aware of the blossoming friendship between the two girls, no one mentioned the fact.

Jane's father at first fretted that it was improper, but was soon won over by Claudia's ethereal charm and aura of deep sadness, which they attributed to grief over the death of her parents, or whoever had cared for her previously, although she never spoke of them.

"I think she needs a good sensible friend like you to cheer her up, Janey," her father told her.

Jane had not questioned her new friend about the black armband she continued to wear, but one afternoon Claudia told a strangely disturbing story. She had insisted that day upon exploring the ground floor of the abbey, and Jane, who had never been inside the main house, gladly agreed.

They crept through the cloister to the warming room, and Claudia said, "Miss Winthrace told me this was the only room where the nuns could come to be near a fire." She shivered empathetically. Claudia hated the cold.

"A fire under that great caldron over there, you mean?"

"No, she said that according to the history of the house, the caldron probably was moved in here from the kitchen. It's big enough to cook a missionary in, isn't it?"

They both giggled fearfully, acutely aware of the churchlike atmosphere, the somber silence, the sense of antiquity pervading their surroundings, which seemed to warn that such levity was sacrilegious.

"Do you think the ghosts of the nuns are watching us?" Jane asked gleefully. "I suppose you know about the one who flung herself from the parapet walk and killed herself and her lover?"

To her surprise, Claudia bit her lip and abruptly turned away.

"I say, I'm sorry. I didn't mean to . . . Why, Claudia, what is it? You're not afraid of ghosts, are you? They really don't exist, you know."

Claudia perched on the cold granite stand that held the giant caldron. "Someone reaches for me," she whispered. "I try so hard, but I can't quite touch her. She's my ghost mother or perhaps my ghost sister."

Jane gave an involuntary shudder. "You're talking about a dead woman?"

"They would never tell me about her, but I always knew she was very dear to me, that she loved me more than life itself. I think they believed that it was a kindness to keep her a secret, that I wouldn't miss her or grieve for her if they pretended *they* were my only family."

"Who were they?"

"The two Abelards who brought me up and pretended to be my mother and my grandmother."

"They're the ones you wear the armband for?"

"Simone died when I was seven. Grandmère passed away six months ago. So now here I am with Lord Marrick, who is every bit as formidable as they threatened he would be."

"I've never actually met him, but I've heard plenty of rumors about him. I've seen him coming and going, riding his horse or whizzing past in his motorcar." Jane glanced over her shoulder nervously. "He won't come and find us, will he?"

"No, he's stayed in his study ever since he came back from abroad, except at dinnertime. I hate dinnertime."

Claudia sighed and wrapped stick-thin arms about her frail body. "He's the most frightening man I've ever met and just as deceitful as the Madame Abelards. I hoped he'd tell me the truth about my ghost mother, but he, too, pretended I'd imagined her."

"Perhaps you did."

The lovely violet-shadowed eyes filled with tears. "Oh, Jane. I thought you were my friend."

"I am. Listen, Claudia, my mother died when I was born, but I've often imagined that she was beautiful and talented, perhaps royalty even, although I know she was just a parlor-maid who married a groom. Royce says all children have fantasies about their so-called real parents, even those who didn't lose one."

"The Madame Abelards were *not* my mother and grand-mother. They were dark, swarthy women, with olive skin and raven hair and eyes like bits of coal."

Jane looked at Claudia's flaxen hair and lily-pale complex-ion. "Perhaps your father . . . ?"

"I didn't have a father."

"Claudia, don't be ridiculous. Everyone has a father."

"Well, I didn't. Simone never married."

Jane decided not to pursue that embarrassing avenue of discussion. Claudia, she'd discovered, was extremely innocent about such things, perhaps because, unlike Jane, she had never attended school with older girls or witnessed the breeding of horses and other animals. Claudia's entire knowledge of the world came from the books she was allowed to read or was filtered through the prudish mind of her spinster governess.

"Besides, they both hated me," Claudia added. "I tried so hard to please them, but I never did. If they were my real mother and grandmother, why did they hate me so? I was never even allowed to call Simone 'Mother.'"

"Don't you see, that's probably why you imagined your real mother had died."

"Someday, somehow, I'll make Leith tell me what happened to her."

"He lets you call him Leith?" It was inconceivable to Jane that anyone was allowed to address Lord Marrick by his given name.

"Oh, yes. But it doesn't make him seem any more human.

Oh, Jane, if you hadn't been here, I don't know what I would have done."

The shadows lengthened, and the chamber grew chill. Jane shivered and said, "We'd better go, or old Miss Whipface will be looking for you."

Occasionally, after that, Claudia spoke of her ghost mother, but as time went by Jane thought her friend had gradually outgrown her childish fantasy.

When Royce came to pick her up at the inn, Jane thought he wore a particularly smug expression. "Your car awaits you, madam," he announced, touching his chauffeur's cap. Even in the uniform of a servant, Royce managed to look dashing. "And I'm supposed to pick up your bags."

He gave her an engaging grin. "See? Claudia came through for you. She will for me, too."

"This isn't an invitation to live at the abbey, you know. Lord Marrick is sending Claudia off on a holiday and I'm to chaperon her."

Royce picked up her single suitcase. "I know all about it. I told Claudia to tell him she wants to go to Brighton; then I can join you there. It's perfect."

Jane didn't comment. There would be time to talk Claudia out of that nonsense before they went to dinner. Picking up her handbag, she said, "Who are the mysterious visitors he's having?"

"Nobody seems to know. A German bloke arrived to make the arrangements. Have you got anything decent to wear tonight?"

"You know I haven't."

"Too bad you're so much taller than Claudia, you could have borrowed something of hers."

"They'll just have to take me as they find me."

"Lord, but you sounded just like the old man when you said that. You're not going to become belligerently working class, like him, are you?"

"Dad didn't have a belligerent bone in his body, about class or anything else. He was kind and gentle and wouldn't have hurt a fly. Where did *you* come from, Royce? You must be a throwback."

"If you're going to start another lecture about Claudia, I'll stop the car and make you walk the rest of the way."

"Go ahead and stop. I won't keep quiet about Edith, Royce, I mean it. Either you break it off with Claudia or I will tell her. I swear it."

She glanced at his profile to assess his reaction, and was surprised to see that he was smiling complacently. Jane felt a cold numbness grip her. She'd seen that particular smile on his handsome face before. It meant that he'd accomplished an objective and therefore nothing could take it away from him.

Claudia had left instructions with the butler that Jane was to be immediately shown up to her room, which proved to be next to Claudia's own bedroom.

"Would you like something to drink?" Claudia asked, hugging Jane in her usual enthusiastic greeting. "Tea or sherry? We've plenty of time to dress before dinner."

"I probably should unpack," Jane began, thinking of her creased skirt and hopelessly crushed blouse.

"My maid will do it. Come on, let's go into my room and talk about our holiday." As they went through the connecting door Claudia asked, "Did Royce tell you of our plan?"

"Yes, and I think it's a rotten one. With Lord Marrick in residence here, how can Royce possibly get away? Even if I allowed him anywhere near you, which I won't."

"I don't understand how you can be so against us. I should think you'd be happy that your best friend and your brother love each other. When Royce and I marry, you'll be my sister and then we'll always be a family."

Jane drew a deep breath. "Claudia . . . he isn't free to marry you."

"What? What do you mean?"

"Please don't ask me to explain any further. I can't. All I can tell you is that there is an impediment to his marrying you . . . or anyone else, for that matter."

Claudia had grown ever paler, but she compressed her lips slightly and asked, "Is there also an impediment to our loving each other without benefit of marriage? I think not. Even if Royce can't marry me—and I can't imagine any impediment that couldn't be removed—I wouldn't stop loving him."

Jane stifled an exasperated sigh. "Look, Claudia, will you at least do one thing for me? For the sake of our friendship?"

"As long as it doesn't involve giving Royce up," Claudia answered cautiously.

"Just agree not to see him for a while. Don't let him visit you during our holiday. After all, if you truly love him, an absence should make your heart grow fonder."

"Oh, you don't know what you're asking!"

"Don't I?" There was a sudden ragged edge to Jane's voice. "Do you think I've never yearned for a man I couldn't have?"

Distracted, Claudia peered closely into her friend's face. "Who? *Who?* Oh, do tell!"

"Don't ask. I feel foolish enough about it."

Claudia thought rapidly of the men and boys they'd known jointly and the male students at the university whom Jane might have mentioned more than once. The first image that came to her mind was the change that had come over Jane when Bran Kingsley rode up the previous day. She'd grown quite pink, and despite the fact that she was somewhat rude to him, her voice had dropped an octave or two and sounded rather self-conscious. Indeed she suddenly seemed to become quite awkward and clumsy in her demeanor, not at all her usual self-confident self.

"Why, Jane!" Claudia's eyes twinkled. "It's *Bran*! You're in love with Bran Kingsley!"

Jane jerked her head away from Claudia's delighted gaze. "Don't be ridiculous."

"You are! You're blushing madly, just as you did yesterday when he arrived. Jane, dear friend, don't be embarrassed to admit it to me. I'm so happy for you. It's a wonderful thing to be in love."

"No, it isn't. Not when it's hopeless and unrequited. It's stupid and futile and possibly the worst form of torment there is."

"How do you know it's hopeless? You haven't given Bran a chance to really get to know you. When he does—starting with this Saturday's regatta—"

Jane seized Claudia's arm and led her to a long oval mirror on a delicately carved rosewood stand. The physical differences between the two young women were striking. Claudia's silvery pale hair and lily-petal complexion, her delicate bones, tiny wrists, and long slender fingers, her perfectly proportioned head and the long, graceful column of her neck, contrasted sharply with Jane's taller, sturdier build, her full bosom and strong, capable hands. Her face glowed with pink-cheeked health, and her luxurious mane of rich brown waves seemed darker, more unruly, beside the smooth silken cap of Claudia's hair. But Jane was looking beyond mere surface differences.

"It won't make any difference how well he gets to know me. He'll always see me for what I am. Look at us, Claudia. We might as well be wearing signs around our necks. 'Aristocrat' for you and 'Peasant' for me."

"What nonsense! The only difference between us is our clothes, and if you weren't so proud and would let me buy you some—"

"It's more than clothes, Claudia. Much more. It's breeding. That indefinable stamp of privilege. An inclination of the head, the way you move, your upper-class accent. I can speak the King's English from here to forever and never acquire that certain inflection of rank, that discreet tolerance for lesser beings, that comes naturally to blue bloods like Marrick and you and the Kingsley twins. It's the product of generations of breeding, the exclusivity of your education and background and training. It can't be learned; it's inborn."

Claudia shrugged, as unconcerned as if she hadn't understood a word Jane uttered. "Love," Claudia announced sagely, "conquers all."

There were only four for dinner, seated at the massive dining table beneath twin chandeliers as large as the polar ice caps. Claudia and Jane sat side by side; Lord Marrick was at the head of the table with Herr Bruner on his right.

Jane was at once aware of an undercurrent between Marrick and his houseguest. There was an air of tension, distrust, perhaps even resentment, between the two men.

Bruner was the exact opposite of Marrick in every way, the German being blond with a pallid complexion and almost transparent blue eyes that, disconcertingly, rarely blinked. He wore a wary, watchful expression that reminded Jane of the demeanor of a policeman who was certain he had the guilty party pegged.

Fleetingly the thought crossed Jane's mind that the two men echoed the contrast between Claudia and herself, the dark and the fair, the high-born and the working class; the light-haired Bruner was out of his element, as Jane was.

Marrick seemed particularly morose, brooding almost, this evening, and she noticed that his eyes rarely strayed from his ward.

Claudia was radiant in a white evening gown, her hair swept into a gleaming flower-encircled coil at her crown. A sapphire and diamond necklace almost matched the sparkle in her eyes. There was an air of suppressed excitement about her that Jane hoped reflected only her anticipation of their forthcoming holiday and not her imagined romance with Royce.

Jane felt ancient and dowdy in a black taffeta skirt that ended awkwardly above her ankles. The ecru lace blouse Claudia had insisted she borrow Jane felt was far too fluttery and feminine to suit her. It was also too tight across the bust, and she was beginning to feel breathless from holding herself in. She was convinced that at any moment one of the tiny pearl buttons holding the blouse together would fly off into Bruner's unblinking blue eye.

"And have you two young ladies decided upon a destination for your holiday?" Bruner asked in his clipped accent.

Marrick looked at Jane, as though the decision were hers alone. She and Claudia had argued for over an hour without reaching a decision. Claudia still wanted to go to Brighton, as Royce had commanded, while Jane had suggested her friend might like to visit France or possibly Spain, where she had spent her childhood. Claudia had immediately exclaimed, "We could search for my ghost mother!" but then her lovely eyes had clouded and she'd added, "No. Royce wants us to go to Brighton so I'll be within reach if he can get away."

They were at an impasse when they came down to dinner. Now they answered Bruner's question simultaneously.

"Brighton," Claudia said.

"The Riviera," Jane said, more firmly.

Marrick gave a small smile that, to Jane, appeared mocking. "Ah," he murmured knowingly, and she immediately bristled.

"I suppose you would have expected the stable master's daughter to select Brighton?" Jane said. "It would be more in keeping with a working-class background than the south of France."

"You do carry an enormous chip on your shoulder about your background, don't you?" Marrick remarked. "It's becoming quite tedious."

Jane flushed and tossed her napkin on the table. "I shouldn't be here. Please forgive my lack of manners in front of your guest. I'll go up and pack."

"Jane!" Claudia cried, aghast.

"Oh, do sit down and shut up," Marrick said amiably. "I was about to say that since you evidently can't agree upon a destination, I should like to suggest one."

"Leith, I really would like to go to Brighton—" Claudia began.

"And I would prefer that you go abroad for your holiday. But I don't think the Riviera is a good idea. Why not go somewhere where neither of you have ever been before?"

Jane sat down. "Do you have somewhere in mind, Lord Marrick?"

"New York. It's an exciting city, and the journey has the added advantage of including a voyage aboard a luxury liner."

"America!" Jane exclaimed, stunned.

Even Claudia appeared momentarily beguiled by the dazzling image of the skyscrapers of that fabled modern city across the Atlantic. Her full lips, with their pronounced Cupid's bow, parted in surprise.

Although neither she nor Jane had actually agreed that New York would be a perfect destination, Marrick immediately murmured, "Good, then it's settled. I'll take care of the arrangements, and you can leave as soon as I've booked passage. Meantime I'll write to an old friend there who will keep an eye on you."

His glance flickered in Jane's direction. "No reflection on your good sense, Jane. But capable and level-headed as you are, America is a foreign country."

"We would be the houseguests of your friend?" Jane asked, disappointed by the implied curb on their holiday freedom.

"Not exactly houseguests. Conrad Baron owns one of

Manhattan's largest hotels. Now, if you young ladies would like to retire to the drawing room and leave Herr Bruner and me to our brandy and cigars, we'll join you later."

They were clearly dismissed, and Jane at once rose to her feet. Claudia hesitated, but followed suit.

The moment they closed the dining room door behind them, Claudia whispered, "America! Can you believe it? Now all we have to do is find a way to get Royce over there, too."

Jane propelled her friend rapidly along the hall. "What would you have him do? Stow away aboard the ship? Claudia, for pity's sake, will you stop living in that fantasy world you've created and try to be sensible about this?"

"We just passed the drawing room," Claudia said. "Where are you going?"

"To Royce's quarters to talk to him. We're going to settle this nonsense once and for all. Come on, we should have time before the men finish their cigars and brandy."

They slipped outside into a warm summer evening and hurried through the rose garden to the chauffeur's quarters above the garage. Jane knocked on the door, but there was no response.

"He's probably asleep," she said as she pushed open the unlocked door.

The room was deserted. Not merely unoccupied, but clearly abandoned. All of Royce's personal possessions were gone, empty drawers gaped open from the dresser, the wardrobe door was ajar, revealing that its contents were also missing.

Claudia looked at Jane questioningly. "Did he say anything about leaving when he picked you up?"

Mystified, Jane shook her head.

In a daze, Claudia wandered into the room. "Why would he leave without telling either of us?"

"Perhaps he saw the error of his ways," Jane said grimly. "Or maybe he was afraid Lord Marrick suspected he's been romancing you and decided discretion was the better part of valor. Claudia, this isn't the first time Royce has disappeared abruptly—it's typical of him. I know this is a shock to you, but it's really for the best in the long run—"

"Jane, look," Claudia interrupted. "Here's a letter." She bent to pick up a sealed envelope lying on the hearthrug. "It must have been propped on the mantelpiece, and it blew down when we opened the door." She read the name written on the envelope and silently handed it to Jane.

"Jane Weatherly, Personal and Confidential" was written in Royce's familiar scrawl. She tore open the envelope.

Her brother's message consisted of only three words, but then, there was no need for him to say more.

He had written: "Edith is loose."

❧ Four ❧

JANE CRUMPLED Royce's note before Claudia could read it.

"What did he say?"

"Just that he had to leave."

"He can't just leave without an explanation."

"You don't know him very well, do you?"

"I can't believe he would do this." Claudia cast a forlorn glance about the deserted room as though willing Royce to materialize.

"He told me the other day that he hated being a chauffeur. He may have been offered another job. But, Claudia, you have to face the fact that it's more likely he came to his senses and decided to run before things between the two of you got out of hand."

"I shall never believe that," Claudia declared. "I'll hear from him soon. I know I will."

"The worst mistake I ever made was to suggest he come to work for you. I always hope he's changed and he never does—he never will. Claudia, you must believe me when I tell you no woman is safe around Royce. I foolishly believed your position as Lord Marrick's ward, as well as my friendship with you, would keep you safe from him."

Jane bent to pick up the plaid blanket that had slipped from the window seat. "Well, at least he left before any real harm was done. You must forget him, Claudia. Come on, we'd better get back to the house before we're missed." She closed the door firmly behind them, as though to shut Royce out of Claudia's life.

As they made their way quickly back through the rose garden, Jane shredded Royce's note with her fingernails.

Lord Marrick did not join them in the drawing room. He sent the butler to say he had further business to discuss with Herr Bruner and would see them in the morning.

Claudia, obviously fighting back tears as the full realization of what Royce's departure might mean, said at once, "I believe I'll retire, then, Jane. You don't mind, do you? I think I'm getting one of my sick headaches."

Jane looked at her sharply. "You're not going to cry into your pillow over Royce, are you?"

"No, of course not. I told you, he'll be in touch soon."

Jane reluctantly bade her friend good night and went to her own room, knowing sleep would not come easily this night.

Edith is loose. Royce's wife had somehow escaped from prison, and if Royce was caught with her he would be guilty of aiding a fugitive.

But there was nothing she could do for her older brother. How often she'd tried, even going so far as to ask Claudia to speak to Lord Marrick about the chauffeur's job. He and Edith were on their own now; Jane made a silent vow never to become enmeshed in their lives again. Royce had forfeited all right to any further help from her. Jane would never forgive him for trying to seduce Claudia. That was unconscionable. She was not yet eighteen and had led such a sheltered life that she was utterly defenseless.

Concern for Claudia and worry about what Royce might be up to drove all thoughts of the coming trip to America from Jane's mind, although she tried to regain her excited anticipation.

She perched on the edge of the enormous canopied four-poster bed, then got up and prowled the spacious room, feeling like an intruder amid the beautiful Sheraton furniture and priceless paintings. As midnight silence fell upon the great house, she decided to go in search of a book to read. There was no other way to escape the turbulence of her own thoughts.

The library was on the second floor at the end of the portrait gallery and she made her way past a long row of oil paintings illuminated by gas mantles in wall sconces. Despite his apparently limitless wealth, Lord Marrick had not bothered to install that modern marvel, electricity, in his country estate, probably because he spent most of his time either abroad or at his London club.

None of the painted faces that regarded her from within their ornate gilt frames resembled the present master of Rathbourne Abbey. She searched in vain for an ancestor as darkly handsome or broodingly Byronic as Leith Marrick, and, intrigued by this, she had already pushed open the library door and walked into the room before she realized she was not the only insomniac abroad in the night.

Lord Marrick was seated in a leather wing chair by the fireplace, an open book in his hand.

"Oh, excuse me—" Jane said, embarrassed.

"Come in. I'm glad to see you're still up. I wanted an opportunity to speak with you alone. Oh, don't look so suspicious. I'll take only a moment of your time, and then you can select some books to take to your room."

Jane approached the fireplace slowly and sat awkwardly on the edge of a chair. "If it's about my brother . . ."

Marrick looked puzzled. "What about your brother?"

"Oh . . . I'd hoped he'd had the decency to tell you. . . . I'm afraid he's gone. Packed his bags and left earlier this evening."

"Damn. He might have given sufficient notice so we could replace him."

Jane cleared her throat nervously. "If his sudden departure will cause any problems, I'd be glad to offer my services, just until you hire another chauffeur, of course. I'm an excellent driver. Royce taught me years ago."

In the flickering firelight and with the gas lamp turned low, Marrick's face was an interesting study in lines and shadows, although she was unsure if his expression was amused, amazed, or annoyed. It occurred to her then that Marrick must have guessed she'd learned to drive in one of his own cars while he was out of the country. In the days when the Weatherlys lived in the stable master's cottage, Royce had ingratiated himself with the bored chauffeur of the time, who had taught him to drive. Royce then took devilish delight in passing along the skill to his adoring young sister, who at the time could barely see over the steering wheel. Their father had remained blissfully ignorant of these transgressions. Oh, why had she spoken so impulsively?

For a moment Marrick was silent and then he said, "I've never met a young lady who could drive a motorcar before. Have you any other hidden talents?"

"There's no need to mock me, Lord Marrick."

"That was not my intent, Miss Weatherly. Perhaps I should tell you why I wanted to speak with you privately, since it will explain my interest in your accomplishments. I wish to offer you a position. I understand you are seeking one."

"What sort of a position?" Jane asked cautiously.

"As a paid companion to Claudia."

"What?" Jane jumped to her feet, indignation causing her to send a cushion flying. She bent to pick it up. "I'm Claudia's *friend,* I'll always be her friend—you don't have to pay me for that."

"My dear Miss Weatherly, there's no need to ruffle your feathers. You do tend to be hotheaded, don't you? You can jump to the wrong conclusion faster than anyone I know. You really should learn to curb that tendency. It will cause you to miss opportunities in life."

"You're not even aware that you insulted me, are you?"

"I see no reason why becoming Claudia's paid companion should in any way affect your friendship with her. In fact, it will enhance it, since it will mean you can spend all of your time together, instead of joining her for brief and infrequent visits as you have these past few years."

"Lord Marrick—" Jane began, but he held up his hand to silence her.

"Please, just listen for a moment. Claudia, as you're well aware, has always been delicate and extremely sensitive. She has led a sheltered life here at the abbey, and sometimes I think she lives in a dream world of her imagination that has rendered her ill-equipped to deal with the world as it really is."

"She should have gone to school," Jane said. "It would have done her far more good than all the governesses and tutors you brought in."

"Claudia was not strong enough to go away to school. Her health has never been good, as you're aware. Besides, I promised her father—" He broke off, frowning, then went on, "If you are unwilling to take the position as companion, I'll be forced to hire someone else. Probably a stern nurse-companion who will terrify Claudia and put a damper on your holiday. If I hire someone else she will, of course, accompany you."

Jane knew her expression registered dismay when he immediately pressed his advantage.

"Would you consider a trial period, say, for the duration of your holiday, to see how it works out for all concerned? Since Claudia's companion would be responsible for her twenty-four hours a day, I'd be willing to pay a generous stipend as well as an advance in order to purchase clothes and other necessities for the voyage." His voice softened slightly. "You know it will be best for Claudia if that person is you."

"What exactly would the companion's duties be?"

"To smooth the way for her, relieve her of the inconveniences of travel. Deal with customs and immigration, the transfer of luggage, and various other arrangements. Mainly, I suppose, to keep her out of trouble, which means preventing any unsuitable men from getting too close to her."

Jane averted her eyes, wondering what he'd think if he knew she had already been responsible for bringing an unsuitable man into Claudia's life. She said, "I should think Claudia would be outraged that you'd hire a keeper for her."

"Then we don't have to tell her. Our arrangement would be between the two of us."

"I couldn't deceive her like that."

He leaned forward. "Tell me, if you merely traveled with her as her friend, would you not take care of all the things I've just mentioned anyway?"

Jane smiled ruefully. "I suppose I would."

"Then let me pay you for it. Let's be brutally frank. You need that advance against salary to buy some decent clothes. From what I've seen of your current wardrobe you're going to look like Claudia's maid otherwise."

Jane knew she was defeated and wondered if this had always been his plan, from the moment he suggested she go on holiday with Claudia. She also wondered if he'd ever been thwarted from carrying out any of his plans and desires and decided that he probably had not. Resentment of his privileged position in society surfaced. Why, a peer of the realm was even above the law; he could be tried only in the House of Lords by his fellow peers.

Like Rathbourne Abbey, the Kingsleys' country estate, Willowford, sprawled along the banks of the river Avon. The day of the regatta dawned bright and clear with the promise of warm sunshine for the private yacht club race, held to qualify a shell for entry in the Royal Henley Regatta to take place in July.

Jane was up early, unsure if she was excited or unnerved at the prospect of mingling with the upper classes. She was looking forward to watching the Kingsley twins race. It had always been a pleasure merely to look at those golden-haired young gods of creation. Tall and lean, both Bran and Roald had the sculpted biceps and pectorals of Greek statues, and their green eyes sparkled with humor and intelligence.

Ever since her encounter with Bran she had thought about seeing him again. A tantalizing little demon at the back of her mind whispered that perhaps, just for today, the class barriers between them might be breached.

Thanks to Lord Marrick's salary advance, she had a new dress to wear. At his suggestion she and Claudia had driven up to London the previous day to apply for passports and buy clothes for their holiday. He had given her a sly glance and said, "You did say you could fill in as chauffeur, didn't you? You can take the Bentley. I'll be using the Daimler myself."

Claudia had been silent and withdrawn following Royce's departure, showing little interest in shopping or anything else. Jane worried that Claudia might plead illness and refuse to go to either the regatta or the party at Willowford afterward.

Please let her want to go, Jane thought, feasting her eyes on an afternoon gown of palest yellow, which the saleswoman had assured her lit up her tawny complexion and found chestnut highlights in her brown hair. The gown certainly made her feel different—more elegant, less clumsy. She would wear a wide-brimmed straw hat with the pastel dress. She even dared hope that Bran Kingsley might notice how nice she looked.

There was also a party gown for this evening, carefully packed in layers of tissue to be delivered to Willowford by a servant later. Jane had selected a simply cut white satin dress that, according to Claudia, showed off her magnificent shoulders and cleavage. Claudia herself decided she couldn't be bothered buying a new ball gown and would wear her mauve chiffon.

Glancing at Claudia's closed bedroom door and realizing it was too early to wake her, Jane decided to go for a walk before breakfast.

Strolling through the grounds of Rathbourne Abbey on a sunlit summer morning, inhaling the fragrance of hundreds of roses and the subtle scent of sweet dew-washed trees and grass was surely as close to heaven as any mortal being could get, Jane thought. She avoided walking near the stable master's cottage, as she knew it would bring back memories of her father, and this was too glorious a day for sadness.

She paused for a moment to look back at the abbey, framed by sun-dappled elm, beech, and willow trees and deep green rolling lawns. How could the master of all this magnificence ever bear to leave? What did he seek abroad that he could not find in abundance here?

After walking for almost an hour Jane was ravenous and returned to the house. The circular morning room, which was part of the tower, jutted out over the garden, creating the illusion that they were floating above a sea of flowers and shrubs. Instead of a sideboard, which would have spoiled the effect by obstructing a portion of the windows that encircled the room, a warming table held silver-covered dishes.

To her surprise, Lord Marrick was drinking coffee and reading the *Times*. She had not expected him to be there as Claudia had told her he usually took breakfast in his room.

Jane started to withdraw, but he laid down the newspaper and said, "Good morning. Why are you acting like a fawn in the forest confronted by a hunter?"

"I . . . I thought perhaps you wanted to be alone." She bit

her lip. "No, that's not true. The truth is, I'm a paid employee and I have no business taking meals with the master."

He picked up the paper again. "If you feel so strongly about it, perhaps you'd prefer to go belowstairs and eat with the staff."

Jane hesitated, unsure what to do, and was relieved when Claudia appeared. She murmured, "Good morning," and sat in the nearest chair, her shoulders slumping dejectedly. Jane was dismayed to see how pale and drawn she looked. There were dark circles under her reddened eyes, and it was obvious she had spent the night crying.

Marrick must have noticed his ward's woebegone expression, for he remarked, "You're looking a bit under the weather, Claudia. I'm glad you young ladies are going to the regatta today. Some fresh air and sunshine will do you good. I expect you'll go to the party afterward, too?"

Jane held her breath waiting for Claudia's reply. She smiled wanly and said, "Oh, yes, we'll be there."

"Good. I might drop in myself for the dinner party. The Kingsleys have imported a French chef, I hear."

"Jane," Claudia said, "would you be an angel and pass me some toast?"

Jane quickly filled a china plate with ham, eggs, fried tomatoes and mushrooms, then grabbed a toast rack and placed it all in front of Claudia. "Eat a decent breakfast, for goodness' sake. You're going to blow away on the breeze if you get any thinner."

Marrick chuckled. "She's right, Claudia. You do need a little meat on your bones." He stood up. "I'll leave you two to your female conversations."

As he passed Jane he added softly, "Perhaps you'd like to take breakfast here, too. You'll find a better selection of food than at Cook and the butler's table. They hardly ever vary their breakfast menu—it's invariably kippers or porridge."

"What did he mean by that?" Claudia asked after he left.

Jane shrugged noncommittally and impulsively hugged her.

Claudia smiled, pleased by the gesture. "What was that for?"

"For saying you will go to the regatta today. I was afraid . . . Well, never mind."

"But how could I deprive you of an opportunity to be with Bran? I'd have got up from my deathbed if necessary. Now listen, we must make plans to—very casually, of course—throw you and Bran together."

❦ Five ❧

UNIFORMED FOOTMEN carrying trays of cold drinks and hors d'oeuvres moved among the deck chairs set up under the trees along the riverbank. Maids in starched aprons spread red-checkered tablecloths on the grass and placed a wicker hamper on each, then flanked them with folded blankets. For those too elderly or infirm to sit on the grass, there were trestle tables and benches.

Claudia found a pair of deck chairs in a grove of willows near the finish line, wrapped herself in a blanket, or promptly dozed off.

"She might at least have stayed awake for the race," a voice drawled at Jane's side.

Jane felt her heart hammer and wondered, in the instant before she turned, whether it would be Bran or Roald standing beside her. Everything about them was identical, including their voices. Even when she looked into quizzical jade-green eyes she wasn't sure. She assumed it was Bran, since Roald probably didn't remember her.

"Sshh, Claudia didn't sleep well last night. I'm sure she'll be wide awake and cheering for you or Roald when the race starts."

"For me or Bran, you mean."

Jane looked more closely at the handsome young man beside her. "Roald? Excuse me, I thought you were your brother."

He gave her a lazy smile that was completely disarming.

"But how could you make such a mistake? I'm far better looking than Bran."

"And just as modest, I see. I'm Jane Weatherly."

"Yes, I know. I remember you very well. When we were children you used to dive behind the hedge if you spotted us coming. We could never get near you. We'd catch glimpses of you and Claudia together, and we asked about her mysterious friend, but she would never tell us about you."

"She probably didn't want you to know her playmate was the stable master's daughter."

"If you think Claudia was ashamed of you, then you aren't worthy of her friendship. Actually, I believe it was Bran and I who failed to measure up. She didn't think we were good enough to associate with you, not the other way around. At any rate, she never wanted to share you."

His eyes drifted to the sleeping Claudia. "God, she's lovely, isn't she? Have you ever seen any creature on earth more exquisite?"

"No, I haven't," Jane said truthfully. She had never felt envious of Claudia's beauty, because she knew it went hand in hand with delicate health and fragile emotions, but Jane felt embarrassed that a man would make such a remark about one woman to another.

Roald must have realized this, too, for he immediately added, "I say, I'm sorry. That just slipped out. If I may say so, you're an extremely attractive young lady yourself." He paused. "Since you're Claudia's friend, you must know that Bran and I are completely besotted by her. I . . . er . . . don't suppose she's ever given you any hint as to which of us she might choose?"

Amused and faintly saddened by the carelessly conceited assumption that Claudia would eventually marry one of them, Jane shook her head. "Sorry."

"Well . . . I suppose I'd better go and change into my rowing togs. When Claudia wakes up, remind her that Bran and I are hoping to share a hamper with her."

"Good luck in the race, Roald."

He smiled. "My friends call me Ro. Not merely a diminutive of the frightful Roald, but a statement about my capabilities as oarsman. I'm going to win today."

Watching him make his way to the boathouse, smiling and greeting his friends, Jane wondered what it would be like to have both of the handsome Kingsley twins madly in love with her. What a waste to lavish their affections on Claudia, who treated them so abominably.

Jane accepted a frosty glass of lemonade from a passing footman and sat down to await the start of the race.

The two eight-man shells were in position, the coxswains hovering nervously near. Jane had overheard a conversation that explained why the Kingsley twins would be in opposing shells. This ensured that a Kingsley would be at the Royal Henley Regatta.

Despite their bantering rivalry, Bran and Roald never really competed with each other, in sports or any other endeavor. The success of one was the success of both, and as long as one twin was first, they considered it a mutual victory. It was a good thing Claudia was unlikely to marry either of them, Jane reflected, since she doubted the loser in that particular contest would be so magnanimous toward the victor.

Claudia awoke at the sound of the pistol shot that signaled the start of the race and watched from her deck chair. Jane was on her feet at the riverbank, jumping up and down with excitement and cheering as the two sleek shells glided by, the muscles of the superbly athletic crews rippling as the oars dipped in perfect unison into the diamond-sparkled water.

The two shells were neck and neck as they approached the finish line, but at the last moment Roald's crew pulled ahead and won.

"Too bad, Jane," Claudia remarked as the applause died down and Roald's crew tossed their coxswain into the river in the traditional victory ritual.

"What do you mean, too bad?" Jane asked.

"Well, Ro's team won, but you were screaming Bran's name."

Mortified, Jane muttered, "Oh, no! Was I really?"

She was so embarrassed that she'd made such a spectacle of herself that when the twins arrived to share a picnic hamper she was completely tongue-tied. She nibbled a cucumber and watercress sandwich, ignored cold ham and chicken, and refused the champagne Roald offered.

Bran—who seemed not at all disappointed at losing the race—bantered with his brother and flirted with Claudia. Jane lapsed into mortified silence after Bran thanked her for being the only spectator who actually called out encouragement rather than offering polite applause. She was relieved when at last it was time for the ladies to go into the house to rest before the evening's party.

What a capacity for enjoying themselves the upper classes had, Jane thought, watching couples dancing on the parquet floor of the ballroom at Willowford. She suspected that capacity for pleasure was the chief difference between the aristocrats and the working classes, who were surely so named because that was their function in life—to work, while their "betters" played.

She was seated in a window alcove on a sofa that was partly concealed from the dance floor by a palm in a marble urn. A plump matron snored softly at her side, and several elderly ladies and gentlemen—all in that state of sated stupor that followed an enormous meal—occupied the adjacent chairs.

Claudia had warned her that if she wanted to dance this was not the place to sit, but Jane still felt ill at ease and was content to hide among the matrons. Not even her new white satin ball gown had helped her through the ordeal of dinner.

She had been presented to Sir Nigel Kingsley, an older version of his handsome sons but with a brusque manner and a sharp, penetrating stare that made Jane feel he recognized instantly that she did not belong in their set. His wife, Lady Alicia Kingsley, a rather nondescript woman who seemed overwhelmed by the male members of her family, greeted Jane vaguely and quickly moved on to other guests.

It was the arrival just before dinner of Lord Marrick that disconcerted Jane the most. He was accompanied by a stunning woman clad completely in black. Her hair was as black as Marrick's, set off by her perfect buttermilk complexion. She had large sloe eyes and full red lips and scorned all jewelry, so that one was aware only of the woman.

Jane stared at her in admiration, thinking that every other woman surely must look overdressed and overjeweled. "Who is she?" Jane whispered to Claudia.

Claudia grimaced behind her fan. "Magdalena de Mora. I can't believe he brought her here. He never invites her to the abbey."

"Is he courting her?"

Claudia snorted indelicately. "You might call it that. She's his mistress."

"Oh," Jane said, embarrassed.

"She has a husband," Claudia added. "He's some sort of Spanish diplomat. But everyone knows Leith and she—"

"Ssh! Here they come!"

Jane felt herself being thoroughly scrutinized by the sloe eyes of Magdalena as Marrick presented her.

". . . and Miss Weatherly will be accompanying Claudia to New York," Marrick concluded.

"How exciting for you both," Magdalena murmured, her English perfect, her tone low and seductive. "I hope you have a wonderful time."

"Would you excuse us?" Claudia said, a little rudely. "We were just about to look for Bran and Ro."

"Of course," Marrick said, but his expression changed almost imperceptibly into one of annoyance. "You look very striking, Jane. The gown is perfect, but you should pay attention to your gait. You walk like a warrior maiden."

Claudia had already moved away and didn't hear the remark. Jane was too dumbfounded to respond before Marrick took his lady friend's arm and moved away. The dinner gong sounded at that point.

During the meal, Jane sat stiffly between two young men whose names she couldn't remember, stinging from Marrick's remark. She supposed it was a not so subtle reminder of her position in his employ, since good manners would have prevented him from saying such a thing to any other woman. Or was she being punished for Claudia's rudeness to his paramour?

Still, she knew she tended to stride rather than take short ladylike steps, and hadn't she screamed like a fishwife at the riverbank today, further demonstrating her peasant status?

Halfway through the meal she added to her shame by knocking over a wineglass. The wine sloshed onto her plate, and a red stain crept across the white damask tablecloth.

When she tried to mop it up with her napkin a footman quickly stepped forward, gave her a disdainful glance, and whisked away everything in front of her. She sat, cheeks flaming, head hung low, as a place mat was brought to cover the offending stain, along with fresh food.

Mercifully Marrick did not bring Magdalena to the ballroom for the dancing after dinner, but Jane was sure he had seen her spill her wine. She had refused any further drinks, although the champagne was still flowing freely, and despite a seven-course dinner, crystal dishes of bonbons, Turkish delight, glacé fruits, nuts, and other delicacies were set out on all the tables.

Jane sank lower in her seat, trying to be inconspicuous, her hand concealing a wine stain that had splashed from the spill at dinner onto her white gown. Would this evening never end? Claudia had come alive when the sun set and had danced every dance since the music began, usually with one of the twins, since they cut in on any other partner. Jane was glad to see Claudia enjoying herself for a change and hoped this meant she was no longer moping over Royce's defection.

The music stopped and a moment later Claudia, dragging the twins with her, appeared.

Roald flashed his infectious smile. "May I have the honor of the next waltz, Jane?"

He had obviously been coerced by Claudia, Jane thought crossly. Probably lost the toss with his brother. She was about to say she didn't wish to dance when Roald added, "You'd be doing me a tremendous favor, Jane. Everyone knows you haven't danced with any of the young blades casting lascivious glances in your direction, so my standing among them would rise considerably. Come on, be a sport. After all, I was on the winning team today. Don't I deserve a reward?"

Bran winked at Jane, and Claudia smiled encouragingly. Roald extended his hand to help Jane to her feet, and feeling herself melt, she rose. Surely—other than Claudia, who was impervious to the charm of any male except Royce—the female hadn't been born who could resist the Kingsley twins.

The rest of the evening whirled by in a happy haze. Jane danced with Roald, then with Bran, then with several other partners. She loved to dance and soon lost her awkwardness with everyone but Bran. In his arms she felt stiff, so tense she could not respond to his comments or even smile at him.

As he led her back to the edge of the floor he gave her a perplexed look. "I have the feeling I made some awful faux pas with you, Jane. Was it the other day when I rode over to the abbey—or this afternoon at the picnic? I've been racking my brains to try to recall anything I might have said to offend you. Whatever it was, please forgive me."

"You didn't do anything to forgive," Jane muttered, tripping over her feet.

His arms went around her to steady her, and crushed against him, she was almost undone. She could smell the faint aroma of the bay rum he'd used to tame his abundance of fine fair hair, and the clean soap and shaving cream smell of his skin. Even through his evening clothes his body felt vital, alive, and she was overcome with a longing that overwhelmed her. She could not look into his eyes or even speak.

He sighed as he released her. "If I haven't done anything specific, then I suppose I'm still on trial for being a useless parasite on the skin of society. You might give us half a chance, you know. We've only just come down from Oxford."

"And do you now intend to find gainful employment?" Jane asked, knowing that it was highly unlikely, in view of their father's wealth.

Bran grinned. "Oh, if we get bored enough, we might see if we can muck up the old man's newspaper or magazines."

As they left the dance floor, Bran looked around. "What happened to Claudia and Roald? I thought they were dancing, but now I don't see them anywhere, do you?"

One of his friends, who had been in his crew that afternoon, answered for her. "I saw them slip out onto the terrace, Bran. Looks like you might lose to Ro with Claudia, too. This really hasn't been one of your better days, has it, old chap?"

Tight-lipped, Bran led Jane back to her sofa and excused himself. She wondered if she should have told him that probably Claudia had merely felt faint and needed a breath of air, that she was infatuated with someone else and Bran certainly didn't need to be jealous of his brother. But the thunderclouds in Bran's eyes told her he wouldn't have believed her.

As he left her, she knew for certain that her fears that Claudia would create a rift between the twins had been well founded. Jane's heart ached for Bran. She would have given anything to wipe that look of misery from his face, even if it meant losing him forever to Claudia.

❦ Six ❧

TWO DAYS after the Kingsleys' party, Jane knocked on Claudia's door to see if she was ready to go to dinner and found the room in darkness. Jane could dimly discern the shadowy shape of Claudia in bed and called softly to her.

"I have one of my sick headaches, Jane. I'll have a tray sent up. Will you explain to Leith?"

"I'll stay with you—"

"If you don't mind, I'd rather be alone."

"Perhaps I could get a tray in my room, too, then? I don't want to go to dinner without you."

"No! I mean . . . one of us has to go down to dinner, because Leith wants to discuss the arrangements for our passage to America."

Reluctantly Jane closed the door and made her way along the corridor toward the south wing.

Awed by the sheer sprawling size of the abbey, she glanced at the various doors she passed, careful to follow the route to the dining room Claudia had shown her. Some of those closed doors, Claudia had told her, led to parts of the abbey that had been left unrestored over the centuries.

Just before Jane reached the double doors leading to the dining room, she saw from the grandfather clock standing in the adjacent hall that she was again too early. Jane had the uneasy feeling that being too early was worse than being too late, since the butler and footmen regarded her with frosty stares whenever she was the first to appear for a meal.

A footman carrying a tray of cutlery passed her. Rather than be present while he finished setting the table, Jane continued along the vaulted corridor, not sure exactly where it led.

She caught glimpses of vast rooms lined with eighteenth-century paneling, of statues in niches, and furniture so beautiful it was sad that most of the time it was seen only by the servants who dusted and polished.

One room was furnished with Oriental pieces—handsome black-lacquered chests decorated with golden scrolls, unusually shaped chairs, delicate vases, and priceless jade. Jane found herself drawn into the room, spellbound by the exotic ambience.

The muted sound of approaching voices abruptly broke the spell. Jane felt a moment's panic. Would it appear she was sneaking about? Trespassing in places where she was not supposed to be? She stepped behind the door, hoping they were not coming into this room.

". . . and they've decided to go to Sarajevo instead. They'll come here later, I'm not sure when. In view of this, Lord Marrick, you might want to postpone your ward's voyage to America." That was the clipped accent of Herr Bruner.

Marrick's voice responded, "No, I want Claudia to leave immediately . . . for reasons other than the visit of the archduke. But rest assured I will see to it that she remains in New York for as long as necessary."

"You're not exactly an ardent prospective bridegroom, are you? Most men would not wish to be separated from their beloved for an indefinite period."

"My marriage to Claudia will not be a love match, Herr Bruner. It is simply a tidy solution to an old problem. And I would prefer you not mention it again, especially not in front of . . ."

Their voices faded away, and Jane remained frozen behind the door, trying to digest what she had heard. *Lord Marrick intended to marry Claudia?*

But Claudia had no inkling of his intentions. And what about his mistress, Magdalena de Mora? Did he intend to maintain his liaison with her after his marriage? Jane felt a surge of righteous indignation at the dissolute morals of the rich.

She was even more perturbed by the burden of knowledge she was not supposed to have and by the dilemma of what to do with it. If she told Claudia what she had overheard, she would immediately confront Marrick—and Marrick would undoubtedly send Jane packing. Besides, this was the twentieth century. No one could be forced into marriage, certainly not Claudia, who, in addition to believing she was in love with Royce, would be horrified by a proposal of marriage from her guardian.

Jane made her way back to the dining room, where Marrick and Bruner were already seated. They rose as she entered the room. A footman pulled out a chair for her, and Marrick glanced at her questioningly. "Claudia did not come down with you?"

"No, she asked that you excuse her. She isn't feeling well."

"Nothing serious, I trust?" Bruner asked.

"A headache. I should think she'll be fine tomorrow."

"I hope so," Marrick put in. "I've booked passage for you to New York on the *Mauritania*, sailing on Saturday. I'll have steamer trunks sent to your rooms first thing tomorrow, as we'll have to send them forward to Liverpool."

He went on to discuss the forthcoming voyage, and Jane listened without concentrating, still troubled by the fact that Marrick actually intended to marry Claudia. The arrangement seemed vaguely incestuous to Jane, and she was exceedingly troubled by it.

Before the meal ended, Bruner rose and excused himself, saying he wanted to finish some last-minute packing. He was leaving the following day for Austria. Jane found herself alone at the table with Marrick as the final course—crackers, a selection of cheeses, and fresh fruit—was served.

"Did you enjoy the Kingsleys' party?" Marrick asked when he had apparently exhausted the topic of the New York trip. "I hear you and Claudia were the belles of the ball."

"We had a nice time, thank you."

He was regarding her with that same speculative stare he'd given her on other occasions, as though determined to uncover her every flaw.

As the silence between them longthened, she could not stop thinking about what she had overheard. What if she goaded him into repeating what he had told Bruner about his marriage plans? Perhaps he'd opened the door when he brought up the Kingsleys.

She cleared her throat. "Do you think Claudia might one day marry one of the Kingsley twins?"

Marrick's expression did not change. "No. The Kingsleys will never win Claudia's heart for one simple reason: They're too decent, too honorable. Claudia will only fall in love with a cad."

Jane almost choked on the piece of cheese as a quick vision of Royce, the ultimate cad, flashed into her mind. Somehow she managed to regain her composure. "What makes you think so?"

"She's like her mother—uncannily so—and she, too, had the utmost contempt for good, kind men."

"Do you mean Madame Abelard . . . or Claudia's ghost mother?" Jane asked before she could stop herself.

"Ah, so she's told you of her imaginary mother."

"Is it her imagination?"

He stared moodily into his wineglass.

Jane said, "It's cruel to keep Claudia in the dark."

"Sometimes it's more cruel to be enlightened."

"Then Madame Abelard was *not* her real mother?"

"I didn't say that. Look, I forbid you to feed any fantasies of Claudia's. There are facts concerning her childhood that you cannot know or possibly understand. Now, if you'll excuse me, I have some work to do before I retire."

The instant after a maid deposited Claudia's dinner tray on her bedside table and departed, Claudia jumped out of bed and locked the door.

She dressed quickly, selecting a dark blue evening dress with matching hooded cape. Earlier, when she was supposed to be napping, she had carefully snipped the decorative rhinestone trim off the cape, for fear the stones might catch the light and disclose her presence as she crept past the servants' quarters.

Before leaving her room, she arranged a bolster under the

bedcovers. Her maid had been instructed not to disturb her, and Jane would respect her wish to be left alone, but if anyone did come to check on her, the bolster would look like a sleeping body in the darkened room.

Holding her breath, Claudia went quickly down the rear staircase. Although most of the ground floor remained unconverted, a wine cellar, storage room, and servants' quarters had been built in the south wing, and Claudia tiptoed past the doors leading to that part of the abbey and made her way to what had once been the nuns' warming room.

She carried an electric torch, but it emitted only a dim amber circle of light and she realized she should have found a new battery.

How cold it was down here! Colder than the grave. She wished she'd worn one of her furs instead of the lighter cape. Shivering, she made her way to the giant caldron set upon the carved stone stand.

A shadow detached itself from behind the caldron and, startled, she cried out.

Royce swept her into his arms. She clung to him as he rained kisses all over her face and then claimed her mouth so passionately he took her breath away. After a moment she stopped shivering with cold and trembled instead with desire. But the dank chill of the cloisters pressed in on her, and she murmured against his mouth, "Let's not stay here. I feel as though I'm committing a sacrilege by kissing you here."

Royce laughed softly. "This is the safest place to be, my darling. No one ever comes to this part of the abbey. Look—I've made a cozy corner for us."

He led her around to the far side of the caldron, and she saw he had placed a blanket on the floor. Drawing her down so that they sat side by side, he wrapped one arm around her and with his other hand fumbled under her cape to find her breast.

"Royce, please, we have to talk. Oh, I've been in agony, not knowing what happened. When your note came today I almost fainted with relief. But why did you want me to meet you here and not tell anyone? Surely you want Jane to know you're all right?"

She felt him stiffen. "No, Jane is the last person I want to know. Claudia, darling, you must trust me. I love my sister, but she doesn't know all of the facts about my life. We've lived apart for years, and she has no idea what I've had to deal with. She doesn't approve of my love for you, you know, and she'll do anything to keep us apart."

"But, Royce, why did you leave so suddenly without explanation? You left a note for Jane, but she didn't tell me what it said."

He pressed a kiss to her hair and gently caressed her breast. "I asked her to take care of you, that's all. I couldn't tell you what was happening; I still can't. All I can do is tell you I love you and ask you to believe in me, to wait for me. We can't be together—not yet—but soon, I promise."

"But Leith is sending us to America, to New York. Oh, Royce, I'll be three thousand miles away!"

"New York? Really? Both of you? Well, that's a surprise." He digested this news silently for a moment.

"I won't go," Claudia whispered.

"You must go. I've got some serious business to take care of, and I wouldn't be able to see you for a couple of months anyway. Maybe longer. Better to do as his lordship wants, keep him happy for the time being. By the time you get back from America, I'll have everything settled, and then we can be together forever."

"Can't you tell me what it is you have to do?" Claudia asked wistfully.

"Someday I'll tell you all about it. For now you must trust me. You do trust me, don't you?"

She nodded, and he gathered her closer and kissed her, his mouth drawing her into a vortex of passion that she was powerless to resist. His hands were warm, his body pressed close, and she no longer felt the damp chill of the cloisters.

Where he touched her, her flesh felt as though warm, sweet wine flowed over nerve endings so acutely receptive that surely they must have lain dormant awaiting his lips, his hands, the urgent, driving force of his manhood.

Lost in the magic he created, when at last he drove her over the brink she experienced a blinding moment of revelation, an instant when it seemed the entire meaning of life was revealed to her. Then tremors of release rippled through her body, and he spoke, breaking the spell.

"Remember, not a word to anyone that you've seen me. When you get to New York, write to me in care of poste restante at the village post office."

❦ Seven ❧

THEY SAILED from Liverpool on a cloudy June morning. The first-class section of the *Mauritania* was a floating palace, and even before they left the river Mersey, Jane was convinced she could happily spend the rest of her life aboard a luxury liner.

Claudia immediately became seasick.

Jane ministered to her in their stateroom, offering dry toast and sips of tea. But Claudia clung to her bed in abject misery, wishing she were dead.

"Perhaps if you came up on deck?" Jane suggested in desperation. "The fresh air might help."

"No! If I have to be sick in front of anyone else I shall die."

"I don't think you've got anything left in your stomach to be sick with. Please, Claudia, the ship's doctor says if you'll sit on deck and keep your eyes fixed on the horizon, you'll feel better. And in a couple of days you'll be used to the motion of the ship and get your sea legs."

Claudia moaned and buried her face in her pillow.

Jane spent most of the day in the stateroom, slipping out for a breath of air only when Claudia dozed. After all, she was a paid companion, and if Claudia could not enjoy deck quoits, shuffleboard, Ping-Pong, and the swimming pool and other amenities provided for the passengers' entertainment, then Jane felt duty bound to ignore them also. It was particularly hard in the evening, when the music of the orchestra drifted from the grand saloon and Jane longed to be dancing instead of watching Claudia suffer from mal de mer.

On the fourth day of the voyage Jane managed to persuade

Claudia to go out on deck. She sat in a deck chair bundled in her sable coat beneath several blankets, looking as frail as gossamer, but admitted she did feel a little better. The lengthy siege of seasickness had taken its toll, however, and she spent the remainder of the voyage regaining her strength.

The ship entered New York Harbor just after dawn on the eighth day, and Jane was on deck to watch the Statue of Liberty materialize out of a thin morning mist. Claudia was still sleeping and didn't appear until the ship docked.

She gazed in solemn awe at the Manhattan skyline for a moment, then said, "You don't mind if I stay in the stateroom until we're ready to disembark, do you, Jane?"

"No, of course not. The cabin steward has taken our bags, and I've completed all the customs and immigration forms. I'll come for you as soon as someone arrives to take us to the hotel. I suppose Mr. Baron will send someone."

In the penthouse suite of the Charlemagne Hotel on Fifth Avenue Conrad Baron pondered the problem that no longer could be ignored.

The *Mauritania* had probably already docked. He'd intended to leave that evening for the West Coast. Marrick couldn't have picked a worse time to demand a favor, especially one that involved a pair of giggling young females.

An extremely tall and thin man of indeterminate age, anywhere from forty to sixty, Baron reclined lethargically in an oversize leather chair before a neatly arranged mahogany desk. His lazy gray eyes, usually half closed, fatigued expression, and drooping shoulders, suggested a man with insufficient energy to run large hotels on both coasts as well as an extremely popular restaurant. But the languor he exuded was deceptive. Nothing escaped that lazy gaze, and those who had challenged Baron, in business or any other way, had learned that he dealt swiftly and ruthlessly with his opponents.

After a moment he rang a bell on his desk, and his secretary, a pasty-faced young man named Wilbur Stockman, knocked on the door and entered the room. "Yes, sir?"

"Has Frankie left to pick up the English girls?"

"Yes, sir. He should be at the dock by now."

"He did remember to wear a white carnation in his lapel? That's how they'll know I've sent him."

"I ordered the carnation sent to his room first thing, sir."

"Good. Now . . . I've decided to leave for the coast as planned tonight. Is my car ready?"

Wilbur gave him a pained expression that indicated he felt hurt that his employer would question his ability to prepare the private railroad car for the three-day cross-country journey. "I checked it myself, sir."

"Good, good. Get in touch with me immediately if there's any problem with these very special guests. I've instructed Frankie thoroughly on the situation, but I want to stress to you, too, that I have an obligation to keep those two free from harm during their visit. I owe a debt of honor to Lord Marrick. You do understand, don't you?"

"Yes, Mr. Baron. You were very clear on that point when you informed us they were coming. I'll wire if one of them so much as sneezes."

"It's not their health I'm worried about. We have to send them back to Lord Marrick *intact*. You do get my meaning?"

Wilbur gave him a pained glance. "I do. But may I say that I am not a ladies' man."

"No, but Frankie is, and I doubt I scared him with any of my threats. I want you to keep an eye on him. I expect the girls will be tweedy, horsey types who won't interest him anyway, especially if they look down their aristocratic noses at him."

"I'll certainly keep close watch on Frankie when he's around the young ladies, sir."

From the sudden gleam in Wilbur's rather flat brown eyes, Baron guessed he welcomed the opportunity to spy on Frankie, whose good looks and popularity were a source of envy to the nondescript-looking secretary.

Baron said, "Let me know the minute Frankie and the girls get here."

Frank Allegro shouldered his way through the crush of people meeting the ship and scanned the disembarking passengers descending the gangway. None were the right age.

Traffic had been heavy, and with so many people meeting incoming passengers, he'd had a problem finding a parking space for Baron's Duesenberg. He hoped they were still on the ship and not loose somewhere in the crowd.

He reached the bottom of the gangway at the same time two young women appeared at the top. For a moment he didn't move. He felt as if the wind had been knocked out of him. Baron had told him that Lord Marrick had written that his ward was a petite platinum blonde, which Frank decided was about as descriptive as saying Niagara Falls was a large waterfall.

Frank had never seen a more beautiful woman. As he watched, she adjusted the brim of her hat, her hand moving gracefully as a butterfly as she checked her hatpins. The sunlight glinted on silver-blonde strands of hair escaping from beneath the fashionable hat. Her willowy figure was clad in a smart travel suit, and a sable coat was draped over her shoulders. Her pale oval face was dominated by huge eyes. She seemed too delicate, too angelic, to be a mere mortal.

He was still gaping at the vision of loveliness when her companion, who had managed to come down the gangway without his noticing, appeared in front of him. "From the way you're staring at Miss Abelard, I expect you've been sent from the Charlemagne Hotel to pick us up?"

She was taller than most women, with an hourglass figure he noted but didn't overtly stare at. Attractive, but not beautiful. She'd probably wear well. There was an honesty in her gaze he liked. He gave her his best smile and pointed to the carnation in his lapel. "I guess this helped you arrive at that conclusion, too? Welcome to America, Miss Weatherly. I'm Frank Allegro."

"How do you do."

"Mr. Baron sends his regrets that he couldn't meet you personally, but he's waiting for us at the hotel. I'll just run up and get Miss Abelard."

"No need. She's on her way down." She was regarding him now with a knowing look that said she was well aware of the effect Claudia was having on him.

Close up, she was even more breathtaking. Frank, no stranger to beautiful women, couldn't take his eyes off her and twice stumbled over his feet. For her part, Claudia acknowledged his stammered introduction with a cool smile and then looked right through him.

Pulling out into the heavy traffic leaving the docks, Frank now realized why Baron wanted him to guard Claudia Abelard twenty-four hours a day. She was gorgeous, and she was an heiress. He wondered what she'd think if she knew of his own humble beginnings.

Frank had been found among the emigrants in the steerage section of a ship that had sailed from Cherbourg in the early nineties. He appeared to be under two years old, an appealing child with big blue eyes, curly dark hair, and a dimpled chin. He could say "Mama" but nothing else anyone could understand.

A thorough check of the passenger list and exhaustive questioning of passengers and crew failed to turn up anyone who admitted to having brought him aboard. The captain decided that, since the ship was past the point of no return, he would continue to New York and turn the little boy over to the authorities on Ellis Island. They could deal with the youngest stowaway. Someone must have slipped him aboard the ship, and someone else must have fed him and kept him hidden until it was too late to turn back, but no one claimed him.

Also aboard the ship, in one of the finest first-class staterooms, was a man who had intrigued both fellow passengers and crew with his reclusiveness. He was traveling under the name Conrad Rudolph Baron, but it was rumored that Baron was his title, not his name, and that he was the black sheep of an aristocratic Austrian family being exiled to America to hush up a scandal.

To the surprise of everyone aboard, Baron emerged from his self-imposed isolation to inquire after the welfare of the tiny stowaway. The baby boy had been taken to the ship's infirmary and was being cared for by a nurse. Baron found him tied to a table leg to keep him from wandering away while the nurse flirted with a good-looking steward.

"Untie that child immediately," Baron thundered, his lethargic countenance for once animated by anger.

The nurse, fright written all over her face, hastened to obey while the steward fled.

"Is he an animal, to be restrained like that? How dare you treat a human being in such a manner? Have you no feelings, no sensitivity? You're not fit to be a member of the medical profession, or of the female sex. I doubt that you're even fit to be a member of the human race."

The little boy looked up at Baron and gave him a dazzling smile of approval. The nurse cowered before Baron's wrath.

"For now he will come with me to my stateroom," he continued, patting the child's dark, curly head. "Send someone down to steerage to see if there is a woman willing to care for him for the remainder of the voyage. I shall require a cabin near my own for the woman and child. I want someone clean and English-speaking. We're going to America, and this child must learn the language."

The ship had picked up Irish emigrants after leaving France, and a young Dublin widow grieving over the death of her own five-year-old son from diphtheria was selected to care for the stowaway.

"What shall we call the poor wee mite, sir?" she asked Baron. Maggie O'Flaherty had black hair and brown eyes, and Baron wondered if the little stowaway was also Irish.

"Why don't you give him a name, Maggie?" he suggested.

"Me sainted father's name was Francis, sir," she answered in her soft brogue.

"Francis it is, then."

But it was Frankie, from the start. He proved to be a happy lively boy, who loved to sing and dance. If he heard music of any kind he would tap his feet and raise his voice in baby babble that was astonishingly melodious.

By the time the ship reached New York, it was taken for granted that Frankie and Maggie O'Flaherty were not destined for the immigrant cages of Ellis Island, but would remain in Baron's care. He took a suite of rooms at the Waldorf-Astoria at Fifth Avenue and Thirty-fourth Street, and they went with him.

It was at the Waldorf that Frankie saw his first piano, and it was love at sight. Instead of pounding the keys in the usual cacophony of toddlers, he carefully picked out several notes, then repeated them, his eyes wide with wonder.

"Perhaps we should call him Frankie Steinway," Baron mused.

"Or Frankie Spinetti," the Italian pianist suggested.

"But he hasn't seen any other instruments yet. How do we

know he won't one day prefer a violin or a horn?" Baron
added.

"If it's a surname you're after," Maggie said, "then you
could call him Melody or Harmony."

"He repeats the melody," the Waldorf pianist said. "'Da
capo.' He plays fast—'*allegro.*'"

"Ah," Baron said. "That one I like. We shall name him
Frankie Allegro."

His piano lessons began the following day, and while he
never became a prodigy, he loved to play and sing and his
music was the only antidote to Baron's periodic bouts of
debilitating depression. No one ever knew if Baron formally
adopted the child, but he raised him, educated him, and after
he graduated, employed him. Conrad Baron never married or
had children of his own.

Jane decided that Frank Allegro was an amusing, brash,
cocky, conceited, quick-witted dynamo of unlimited energy.
Claudia tolerated him in the same way she accepted the
presence of any other person charged with her comfort—the
chambermaid who brought fresh linens, the waiter who presided over her meals, the desk clerk who took her messages.

Claudia and Jane had met their host only briefly. Conrad
Baron had explained that he had to leave on business and that
they should let Frank know if they needed anything. He would
also be their driver, showing them the sights of the city, and
their escort when they went out in the evening.

Claudia was so delighted to be on terra firma again that she
wanted to see everything, do everything, enjoy all of the sights
and sensations this fabulous city had to offer, and she wanted
to do it all immediately.

Jane was plunged into a dizzying whirl of dining, Broadway
shows, sight-seeing tours, and shopping expeditions that left
her breathless. At first she was happy that Claudia seemed to
be enjoying her holiday so much that she was too busy to
lament about how much she missed Royce. Then it occurred
to Jane that Claudia had not brought up the subject of Royce
since they left England. Of course, she had been ill on the
voyage . . . but it did seem strange that she had not uttered
Royce's name even once.

Shortly after reaching New York, Claudia discarded her furs and wool suits and happily announced that she felt truly warm.

Frank said, "Mr. Baron thought maybe you'd want to get out of town—maybe take a trip up to Maine to escape the heat."

"Escape from it? Oh, no, I adore it."

"Good." Frank grinned. "I always feel like a foreigner outside of Manhattan."

Claudia frowned slightly. "Well, you don't have to go everywhere we do. Besides, we'll be returning to England shortly."

"I thought you liked it here," Jane put in, reluctant to leave before she had seen more of the country.

"I do. But I want to go home as soon as we can leave without hurting Mr. Baron's feelings. I do wish he'd come back from the West Coast."

So she was still pining for Royce, Jane thought, despite the fact that she never mentioned him.

"Mr. Baron could be gone for months," Frank said. "I hope that means you'll be staying."

"In that case," Claudia answered, "I shall write to my guardian and ask how soon we can politely leave."

They were dining at a French restaurant, and a pianist was playing Chopin in a desultory manner. Frank drained his wineglass and said, "That's going to put me to sleep. Excuse me, ladies."

A word with the maître d', another with the pianist, the surreptitious exchange of currency, and Frank sat down at the piano and began to play.

Spellbound, Jane leaned forward to listen. She had never heard such music. Lively, happy, sometimes raucous, occasionally melancholy, constantly changing, always surprising. The piano seemed to be telling several different stories at once, yet they blended beautifully, connected in some vibrant, compelling way.

He returned to their table amid the enthusiastic applause of the other patrons, and Jane exclaimed, "That was the most exciting music I've ever heard. What was it? I've never heard anything like it."

"Something I learned on a trip to New Orleans. It's called ragtime." Frank looked at Claudia. "Did you like it?"

She gave him an uninterested glance. "I was rather enjoying the Chopin."

"Tell me more about your ragtime," Jane said quickly. Perhaps, she thought, that was the secret of Claudia's power over men. She treated them so abominably.

Jane stared at the *New York Times* headline of June 28: "Heir to Austria's Throne Slain with His Wife by a Bosnian Youth to Avenge Seizure of His Country."

Peering over her shoulder, Claudia said, "Oh, dear. Poor Archduke Ferdinand. I believe Leith was expecting him and his wife to visit the abbey this summer."

Jane remembered the conversation she had overheard between Marrick and Karl Bruner: "They are going to Sarajevo instead."

To their death, she thought now, and wondered at the possible political and international repercussions of the assassination.

There was no time to wonder, since Claudia was ready for another evening on the town. She exhibited a brittle gaiety, filling every minute with some frenetic activity, as if by doing so she could make the time pass more quickly.

Jane worried that Claudia's frail health could not withstand the onslaught of sleepless nights and fast-paced days. Jane herself was becoming weary and longed for a quiet hour with a book.

She had finished dressing when there was a knock on her door, and opening it, she was confronted by Frank. He gave her one of the winning smiles he usually reserved for Claudia.

"I came to ask a favor," Frank said. "I wondered if I can persuade you to come down with a headache tonight."

"So that you can be alone with Claudia? No, you can't."

"Her guardian's paying you to be her chaperon, is he?"

"As Mr. Baron is paying you to be our escort?"

"Ouch! Look, I swear I'll be a perfect gentleman. I just want a chance to get to know her a little better."

"You're wasting your time. She isn't interested in you. Besides, there's someone back in England she cares about."

"I'd still like an evening alone with her Or even an hour. How about I take her for a carriage ride around Central Park and you retire early?"

"Out of the question. Besides, I have a feeling that, in view of today's news from Sarajevo, we may soon be returning home. Why start something you can't finish?"

"I guess you wouldn't understand. I'll see you down in the lobby."

In July the letter Claudia eagerly awaited came from Lord Marrick. He was back in residence at the abbey, and they could return whenever they chose. Jane should contact the Cunard Steamship Company and select a suitable sailing.

Claudia was overjoyed. "Oh, do let's call them today and get on the first ship."

Jane hesitated. "Are you sure you wouldn't like to take a short trip out of town? We haven't seen anything outside of New York, and I doubt we'll ever come back—"

"I want to go home on the fastest ship," Claudia said firmly. "Will you call Cunard right away? I think I'll lie down for a while; I'm rather tired today."

An hour later when Jane went to wake Claudia and tell her passage to Southampton was available in three days, she found her lying on the floor near her bed.

Flying to her side, Jane dropped down on her knees and cradled Claudia's head. She was breathing shallowly, and there was a bluish cast to her lips. Jane grabbed the telephone from the bedside table and screamed into it that she needed a doctor immediately.

Frank waited with Jane in the adjoining room while the doctor, assisted by his nurse, examined Claudia. Frank seemed to feel he was personally responsible for Claudia's collapse.

"She's so tiny, so delicate. I shouldn't have let her burn the candle at both ends the way she's been doing. She's been getting by on two hours sleep a night. . . . Baron will have my hide. Oh, God, I hope it's nothing serious. Maybe I should call another doctor. A specialist."

"Specializing in what?" Jane asked, her own fear for Claudia sharpening her tone. "We don't know what's wrong yet."

"They've been in there with her a long time. I don't like the look of this. Did this ever happen to her before?"

At that moment the door opened and the doctor, a portly, pink-cheeked man, emerged. "My nurse will stay with her for the time being," he said. "I would like her to see a cardiologist as soon as possible."

"Her heart? It's her heart?" Jane asked.

"She's never been told that she has a weak heart?"

"Not as far as I know. . . . No, she would have told me, or her guardian would have."

"Well, let's get a cardiologist to examine her before we jump to conclusions. For the time being, just keep her quiet. A light diet, no exertion, bed rest. Keep her calm."

"Doctor," Jane said, "you haven't told Claudia of your suspicions, have you?"

"No. To her, I diagnosed simple exhaustion and prescribed rest. But if she has a weak heart, she should be told. There are precautions she must take."

"We'll take care of her," Frank said. "I'll call the best heart man in New York."

The following day a renowned cardiologist confirmed the doctor's suspicions, and Jane sent a cable to Lord Marrick. His wired reply was prompt and definite: "Remain in New York. Arriving shortly aboard *Aquitania*. Marrick."

⊰ Eight ⊱

EDITH WEATHERLY sighed contentedly and rolled away from Royce. He reached for the gold cigarette case Claudia had given him, hoping that a cloud of smoke would obscure his expression of distaste.

During the four years Edith had spent in prison her formerly voluptuous body had become soft as dough, flabby and unpleasant to the touch. She perspired profusely during sex and he almost drowned in her saliva. S'truth, she slobbered worse than a bloodhound, he thought, inhaling the acrid smoke deeply.

He had been able to climax only by imagining himself making love to Claudia, closing his eyes and picturing her delicate body, her rib cage so fragile above a handspan waist that he could crush it in his hands if he chose. He thought of Claudia's cool skin, as delicate as silk, of her sweet lips, her clean hair.

"Tell me about the rich girl. Was she bloody awful in bed?" Edith asked slyly, pushing her tangle of carrot-red hair out of her eyes and accepting the lit cigarette he passed her.

"I expect she'd have been a corpse if I'd given her a tumble, but I didn't," Royce said. It was uncanny how Edith could read his thoughts. He made an effort to think about other things, but there was little to distract him. The room they had taken in a third-rate inn depressed him. Being with his wife disgusted him.

Edith snorted in derision. "A lovely young virgin in the house and you kept your hands off her? Never. But you just mind yourself from now on. Edie's back, and she's going to take care of you in that department." She sat up, humming under her breath.

"Edie, I'm nearly out of cash," Royce said. "We're going to have to move on. I've been thinking. Maybe we should go up north and see if we can find some nice estate tucked away somewhere in the country that needs a chauffeur. Some county we've never been in before, like Yorkshire. Maybe even Scotland. If we change our appearance a bit and our names, with luck we shouldn't run into anybody who knew us before. Maybe you could change the color of your hair. You're going to have to lie low for a long time."

He avoided looking at her, for fear she would guess what he was up to. He had to make her believe that he was concerned about her being captured and returned to prison. In truth, he wanted her back there as soon as possible, but he had no wish to be incarcerated himself for harboring a fugitive or, worse, for any other crime in which she decided to implicate him.

Damn her. He would have divorced her in a minute had it not been for the fact that as a wife she could not be forced to testify against her husband, nor did she want to. As a discarded woman it would be another story. Her vengeance would be swift and terrible.

He would have to move very carefully. Edith had to be recaptured while he was elsewhere so that she would never suspect he had turned her in. But so far, except for one evening, when he'd pretended he was going to collect back wages owed him by Marrick and instead had gone to see Claudia, Edith hadn't left his side.

Another burning question was how much the authorities here in England would cooperate with the Irish police. Would they extradite her to Ireland?

Edith's rough fingers grabbed his chin and turned his face toward her, her cat's eyes suddenly alert. "And how are we going to get up north? Just walk into a railway station and buy tickets? The Irish police will have notified the scuffers here to keep a lookout for me. They'll expect me to come home. My photo's probably posted in the railway stations by now."

"You made your way from Liverpool down here without getting caught, didn't you?"

"I had a bit of help, ducks," she answered enigmatically.

He decided against questioning her about her escape, feeling the less he knew about it the safer his own skin would be. "Well, I suppose I could get a car and drive us."

She gave him a mocking glance. "Who do you know who'd lend you a car?"

"Nobody. But when Marrick goes away his cars aren't used, they're just left in the garage. And he doesn't have a chauffeur now to keep an eye on them. I could get in and borrow one. We could abandon it after a while and pick up another along the way. As long as we don't keep a car too long, we should get away with it. When we're far enough north we'll get on a bus."

Her eyes narrowed. "How did you find out he's going away—Marrick, I mean?"

"He's away more than he's home. Sooner or later he'll be off again. We'll just wait."

She considered. "All right." She stubbed out her cigarette and nestled close to him again. "We need to find you a rich old widow to romance."

His stomach churned. "What about Claudia Abelard? There's more money there than we could count—"

"Forget her, Royce," her voice hissed in his ear like a snake. "Now I'm out, if I ever catch you with another woman under the age of fifty, I'll cut it off."

He winced as she squeezed viciously to accent the threat. She laughed then and kissed him. "Besides, you said her guardian had shipped her off to America, didn't you? She's no good to us there."

Raising her head she looked at him, then traced the cleft in his chin with her finger and said softly, "You're a good-looking swine, Royce. I missed you. And I worried about what you were up to when I was inside. I should've made sure you were out of circulation, too, shouldn't I? Next time I will."

❖ Nine ❖

IT WAS FRIGHTENING, Jane thought, how quickly Claudia's already limited strength deserted her. By the time Marrick's ship was due to arrive, less than two weeks later, she could barely get out of bed.

Conrad Baron returned from the West Coast in a state of high anxiety about his guest. He put Claudia in his own spacious suite on the top floor and moved onto a lower floor himself, so that she could have complete peace and quiet. He wanted to hire a full-time nurse but Claudia refused the offer.

Frank was even more devastated than Baron by Claudia's illness, and blamed himself for allowing her to burn the candle at both ends. Only Jane, fearing that such obvious worry would frighten Claudia, managed to keep a cool head and take a matter-of-fact attitude toward her friend.

On the day the *Aquitania* docked, Jane accompanied Frank

to the pier to meet Lord Marrick, and as they waited for the passengers to disembark Frank asked, "What's he like?"

"You've never met him? He's abroad so much I thought maybe he came here sometimes."

"Mr. Baron goes to Europe at least once a year. I guess they get together then, but Lord Marrick has never visited him here."

"He's in his late thirties. Tall, dark, and sinister-looking. If he were an actor he'd play the villain."

"Yet he came all this way to be by the side of his sick ward."

Jane thought of the conversation she'd overheard between Marrick and Bruner and muttered, "Claudia is more than his ward; she's his prized possession."

"Doesn't sound as if you like him very much."

"He's a member of the privileged English upper class. You're American; you wouldn't understand what that means."

"Oh, we've got our own version of your blue bloods."

"Mr. Baron, for instance?"

"No, he's your European variety. I'd have thought you knew that."

"I know nothing about him, except that he always looks ready to fall asleep. What makes you think I did?"

"Well, he was one of the Three Musketeers." Seeing her baffled expression, Frank went on, "Lord Marrick was another. I don't know much about the third member because Mr. Baron never talks about him."

"I still don't understand."

"They were students together at Heidelberg. Three close friends. They didn't call themselves the Three Musketeers, by the way—that's what I dubbed them. There's a picture of them in Mr. Baron's bedroom, looking very young and full of their own importance. If you're interested I'll show it to you sometime. When I was a small boy I asked him about it, because it's the only photograph he has. No pictures of his parents, family—just the one of the three students taken in front of the library at Heidelberg University."

"And what did he say when you asked about the photograph?"

"That the three of them were close friends. That there was nothing they could not ask of one another."

"I can't believe Lord Marrick echoes his sentiment. At least, Claudia never mentioned any undying friendship—" Jane broke off. "Here he comes now."

"I thought you said he was sinister-looking," Frank whispered as Lord Marrick strode down the steeply sloping gangway toward them.

Marrick nodded briefly to Jane, then interrupted her introduction of Frank by asking, "How is Claudia?"

"She's very weak. Frankly, Lord Marrick, while I'm sure she does have a heart murmur, as the doctors say, I wonder if they're focusing so much on her heart they're missing another reason for her illness."

"So your field of knowledge extends to medicine also, Miss Weatherly?" Marrick handed his valise to Frank, who winked at Jane as he took it and led the way to the car.

Jane felt her jaw clench. "Since Claudia became ill I've read every medical book I could get my hands on. The cardiologist said she has paroxysmal tachycardia. I looked it up. It isn't a serious disorder, especially in someone so young, so I don't think Claudia should have turned into an invalid overnight. But the cardiologist isn't interested in anything but her heart."

"Then we'll find someone who is." He gave her a bemused glance. "Unless you've already diagnosed her malaise?"

"Of course not." She decided to ignore his sarcasm. "But I suspect anemia. She's run-down and exhausted and needs a rest, but the doctors have frightened her about her heart, and I don't think it's good for her not to do anything at all, she'll just get weaker."

Marrick helped her into the car. "You'd make a good nurse, Miss Weatherly. Don't worry. We'll have other doctors look at her. I do believe you're correct in your assumption that it might have been better not to tell Claudia she has a weak heart. There's no doubt she'll brood about it. She tends to brood about a great many things."

He climbed into the front seat with Frank. "And how is my old friend Conrad?"

"Worried to death about your ward. As we all are," Frank answered.

In the backseat Jane noted with some satisfaction that Frank addressed Marrick as an equal, showing him none of the deference to rank he would have received at home.

Claudia reclined on a brocade chaise longue in the sitting room of the suite, awaiting the arrival of her guardian. She twisted a handkerchief nervously and stared at the china clock on the mantelpiece.

Leith had always had this effect on her. Any conversation with him seemed akin to facing judge, jury, and executioner. He probably thought she'd brought her present malady upon herself by engaging in a mad whirl of social activity since her arrival in New York. No doubt that awful Frank Allegro had already reported that she'd stayed up all night and been out gallivanting all day and had drunk too much champagne and lived on caviar and desserts. But she hadn't known then she had a weak heart. She had to fill every minute to make the time pass quickly. But the passage of time had not brought her heart's desire.

Her heart was broken, of course. Claudia had convinced herself that was the real cause of her palpitations and mind-numbing lethargy. She had written to Royce every day on the voyage, posting a batch of letters and cards the moment they docked, and almost every day since. But there had not been a single response from him. Not even a card. Little wonder her poor heart had shattered into a million pieces. Royce had already forgotten her.

She wished Jane could have stayed with her, but Leith wanted to see her alone. Jane had tried to reassure her that a heart murmur wasn't serious, but Claudia knew the truth.

Her bedroom door opened suddenly, and Claudia jumped as Leith came into the room. He always seemed to overpower his surroundings, dwarfing lesser beings, making her feel especially insignificant, more conscious than ever of her physical frailty and lack of sophistication. But today when he spoke his voice was gentle. "Hello, Claudia. How are you feeling?"

"Much better, thank you. I really didn't mean to drag you all the way across the Atlantic like this."

"I was worried about you."

"I'm just a little tired, that's all."

He pulled a chair close to her chaise longue, sat down, and picked up her limp hand.

The physical contact disturbed her. He had never touched her before. Was she dying, was that it?

Seeing the alarm on her face he released her hand quickly. "We're going to take good care of you, Claudia. I'm bringing in some other doctors to examine you."

"Couldn't I wait until I get home and see our doctor there?"

"You're not going home, Claudia. Not for a while."

"But I'm not that ill! Please—"

"Listen to me. I have several important matters to discuss with you. First of all, at any minute England and France will be at war with Germany. There's no way to anticipate what this will mean at home, but you can be sure life will change for us drastically. You and Jane will be much better off if you remain here."

"No! No, I can't—I must go home." Claudia heard the rising panic in her voice and her heart began to thud painfully. I must go and find Royce, she thought. When we're together he'll fall in love with me again. Absence doesn't make the heart grow fonder. It's out of sight, out of mind.

She drew a deep breath. Her guardian mustn't suspect she was feeling ill, or her cause would be lost. "Leith, I've fallen in love. I wanted to tell you before I left, but . . . well, he had to go away for a little while, but we are going to be married one day."

He frowned. "The Kingsley twins didn't go away. They're both still at Willowford enjoying a lazy summer."

She looked down at her hands, folded tightly on her lap. "I . . . didn't mean Bran or Ro."

"Who, then? Young Carstairs? Richard Ward's son? That terribly nervous young viscount, what's his name?"

"No, no . . . none of them." Claudia felt her panic grow. If she were to admit to being in love with his former chauffeur, would he be so angry that Jane would suffer guilt by association? Would he send Jane home without her? Claudia said quickly, "You don't know him. I met him at one of the Kingsley parties while you were abroad. He's . . . a student in London."

Marrick rose to his feet and paced about the room, coming

to rest at the window. He stared down at the bustling street below. When he spoke he did not turn to look at her. "What you felt was infatuation. There's no such thing as lasting love, take my word for it. Except perhaps between parents and children, and then not always."

"But I *do* love him! I *will* marry him."

He turned and surveyed her with a speculative look. "I hadn't meant to tell you this now, especially in view of your illness. But I think perhaps it's time. I'm going to tell you why your choice of a husband was perhaps preordained. I'm also going to tell you how you came to be my ward."

Her heart had begun a familiar erratic fluttering. She pressed her hand to her chest to try to calm it.

"Let me go back to when it started. To three young men who formed a close friendship in their student days."

"Mr. Baron told me you were at Heidelberg together," Claudia said. "I wondered why you went to a German university."

"I also went to Cambridge. In the latter part of the last century Heidelberg was world famous, particularly in the fields of medicine and law. Many Americans went there also. The three young men whose friendship I mentioned were graduate students. Few men form friendships as close as those three. Closer even than blood relations. In fact, it's possible the bond between them was formed because their families had let them down in that regard."

"In what way?" Claudia asked, noting that he referred to himself in the third person and wondering if he was somehow ashamed of what he was about to tell her.

"One of the trio—Conrad Baron, our host—was something of a rogue who constantly embarrassed his family. Eventually they shipped him over here, turned him into what the Americans call a remittance man. They paid him to stay abroad."

He paused, frowning. "Another of the three was of such high rank and great wealth that he was quite literally lost amid his family possessions. His parents virtually ignored him. The third was sired by a man so cold and distant that his wife ran away, abandoning both him and their son, who was sent away to boarding school at the tender age of five. Since the other boys were all at least two or three years older, he always felt out of step, unsynchronized. During his student days he was always the youngest, which is perhaps why his friendship with the other two, who were several years older, meant so much to him."

Claudia knew instantly which of the three was Leith Marrick, but made no comment.

"But to get back to those student days. Our situation was far from unique. We were careless young men with access to unlimited wealth we had not earned. Possessions, money, meant nothing to us. We spent with reckless abandon, and one way we disposed of our families' money was by gambling.

"Most of the time we came out more or less even. We gambled with one another, with other students, rarely with outsiders. It wasn't a serious problem." Marrick paused. "Until the American came."

"He taught us to play poker. Now, I'm not going to tell you that what followed would not have happened had we been playing whist, but I do believe the unfamiliar game precipitated a series of bets that we wouldn't have made if we'd stayed with our usual games. There was the novelty of the new game, and we were fascinated by the chance to bet on a single turn of a card. In all fairness, I must say the American warned us that fortunes could be made and lost on the turn of a card. He said back home a player would wager anything from the family farm to the shirt on his back. We countered that, both in England and on the Continent, country homes and much more had changed hands after a night at the gaming tables.

"One night we began to play in deadly earnest. The stakes rose higher and higher; the bets became more and more complicated. We played all night, all the next day, and into the small hours of the following morning. That certain sense of unreality, of abstract energy, that comes about through sleep deprivation, had us all in its grip. Nothing had any substance beyond the next hand of cards.

"Someone—I don't remember who—suggested we play for the most valuable piece of property—a plantation in Kenya, a country home, for instance—that each of us would one day inherit.

"One of us, and I'm not going to identify him because we were sworn to secrecy, then said he'd be willing to wager a large and valuable property on condition that he receive assurance it would one day be shared with someone he would name. Naturally we told him to leave some other portion of his estate to this person, but he insisted this was impossible.

"We then learned that at the tender age of eighteen he had had a brief fling with a member of a Paris ballet company, who had borne him an illegitimate daughter. He was paying for the child's care in a foster home, but worried about what would become of her if he were to meet with an untimely demise. Because she was not his legal offspring, she would have no claim on his estate."

Claudia listened intently now.

"During the course of that infamous poker game, he saw an answer to his dilemma. His property, and the land that went with it, was by far the most valuable of the wagers, but before he would make the bet he wanted a sworn promise that whoever won would take care of his daughter should it become necessary—that is, in the event of his death.

"It seemed a simple request. What more could it involve than writing a check for the child's care? But he wanted more than that. The winner was to agree to make the child his ward and see to it that eventually she go to live in the family's country home."

"Rathbourne Abbey," Claudia whispered. "And I am the child of the ballet dancer. I always knew that the Abelards were not my real mother and grandmother, you know."

Marrick turned to face her, his expression guarded, but she detected a plea for understanding. "Your father asked me not to tell you. He said he would tell you himself when you were old enough to forgive human weakness. You see, he felt that since Simone and her mother had taken care of you from birth, there was no reason to burden you with the knowledge that your birth was illegitimate. Nor did he want his family to know of his indiscretion."

"Is that what I am?" Claudia asked sadly. "An indiscretion?"

"I'm sorry. That was clumsy of me. Your father genuinely cared about your welfare, Claudia. He went to elaborate lengths to ensure you would always be taken care of, didn't he? Looking back with the wisdom of hindsight, I see now that he never had any intention of winning that poker hand. He wanted to be sure there would be someone other than himself to care for you."

"But why didn't he simply marry my mother?" Claudia asked in a small voice.

"I didn't learn the answer to that question for years. Probably his male pride would not allow him to admit the truth, which was that your mother refused to marry him. She didn't want to be tied down with either a husband or a child."

Marrick was silent for a moment, perhaps thinking of his own mother who had abandoned both him and his father. He went on, "Your father deeded Rathbourne Abbey to me four years later when he inherited it, and two years after that he was killed in a hunting accident in Africa. I made you my ward."

Claudia finished for him. "And when first Simone and then Grandmère died, I came to live with you." She was silent for a moment, contemplative. "Is that why you spent so little time at the abbey? Because it wasn't your own family home?"

"Perhaps. But I doubt I'd have spent much time in Scotland, either, where my family's country estate was—I disposed of it years ago. Rathbourne Abbey was more convenient, closer to London and the European capitals."

Claudia had to force herself to ask the question she most needed to have answered. Her throat had constricted, her mouth was dry, and her heart still raced. "What . . . what became of my mother?"

"She died of tuberculosis a few months before your father was killed."

Her breath shuddered from her body, leaving her feeling drained, lifeless. She couldn't speak. "She wanted to see me. I know she did. She reached for me—"

"Stop it, Claudia," he said sharply. "She never made any attempt, to my knowledge, to see you."

She bit her lip. "I should think, in view of what you've just told me, that you would be delighted to be rid of me. That you'd be glad to hand me over to the care of another man."

"Be honest with me, Claudia—this man you profess to be in love with, he has no money, no background, does he?"

"How did you know?"

"I guessed, from your reticence to tell me more about him. Claudia, listen to me carefully. I had no idea when Rathbourne

Abbey became mine that it would be filled with almost priceless objets d'art or that the tenant farms that came with it would be on such valuable land. Nor did I foresee that my own family's fortunes would decline drastically before I came into my own inheritance. You know I have an uncle—my father's younger brother—and several cousins, who live in Cape Town. They are a family of wastrels, cunning and devious, and . . . Well, no matter how carefully I prepare my will, leaving Rathbourne Abbey to you, I'm afraid they will contest the will and you will not prevail in a legal battle with them."

Claudia considered this silently. Since Royce was indeed penniless, as Marrick had guessed, it would be nice one day to inherit Rathbourne Abbey. But Marrick was not an old man, he seemed far too strong and healthy ever to die.

"I want it to be yours, Claudia," Marrick said. "I owe it to your father. There's only one way I can be sure of that. I've thought of this for some years now, even as I worried about that weasel of an uncle of mine and his greedy sons in Cape Town. The one way to thwart any possible assault on my estate, and to ensure it becomes yours, is for you to marry me."

She was so stunned she could only stare at him with such revulsion that she saw his expression harden.

He snapped, "Before you tell me you'd rather die, let me assure you I have no romantic inclinations toward you. The marriage would merely be on paper, a business arrangement to protect your inheritance. If you wished to see your penniless student I would not object, as long as you were discreet."

The idea of marriage to her guardian was so repulsive she could hardly speak. She had to force herself to say quietly, "Leith . . . I don't care about the abbey. I've never liked living in it. I don't care about the paintings and the porcelain and all the other things. I can't marry you. It would be a betrayal of my love for—" She broke off in time. Not that he appeared to be listening to her; a mask had descended over his face.

"There's no need to say any more just now. For now you must concentrate on getting well. You and Jane will stay here until you are fully recovered. I don't want you at the mercy of some ship's doctor. Conrad has a home on Long Island that he rarely uses and has offered it to you for your convalescence. You can think about what I've said, and we'll talk about it again when you come home."

He walked to the door, paused, and looked back at her. "You might find that when you see your young man again one or both of you has already fallen out of infatuation."

"Let's get Frank to take us to the park. It's such a lovely day; an outing would do you good," Jane urged.

Claudia shook her head wanly. "I don't feel strong enough."

"You've got to get out of that damned chair," Jane said, her patience stretched to the breaking point. "All you do is flop on the bed or the chair. It's no wonder you're so weak."

A tear slid down Claudia's sunken cheek. Jane dropped to her knees beside the chaise longue. "I'm sorry. I didn't mean to shout at you."

"Don't you think I *want* to get well? Jane, I want to be strong enough to go home! I *yearn* to go home!"

"If you would just walk a little way—up and down the balcony, perhaps. I'd help you."

"I'm too tired." Claudia began to whimper piteously.

"All right. Don't cry, please. Perhaps the new doctors who are coming tomorrow will be able to help. But you've got to help yourself, too."

Claudia wadded her sodden handkerchief into a ball. "It's not the same between us, is it? We aren't the same kind of friends we used to be. It all changed when we left home."

"What do you mean?" Jane asked cautiously, feeling guilty because it was true. They were no longer friends and confidantes. She had not told Claudia the truth about Royce, had not told her of the conversation she'd overheard about Lord Marrick's marriage plans, and had certainly not told her that she was now a paid watchdog.

"You know what I mean. There was a time when we told each other everything. Now I'm afraid to confide in you because I hate it when you're angry with me."

"Oh, Claudia . . . have I turned into such an ogre? I'm sorry. I do have a guilty secret." She told quickly of Marrick hiring her to be a paid companion.

"Goodness, is that bothering you? Why didn't you speak up

sooner? I knew all about it. I didn't mention it to you because I thought . . . well, perhaps it would embarrass you. You have such fierce pride about such things. Jane, it isn't important. Please don't let it put a barrier between us."

Jane's shoulders slumped. "I loathed the idea of deceiving you. I wish I had spoken up before now. While I'm unburdening myself, I want to tell you why I was so outraged that my brother had been courting you. Now that he's out of your life I hope it won't hurt you so much—"

Claudia held up her hand. "Please stop! Royce is far from out of my life. I still love him. Until I became ill, I wrote to him every day."

"How could you? You don't know where he is."

"I saw him just before we sailed. He told me to write to him in care of poste restante."

"My God, Claudia! He's *married*."

"I guessed that much from what you—and he—told me. It doesn't matter. He can get a divorce. And please don't lecture me about how society views divorced people. I'm well aware of the stigma—but I don't care."

Jane thought rapidly. She had a good idea why Royce would never divorce Edith, but no real proof that her theory was correct. "Where is he? What is he doing?"

"I don't know. He didn't reply to any of my letters," Claudia answered miserably.

Inwardly Jane breathed a sigh of relief. "There's something else I must tell you. I'm afraid I have to add eavesdropping to my sins—I overheard Lord Marrick say he intends to marry you himself."

"I know." Claudia lay back limply on her pillow.

Jane blinked, astonished. "You do? You never mentioned it."

"I just found out this morning. I was going to tell you, but you started bossing me again about getting out of my room, and . . . well, I didn't get a chance."

Jane picked up a crystal decanter from the bedside table, poured a glass of water, and handed it to Claudia.

She sipped the water, handed back the glass, and related her conversation with Marrick. .

"Phew," Jane said when she finished. "How do you feel about all this?"

"I shan't marry him, of course."

"No. I didn't think you would."

They sat silently for a while, each lost in her own thoughts. At length Claudia spoke, as though to herself, "My mother isn't lost to me. I don't care what he says."

"You think he lied to you about your mother?"

"No. He told the only truth he knows. He wouldn't deliberately lie to me. He's never done that. He simply doesn't talk about that which he doesn't want me to know."

"Isn't that a form of deception? Isn't that what happened between the two of us?"

"You misunderstand. I didn't say my mother is still alive. It may be that she is truly dead, as he says. But some part of her reaches for me . . . tries to connect with me in some way. I've always known that if I could only discover what it is she's trying to tell me, I'd understand what my life is *for*."

"I doubt many of us ever learn that, unless we're destined for sainthood, or to make some major contribution to the welfare of mankind."

"Leith says life is all a barbaric game."

"He's a cynic. Don't listen to him." Jane smiled suddenly, a feeling of relief washing over her. "Have you noticed? That invisible barrier between us is down. I'm so glad."

"Me, too. And, Janey, I really will try to walk with you tomorrow."

"Good," Jane said. "We've got to get you well."

The following day Claudia was examined and tested by a team of physicians, and a few days later they diagnosed exhaustion brought on by poor eating and sleeping habits but due mainly to anemia. Claudia was put on a high iron diet and a tonic, and for a while seemed to rally.

Marrick returned to England. He sent a cable confirming his safe arrival, and Frank delivered it to Jane. She was packing to move to Conrad Baron's Long Island home and quickly scanned the message. "I'll give it to Claudia later. She's taking a nap."

Frank stood in the hall outside her door, regarding her with a grave expression. She looked at him questioningly. "What is it?"

"Bad news. The newsboys are screaming that England and France are at war with Germany."

❧ Ten ❧

THEY MOVED into a large, comfortable home on Long Island, with a competent staff and weekly visits from a doctor. Baron also offered Frank's services as escort, but since Claudia didn't want to go anywhere, he found other excuses to visit.

It seemed to Jane, as the days turned to weeks and the weeks faded into months, that although Claudia recovered physically, her state of mind kept her imprisoned in an endless convalescence. She simply lost interest in everything, including, to Jane's distress, going home. Whenever Jane brought up the subject of returning to England, Claudia would sigh and say, "But I'm not sure he's even in England. Let's wait another week and see if we hear from him."

Jane blew up the first time. "Hell's bells, Claudia, you can't spend your whole life waiting to hear from Royce."

"Do you think he joined the army?"

"I don't know. But it doesn't matter where he is or what he's doing, you've got to accept the fact that he's gone from your life forever. I hate to be so brutally frank, but to Royce you were a passing fancy, nothing more."

"Something happened to prevent him from writing to me, I know it. Perhaps he had an accident— Oh, dear, he could be suffering from amnesia."

Jane groaned and didn't mention going home again for a couple of weeks.

Claudia fell into the habit of sleeping late each day and taking long afternoon naps, leaving Jane to her own devices.

One day when Frank arrived, on the pretext of bringing delicacies to tempt Claudia's appetite, Jane greeted him warmly, glad to have some company. "Claudia's napping. Come for a walk with me; it's such a perfect afternoon."

He gave her a comical grimace. "Walk among all those trees and flowers and bees and things? Is it safe?"

"I'll protect you," Jane promised solemnly. "I was brought up in the country."

"Well, I don't know if I can walk on grass. On water, maybe . . ."

She punched his arm playfully, and they went out into mellow sunshine. The grounds were green and tranquil, birds serenaded the last days of summer, and the scent of flowers hung in the warm, still air.

"It's so peaceful," Jane said, "I find it hard to imagine the horror of the war in Europe. Makes me feel guilty. As an Englishwoman I should be home, doing something for the war effort."

"What, for instance? Sewing cordite into bags? Making army uniforms?"

"You think women can only be seamstresses?"

"I'd hate to see you in the trenches. You could be a nurse, I guess, but you'd need training for that. Besides, I hope you won't leave Claudia. I don't think she could stand another abandonment."

"She told you about my brother?" Jane was surprised.

Frank nodded. "A little. What happened?"

Jane didn't want to talk about Royce. She stared straight ahead and mumbled, "He's married. He was a cad to lead her on."

"You think she's ever going to get over him?"

"Of course, in time." Jane wasn't really convinced, but what else could she say? "Frank, to tell you the truth, I'm getting bored, with so little to do. You're right; I can't leave Claudia. But you just said something that gave me an idea. Perhaps I could volunteer for nursing service in France after I've taken Claudia home to Rathbourne Abbey. In the meantime, would it be possible for you to bring me some books I could study? You know, first aid, basic nursing techniques, and so on?"

"Sure. Be glad to. I have a friend who's in medical school. I'll ask him for a recommended reading list."

"Thank you. I'd be grateful."

They walked on in silence for a while, then Frank asked, "You think Claudia will come down to dinner?"

Jane knew that when Claudia learned he was present she definitely would not leave her room, but she said, "It depends on how she's feeling. She may." Jane couldn't fathom why Claudia disliked Frank so, as she herself found him to be a witty and entertaining companion, full of fun and vitality. She also admired his dependability. If he said he would do something, it would be done, no matter what. She added, "I hope you'll play some more of that wonderful ragtime music for us after dinner."

He gave her a look of exaggerated dismay. "What, and have Claudia run screaming into the night? She hates it. If she's up, I'll play you some nice Chopin."

How was it possible that what had been intended as a few weeks' holiday could have stretched into months? Claudia had become an invalid and Jane her nurse. Despite Jane's best efforts, Claudia had lost interest in everything, including, it seemed, life itself.

Frank had suggested they would love a Broadway show called *Daddy Long Legs*, and told Jane she should see the new moving picture, *The Escape*, but that perhaps it wouldn't be Claudia's cup of tea, and therefore he would be glad to volunteer to stay with her while Jane went into town to the picture show. But Claudia continued to languish in her room, rarely leaving it even for meals.

"Damn it, Claudia," Jane said one day as they finished eating breakfast and Claudia objected to all of her suggestions as to how they might spend the day. "You're worse than any nineteenth-century maiden who goes into a decline because she's lost her beau. Why are we staying here? Let's go home. I hate being abroad while England is at war. The Americans seem to be terrified that they'll be drawn into the war, and . . . well, I feel we should be doing something for our country."

"Leith doesn't want me to go home," Claudia said flatly.

"Why not? Is he embarrassed by the fact that he isn't in the army?"

"Jane! He's far too old . . . isn't he? Thirty-eight or -nine."

"He's strong and healthy, and I think older men than he have gone to France."

"He says he's very busy just now and doesn't spend much time at the abbey. He says with the war everything has changed and that I should stay here until he sends for me." She paused, twisting her napkin into a snake. "Besides, if I go home, Leith might bring up the subject of marriage again."

"Ah, so that's it. Surely you don't intend to spend the rest of your life here just to avoid marrying your guardian? Tell him you don't want to, and be done with it."

"I don't think I'm up to the journey just now." Claudia gave her a piteous look.

"Then for heaven's sake start walking with me every day. Your appetite would improve, your strength would increase."

Claudia sighed. "Perhaps tomorrow."

"I don't understand. When we first came to America you *wanted* to go home. What changed? Something did, I know. Even after you became ill, you were still desperate to go home. Then abruptly you didn't care anymore. I can't believe it's simply because Lord Marrick told you to stay, or because he wants you to marry him."

Drowning blue-violet eyes regarded Jane with a look of utter despair. "I know I should have told you this before. I received one brief note from Royce. It came while Leith was here, and I was afraid he'd find it. Royce said he would try to work his passage to New York and join us here. That it might take a few months before he could get a ship."

Jane pushed an unruly strand of hair back behind her ear. She felt like tearing it out by the roots. "So you intend to wait for him."

"Forever, if necessary."

"He's no good, Claudia. He has no respect for women."

"Nothing you can say will change my mind about him. I'll love him until I die."

"Then there's nothing more to be said. I can't stay here any longer. I'm going home. I'm sorry."

Tears streamed down Claudia's sunken cheeks. "Please don't desert me!"

"Then come with me."

"No, I can't. Jane . . . what will you do if you go home?"

"I'm going to volunteer for nursing duty in France. At the front line if possible, in a field hospital. From what I've read there's a desperate need for nurses."

"But you'd need training for that. More than you can get from studying books."

"I'll go to a teaching hospital, I suppose."

"You could do it here. We could move back to Manhattan, and you could go to nursing school. At least I'd see you every day, and I wouldn't feel so alone."

Jane considered. "When my training is finished, I'll definitely be leaving. You do understand that?"

"Oh, yes. By then I'm sure Royce will be here."

But Royce didn't arrive, although Claudia grew stronger and Jane became absorbed in her studies. Autumn came, then winter. They spent Christmas with Baron and Frank and a collection of their friends—politicians and hoteliers and what Frank called robber barons.

In January Claudia caught a cold, which lingered, but the sunshine of early spring revived her. Still Royce didn't arrive, and even Claudia gave up hope that he would. They now waited for Jane to complete her nursing training, but in early April a transatlantic cable arrived for Claudia: "Sorry. Long illness delayed plans. Joining army. Will be leaving for France soon. Can you come home at once? Letter with details of rendezvous waiting poste restante. Love always, Royce."

❦ Eleven ❧

May 7, 1915

JANE WONDERED how long she had been treading the frigid water of the Atlantic. Claudia lay on the hatch cover, one arm and one leg trailing in the sea, as Jane held on with one hand and resolutely pumped her feet to stay afloat. She worried that the makeshift raft was becoming so sodden it would soon sink.

They had drifted away from the few lifeboats they had sighted, and she could no longer see any other swimmers. There were many floating bodies, and once she gasped with fright as the corpse of an elderly woman gently bumped into her.

Debris of all kinds drifted by—a hairpiece, a man's white silk scarf, a feather boa, planks, gratings, an empty suitcase.

Surely the German submarine that had sunk the ship must have been aware of all the innocents in the water? Could they not have surfaced at least long enough to pick up the women and children? How could they violate every convention of civilized people?

"Claudia?" Jane said hoarsely, salt water splashing into her mouth as she spoke. Claudia's eyes were closed, and she didn't respond. Jane comforted herself with the thought that Claudia had merely fainted again and perhaps it was just as well she was unaware of what was happening.

Don't die, Jane willed her silently.

The irony was that Claudia's health had been so much better this past week aboard the *Lusitania*. A combination of the sea air, rest, tempting food, and—not least—the anticipation of seeing Royce again had worked wonders.

She was so eager and filled with excitement that Jane had been reluctant to burst the bubble for her and had decided to let her enjoy the voyage. Jane herself had been deeply concerned about the warnings to transatlantic travelers, printed in American newspapers by the Germans, that a state of war existed between England and Germany. Men on the quay had handed leaflets to embarking passengers warning of U-boat attacks in the Atlantic, although she personally had not been given one. She had tried to persuade Claudia to travel instead on the *New York*, which also had staterooms available, but Claudia had pointed out that the *Lusitania* was the fastest ship plying the Atlantic and would save them two days.

The morning they boarded her Jane had looked across the Hudson and seen the ensigns fluttering from the sterns of the German ships interned at Hoboken, and she had felt a stab of apprehension, but the crowd on deck had been so joy-filled and lively she had stifled her qualms. She did wonder if any of the carefree passengers considered that they were sailing on a British ship to war-torn Europe.

But the appointments of the *Lusitania*, the undisputed queen of the Atlantic, were so luxurious, the passenger list was so prestigious, and Jane was so excited to be going home that she soon forgot her misgivings about German submarines.

She could not, however, ignore the nagging worry over Claudia's forthcoming rendezvous with Royce. Each day of the voyage Jane considered and rejected several courses of action. That morning she faced the fact that time had run out. They would be home tomorrow.

As the ship emerged from a heavy fog bank into brilliant sunshine and Jane caught her first glimpse of the Irish coast, she had known that there was nothing for it but to tell Claudia the truth about Royce and Edith.

Claudia had ordered breakfast in her stateroom as usual while Jane took a brisk walk around the deck and then went to the magnificent high-domed white and gold dining room with its marble Corinthian columns and attentive table stewards.

Scanning the menu, she couldn't help but overhear an indignant conversation at the next table.

"Have you read the *Daily Bulletin*?" one man asked his companion, referring to the Cunard on-board newssheet printed each day. "There are reports from the Dardanelles and the Western Front that the Germans are experimenting with new chemical devices, glass bombs of ether and shells charged with inflammable materials. They're also conscripting sixty-year-old men. If they're that desperate, they're going to start torpedoing *all* British ships, including passenger liners, you mark my words."

"For God's sake, don't mention that in front of our wives. I suppose you noticed that our ports have been blacked out as we approach land and we've slowed our speed? I can understand the blackout, but you'd think they'd want to get out of these waters as quickly as possible. I asked one of the ship's officers about it, and he said it was to save coal."

"Hush, here come the women."

Their voices were joined by female conversation, and the talk turned to plans to enjoy the shipboard swimming pool that day.

For once Jane's hearty appetite had deserted her. She had put off for too long telling her dearest friend all she needed to know about Royce, yet even now she felt guilty about breaking her promise to her brother.

Jane found Claudia peering into the mirror of the stateroom's Sheraton dressing table. When Jane appeared, Claudia asked, "Do I look . . . you know, pinched? As if I've been ill?"

"No. You look beautiful."

"Oh, I do hope he thinks so."

Jane sat on the edge of the bed, her gaze drifting from the tapestries on the walls to the window, which rather than being a porthole was the size and shape of a window in a house. They could have been in the guest room of a luxurious home ashore, except that beyond the window the sunlight sparkled on the calm surface of the sea.

"Claudia, I have to tell you about Royce's past. I must convince you that he will use you but never marry you. He can't divorce his wife. Ever."

Claudia swiveled around to stare at her. "What nonsense. Of course he can. We'll give her grounds—he can commit adultery. I'd be willing to let her name me as corespondent."

"Oh, dear heaven! Claudia, please, listen to me, don't interrupt. Royce has always been attracted to . . . well, I'll call them the nonconformists of society—the political radicals, the dissidents, the . . . people who thumb their noses at the rules. When he left home and went to London he became involved with a wild crowd who trod the fringes of the law. He never actually got into any trouble himself, but I think he came close a few times. Anyway, he met a woman . . ."

Jane paused, remembering the first time she had met Edith Braddock. Her first impression, after the shock of the heavily painted face and the blaze of nearly orange hair, which surely wasn't natural, was of a Rubenesque figure, obviously tightly corseted, wearing a bright green coat with an astrakhan collar. Eyes that were not quite green, not quite amber, regarded Jane somewhat in the manner of a cat that had just dragged in a sharp-toothed rat almost as big as herself, a mixture of pride and defiance. *Here is my prize and I dare you to try to take it away from me.*

At the time Jane met the woman her brother would marry after a whirlwind courtship, she thought Edith looked and sounded as common as any Piccadilly Circus tart, despite the fact that she had a respectable position as a shop assistant.

When Jane later asked Royce what he saw in Edith, his eyes glazed in erotic stupor and he replied, "Edie has a few tricks up her sleeve you couldn't even imagine, Janey. What she can do to a man . . . Well, let's just say that what happens between us when we're alone is what I see in her."

"Jane? What is it you're trying to tell me?" Claudia's voice broke into the memory.

Jane went on hurriedly, "Edith Braddock is a common piece of goods, attractive I suppose in a flashy, tarty sort of way. Very flamboyant, very obvious. Royce was young and foolish—oh, there I go again, making excuses for him. Anyway, they were married within a few weeks of their first meeting.

"Their troubles began almost at once. Royce lost his job, and Edith was arrested for shoplifting. I'm not sure exactly what happened after that. As you know, I hadn't lived with Royce or even seen him for years, except for a flying visit every now and then. But I think Edith was given a suspended sentence and then got into trouble for stealing again. Anyway, they beat a hasty retreat from London, and the next I heard from Royce they were working for a widow up in Cheshire, Royce as a chauffeur and Edith as a parlormaid."

She broke off as the ship rolled slightly. Claudia clutched the bolted-down dressing table for support and murmured, "I shall be glad to get back on dry land. The thought of all those fathoms beneath our hull frightens me sometimes. Go on, I can't wait to hear why you feel Royce is bound to this awful woman for life."

"They left the widow's employ very abruptly and went to work in a similar capacity for an elderly gentleman and his younger wife. Claudia . . . there was a succession of similar positions, always involving either a wealthy widow or a rich old man with a frustrated younger wife."

"What are you implying?" Claudia asked, her tone frosty.

"That Royce romanced a series of lonely women and made off with large sums of money from each of them—aided and abetted by Edith."

"What a ghastly thing to say about your own brother!"

"Do you think I ever wanted to tell you this? I'm so ashamed that I sent him to Rathbourne Abbey, to you. I blame myself more than you'll ever know. But Royce is so persuasive that I truly believed he was innocent of any wrongdoing, that Edith was the villainess and without her influence Royce would never behave like a cad again. How wrong I was!"

Claudia's voice trembled with emotion as she said, "These accusations you're making are without any foundation, any proof."

Jane bit her lip. "What I'm telling you about their exploits in England isn't known to anyone but me, and I only realized what they had been doing in retrospect. You see, they moved to Ireland. I didn't see them or hear from them for over a year. When I did I learned their last position was with a woman named Mrs. O'Neil who owned a country home in Ireland."

"Yes? What happened?"

Drawing a deep breath, Jane said quickly, "Mrs. O'Neil was murdered. Edith was tried and convicted. She was sentenced to life in prison."

"Dear God! Oh, poor Royce!"

"At the trial other staff members testified that Royce had been seen in compromising situations with Mrs. O'Neil and

Edith had been throwing jealous fits about it. There was other evidence that they'd left two previous positions because Royce became involved with his employers' wives and that Edith had stolen money and jewelry from them. Her defense counsel said the women involved had given her gifts, to ease their guilty consciences over their affairs with Royce. The prosecutor countered that she was then also guilty of blackmail. Apparently neither of their previous employers would press charges or testify."

"How . . . how did she do it? The murder, I mean."

"Mrs. O'Neil drowned in her bathtub. There were bruises . . . it appeared she'd been held under the water."

Claudia shuddered. "I've always been afraid of drowning—of fighting for breath. . . ."

Jane went on, "I was at university at the time, getting along on the skimpiest funds. I couldn't afford to go to Ireland for the trial, and no one would lend me any money. There was only a brief mention of the case in the English newspapers, but I bought all the Irish papers I could get my hands on. It seems Edith had been seen leaving the bathroom, and earlier a footman had overheard his mistress telling Edith she was being dismissed. He testified that Edith screamed at her that if she left Royce would go, too, and Mrs. O'Neil answered that Royce would be staying on, that he'd had enough of Edith's jealous rages and was leaving her. The butler confirmed that Mrs. O'Neil had told him she was dismissing Edith, but not Royce, and he was to hire another maid."

"Jane, how awful this must have been, for you as well as for Royce. But surely he has ample grounds to divorce Edith. I don't understand why you say he can't."

"One reporter wrote that he was sitting near Royce when Edith's sentence was read. As they took her from the courtroom she looked at Royce and said, 'You'd better do something about this, or else you know what I'm going to do.' The reporter asked why Royce hadn't been charged with any crime and what his wife had meant by that remark. But nothing further happened. Edith went to an Irish prison, and Royce came back to England. The first time I saw him I asked about Edith's parting remark and what it meant. He said that she wanted him to get her barrister to appeal the sentence and that he would try to put together some money and go back to Ireland.

"I was deeply troubled, as you can imagine. There were prelaw students at the university and I—hypothetically, of course—discussed the trial with them. One of them kept harping on the fact that it would be extremely difficult for a woman to hold another woman's head underwater long enough to drown her. I insisted that there was an eyewitness, which was stretching the truth a little, but he asked if anyone had bothered to check to see where Royce was at the time of the drowning, and even if he didn't help her, they were both guilty, because it was Royce who created the situation that led to murder."

"Jane, you surely didn't subscribe to such a dreadful theory about Royce, did you?"

"No, of course I didn't. Edith is a big woman and quite strong. I'm sure she did it. But I kept thinking about the women Royce had worked for here in England, and how he and Edith kept moving from one position to another. They seemed to have plenty of money—they often took long holidays. How many chauffeurs and maids can afford to do that? Had he seduced his employers here, too? In any case, he'd clearly been romancing Mrs. O'Neil, so it seemed to me that that fact alone made him at least an accessory. Besides, surely he should have seen how dangerously close to violence Edith was and prevented it?"

"That isn't fair! How could he have known she would kill the poor woman? We can't be held responsible for what other people do, Jane, only for our own actions."

"But think how close a husband and wife are. Royce must have known her state of mind. Besides, Mrs. O'Neil had told Edith she was dismissed much earlier that day, hours before she was drowned. There would have been ample time for Royce to pack up and leave with her and avert the tragedy."

"I still think you're being unfair to him. He couldn't anticipate what his wife was going to do."

"All right, let's assume that. Some time later he came to see me in Manchester and I asked him what he intended to do about Edith. Was he going to stay married to her, or, in view of her conviction would he try to obtain a divorce? He replied that he couldn't divorce her. '*Couldn't*'—not 'wouldn't.' When I asked why, he answered, 'Because a wife can't testify against her husband.' I immediately asked if he'd been involved in the murder, and he said no, he hadn't, but that one never knew what somebody like Edith might do or say if she was crossed, that she had a violent temper. Claudia, I believed in him, too. He's my brother, and I didn't want him to be a conscienceless womanizer who drove his wife to murder. I wanted to blame Edith for everything."

Jane ran her hand through her hair distractedly, dislodging several pins. "You know this is so, because when you wrote and said Lord Marrick's chauffeur was retiring, I asked if you could get Royce the job. Do you think I would have done that if I hadn't thought Edith was the guilty one and Royce had just fallen into bad company again, as he had so many times in the past? He seemed so full of remorse and so sorry for what had happened to Mrs. O'Neil that I was sure he would lead an exemplary life from then on."

"But you changed your mind about him," Claudia said quietly. "Why?"

"Because he was repeating the old pattern, Claudia—he was trying to seduce *you*. You're my best friend, and you were only seventeen years old! I couldn't believe it. I saw then that it wasn't Edith's influence that made him behave as he did. He didn't need any prompting."

"But it's different with me, Jane. It really is. He loves me." Claudia's eyes glistened with tears. "And I love him enough to die for him."

Jane gripped Claudia's shoulders and shook her. "For God's sake, don't say that. Claudia, I was as blind as you. I rationalized it all away, too—it was Edith, she was the wicked one. Royce was blameless. But think about it. He was the one who preyed on those women, romanced them, seduced them. Oh, she profited by it, but Royce was just as guilty, if not more so. When my eyes were finally opened, I began to wonder if there was more to Mrs. O'Neil's murder than had come out at the trial. Why had he told me that a wife can't testify against her husband?" She paused. "Actually, one of the law students told me he believed the law states a woman can't be *forced* to testify against her husband. Either way, that's the reason Royce won't divorce her."

Claudia looked down at Jane's hands, still holding her frail shoulders, and Jane released her. Claudia said, "How can you even *think* that Royce could have had anything to do with such a hideous crime?"

She picked up her sable coat and pushed past Jane to the stateroom door. Jane called after her. "Edith escaped from the Irish prison. That's why Royce disappeared just before we came to America. Claudia, please don't go to him. I'm so afraid for you—not just that you'll have your heart broken, but that your life might be in danger."

Claudia gave her one stricken look and fled.

Jane had remained motionless for several minutes. She had been forced to choose between her loyalty to her brother and her friendship for Claudia, and she knew in that moment that she had probably lost both of them.

Her eyes stung and she could no longer feel her feet. How cold the Atlantic ocean was in May. Rising on a gentle swell, she looked toward the mountains of Kerry, clearly visible on the Irish coast, and could make out a lighthouse and trees, all seeming tantalizingly near and yet hopelessly out of reach.

"Damn it," she said aloud, "I'm not going to drown."

She reached down and managed to get one shoe off, giving her more freedom to flex her toes. As she reached for the other shoe she saw to her horror that the makeshift raft carrying Claudia was slipping below the surface.

A moment later Jane was desperately trying to support the limp body of her friend as the sodden grating sank out of sight.

Keeping her hand under Claudia's chin, Jane again turned on her back and started to kick for the distant shoreline, knowing the impossibility of reaching it. But she had to have a goal, something to strive for. Hadn't her father always told her that human beings had to set their sights on future achievements or they might as well give up?

The top of her head touched something hard and, twisting to look over her shoulder, she saw she had bumped the gunwale of a boat, floating barely an inch or two above the surface of the sea. Would it support their weight? The boat was stove in, of course, and almost filled with water, but she would have to take a chance. She couldn't keep Claudia afloat much longer, and there was still no sign of rescue ships.

She gritted her teeth to stifle a moan at the exertion of lifting Claudia over the side, then held her breath as she waited to see if the boat would sink. But Claudia's slight weight made no difference. Jane was so exhausted she knew she would have to rest, if only for a little while. She dragged herself over the gunwale and lay back, panting, rejoicing in the respite, however temporary, feeling the warmth of the sun on her face, despite the icy water in which she was still half submerged.

But her weight was too much for the stove-in boat; she could feel it going down. Reluctantly she slipped back into the water.

"Miss . . ." a voice called across the shimmering expanse of the sea. At first she thought she was hallucinating, as they hadn't seen any live swimmers for some time. But then it came again. "Miss . . . over here."

Turning to look behind her she saw a man paddling a collapsible canvas boat toward her.

As he drew closer she saw he was a crewman, and he had two passengers in the boat with him, one of whom was frantically bailing water. The collapsible rode perilously low in the water and was obviously leaking badly.

The crewman reached out his hand toward Jane, but she said, "My friend—we have to get her out of this boat; I don't know how much longer it will float."

The bailing passenger objected. "This boat won't stand the weight of two more. We're almost full of water now."

"Then I'll go into the sea myself," the crewman said. "I'll not leave two women to die."

"We could take turns in the boat," Jane offered. "If I could just rest for a few minutes . . ."

A strong hand gripped hers and pulled her into the collapsible and a moment later the crewman lifted Claudia in beside her. She looked so peaceful she might have been asleep. Jane raised a numbed hand to Claudia's neck to feel for a pulse, and breathed a sigh of relief as she found a faint sign of life.

The crewman and the passenger were bailing as fast as they could. Jane saw that the other passenger was injured and unconscious.

She was shivering and her teeth chattered. She estimated from the position of the sun that at least two hours, perhaps longer, must have elapsed since the *Lusitania* went down. Why was it taking so long to send rescue vessels?

Jane found Claudia's cold fingers and held them, hoping somehow to convey through her touch her own will to live.

The next moment a swell caught the damaged boat, capsizing it, and they were all tossed into the sea. The collapsible disappeared beneath the surface and Claudia's limp hand slipped from Jane's grip.

Desperately Jane dived, clutched at a sinking body but was unable to hold it. Lungs bursting, she broke the surface again.

Taking a deep breath, she was about to dive again when she saw the crewman holding up Claudia. There was no sign of the other two men.

Jane floated for a second, hopelessness claiming her. Then, seeing that the crewman was having trouble keeping Claudia's face out of the water, swam over to them.

"Sorry—can't hold her," the crewman said apologetically. "I think my collarbone's broken."

Once again Jane hooked her arm under Claudia's chin and started to backstroke.

A sudden turbulence struck them, and she had to fight to hold on to Claudia as they were tossed about in the Atlantic swells. Salt water splashed into Jane's mouth and she coughed, choking. Her eyes burned as though red-hot needles had been driven into them, and she couldn't see what was causing the frothing swells upon which they were being tossed.

A moment later she heard the throb of engines.

Floating up over a foaming wake, she saw that the first rescue ship had arrived to pick up survivors.

She heard the crewman yelling and saw him waving one arm to attract the attention of the approaching ship. Jane clung to Claudia for dear life and called for help also, but her voice sounded as though she were crying underwater.

Boats were being lowered from the rescue ship, and within minutes she could see the sailors pulling lifeless bodies from the water. *Oh, please look over here! We're alive—come to us.* She shouted again, but no boat started toward them, so she kicked harder, unsure where she found the strength to drag Claudia toward the rescuers.

Suddenly strong arms went around her and she was relieved of the burden of Claudia's limp body.

The next moment she was lying in the bottom of a lifeboat, blinking through salt-crusted eyes at the concerned face of a young sailor bending over her.

"Claudia . . ." she whispered. "Is my friend all right?"

"She's alive, ducks," a Cockney voice responded. "Just barely."

"There's a man in the water . . ."

Jane felt herself drifting off into an incredibly peaceful sleep.

❧ Twelve ❧

JANE AWOKE to the sound of tolling church bells. She was in an unfamiliar bed in a tiny room, with a crucifix on one rose-papered wall and a picture of the Virgin Mary on another.

Vaguely she remembered coming ashore, on legs that no longer seemed to belong to her, to the glow of gas lamps and the soothing murmur of Irish accents. Wanting only to sleep away utter exhaustion and the wrenching ache of her limbs, she had sat shivering on a bench on the cold wharf wrapped in a blanket. She dozed again, then drifted to consciousness to hear someone softly urging her to come away now to a nice soft bed.

Groaning as stiff muscles protested, she eased herself from the feather mattress and hobbled to the window. Lifting the lace curtains, she was surprised to see her hand was black-and-blue. Slowly she rolled up the sleeve of the flannel nightgown someone had put on her. The bruises extended all the way to her shoulder. Her other arm was equally discolored.

Turning her attention to the view outside her window, she looked down on a harbor, undoubtedly Kinsale, and could see five of the *Lusitania*'s lifeboats roped together. Boys were wading in the water, probably searching for souvenirs.

More memories flooded back, and with them a stab of panic. Where was Claudia?

Jane moved stiff-legged to the door, opened it, and called out, "Is anyone there?"

A young woman with a cloud of dark hair and a buttermilk complexion appeared at the foot of a narrow staircase. "Sure and 'tis safe you are now, and on dry land, miss. My name's Mairead, and me and my man took you in last night because they ran out of hospital beds and hotel rooms. Would you like a cup of tea?"

"Oh, yes, please." Jane's voice was hoarse and whispery. "And I'm very grateful to you for taking in a complete stranger."

"Sure and 'tis a terrible thing the Germans did. So many lost souls!"

"Is my friend here, too?"

Mairead looked blank and shook her head.

"Her name is Claudia Abelard. She's petite and has very fair hair, almost silver. Do you know where they took her?"

Mairead gestured helplessly. "There's no way of telling. I'm sorry. Was she hurt? The injured ones were separated, you see."

"She was picked up by the same boat as I was," Jane added.

"Don't worry, then. I'm sure your friend is all right. You go back to bed and I'll bring you some nice hot tea and toast."

"If I could borrow some clothes . . ." Jane said. "I must go and look for her."

"First you'll have a hot bath and something to eat," Mairead said firmly.

Jane bathed in a hip bath in front of the kitchen fire and was shocked to see she was bruised virtually all over her body. Her anxiety intensified. How could the frail Claudia have survived such an ordeal?

The hot water did ease some of Jane's stiffness. Mairead provided underwear, a dress, and a woolen shawl, as well as shoes that were a little loose. Jane gulped some scalding tea and ate two slices of toast and drippings, then despite Mairead's misgivings, set off to look for Claudia.

All of Kinsale's flags flew at half mast, and with the tolling church bells it seemed the entire town was shrouded with death. She encountered other survivors, clad in an assortment of borrowed or newly bought clothing, wandering about searching for loved ones or friends. They exchanged snatches of news.

"Someone said Mrs. Morell is all right. She was the oldest woman aboard. . . ."

"I heard someone saw Alfred Vanderbilt in the water. . . ."

"Did you hear, Charles Frohman is dead." Jane had met the impresario briefly during the voyage and thought of the terrible loss to the theatrical world.

"Captain Turner was saved. One of the crew said the captain was convinced the ship wouldn't sink, and he waited too long to order the boats lowered."

"But the deck was almost perpendicular. The boats couldn't be launched on one side of the ship and on the other they were swinging wildly. I saw one swing inboard so far it smashed into passengers on deck and then careered into a collapsible. Another boat hit the side of the ship and disintegrated."

"Why didn't the rescue boats get to us sooner? We were only ten miles off the coast. . . ."

"They say every German in town is hiding from the wrath of the people. Dear God, I heard the death toll will be well over a thousand. Murder, it was, cold-blooded murder."

Claudia was not in the hospital or in any of the town's hotels.

With a cold sense of dread gripping her, Jane forced herself to visit the temporary morgues that had been set up on the Cunard wharf.

At the door of the first she reeled backward, clutching her throat, tears springing to her eyes, at the sight of a pile of dead infants, their tiny bodies battered and discolored. The shed also contained women, hastily laid out in whatever they had been wearing when the liner went down. There had not yet been time to cover the corpses.

Numb with horror, Jane walked past the grim rows of

bodies, some clasped in each other's arms. So many women, so many children. There were women with babies strapped to their breasts. Sunlight filtered in through a window and found a blond head, and Jane's heart turned over. But it was not Claudia.

A wave of weakness assailed Jane, and she staggered outside again, unable to continue the search. She found her way back to Mairead's house and was presented to her husband, Seamus, who told her, "I heard tell there are many survivors in Queenstown. Your friend may be there. I'll go and find out for you."

"How very kind you are," Jane murmured, collapsing onto the nearest chair.

He returned two hours later. "There's a Miss Claudia Abelard in a private nursing home."

"Thank God," Jane breathed. "I'll send a wire to her guardian."

Seamus's face creased with concern. "The doctors think she has pneumonia. I'll take you to her."

Jane was sitting at Claudia's bedside when Lord Marrick arrived. Claudia had been drifting in and out of consciousness and was very ill. A priest wanted to give her last rites, but Jane sent him away. Claudia was sleeping when her guardian arrived.

Marrick looked down at his ward for a moment, then gestured for Jane to leave the room. She felt her welcoming smile freeze on her face.

He followed her into a Spartan waiting room and stared at her silently for a moment. "I do not recall receiving word of your intention to terminate your position as my ward's paid companion. As your employer, I expected you to follow my orders. You were supposed to remain in America until I told you otherwise, or at the very least let me know that Claudia intended to return home. Had I known, I would have insisted that you travel on an American vessel."

What had she expected? Jane wondered. His gratitude? Some expression of relief that they had both survived? A query as to the state of her own health? The tension of the ordeal, her fear for Claudia, and anger that he would berate her in such a manner, all combined to produce her answer.

"Oh, would you, now? Not very patriotic of you, Lord Marrick. Or perhaps you knew in advance that the *Lusitania* would be sunk? There were rumors of saboteurs and German agents in New York, and I recall you have close German and Austrian friends."

"I refuse to dignify such a comment with a response. As far as I am concerned, your position as paid companion has now ended. I will take care of Claudia. I understand Cunard will be arranging transport to Liverpool for you." He withdrew an envelope from his pocket and tossed it onto the waiting room table. "Please accept three months' wages in lieu of notice."

"I should like to see Claudia before I go," Jane said, in a more subdued tone. "She hasn't been able to talk to me yet."

"I'll send for you when she feels well enough. Where are you staying?"

Marrick wasn't present when Jane arrived to see Claudia the following afternoon.

Jane kissed her feverish brow. "How are you feeling?"

"A little better. Jane, you saved my life."

"Lord Marrick seems to think I almost caused you to lose it. He's furious that we were on the *Lusitania*."

"I know. Don't pay him any attention. Is it true that twelve hundred people were lost?"

Jane nodded. "Cunard put out the figures today: 1,150 lost and 767 saved."

Claudia chewed a fingernail and said distractedly, "I can't comprehend the tragedy of it. I simply can't think about what happened just now. Is that dreadful of me?"

"No. You need to save your strength and direct all of your energy to getting well."

After a moment's silence Claudia said, "You must go and pick up Royce's letter, Jane. Find out where he is, and let him know I'm all right and I'll come to him as soon as I can."

"Oh, Claudia!" Jane exhaled sharply in exasperation. "I won't do any such thing. I've told you I won't be a party to delivering you into my brother's clutches."

Claudia's eyes, already bright with fever, glittered with

tears. "Don't force me to choose between you, Jane, please."

"I intend to do everything I can to keep him away from you, Claudia. I'm sorry, but there it is."

"Then go. There's nothing more to be said." She turned her head away.

Jane opened her mouth to speak, but bit her lip instead. She stared at the back of Claudia's head for a moment, raised her hand to touch her, then let it fall to her side again. She turned and walked stiffly from the room. She didn't see Lord Marrick again before she left Ireland.

Jane arrived in Liverpool to find the city torn by anti-German riots. Hundreds of homes in the seaport had been robbed of their breadwinners, and there was fury abroad on the streets.

Seamen and dockers and their families attacked everyone suspected of being German or Austrian. Shop windows were smashed, stock and furniture tossed out on the street, as a mob waving Union Jacks and wielding sticks moved through town, dragging shopkeepers from their premises, ignoring the police, even pulling some of the mounted police from the backs of their horses.

According to the newspapers, rioting had broken out in London also and had spread abroad. Germany was condemned as a wild beast, while it appeared the captain of the *Lusitania* would most certainly face an inquiry into the sinking.

While Lord Derby appealed for public restraint in Liverpool, there was already a mounting demand in London for the internment of all Germans. The non-naturalized aliens had already been interned.

Jane took a room in a modest hotel while she decided what to do next. She had intended to resume her nursing training, but now felt she did not have the patience or even the compassion necessary to enter the healing profession. She was too filled with rage, with a need for vengeance, wanting to strike back at the Germans, to punish them for the monstrous crime they had committed.

She concentrated on her anger toward the enemy because it was a way to overcome her hurt, to subdue the grief she felt at the loss of Claudia's friendship.

❧ Thirteen ❧

JANE STEPPED down from the London train and looked around. So many soldiers for such a small village station. Were they coming home on leave or returning to Flanders? They wore their uniforms proudly, Sam Browne belts gleaming on fresh-faced boys who looked far too young to be lieutenants, boots shining like black mirrors as stern-faced sergeants and eager recruits clattered purposefully around her in a khaki wave.

She was almost sorry she had not worn her own uniform, for she wanted to proclaim her membership in that patriotic throng, but of course it would have been inappropriate for a visit to Rathbourne Abbey.

There was no sign of anyone wearing a chauffeur's uniform waiting on the platform to meet her, despite Claudia's assurances that they would send a car for her, so Jane picked up her suitcase and made her way toward the turnstile.

"Jane!" a male voice called. "Jane Weatherly! Whoa . . . hold on, there."

One of the Sam Browne belts detached itself from the khaki-clad crowd, and its wearer shouldered his way toward her.

She stood still, staring at the approaching lieutenant, her heart turning over. Bran Kingsley had been devastatingly good-looking as a careless boy; he was even more heart-stoppingly handsome in his uniform.

But as he drew nearer she could see there were subtle changes in his face. Tiny sun wrinkles had appeared around his eyes, and his guileless, boyishly eager look had been replaced by a reckless, fatalistic expression she had seen on other soldiers home from the front. It was a look that said their expectations of life extended no further than the moment at hand, a look that filled her with dread.

When Bran reached her side he surprised her by sweeping her into an embrace and planting a brief kiss on her lips. For one dizzying instant all of her dreams were within her grasp. Then he laughingly released her and said, "Sorry, couldn't resist. Besides, I believe it's against the law for a soldier and a pretty girl to meet on a railway platform without kissing."

She said something—she wasn't sure what—and he took her suitcase from her. "Claudia asked me to pick you up. Naturally I jumped at the chance to prove to you that I was good for something besides being a parasite on the skin of society."

"You're never going to let me forget that, are you?"

"Probably not. Actually, the staff at Rathbourne Abbey— and at Willowford, too—has been seriously depleted since the war started. We're managing with old geezers on their last legs and boys too young to drive. Which reminds me, what's this I hear about you joining the Ambulance Corps?"

"Well, I knew how to drive; it seemed to be the thing to do. I volunteered to go to France months ago, but my orders haven't come yet, even though I understand there's a desperate need for ambulance drivers at the front."

"There is," Bran said grimly. "Getting the wounded to a field hospital quickly saves lives. You'd be appalled at how long horribly mangled men remain in the trenches without proper medical care. The motor ambulances take them from divisional units to the casualty clearing stations, a few miles from the hospital trains. But, Jane, the ambulance drivers come under fire too, from stray shells, even aeroplane guns. The red cross on the ambulance isn't always protection. It's no job for a woman."

"You haven't noticed that there are women driving ambulances at the front, then?"

He gave a rueful grin. "I suppose what I'm saying is that it's no job for one of my friends—for a woman I know."

The comment caused a surge of happiness to infuse her, for she interpreted it to mean he cared a little about what happened to her. She allowed herself a quick fantasy wherein he was wounded—very slightly, of course—and she was driving the

ambulance that picked him up. Later she could visit him at a
field hospital to see how he was coming along. . . .

Walking beside him, she was very much aware of the
envious female eyes cast in her direction, and she felt proud,
almost proprietary, allowing herself to pretend they were a
couple.

She added, "I'm still transporting the wounded from boat
trains to various hospitals in and around London."

"Good. I hope you won't go to France." Bran took her arm
to guide her. "My car's over there."

"How long have you been home?" Jane asked as he put her
suitcase into the boot.

"Six days. I have to go back tomorrow. I'll miss Claudia's
birthday party—I suppose that's why you're here? Ro will be
here in time, though, lucky dog. We couldn't get leave at the
same time because we're in the same unit. Claudia looks
wonderful. I've never seen her so radiant. When did you last
see her?"

"Not since shortly after we were rescued. I left her in
Ireland. It's been over a year since I saw her." Jane stared
straight ahead.

"This is the first opportunity I've had to add my voice to all
the others who must have thanked you for saving her life. What
a heroine you were! We're all so proud of you."

"I didn't do anything," Jane mumbled, embarrassed. She
was more than a little surprised that either Claudia or Marrick
had told of her part in the rescue, in view of their stony silence.
"Bran, to be honest with you, I was surprised when Claudia
wrote and asked me to come for her birthday.
We . . . quarreled. In fact, I parted from both Claudia and
Lord Marrick under a cloud. Before Claudia's invitation came
our only communication was a card I sent to her, giving her my
address."

He glanced sideways at her in surprise. "Pretty ungrateful of
them, I'd say. What on earth happened?"

"Claudia and I disagreed about something. Lord Marrick
was furious because we'd booked passage on the *Lusitania*
without telling him. But it was a spur-of-the-moment decision."

"You could hardly have anticipated the Germans would sink
a passenger liner. She was very ill for a long time, you know,

and there was a long convalescence after she came home. Perhaps that's why you didn't hear from her. What did you quarrel about?"

"Nothing of any consequence," Jane answered. "I can't wait to see her. We've a lot of catching up to do."

Claudia flung herself into Jane's arms and greeted her tearfully. "Oh, Jane, I'm so happy to see you. I've missed you so."

"I've missed you, too," Jane answered truthfully.

"Come on, let's go up to my room and talk all day and all night." Claudia broke off and gave Bran, who stood behind Jane in the entry hall, an apologetic smile. "Will you excuse us, Bran?"

He looked crestfallen. "I have to go back to France tomorrow, Claudia. I'd hoped to spend this evening alone with you."

She gave him an exasperated look. "Bran, there's no point. You're a dear friend, but that's all you're ever going to be. How many times must I tell you?"

Jane stared at the marble floor, aching for Bran. He flushed, and the pain in his eyes was more than she could bear. She said quickly, "Thank you so much for picking me up at the station, Bran. If you need someone to drive you back tomorrow, I'd be happy to return the favor."

"Thanks. I take it I'm being dismissed?"

"Well . . ." Claudia said, "if your leave really is all over, then you'd better come back this evening for dinner."

He gave her a ghost of a grin. "Bless you. I'll be eating ghastly slop out of billycans in the trenches soon enough."

"Oh, Bran!" Claudia forced a giggle. "Willowford has the finest chef for a hundred miles."

"Won't your parents be upset if you don't stay home tonight?" Jane asked.

"The pater had to go back to London, and the mater cries every time she looks at me. It would be a relief to get away."

"We'll see you about eight, then," Claudia said, and stood on tiptoe to kiss him lightly on the cheek. Jane saw him tense, his expression one of intense longing. He raised his arms slightly, as though to clasp Claudia to his heart, then lowered them again. Jane thought of the careless embrace he had given her at the railway station and was painfully aware that it had meant nothing to him. He loved Claudia with all the passion a young man could feel, and obviously dared not take her into his arms for fear he would never be able to let her go.

As she followed Claudia up the stairs that led from the marble entry hall to the upstairs living quarters of the abbey, Jane decided Bran had been right about how wonderful Claudia looked. She was glowing with health and happiness. All the gaunt hollows and protruding bones of her illness had miraculously disappeared, giving her a more womanly figure. But the changes were more than physical, for Claudia seemed serene in a way she had never been before. Gone was the lost little waif, and in her place was a woman of such great beauty that it dazzled the eyes to behold her.

A maid brought up a tea tray, and Claudia asked about Jane's experiences driving an ambulance, and did she intend to finish her nurses' training, and why for heaven's sake hadn't she taken the opportunity to let Bran know she was interested in him? Didn't she realize why Claudia had asked him to pick her up at the station? "So you two could be alone, of course. But you obviously wasted the opportunity," she finished indignantly.

Jane, unable to get a word in, could only wait for her to run down.

". . . I only asked him back tonight for you, you know. So after dinner I'll leave you alone—"

At this Jane held up her hand. "Stop! Please don't play the matchmaker. Bran isn't interested in me. He's hopelessly in love with you and always has been."

"Then he'll just have to get over it." Claudia waved her hand airily, and Jane was tempted to ask if she had managed to get over her infatuation for Royce, but didn't. She wanted to repair the rift in their friendship and had decided not to let Royce come between them again.

"I'm so glad you came," Claudia went on. "There's a big party planned for my birthday, but"—she was obviously brimming over with suppressed excitement—"*we won't be here!*"

"I don't understand," Jane said, noting that although Claudia had asked a great many questions, she had not waited for answers from Jane. Whatever her news was, it was of such tremendous importance that it eclipsed everything else.

"We shall leave for London the day before my birthday," Claudia went on in a conspiratorial whisper. "I've already booked rooms at a little hotel on Regent Street."

"Wait a minute. . . . Are you telling me you intend to run away from Lord Marrick? Has he been after you to marry him again?"

"No, no. He's been away almost constantly and quite preoccupied when he's here. He did say we could talk about it again after my birthday. But by then I'll already be married."

"*What*?"

Claudia stared at her. "You haven't heard from him? He promised he'd let you know."

"Who? Who would let me know what?"

"Royce. He said he'd get in touch with you. Didn't he?"

Jane experienced a sensation of everything falling away, blurring, then rushing back to engulf her. She swallowed hard. "I haven't seen or heard from him since before we left for America. But you have, I take it. Is he in the army?"

Claudia glanced away. "He was going to join up. He really intended to, but he had a recurrence of his illness."

"What illness?" Royce, like herself, had always been as healthy as a horse, and Jane didn't believe an illness had prevented him from keeping his promise to write to Claudia in America.

"He has an ulcer. When it flares up he's completely incapacitated."

"I see." Jane still found this difficult to believe, but decided to give him the benefit of the doubt. "What about Edith? Where is his wife?"

"She was caught and sent back to finish her sentence."

"Are you sure about that? Was it in the newspapers?"

"Well, I didn't exactly read it for myself, but . . . Jane, I can't believe Royce didn't let you know all this. I gave him your address. Perhaps his letters went astray."

"Yours didn't," Jane pointed out dryly, but Claudia wasn't listening.

"Anyway, I sent my maid to pick up his letter, and we were able to correspond, even while I was ill. I didn't see him again

until about four months ago, but we've managed to meet fairly
frequently since. Leith doesn't know, because Royce had to see
about his divorce, and, well, he just thought it would be better
not to tell Leith yet."

"Royce is getting a *divorce*?" Jane couldn't believe it.

Claudia nodded. "You see, we're going to live happily ever
after despite all your fears for us. Please say you're happy for
us, Jane. We both love you so much."

"I've always wanted your happiness, Claudia. And I love
my brother, but . . ."

"Please, no buts!"

"I just wish you wouldn't sneak off like this, behind Lord
Marrick's back."

"But you know he'll never give us his blessing. We have no
choice."

"There's always a choice. Where is Royce now? I'd like to
see him."

Claudia avoided her searching gaze. "He's in London taking
care of the last-minute details of the divorce, getting a marriage
license, and so on. But we'll see him in a few days."

"Is there anything I can say to you to persuade you not to
leave without a word to Lord Marrick?"

Claudia's eyes filled with violet shadows. "Janey, I shan't
feel safe from Leith until I am Royce's wife. If Leith knew,
he'd find a way to stop us, I know he would."

Jane sighed. "I'll go with you—but keep in mind that my
leave ends the day after your birthday."

"That will also be the day after my wedding, Jane. Royce
and I will be on our honeymoon."

Jane could not meet Marrick's eye during dinner. There
were only four at the long, elegantly set table. Bran never took
his eyes off Claudia and answered Marrick's questions about
conditions in France in what to Jane seemed a somewhat curt
manner for a guest. She wondered if Bran resented the fact that
Marrick was not in uniform. There was a great deal of ill will
toward able-bodied men who shirked their duty to king and
country. The practice of anonymously sending civilians white
feathers, the symbol of cowardice, was increasing.

Occasionally Claudia turned a starry-eyed glance in Bran's

direction, but Jane knew she was really looking right through him to the moment she would be reunited with Royce. Bran, mesmerized by her beauty, didn't notice. He was happy she deigned to look in his direction at all.

"I hear you're an ambulance driver, Miss Weatherly," Marrick said.

"Leith, for heaven's sake, couldn't you call Jane by her first name?" Claudia said before Jane could reply.

He raised a black eyebrow. "When Miss Weatherly gives me her permission, I'd be happy to do so."

"Please call me Jane. But be warned that I'd be uncomfortable addressing you as anything other than Lord Marrick."

"Then I shan't suggest it."

An awkward silence fell. Bran continued to gaze adoringly at Claudia, who returned to her dream world. Jane said to Marrick, "I didn't mean to be rude. I . . . Yes, I am an ambulance driver. But unless they send me to France soon, I'm going to request a transfer to the Nursing Corps and try to get to the front that way. I do have enough training to be an auxiliary."

"The Western Front is no place for a woman," Marrick said.

"Exactly what I told her, sir," Bran said. "There are those who believe it's no place for a man either, are there not?" His eyes raked his host overtly, and Jane squirmed inwardly. Marrick had no business talking about battlefields he knew nothing about.

But Marrick ignored Bran's baleful glance and replied, "What do you expect, with a War Committee made up of civilians and politicians? Their orders represent a consensus—vague guidelines rather than firm direction. Then you have a certain field marshal who still thinks in terms of cavalry charges. A disaster is in the making on the Western Front."

Bran's green eyes glittered angrily, but his tone remained reasonably civil. "Is that why you have chosen to remain out of uniform, sir? One would have thought that a man with such a badly needed skill as you have would have rushed to serve his country."

"One would, would one?" Marrick asked, calmly breaking his bread into small pieces.

"What skill is that?" Jane asked, interested.

"He's a flier and we need pilots desperately."

Marrick turned to Jane and said dryly, "That's because they don't last long. A few hours, some of them. I've no intention of going out in a blaze of glory in some dogfight over no-man's-land. I fully intend to die in bed."

Bran was glowering and obviously fighting a silent battle with himself over the conversational limits a polite guest was expected to maintain.

Jane said quickly, "How exciting that you know how to fly an aeroplane, Lord Marrick. Where and when did you learn?"

"In Africa when I was a very young man. It's the best way to cover considerable distances where no roads exist."

Claudia, who had remained silent as she gazed dreamily into space, yawned behind her napkin. "I'm awfully tired, Leith. Would you mind if I retired early? You'll entertain Bran, won't you, Jane?"

Although at that moment she was intensely curious about Marrick's flying prowess and how he had come to be in Africa, at the mention of Bran, Jane felt herself flush. She stammered, "I . . . I'm sure Bran would prefer to spend his last evening with you, Claudia."

Bran rose stiffly to his feet. "Actually, I should turn in early myself. I have to make an early start in the morning. Jane, I would like to take you up on your offer to drive me to the station tomorrow—if you don't mind getting up at the crack of dawn, that is."

"Not at all. What time is your train?"

"Seven. I could be here by six." He looked longingly at Claudia. "Would you walk me out to my car?"

She hesitated, giving Jane a stern look that spoke volumes, but went with him.

When they were alone, Marrick commented, "That blush gives you away, you know, Jane. You turn scarlet every time he speaks to you. It wouldn't be noticeable in some simpering miss with a string of beaux and nothing more consequential on her mind than which gown to wear. But when a woman like you blushes and stammers in a man's presence, one suspects her feelings toward that man are much more serious."

Jane rose to her feet instantly. "I think I'll retire, too."

He raised his glass to her in a silent toast before taking a sip of wine. "You are here as a guest, you know. No need to swallow your irritation. You do feel irritated, don't you? Steel sparks are flashing from your eyes. You believe a gentleman should not have mentioned the lovelorn glances you were bestowing on young Kingsley. But I thought it better that you were made aware of the fact that you were wearing your heart on your sleeve. Men are hunters by nature, you see, and tend to ignore the easy conquest."

"How dare you presume to speak to me in such a manner?" Jane's voice shook. For one wild second she considered hurling a plate at his arrogant head.

A mocking smile hovered at the corners of his mouth. "I suppose because you are Claudia's friend, of her generation and not mine. One recalls the follies of one's own youth, you see. With maturity comes an irresistible urge to pass along the lessons taught by bitter experience. As a young man I—and every other young man I knew—would have been intrigued and challenged by a young lady's attitude of complete indifference. I am merely advising you that you would stand a better chance of catching Bran Kingsley's eye if you were to affect such an attitude rather than that melting look of invitation you give him."

"I find this conversation insulting and inappropriate," Jane said. "Good night, Lord Marrick."

She had almost reached the double doors when he called after her, "Good night, Jane. Pleasant dreams."

Jane went to her room and prepared for bed and, expecting Claudia to join her as soon as Bran left, curled up with a magazine to wait. But Claudia did not come, and after a time Jane went to sleep.

Claudia had never become accustomed to the dank chill and the menacing shadows of the ground floor of the abbey. She crept through the cloister into the misnamed warming room and made her way to the great caldron perched upon its granite stand.

Royce came out of the shadows and opened his arms. She pressed close to him and kissed his mouth. "I hate meeting you down here," she whispered.

"I offered to come to your room, but you wouldn't hear of

it." He pulled back to scrutinize her face in the flickering glow of the candles he had lit. "Did Jane arrive?"

Claudia nodded. "I thought you were going to write to her. She said she hadn't heard from you."

He solemnly crossed his heart. "I swear I wrote to her. The letter must have gone astray."

"Oh, Royce, I hate deceiving her. I told her you were waiting for us in London."

"What did she say when you told her we were getting married?"

"She seemed most concerned that we were eloping. She wanted me to tell Leith."

"Of course she did. My astute sister knows very well that your guardian would find a way to stop us, because he wants you for himself. I told you not to invite her, but you wouldn't listen to me. Darling girl, we don't need anyone but each other, do we?"

"Royce, Jane is your sister and my dearest friend. I need her in my life and so do you. Once we're married she'll come around, you'll see. But you must talk to her. Will you? Tomorrow?"

He drew her closer into the dearly familiar contours of his body. "Now, you know I have to go up to London tomorrow. If I don't get the money to the estate agent by tomorrow night, we won't get the house."

"Bran Kingsley is going back tomorrow on the seven o'clock train, and Jane offered to drive him to the station. Is that the train you're going to take? If so, you could talk to her before you leave. I'd feel so much better if you did."

He murmured, "Ah, Claudia, how lovely you are." He kissed her eyelids, then covered her mouth with his, and that blissful connection blotted out all questions and doubts. His hand slid from her waist to her breast, and she lost herself in the magic of his touch. When she was in his arms everything was perfect, whole.

After a moment he whispered, "Did you . . . you know, get the necessary?"

She fumbled in her pocket, withdrew a bankbook, and handed it to him. "The bank said they couldn't add your name to the account because we're not married yet. So I just had it put in your name, and then we'll add 'Mrs. Royce Weatherly' later. The account has been transferred to the London branch, and they have a sample of your signature. There's also a certified check that you can give to the estate agent as a deposit. I didn't know the agent's name, so it's made out to you, and you can endorse it over to him."

He held the bankbook closer to the candlelight to read the amount, glanced at the certified check, and nodded, satisfied. "This is our future, Claudia my love. Our love nest. Just think, we'll never have to make love with the ghosts of the nuns watching, ever again."

She shuddered. "Please! Don't remind me."

Chuckling, he slipped the bankbook and check into his own pocket and bent to kiss her again.

"I can't wait to see the house you've found."

"You'll love it. A mews house, near everything. I was lucky to find it, with London as jam-packed as it is." He deftly removed her clothes and his own as he spoke, and then covered her shivering flesh with his warm body.

Their lovemaking was different now, Claudia thought happily as she yielded body and mind to him. Each was familiar with every nuance of the other's response. He had taught Claudia how to touch him, how to please him, and she had been an eager pupil. How desperately she desired him, even more so now. Her body had changed in subtle ways, her senses were sharper, more receptive. Her breasts were exquisitely sensitive, and when he licked her nipple she cried out and wrapped her legs around him to draw him inside her.

Royce prolonged their pleasure this night, slowing the driving force of his passion, delaying his climax, until she, lost in ecstasy, reached a zenith that had no end, sending tremors rippling through her like the aftershocks of an earthquake. How had she ever existed without the pleasure Royce's lovemaking gave her? She felt like one of those morphine addicts she'd heard about, who needed the drug long after their battle wounds had healed.

His mouth found hers again, and he quickened his thrusts until he, too, climaxed. She clasped him to her breast and stroked his hair, and he lazily nuzzled her soft flesh and murmured, "You're getting quite plump, love. Do you think your breasts are getting larger because I can't stop playing with them?"

She laughed softly and kissed the top of his head. She hadn't intended to tell him her wonderful secret yet, as she was saving it for their wedding night. But tonight their lovemaking had been so perfect and she felt so fulfilled, so perfectly in tune with him, that telling him seemed natural. Besides, their wedding was less than a week away, and he should be sharing her joy.

"Royce, darling . . . I love you so much. I'm so happy that in a few days we'll be married. I shall never ask for anything in the whole world other than to be your wife. Do you know how much I worship you?"

He raised his head and smiled at her. "And I adore you."

"Even though I'm getting fat?"

"You won't get too fat, will you?" He feigned alarm, since except for her developing breasts, she was as slender as a reed.

"I'm afraid so. But it will be just a temporary condition. Royce, my darling, I'm carrying your child."

For a moment he didn't speak. He continued to lie close to her, their bodies joined from the waist down, he supported by his elbows, and his gaze didn't waver. But Claudia had a fleeting feeling that for a split second he was not there.

Then he let out a long breath and said, "Well, that's certainly a surprise. I thought you were using the diaphragm I got for you."

She felt a small stab of alarm, but answered, "I tried, honestly I did. But I couldn't get the wretched thing to go in."

"You should have told me. I'd have done it for you."

She shuddered. "How unromantic! Royce . . . you don't mind, do you? About the baby? After all, we *are* going to be married. I'm only about two months along, and we can tell everyone it's a seven-month baby."

This time there was no hesitation in his reply. "Of course not." He paused, then added, "As long as you're happy about it."

"It's a little late not to be happy, isn't it?"

"No, not really," he answered casually. "If you didn't want it, there are people who take care of such matters."

She gasped. "Don't even think such a thing! I want lots of children. I always hated being an only child."

He kissed her again. "Sounds as if I'd better hurry up to London and buy our house, love, while we can still manage with three bedrooms."

⪻ Fourteen ⪼

BRAN WAS SILENT for most of the journey from the abbey to the railway station, responding in monosyllables to Jane's comments and questions.

At length he turned to her and said, "I know you're trying to distract me from thoughts of my destination, not to mention my complete lack of success with Claudia . . . but it isn't necessary. I fully intend to live to fight another day."

She wasn't sure if he referred to fighting the enemy or fighting for Claudia, and she fell silent herself.

Just before they reached the station he said, "No need to see me off. Just drop me out front. There's nothing worse than saying good-bye on a railway platform. It has such an air of . . . finality, I suppose."

Thinking of his exuberance when he met her the previous day, Jane was saddened. She had no doubt his melancholy mood this morning had more to do with Claudia's indifference toward him than with dismay about returning to the front.

As if prompted by her thoughts, he said, "I expect Claudia will tell you, so I might as well let you know that I asked her to marry me last evening . . . a rather hurried proposal at the front door. Lord knows I had planned to create a more romantic atmosphere and build up to my declaration of undying love, but well . . . Anyway, she turned me down." He strove to affect a light tone, but Jane heard the heartbreak in his voice and wanted to weep for him.

As she tried to find the words to comfort him, he added with a ghost of a smile, "Perhaps Ro will have better luck when he gets here."

"Claudia is still very young," Jane managed to say. "Give her time."

Jane sat in the car and watched as he made his way into the station. He held his head high and moved with easy grace, like a sleek racehorse. "Oh, Bran," Jane whispered to herself, "how can anyone not love you?"

"Dear heaven!" Jane exclaimed, surveying the formidable array of trunks, suitcases, and hatboxes Claudia and her maid had assembled. "How will you ever get all of this out of the house without Lord Marrick seeing it?"

"You can go now," Claudia said to her maid. "We'll take the suitcases and hatboxes when we leave; I'll send for the trunks later. Remember, not a word to anyone."

Jane sat on Claudia's bed. "Isn't it time you told Lord Marrick of your plans? Better than having him catch you sneaking off like a thief in the night."

"He won't catch me," Claudia said confidently. "He has to leave this afternoon. Another of his mysterious jaunts that he never explains. You and I will take the evening express."

"Lord Marrick isn't going to be here for your birthday?"

"He said he'll be back in time for the ball if not for dinner. But by then I shall be Mrs. Royce Weatherly. Jane, just think, we'll really be sisters at last."

"Well, sisters-in-law, at least," Jane demurred, although she did not believe for a minute that Royce had divorced Edith or, if he had, that he would marry Claudia.

"*Sisters*," Claudia said firmly, "and we're never going to quarrel again, ever, are we? Swear it!"

"I do solemnly swear," Jane said, crossing her heart.

"Shall I leave a note for Leith or phone him when he gets back?" Claudia asked.

"Phone him," Jane said promptly. Her father had been fond of quoting proverbs, and two came to mind: that there was many a slip twixt cup and lip, and that it would be premature for Claudia to burn her bridges.

As Claudia had predicted, Lord Marrick departed immediately after lunch. The two young women had an early dinner and then called a taxi.

Following two footmen who carried their bags out to the cab, Jane looked around with a twinge of regret. This was probably the last time she would ever be invited to Rathbourne Abbey. She had no illusions about how Marrick would react to his ward's eloping with his former chauffeur.

Then they were on their way, Claudia eagerly ticking off the miles as they approached London. "After we're married, Royce and I have some wonderful news to share with you. I'd tell you now, but I'm sure he will want to be with me when I do."

Jane had inquired as to where Claudia and Royce intended to live, and Claudia had given her an impish smile and evaded the issue, so Jane assumed the "wonderful news" was that Claudia had already found her honeymoon cottage—although with Marrick's generous allowance, Claudia probably had acquired a honeymoon mansion. Jane speculated briefly as to whether Marrick would continue the allowance and decided that, in view of what he had told Claudia about his acquisition of Rathbourne Abbey, he probably would. Undoubtedly he would find a way to keep Royce from getting his hands on the bulk of her fortune, and that, Jane thought, was a good thing.

It was late when they reached the modest hotel on Regent Street where they would spend the night. Two rooms had been booked in Claudia's name.

As they followed an elderly porter who staggered under the weight of their bags, Jane whispered to Claudia, "Shall we share a room?"

"Whatever for? We have two."

"But what about Royce?"

Claudia looked at her oddly, and Jane, confused, muttered, "I just thought Royce would take one room and . . . I'm old-fashioned, I suppose."

"Oh, don't get yourself into a state!" Claudia giggled. "As a matter of fact, Royce isn't staying here tonight. I insisted that he mustn't see his bride until the ceremony. Even though it is only a Registry Office affair."

The porter, puffing, preceded them into the lift, which rattled up to the third floor. There seemed to be virtually no young men left in the entire country to work in service jobs. Jane recalled hearing on the *Lusitania* that the Germans were conscripting sixty-year-old men, and she wondered how long it would be before Marrick's age group was called up for military service. Or had it already been called and he had somehow evaded conscription? She thought of Bran, so heartbreakingly young and brave, and decided it was unfair to kill and maim the young men first. They had not yet had a chance to live. It would make more sense to send the old men who were already world-weary. Marrick, of course, came instantly to mind.

Claudia was tired from the journey and the excitement and retired at once. Jane lay awake, wishing she knew where Royce was staying so she could talk some sense into him. Eventually she dozed fitfully and awoke just before dawn to the sound of rain pattering against the window.

She had arranged to meet Claudia for breakfast at eight o'clock, and when that hour arrived the rain was falling from leaden skies in a solid sheet. Jane sat in the hotel's deserted dining room sipping tea and wishing Claudia had not been so secretive about her wedding arrangements. If she had decreed that Royce not see her before the ceremony, then they would be meeting at the Registry Office, which meant there would be no time for Jane to talk to her brother. Did he intend to go through with a bigamous marriage? Surely not under his real name? Was it possible he had in fact obtained a divorce? Questions without answers pounded inside Jane's head as her stomach growled with hunger.

At half past eight Claudia came into the dining room, smiling as though the sun were shining. To Jane's astonishment, she ordered a huge breakfast—a fruit compote, a pair of kippers, poached eggs, muffins, and marmalade.

"Lost your appetite and found a horse's?" Jane inquired mildly.

Claudia's smile widened. She popped a fresh fig into her mouth.

"Is Royce staying somewhere nearby?" Jane asked.

She had to wait for an answer until Claudia swallowed a peach slice. Then she nodded and said, "We'll meet him at the Registry Office at two o'clock. We'll have all morning to find the dresses we'll wear."

"I'm surprised you haven't already chosen one."

"I did." Claudia giggled, a frequent habit nowadays, Jane noted. "But it's too tight."

"I noticed you'd put on a little weight. It's quite becoming. But, Claudia, if you don't mind, I won't go shopping with you. I really have no need for a new dress. I wear my uniform most of the time. What I'd really like to do is talk to Royce. I haven't seen him since we left for New York, you know, and you'll be whisking him away on a honeymoon right after the wedding. Where is he staying?"

Claudia's smile faded, replaced by a look of alarm. "Jane, if I tell you, you won't . . . I mean . . ."

"No, I won't try to talk him out of marrying you—that is, as long as he shows me evidence of his divorce."

"Well, of course, he'll have his decree," Claudia said indignantly. "He's staying with a friend who has a flat in Camden. I'll give you the address if you promise not to quarrel with him. But he might not even be there—he has lots to do, and there's no phone so we can't call."

"I'll take a chance," Jane answered.

Jane was drenched by the time she reached the address Claudia had given her, a two-room flat in an aging terraced house. The taxi driver had dropped her at the wrong house, and she'd dashed along an oppressively gloomy street to the right number under a deluge of rain.

Shaking the raindrops from her hat, she waited on a musty-smelling landing for someone to respond to her knock and after a minute knocked again. This time a peevish female voice called, "I'm coming."

Jane's heart dropped into her rain-sodden shoes. Royce was staying with a woman friend and had actually given Claudia her address? Oh, please, Jane prayed silently, let her be married with a husband on the premises.

The door opened a crack, and to Jane's intense relief, a middle-aged woman appeared. "What is it?"

"I'm looking for Royce Weatherly. I understand he's staying here."

The woman started to close the door in her face, but Jane

added quickly, "I'm his sister—Jane. He must have mentioned me."

"He never mentioned anybody to me, because I never met the dratted man, though I've heard enough about him to curl my hair. Seems him and his wife were always fighting and disturbing the other tenants. That's why they were evicted."

"He . . . was here with his wife?" Jane's sense of foreboding deepened.

"That's what I said, didn't I? But they're gone now. This is my flat. Moved in late last night and I'm tired, so don't pester me with your questions. Good day, miss."

"Do you have any idea where they moved to, or can you tell me who could give me their present address?"

"The landlord lives on the ground floor." The woman slammed the door shut.

Jane hurried downstairs, her heart thudding. Edith was still with Royce. *What were their plans for Claudia?*

The landlord was even more curt than his new tenant. "I threw them out a week ago, lock, stock, and baggage. No, I don't know where they are and I don't care."

"His wife," Jane asked quickly, "did she have bright red hair—a tall, rather well-endowed woman?"

"She was big, all right, and she had a voice as low as a man's, but her hair's black as coal."

Edith had probably dyed her hair. She did have a deep contralto voice. There was little doubt she was still with Royce.

A sickening thought occurred to Jane, and after thanking the landlord, she raced back out into the rain-swept street. There were no taxis about, so she made her way to the nearest tube station.

By the time she arrived back at the Regent Street hotel, Jane had worked herself into a state of anger and anxiety. Claudia had not returned from her shopping expedition.

Jane put on dry clothes and then paced up and down the corridor, awaiting Claudia's return.

She appeared just after noon, carrying several packages. "Hello, Jane. What on earth are you doing out here?"

"Waiting for you. Here, give me those while you find your key." She took the packages as Claudia unlocked her door.

"Wait till you see the dress I found! It's a very fine white wool and there's a matching cloak—very dramatic, yet sort of virginal, too—"

Jane interrupted, "Claudia, he's not there. He moved out a week ago."

Claudia unpinned her hat. "I warned you. He probably took a hotel room nearby. Can you help me do something with my hair?"

"He's gone, Claudia. I feel it in my bones. You . . . you didn't give him any money, did you?"

Claudia's eyes widened, and although she tried to maintain her unperturbed expression, Jane knew that her worst suspicions were confirmed.

"He'll meet us at the Registry Office. Don't worry," Claudia said quietly.

Jane walked around the room, absently picking up Claudia's scattered belongings. "Don't go to the Registry Office. I couldn't stand it if he left you waiting."

"Don't be ridiculous! He'll be there. He promised."

"No, no, he won't. Claudia, you have to go home to the abbey before Lord Marrick returns. There's no need for him—or anyone else—to know about this."

"You're not listening to me, Jane."

"I'll never forgive him for this. I didn't think even he was this low."

"I have to take a bath. Would you excuse me?"

Jane knew it was useless to beg, plead, or argue. She could only stand by helplessly while Claudia prepared for a wedding that was not going to take place.

For once Claudia was ready early and insisted on ordering a taxi long before they needed it. When the taxi reached the Registry Office a full half hour early, Jane had a sudden idea. "Would you park across the street," she asked the driver, "where we can see the entrance? We'd like to wait." To Claudia she said, "We'll be able to see him arrive. You know the groom should be there before the bride."

Since the rain continued to pour down, both Claudia and the taxi driver were agreeable.

A little after two Claudia said, "What if he got here really early and he's waiting inside?"

"I'll go and find out," Jane answered.

"You got a brolly, miss? You can borrow mine if you like," the taxi driver said.

Jane gratefully accepted the umbrella and dashed across the street. When she returned a little while later and slid into the backseat, she could not look into Claudia's eyes.

"He'll come," Claudia said. "He's a little late because of the rain."

"He's not coming, Claudia. He didn't take out a special license or make an appointment for a wedding for today or any other day. I made them check."

"There's been some mistake, then—"

"Claudia, for God's sake, face reality! Let's go. Let's not sit here in the rain."

"You can go if you want to. I shall wait. He wouldn't leave me like this."

Another half hour passed, the silence broken only by the drumming of the rain on the taxi roof.

Claudia said, "Something has happened to him. He would have come. He must have had an accident."

"Let's go and ask at the police station," Jane suggested.

"Not yet. Let's wait just a little longer."

The minutes ticked by. Claudia began to shiver uncontrollably. Jane put her arm around her. "Let's go back to the hotel. He knows where you're staying; perhaps there's a message." She didn't expect there would be, but it was a way to get Claudia back to the hotel.

Claudia nodded, her expression still determinedly hopeful.

There was no message and no report of an accident. At Claudia's insistence, Jane also called several hospitals. Claudia stood at the window watching the street below.

At six o'clock Jane said, "We should go and get something to eat. We missed lunch." They had intended to have a wedding breakfast after the ceremony.

"I'm not hungry. You go."

"Shall I have something brought up?"

"If you wish."

"Will you please come away from that window?"

Claudia ignored her. Jane paced restlessly around the room.

"You know I have to go back tomorrow, Claudia. My leave ends at midnight. What are you going to do?"

"I'll be all right."

"I can't just leave you here. Please go home."

Claudia turned away from the window at last. Her eyes seemed empty; all her newfound vitality had drained from her. "I will . . . but not today. Leith won't be back until tomorrow evening, so there's no hurry."

Jane ordered tea and sandwiches, and Claudia ate with her, in a purely mechanical way. There was little conversation between them. Shortly after eating, Claudia decided to take another bath and go to bed. Jane went back to her own room, wishing passionately that she could do or say something to ease Claudia's pain, wishing she could get her hands on Royce to throttle him.

Just before Jane fell into a tense, dream-filled sleep, she reminded herself that her father always said every cloud had a silver lining. Perhaps Claudia needed this cloud in order to finally see Royce for what he was.

The following morning they bade each other a strained good-bye. Jane made Claudia promise again that she would return to her guardian. Hugging her friend, Jane said softly, "The pain will pass, Claudia. It's really all for the best, believe me. He would have made you miserable. Take care. I'll write to you as soon as I get my new orders."

Claudia felt like a sleepwalker who had awakened to find herself in a strange place with no knowledge of how she arrived there. On the morning of her twentieth birthday she made her way to Euston station and bought a first-class ticket on the ten o'clock train. Even if the train was a little late, she would arrive at the abbey before her birthday guests.

Not that she wanted to go back to the abbey. She would have done anything to avoid it, but she had transferred all of her available funds to Royce. A phone call to the bank confirmed what Jane had suspected: the account had been closed two days earlier. The certified check had undoubtedly been cashed by Royce rather than the estate agent, and in any event Claudia did not know the agent's name or the address of the mews house Royce was supposed to buy, if indeed such a house had ever existed.

The train was late and the platform so crowded there was nowhere to sit. She felt a little faint and so sat on her suitcase. She had been lucky, suffering none of the nausea or faintness she'd heard were common in early pregnancy, but perhaps her present weakness was due to her loss of appetite. In her misery her throat had constricted, her stomach had knotted, and she had been unable to force down any food that morning.

Soldiers and sailors milled about, and she watched them idly. One young officer strolled along the platform, glancing at his watch. Probably he was waiting for the same train as she was. As he came closer she leaned forward, peering through the wisps of steam left by a departing train.

There was no doubt—the height, the set of the shoulders, a glimpse of gold hair beneath the peaked cap—it was Bran Kingsley. No, wait, it couldn't be Bran. He had returned to the front on the day she and Jane came to London.

She stood up and waved. "Ro! Ro . . . over here."

Roald Kingsley's face lit up, and in a few long strides he was at her side, pulling her to her feet to kiss her. "Claudia, by all that's holy, what on earth are you doing here when I'm desperately trying to get to the abbey in time for your birthday party tonight?" He paused. "Your party is still on, isn't it?"

"Oh, yes. Not that I'm looking forward to it."

He glanced at her pile of luggage. "You must have been on a long trip."

Claudia gave him a vague smile.

"If you're not looking forward to your party, then let's not go," Ro said, a devilish glint in his eye. "Let's stay in town and celebrate your birthday all by ourselves."

"All right," Claudia said, surprising herself as much as him.

"What? Do you mean it?"

"Yes."

"But . . . aren't they expecting you?"

"We can call and tell the housekeeper we aren't coming. I don't think it will be much of a surprise to the staff. They knew I didn't want a party this year."

"What about Lord Marrick?"

"Ro, do you want to spend your entire leave arguing with me in a railway station?"

"Of course not." He laughed joyfully, signaled a porter to pick up her luggage, and took her arm.

❦ Fifteen ❧

ON THE DAY Jane received her orders to leave for duty in France, a letter arrived from Claudia. The return address caught her attention immediately. Why on earth was Claudia writing her from Willowford, the Kingsleys' country estate, instead of from Rathbourne Abbey? Jane tore open the envelope.

> Dear Jane,
>
> Your letters were sent over from the abbey and were waiting for me when I arrived here today. Roald Kingsley and I were married in London yesterday and he has returned to France. I will be staying at Willowford until the war is over.
>
> Take care of yourself.
>
> > Affectionately,
> > Claudia

Jane read the letter three times and was as baffled by it on the third reading as the first. Ro Kingsley had obviously caught Claudia on the rebound from Royce, but so swiftly! The date on Claudia's letter indicated that scant days had passed from the time she was jilted by Royce to the time she had married Roald. Marrick surely had not given his blessing, so they must have eloped.

But much more than the details of the wedding were omitted. There was a curiously remote feeling to the bare facts recited, which read almost like a dismissal. Jane's first reaction was to wonder if between the lines Claudia was politely informing her that she had turned her back on both Royce and her, and if that was the case, Jane certainly couldn't blame her.

She put through a trunk call to Willowford, but was informed by the butler that Mrs. Roald Kingsley was not at home. "May I give her a message, Miss Weatherly?"

"Yes . . . no, thank you. Just tell her I'm going on duty but I'll call again when I can."

During the following week she called several times, but Claudia was never at home. Jane began to wonder if the staff at Willowford had been instructed not to put her calls through. She found a small antique beaten silver frame on a miniature music stand that seemed perfect for a wedding photograph and sent it to Willowford.

Eventually, on the eve of her departure for France, upon phoning and again being told Claudia was not home, Jane snapped, "Then please tell me where she is. I must speak with her."

There was a pause. "I'll bring Lady Kingsley to the phone, miss. Would you hold on, please?"

Static buzzed in her ear as she waited. The operator interrupted to demand more money, and Jane fed all of her available coins into the telephone. More minutes passed; then the line went dead. She stepped out of the telephone booth. She hadn't particularly wanted to speak to Claudia's mother-in-law anyway.

Jane glanced at her watch. If she went straight to Euston she could be on the midnight train and arrive at Willowford early the following morning. She had the weekend off, prior to embarking for France. She was still wearing her uniform, and there wouldn't be time to pick up a change of clothes, but if Claudia invited her to stay, she could buy a change of underwear in the village.

The following morning she presented herself at Willowford and was informed by the butler that neither Sir Nigel nor Lady Kingsley was in residence and that Mr. Roald's wife was out for the day. He was sorry, but he didn't know when she might return.

Retracing her steps down the driveway, she looked up to see

Rathbourne Abbey in the distance, etched against the summer sky. Perhaps Claudia was visiting her guardian? Almost with a will of their own, Jane's feet turned in the direction of the abbey.

A new butler responded to her ringing the ancient bell at the abbey door. He looked at least ninety, Jane decided. His predecessor no doubt had been taken by the army. She wondered again how Marrick managed to stay out of uniform and tried not to think of the mangled men her ambulance carried. They were all so pathetically grateful to be alive and back home, even with the most fearful wounds and disabilities. If the war didn't end soon, it seemed an entire generation would be lost or would be hobbling around without limbs, without sight, or horribly burned. Worst of all were the victims of poison gas. She had thought perhaps after a while she would become, if not inured, at least accustomed to the suffering of the casualties of war, but she had not.

"May I help you, madam?" the butler asked, and she realized she had been staring at him. She said, "My name is Jane Weatherly. I wonder if perhaps Miss Claudia is here?"

"Mrs. Kingsley lives at Willowford now, madam."

"Yes, I know. Is Lord Marrick at home? Would you tell him I'd like to speak with him?"

He hesitated, then said, "I'll see if his lordship is receiving," and shuffled off. Jane waited, wondering if she'd have the nerve to ask Marrick how he felt about Claudia's marriage.

What seemed a long time later the butler reappeared and conducted her upstairs to the living quarters. Watching his stiff-limbed ascent of the staircase, arthritic joints creaking on every step, Jane was tempted to ask him which room his lordship was in so she could find it for herself. Despite having been born and brought up on large estates, Jane considered the whole concept of service, of one person doing for others what they were perfectly capable of doing for themselves, distastefully feudal. Especially when decrepit servants were at the beck and call of robust masters.

Marrick was in his study, seated at his desk. He rose when she entered the room. "This is an unexpected pleasure, Jane." She felt rather than saw his almost-black eyes flicker over her uniform. "You're looking very well."

"Thank you. I'm sorry to disturb you, but I'm leaving for Flanders on Monday, and I was rather hoping to find Claudia here. I haven't been able to reach her at Willowford."

He gestured for her to take the leather armchair across from the desk, and she sat down. "I saw Claudia only briefly after she returned from London. She hasn't been back here. Could I offer you some refreshments?"

"No, thank you. I had breakfast in the village. I . . . suppose Claudia's marriage was as much of a surprise to you as it was to me?"

A dark eyebrow arched in surprise. "A surprise to you, Jane? But you accompanied her to London. She surely must have told you of her intent?"

Jane couldn't meet his eyes. She certainly couldn't deny she knew Claudia planned to marry, but neither could she tell him her surprise had been the identity of the groom. She mumbled, "I tried to get her to talk to you about her intentions, but she was afraid you'd disapprove."

" 'Disapprove' is hardly the word for it. A lonely soldier comes home on leave and manages to convince an impressionable girl that it's her patriotic duty to give him a few hours of happiness before he returns to the front. Neither of them stops to consider that he could come home maimed or that she could be a widow faster than she became a wife."

"I hope neither of those dreadful possibilities comes to pass. Lord Marrick . . . I really am sorry she eloped. Claudia and I hadn't been in touch since we returned from New York. When I accepted her invitation to come for her birthday, I had no idea what she was planning. I did try to dissuade her."

He studied her face for a moment. "Why are you having such trouble looking me in the eye? Is there something I don't know about this hasty and ill-advised marriage? Ah, I see by your rising color that there is."

He paused, then said, "I might as well tell you that I am investigating the possibility of annulment."

"Is that why Claudia is hiding?"

"Possibly. If you know anything that might be useful . . ."

"I think we should respect Claudia's decision. Whether we like it or not, she has chosen Roald Kingsley to be her husband."

He regarded her with a strangely troubled gaze. "She selected one of the Kingsley twins. I'm not sure it mattered to her which twin. On a whim she decided to marry, and Roald was handy. A few days earlier it could just as easily have been Branston."

Jane stood up quickly. "Perhaps I'd better leave. I feel uncomfortable discussing Claudia behind her back."

"As uncomfortable as you do contemplating that she might have come close to marrying your own true love? Well, fear not. Bran is still a bachelor."

He picked up an envelope from the desk blotter. "I received your message, by the way. I hope you won't be too disappointed to hear you weren't the first to send me one of these. I'm acquiring enough of them to stuff a pillow."

As he spoke, he allowed the contents of the envelope to fall out. Jane watched in stunned disbelief as a white feather drifted toward her.

❦ Sixteen ❧

July 1, 1916

BRAN KINGSLEY glanced at his wristwatch. It was exactly 7:30 A.M., and an eerie silence had fallen over the battlefield. By a strange coincidence, both the British and the German guns had suddenly ceased their barrage.

Roald, crouched at Bran's side, looked up as a bird swooped down over the trenches, singing a joyous salute to a sunlit morning and cloudless skies. Turning to his brother he whispered, "Bran . . . if anything happens to me—"

"Shut up," Bran hissed. "Don't even think of it. We're going to live through this, both of us."

"But . . . just in case, you will take care of Claudia for me, won't you?"

"You'll take care of her yourself. For God's sake, don't give up before we've started."

Bran made a pretense of checking his bayonet again. He and his twin had always been able to read each other's mind, and Bran hoped Roald, in his own joy at capturing the fairest of the fair, did not recognize the depth of his brother's torment over losing Claudia.

Even when Bran told himself that if she had to belong to another man he'd rather it be Roald than anyone else, the pain of losing her was more than he could bear. Nor did he want his twin to know that in some dark corner of his soul he didn't care whether he lived to see the sun set this day.

The quiet was abruptly shattered as the British barrage fell upon the next line of enemy defenses. In their own trenches whistles blew, shouts came from the platoon and section commanders. The battle of the Somme had started.

The long line of men lying out in no-man's-land rose first, looking from right to left as though on a parade ground, then set off after their officers toward the enemy.

Bran and Roald, both lieutenants, were among the first up the ladders and over the top. Behind them the heavily laden men struggled to climb out of the trenches, and the officers ran along the parapet shouting encouragement, leaning in to pull the overburdened soldiers up and out.

They passed first through their own barbed-wire defenses, some units making bridges of duckboards, but most passing through paths cut in the wire the previous night.

Bran had just got through the wire, and Roald was ahead of him, when he heard a German bugle blow. Instantly a hail of deadly machine-gun fire found easy targets.

British soldiers struggling out of their trenches were hit and tumbled back, some of them dead before they fell. Others were caught in the narrow alleys in the barbed wire, which became deathtraps as men trying to avoid their dead and wounded comrades got caught and were themselves hit.

In spite of the unexpected opposition there was no hesitation as more and more men left the trenches and joined the waves of soldiers moving along the eighteen-mile front, crossing ground where no man had stood in sunlight for two years.

The Kingsley twins led their men forward into hell.

Weren't the German guns supposed to have been silenced, weren't the Germans all supposed to be dead? But discipline and control took the place of logical thought, and every man pressed forward toward the objective, ignoring fallen friends, trying not to hear the moans of the wounded.

Roald paused beside their captain as he was hit, but Bran shoved him away. "He's dead. You can't help him. Keep going."

A moment later a fountain of earth and black smoke leapt into the air ahead of them, and Bran cursed in surprise as he was almost knocked off his feet by the blast.

The German artillery, realizing the British were advancing, had switched from firing on their gun positions and trenches to pounding the center of no-man's-land. Men fell all around them, screaming above the noise of shellfire and the rat-tat-tat of machine guns.

The twins plunged ahead into the smoke and dust, passing over long rows of dead. Bran had expected to feel fear, but now that the action had begun, he felt only a curious detachment, as though nothing that was happening was real.

From time to time he glanced at his brother, now moving along at his side, trying to assess Roald's state of mind. Men with the newfound responsibility of a wife sometimes wanted so badly to survive that they became overcautious and made careless mistakes. But Roald appeared to be in perfect control of his emotions, despite the deadly shellfire exploding all around them.

At last the barrage fell behind them, and the German wire appeared ahead. Although the leading waves of infantry had been broken by the terrible fire, individual survivors kept going.

Now the sound of German machine guns replaced the shellfire, and the Kingsley twins, plodding resolutely forward, could see their comrades falling silently into the grass or crying out as bullets struck home.

Bran felt a sudden acute fear, not for himself, but for Roald. He shouted. "It's hopeless. We're too few—"

Roald gave him one startled glance in the instant before a group of German soldiers loomed up out of nowhere.

The twins fired simultaneously and two Germans fell. There was another burst of rifle fire at their side as a corporal joined them and killed a third German. Bran saw his enemy's face as he fell and thought, My God, he's a boy. The last remaining German raised his hands in surrender.

A harsh voice yelled something in German, and an officer appeared. The soldier dropped his hands, and the officer pulled the pin from a grenade, apparently determined to take on the entire advancing army single-handedly.

Roald's shot hit the officer, and the grenade blew, killing both Germans.

As the smoke cleared, Roald muttered, "Good God, Bran—look!"

In front of the German barbed wire lay what appeared to be hundreds of unexploded mortar shells. They looked like outsize oranges in the sunlight, as they were a bright orange-yellow. They were supposed to destroy the German wire, but the recently introduced mortars—attached to sticks, which often came off when fired—had proved to be duds.

British troops struggled to get through the wire and became hopelessly enmeshed, their equipment caught on the barbs, rendering them helpless. They were picked off by the German riflemen, bodies jerking in their death throes as they were riddled with bullets.

"Find a gap!" Bran yelled, and the twins raced along the wire, dodging bullets.

But the machine gunners had the gaps in the wire covered, and the two brothers dropped into a shell hole as a burst of fire swept the grass around them.

For a moment they lay side by side, panting. Two other men, one their corporal, slid into the hole beside them, which was still filled with smoke and reeked of the recent explosion.

Bran rolled over onto his stomach. "Stay down, I'll take a look."

He raised his head and instantly felt something smash into his helmet with the force of a sledgehammer. He dropped his head, pulling off his helmet. It was smashed in, but apart from a severe ringing in his ears, he felt no pain. The machine gun bullet had not penetrated the steel.

The corporal opened a pouch he was carrying and produced several grenades. "Fink we oughta knock out that bleedin' machine gun nest before we shove on?" he asked in a thick Cockney accent.

Roald took a grenade as Bran put his smashed helmet back on. Roald and the corporal threw their grenades simultaneously. "We got 'em," Roald cried, elated. He looked at Bran. "Are you all right?"

Bran was still trying to gather his wits, but he nodded.

"Let's go," Roald said, a reckless note of bravado in his voice now.

Bran peeped over the top of the shell hole, saw a round helmet rising above the German trench, and fired. The four British soldiers jumped up, rushed the last few yards, and jumped into the trench. Aside from the single dead German sprawled over the edge, there was no one there, friend or foe.

They scrambled out and ran for the second-line trenches. Bran had the same eerie sense of unreality, as if it were all some sort of surreal nightmare. They could see for quite a distance on either side, and there was not a single soul in sight. They might have been the last four men on earth.

As they reached the second-line trench they saw a German soldier lying on the parapet. The corporal approached him with fixed bayonet, but Bran grabbed his arm to stop him. The German's face was gray, contorted with pain, and it was obvious he had been mortally wounded.

To their surprise, the German slowly raised an arm and saluted. He murmured, *"Waser, Waser."*

Unhooking his flask, Bran held it to the German's mouth, and he took a sip of water. His eyes glazed and he whispered, "Mutter, Mutter."

Bran felt a wave of compassion overlaid by guilt. He had not personally killed this boy, who could not have been more than eighteen, but he felt like a murderer nevertheless. He reached down to close the German's staring eyes, and his eyelids felt as delicate as a butterfly's wings.

Bewildered by the sudden intensity of his feelings after

previously moving through the battlefield without emotion, Bran froze, unsure what to do next.

He felt someone shake his arm, and Roald's voice snapped, "Our orders are not to wait at the front-line trenches; we're supposed to press on. Bran? Are you listening to me? Come on, we can't stay here."

"Four of us?" Bran asked. "You want four of us to attack the whole bloody German army? Where the hell is the rest of our company?"

"Out in no-man's-land, sir. Dead," the corporal answered. "P'raps we'll find some more of our boys up ahead," he added doubtfully.

"Right," Roald said. "We're bound to meet up with other units who've got this far. None of us are wounded. We've got to go on. We've no choice."

He leapt out of the trench and began to run.

Bran followed, a cry of protest at the futility of it all dying on his lips as a bullet slammed into his lower jaw. He fell to the ground, amazed at the intensity of the pain, choking on the warm gush of blood.

Roald turned, his expression one of disbelief, as though he had truly believed they were invincible. He raced back and bent over his brother, and Bran tried to understand what he was saying.

They had not seen the sniper, nor did they see the Germans who hurled grenades at them. The first grenade killed their two comrades instantly.

The sound of explosion from the second grenade was sharper than the din of the battlefield. The space around them filled with a red haze. Then everything seemed to be moving in slow motion toward smoke-filled oblivion.

One badly wounded Kingsley twin lay on the battlefield for several hours beside the body of his dead brother.

❦ Seventeen ❧

As DARKNESS FELL over the battlefield the medical services realized the enormity of their task. Casualties exceeded all estimates, and the clearing stations were already packed with walking wounded.

With the onset of dusk the stretcher-bearers began to recover the thousands of wounded men lying in no-man's-land. They were in terrible condition, having been left untreated for many hours, and some had been wounded more than once.

Every available man was pressed into service, as heavy casualties had also occurred among the stretcher-bearers. There were not enough stretchers, so sheets of corrugated iron were used. Often two men were carried on one stretcher. Before long the bearers lost the use of their hands and had to carry the stretchers by slings around their necks.

The stretcher-bearers who brought the badly wounded young lieutenant to the battalion aid post told the medical officer, "He's lost half his face, sir, and one arm's mangled, but he had a death grip with his good hand on the body of another officer. We had to pry his fingers off the body. I think he wanted us to bring it, too. He can't talk . . ." The stretcher-bearer, an artilleryman who'd been pressed into service and was unaccustomed to the sights he had witnessed that night, became aware of the shadowy piles of bodies stacked like sandbags all around the trestle table on which the M.O. was providing rudimentary medical care. He turned away, aghast.

Glancing at the badly wounded lieutenant, the M.O. said, "I doubt he'll survive. Don't blame yourself if he doesn't. We're all just trying to cope. Take him back to a dressing station."

Immediately behind the trench system, the dressing stations

were operated by the field ambulances. There were no facilities for surgery, but at least the wounds could be dressed properly before being sent back to the casualty clearing station.

The bearers carried the wounded lieutenant who had clung so desperately to his dead companion to a dressing station set up in a basilica, where he became part of a flood of wounded pouring in on foot, on stretchers, in wheelbarrows and carts. Their wounds were dressed and they were laid out on the floor to await evacuation.

Soon the whole church was packed, and orders were given to stop all vehicles and make them take the wounded to the rear. Those who were not expected to survive were put on one side and left, their cries for help haunting forever the ambulance drivers forced to leave them behind in order to concentrate on those who could be saved. The wounded lieutenant, whose smashed jaw would not permit him to speak, was laid among the men not expected to survive.

He lay there all the following day. Occasionally German shells crashed against the walls of the basilica, but the massive walls had survived almost two years of shelling and protected the men inside.

At first his only wish was for oblivion. An end to the pain, to the maddening thirst, relief from the flies that buzzed hungrily about the bloodstained bandages swathing his head. Peering with one eye out of his gauze cocoon, he saw that everyone was too busy to tend to him.

Maybe the next shell would break through those stout walls and end his misery. He prayed for death. Perhaps the fever raging through his shattered body would rise so high that he would roast.

What would dying be like? A sudden darkness, like the switching off of a light? A gentle sensation, like drifting off to sleep? Was some cool eternity waiting just beyond the barrier of pain in which he was trapped?

Around him men moaned and cursed the God who had made them. They called out for loved ones, and one pathetically young voice kept asking plaintively, "Help me? Please help me." At midday the voice fell silent.

By early evening, twenty-four hours after he had been

brought to the basilica, the lieutenant had a new fear, that he was *not* going to die.

Had gangrene set in yet? Would he lose his arm? What about his face, how bad was it? At least he hadn't been blinded; one eye appeared to be working. He forced himself to raise his good arm and wave it, in the slender hope that someone would notice he was still alive and in danger of remaining so.

He didn't think about his brother at first. His mind could not deal with such intense grief.

Ambulance drivers who had made many trips from the dressing station to the hospital trains noticed the lieutenant whose head was completely wrapped in bandages except for one tiny peephole over his left eye. As the evening wore on they saw that he waved whenever anyone came into view of that tiny window in his bandages. Then he changed the wave to a feeble salute. The gesture was gallant, heartbreaking.

To counteract the pain, he forced himself to remember happier times. But all the happier times had been shared with his brother. They had never been apart. The future, if indeed he was going to have one, stretched bleakly before him. Twins who had been born together were meant to die together, weren't they?

A voice floated over his head. "I don't care. I'm taking this one. He's been here all day, and I say a man who can salute can recover."

Miraculously hands touched him, sliding him onto a stretcher. He thought it was probably a good thing he couldn't make a sound, as he might have screamed in agony and been promptly returned to the ranks of the doomed.

Minutes later he was in an ambulance, bouncing over the rough road toward the rail lines. It was then that he thought about Claudia, with a yearning need that made him want to live.

All day the ambulances had brought the wounded to the casualty clearing stations. Jane had been part of that shuttle service, driving the ten miles from the dressing stations, unloading, and racing back.

She had heard shells scream overhead and had passed the burned-out wreckage of an ambulance that had received a direct hit, but her main fear was of falling asleep at the wheel. Never in her entire life had she experienced such bone-wearying, mind-numbing fatigue. And still the casualties waited in ever-increasing numbers, their wounds festering, their agony unending.

Only her anger at the bungling incompetency of the army's plans for casualties kept her going. Eighteen ambulance trains had been ordered for the Fourth Army, but only three had appeared. Urgent messages to other parts of the British zone had produced two more, making a total of five for the day. Three thousand or so wounded had been moved, but the total casualties exceeded thirty-two thousand in the Fourth Army alone. Now it was almost eleven at night, and thousands more wounded men were coming in from the front. She had just been turned away from a clearing station that was full.

She drove through the darkness, trying to find someone to take her cargo of human suffering. Her wounded passengers were quiet except for an occasional stifled groan, confident they were on their way home to Blighty.

Jane felt a great weight of responsibility, of frustration, and a deep sense of compassion. There were so many wounded at the basilica and in the village square who would probably remain there all night, dying from untreated wounds or from the German shells that still fell among them. Many of them lay out in the open. What if it rained?

Before the battle of the Somme began everyone had been confident of a decisive victory. Jane could not imagine now that these brave men were fighting a war that could be won. They were engaged in a conflict that they could only endure.

She didn't dare allow herself to wonder how the Kingsley twins were faring. Please let them be all right, she prayed silently whenever a wounded lieutenant who reminded her of Bran was lifted into her ambulance.

Damn, but someone must be made to answer for those missing ambulance trains. How many would die because someone had bungled?

The faint red glow of rear lights ahead alerted her to the fact that she had caught up with another ambulance whose driver, like her, was undoubtedly searching for a place to unload.

Minutes later she saw the headlights of a third ambulance behind her.

Afterward, she was never able to recall exactly what caused the ambulance in front of her to come to a sudden halt. A vehicle emerging from a side road? An animal crossing? Jane braked, feeling the wheels lock and slide. Her ambulance came to a stop only inches from the rear of the one in front.

She barely had time to turn off her engine before she heard the screech of brakes and then the grinding of metal as the lorry behind slammed into her vehicle. She felt a sharp pain as she was flung forward and her head struck the windscreen.

For an instant she was aware of voices, shouts, footsteps, and couldn't understand why she seemed to be in complete darkness. Then all the sounds faded away and she found herself floating lazily in the air just above the parapet walk at Rathbourne Abbey, and realized she was dreaming.

❧ Eighteen ❧

CLAUDIA SAW the telegraph boy ride up to Willowford on his bicycle. She had been sitting in the gazebo, which had been built on a slight rise to offer a view of the river, and at first the significance of the arrival of a telegram did not register.

She spent much of her time hiding from her mother-in-law, who regarded her with a pained expression that suggested she was fully aware that Claudia had married her son out of necessity. Not that Lady Kingsley had hinted in any way that she suspected her daughter-in-law was enceinte and that the child was not her husband's. But she watched Claudia with an air of expectation and suspicion, and Claudia had no intention of confirming those suspicions. She had not written Roald about the coming baby either. It was simply easier to put it off.

Claudia had no real feelings of guilt about her deception; she was too unhappy that Royce had abandoned her for any other emotion to intrude. She tried to hate him for his betrayal, yet longed for him with a yearning that transcended reason. With her mind occupied almost completely by Royce, she had not given much thought to her marriage to Roald.

Both Bran and Ro had proposed to her so many times that when Ro repeated his proposal on the evening of her birthday in London it had been easy to accept. Marriage to Ro meant that she would not have to face her guardian with the admission that she was carrying an illegitimate child and had given away every penny of a considerable bank account. When Roald recovered from his delighted surprise at her acceptance, he immediately took out a special license.

A warm breeze whispered through the gazebo, eliciting a sigh from Claudia. Such a perfect summer day! How she longed to spend it with Royce. The telegraph boy had now disappeared around the bend in the driveway.

Occasionally, when Claudia roamed through the elegantly appointed rooms of Willowford she caught a glimpse of a photograph of Ro or Bran or passed by the portraits that had been commissioned just after they joined the army. She would gaze at their handsome, laughing faces and remind herself that she was Mrs. Roald Kingsley. But deep down, she didn't really believe it. She was Royce's woman and always would be, and she continued to exist—other than for the remote hope that he might one day return to her—because she carried his child.

Glancing toward the house, she saw that the butler was walking across the lawn toward her. What did he want? She hoped Lady Kingsley was not sending another request that she join her for tea. Why couldn't they simply leave her alone? The telegraph boy was now pedaling furiously back down the driveway.

Claudia had dreamed of her ghost mother almost constantly since Royce left. She felt closer to her than ever before—hadn't she also known the terror and the excitement of creating a new life? The difference between them was that her mother had not wanted either the man or the child. Claudia wanted both, desperately.

A letter had arrived that day from Jane. She was in Flanders but did not mention the war. The newspapers were filled with stories about a major battle taking place on the Somme. Claudia had not replied to any of Jane's letters, except to send her a brief note thanking her for her wedding gift. It wasn't that Claudia blamed Jane for Royce's defection, but that Jane had warned her all along what to expect and Claudia was not yet ready to face her friend and divulge the extent of Royce's betrayal.

The butler reached her side, breathing heavily from the long walk. His face seemed to have fallen in on itself, and his eyes were red-rimmed. "Excuse me, madam, but her ladyship would like to see you in the south drawing room."

"Tell her I'll be along shortly."

"It is a matter of grave urgency, madam. Her ladyship requests your immediate presence."

"Oh, very well." Claudia sighed.

Halfway across the lawn the significance of the arrival of the telegraph boy dawned on her. She caught up with the butler. "A telegram came, didn't it? Dear heaven, it wasn't . . . from the army?"

The butler shuffled his feet, his face turning gray. He had been with the Kingsleys for many years and had watched the twins grow up. "Madam, it isn't my place—"

"Which one?" Claudia demanded. "Ro or Bran? *Tell me!*"

"Please . . ." He brushed his fist across his eyes, and she saw now that tears were coursing down his face.

"Was the telegram for me?" Claudia asked, planting herself directly in front of him.

Seeing no escape, he replied heavily, "There were two wires, madam. Lady Kingsley has summoned Sir Nigel from London. I believe one of the young masters was wounded and the other . . ." He couldn't go on. He pulled a handkerchief from his pocket and blew his nose.

"*Which one*?" Claudia's voice had risen to a scream, but it was clear the old man was too overcome to reply.

Then she was running toward the house, frantically trying to conjure up a vision of her husband's face.

The nurse taking Jane's pulse bristled with starch. Her cap, apron, and manner presented a formidably stiff and unyielding facade. A thermometer in Jane's mouth further hindered conversation. All she knew for certain was that she was aboard a hospital train, for she felt the motion of the carriage and heard the wheels clattering their familiar refrain over the steel tracks.

Sliding the thermometer to one corner of her mouth, Jane said, "I can't seem to remember how I got here."

Was it her imagination or did the nurse's nose twitch ever so slightly in disapproval? She replied, "The ambulance you were driving was in an accident. Personally, I don't think women have any business driving ambulances. They're just not physically capable of handling those big lorries."

Jane decided to ignore this and asked, "Was anyone else hurt?"

The nurse gave her an accusing look. "There were *wounded men* in your ambulance *and* the one you crashed into." It was clear she held Jane responsible for the accident.

There was no point in explaining. "Do I have a concussion? I remember my head striking something."

Sniffing, the nurse dropped her wrist and yanked the thermometer out of her mouth, then moved on to the next patient. Jane didn't really blame her for her attitude. The train was packed with badly wounded men, and in her shoes Jane would also have resented the presence of a woman who seemed to have little in the way of injuries.

A younger nurse approached her moments later and whispered, "Don't take any notice of Sister; she's been on duty for nearly forty-eight hours. You've got a concussion and some cracked ribs, but you'll be all right. You're going home."

Jane nodded and thanked her. She was about to add something—she wasn't sure what—when all at once she found herself crouching behind the hedge that bordered the lawns at Willowford where the Kingsley twins and their friends played polo. As usual, Bran and Ro were thundering across the turf, laughing as their mallets whacked the ball simultaneously.

She sighed and gave herself up to the dream.

Back in London she was examined by a doctor and ordered to spend the night in hospital for observation. The following morning she was told to take two weeks' leave while her ribs healed, then report back for duty.

Among the letters she picked up a few days later was a heavy vellum envelope bearing Lord Marrick's crest. She stared at it for a moment, her first reaction being fear that something had happened to Claudia. There had been no word from her other than a brief thank-you note, despite Jane's letters, since the announcement of her marriage.

Slowly Jane slit open the envelope with a knife and withdrew the single sheet of notepaper.

"Dear Jane," Lord Marrick had hand written in a bold script, "I am writing to advise you that Willowford is in deep mourning, as they have received word that Branston was killed on the Somme during the first day of the battle. . . ."

The writing blurred, and Jane could not read any further. She could hear a low moaning, not unlike the sound made by a wounded soldier, and for a moment didn't realize it was coming from her own lips. Oh, no, not Bran, dear God, not Bran!

Grief, anger, denial, washed over her in scalding waves. She couldn't cry; she wished she could. The pain was trapped inside her, bursting to get out, but there was no exit.

At length she read the rest of Marrick's letter:

As though this were not tragic enough for one family to bear, the Kingsleys have also been informed that at the same time Branston was killed, Roald was critically wounded. From what I can gather, he is too badly off to be brought home yet and remains in a French hospital.

One of his fellow officers visited Willowford to break the news of his injuries to his family, as gently as he could, as apparently there is much disfigurement of his features.

I spoke with Claudia, and she is in a state of utter panic, terrified that she will be forced to go to see her husband, which, of course, eventually is inevitable.

Would it be possible for you to visit Claudia at your earliest convenience? She needs your level head and calming influence in this present crisis. It would be best for you to stay here at the abbey rather than at Willowford.

Very truly yours,
Leith Marrick

Jane stared at the final paragraph. Typical of him to assume she would—or could—drop everything to do his bidding. But, of course, she had to go to Claudia at once. Poor Claudia, how would she be able to deal with a disfigured husband? Jane tried to suppress the thought that sprang unbidden into her mind, that it would have been easier for Claudia if Roald had been killed rather than Bran.

❧ Nineteen ❧

ALL OF THE SHUTTERS were closed and all of the curtains drawn at Willowford. A somber wreath adorned the front door, and the aging butler wore a black armband. He regarded Jane with polite surprise. She had ignored Marrick's suggestion that she go to Rathbourne Abbey and had arrived here without calling first.

"I've come to see Miss Claudia—Mrs. Roald Kingsley, I mean. I'm her friend Jane Weatherly," Jane said in a tone that brooked no refusal. "Please announce me right away."

After a moment's hesitation he replied, "Very good, madam."

He disappeared along a vaulted corridor, and a few minutes later a footman returned. "If you will follow me please, madam, I'll take you to Mrs. Kingsley."

Jane was conducted to Claudia's rooms on the second floor. The footman knocked and when they heard Claudia's voice calling for her to enter, Jane stepped inside into near darkness, despite the fact that it was midday.

She paused on the threshold, peering into the gloom to try to find Claudia in the unfamiliar room.

"Hello, Jane. I'm over here by the window."

Jane followed the sound of Claudia's voice, groping her way past a canopied bed and a massive dressing table to a window alcove, where she could dimly make out the shape of a sofa and a pair of chairs. A huddled shadow on the sofa appeared to be Claudia. "Claudia, what are you doing sitting here in the dark? Could we open the curtains?"

"No! Wait—I'll turn on a lamp."

The dim light did little to relieve the darkness, but it was enough to illuminate Claudia's ravaged features. Jane drew in a sharp breath. "Oh, Claudia!"

"Jane, I'm so frightened, I don't know what to do. I must get away from here."

"I agree," Jane said. "Let's go for a walk in the fresh air. If this utter gloom is the Kingsleys' idea of mourning—"

"No, no! I mean far away. I've made a dreadful mistake, but I shouldn't have to pay for it for the rest of my life, should I? I thought perhaps I could go to London with you. I even considered going back to New York—Mr. Baron and Frank were very kind—but I couldn't face crossing the ocean again."

"Claudia, what on earth are you talking about?" Jane asked.

"They're going to make me go to the hospital to see Roald, and I don't want to. I can't bear ugliness, and he's . . . he's been maimed horribly. . . . They say his face was almost shot away and they had to amputate his right arm."

"Oh, dear God," Jane murmured. "Poor Ro! How he must be suffering. How can you even think of deserting him? You can't just run away and pretend he isn't your husband. Claudia, you'll just have to steel yourself. He probably doesn't look as bad as you imagine."

"It's all right for you to say that—you're used to seeing ghastly wounds, but I'm not. And Roald used to be so handsome! Oh, I can't bear it!"

"You're going to have to bear it," Jane said shortly. "Think about Ro—what he has to bear. Where is he, by the way?"

"They're moving him to a hospital in London sometime during the next few days, so I know I'll be expected to go and visit him. I must get away, I tell you. I can't see him. I won't!"

Recognizing rising hysteria, Jane said in a gentler tone, "I'll go to the hospital with you. It won't be so bad, honestly. Once you get through that first meeting, you'll get used to how he looks, no matter what. And surely, with time—"

"No! No, I refuse to go. I can't be married to a man with no face!"

"For God's sake, pull yourself together. You married a soldier; you knew the risks. You can't desert him now."

"Yes, I can. I will."

"For pity's sake, if you have no feelings for him, why did you marry him?"

"Because I'm going to have a baby, that's why."

Jane stiffened. "How can you be sure? You haven't been married long enough to be really sure."

"It's Royce's baby, Jane."

Jane felt as though she had been slapped. She was silent for so long, contemplating her brother's perfidy, that Claudia asked anxiously, "Jane? Did you hear what I said?"

"Yes, I heard," Jane replied heavily. "And I don't know what to say, other than to tell you I'm sorry, that I blame myself for sending Royce to the abbey—and I'll never forgive him for this. Oh, God, what a mess he's made—of your life, of Roald's . . ." She broke off, a ghastly possibility occurring to her. "Roald doesn't know about Royce, does he? I mean, he thinks the child is his?"

"He doesn't know I'm pregnant. I haven't seen him since the day after the wedding. Oh, Jane, I can hardly remember what he looks like!" She shuddered. "*Looked* like, I mean. Before . . ."

"Claudia, only you can decide on the right thing to do, but . . . well, Roald is the innocent party in this situation. Whatever happens, he shouldn't have to suffer any more than he has already."

"That's why I must leave. He doesn't have to know about the baby. But I . . . well, I don't have any money, and I can hardly ask the Kingsleys for any. I wondered if you'd talk to Leith for me. You see, he was furious that I married Roald. . . . He even talked about having the marriage annulled."

"What changed his mind?"

"I told him I was going to have a baby."

"He stopped your allowance, I take it? But didn't he settle a large sum of money on you when you were eighteen? You said he was going to."

In the semidarkness Jane heard Claudia's soft sigh, but could not see the expression on her face. "Yes. He also gave Roald and me a handsome dowry, but of course the dowry now belongs to my husband."

"What about the other settlement? Was it a trust fund?"

There was a long silence, then Claudia's whispered response: "I don't have it."

Jane drew a sharp breath. "Please don't tell me you let my brother get his hands on it! Oh, Claudia, how could you have been such a fool—after I warned you, after I told you of his past history?"

Claudia began to cry. "Don't scold me, Jane, I can't stand it. Tell me you'll go to Leith and ask him to give me an allowance again so I can go away."

"I'll do no such thing. You promised to love and honor Ro Kingsley, and that's exactly what you're going to do. Stop and think, Claudia. You're going to have a child. Your child could be the Kingsleys' only heir, since Bran is dead . . ." Her voice broke and she went on hurriedly, "And it isn't certain that Roald is going to survive either. Many men die from their wounds, weeks, months later."

"But my child *isn't* a Kingsley."

"Nobody knows that but you." Jane paused. "Or does Royce know?" She could barely make out Claudia's nod. "Ah, I see. That's why he disappeared again. He couldn't face fatherhood."

"That's not true. He was thrilled when I told him. Something else drove him away—I don't know what."

Realizing there was no point in attempting to get Claudia to face the truth about Royce, Jane decided to try another approach. "Apart from any other consideration, you must think about what's going to happen to your child. You can't just go off by yourself, Claudia. To be brutally frank, you can hardly take care of yourself, let alone a baby—assuming Lord Marrick would reinstate your allowance, which is doubtful. So you have two choices. Either stay with Roald and the Kingsleys, where your child will have a secure future at least . . . or ask Lord Marrick to take you back, which he probably would. But I hope you'd be able to live with the knowledge of how much you'd added to the suffering of an innocent man . . . who has already lost so much."

"I don't want to go back to the abbey," Claudia said forlornly. "But I don't want to stay here either. Oh, what will become of me?"

Jane slipped her arms around her friend as she again dissolved into tears. "Don't make any decisions yet. Let's go and see Roald, and then I'm sure you'll do the right thing."

"Promise me you'll stay with me," Claudia begged between sobs. "Every minute."

"Of course I'll go to the hospital with you. But I can't stay here. The Kingsleys are in deep mourning; I couldn't impose."

"This is my home, too, isn't it?" Claudia said, sniffing.

Jane found a handkerchief for her. "Actually Lord Marrick has invited me to stay at the abbey."

Claudia looked up in surprise. "He did? What on earth came over him? He's been very cold and distant to me. Please stay here, Jane. I'll send for a maid to make up a room for you."

In the hospital they were caught up in a group of visiting relatives and friends and swept along the corridor toward the ward. At the door Claudia faltered, and Jane had to push her forward.

They walked down the aisle between the long rows of beds, and Claudia kept her eyes fixed straight ahead, looking neither right nor left. Even Jane felt her heart thump painfully against her ribs in anticipation of seeing Roald.

The doctor had informed them that Roald was unable to speak because his jaw had been wired together, but that he could hear perfectly well. There had also been a stern admonishment that the last thing the badly wounded man needed at the moment was a flurry of tears and wailing laments.

"Don't bring up the subject of his dead brother," the doctor warned. "Try to be cheerful, give him hope for the future." His practiced eyes took in Claudia's loosely fitting clothes, and he added, "If he doesn't already know he is to become a father, this would be an excellent time to tell him. It might be just what he needs to make the difference between fighting for his recovery and giving up."

"You heard what the doctor said," Jane whispered as they walked through the crowded ward, aware of the smell of ether and carbolic and of the low murmur of agony that hung in the air. "You've got to give Ro hope for the future."

He was in the last bed and before they reached him Jane saw, to her guilty relief, that his head was completely swathed in bandages with only a narrow opening for one eye to peer out at the world. Perhaps by the time the bandages were removed Claudia would have become used to the idea of his changed appearance. For now Jane felt the best she could hope for was to delay any precipitate moves on Claudia's part.

Claudia waited until the last moment to look at her husband. The sheets had been drawn up so that his missing right arm was not immediately obvious, but Jane noted the ominous flat area just below his right shoulder. She looked away quickly and waited at the foot of the bed as Claudia tentatively approached her husband.

As she drew near, he slowly brought his left arm out from under the covers and reached for her. Claudia took his hand in hers and raised it to her lips. "Oh, my dear," she said softly.

Jane felt tears sting her eyes as she said a silent thank-you. She made a pretense of fumbling with a bedside chair, then pushed it forward for Claudia to sit down.

Still holding her husband's hand, Claudia said, in a calmer tone than Jane expected, "The doctors say you are going to feel better soon. Darling, Jane came with me. She's home on leave because she was hurt while driving an ambulance in Flanders. Just think, she could have been the one who took you to the hospital."

"I just came to say a quick hello, Roald," Jane said hastily, "and to tell you that we're all hoping you'll make a speedy recovery. I'll wait outside for you, Claudia."

Claudia turned and nodded, her expression saying that she was in control of her emotions. As Jane walked away she heard Claudia say, "I can only stay a moment, the doctor says, so I must share my wonderful news. . . ."

Ten minutes later when Claudia joined Jane in the waiting

room she seemed almost in a trance. Jane took her arm and led
her outside. .

"You told him about the baby?" Jane asked as they tried to
hail a taxi.

Claudia nodded. "He squeezed my hand, and I could see
tears in his eye. Jane . . ."

"Yes?"

"He didn't look so bad—well, I mean, his face was all
covered with gauze and bandages, but there still seemed to be
a face underneath, don't you think? Jane"—Claudia broke off,
a look of wonderment on her face—"you'll never guess what
happened while I was talking to Ro. . . . I felt the baby
move! Of course I told him what was happening. He even tried
to put his hand on my stomach, but I wouldn't let him, not with
all those other people watching. I believe the baby is going to
be our salvation. All of us. Me, Ro, his parents . . ."

A taxi drew alongside them and stopped. Jane didn't know
why she didn't feel relieved at Claudia's change of attitude.
She felt a little like a runner who has cleared the first hurdle but
knows that even more formidable barriers remain in her path.

❦ Twenty ❧

FOR THREE MONTHS Jane's information about what was happening to Claudia came in the form of brief, often almost
incomprehensible notes from her friend.

Dear Jane,

What was your father's name? His Christian name, I
mean. I don't think you ever mentioned it. I expect you
know why I ask.

I'd love to come up to London to see you on your day
off, but if I did I'd have to go to the hospital to visit

Roald . . . so I tell the old dragon that I can't travel just now. I'm getting as big as an elephant, and I feel poorly, so it's not really an excuse. But I do wish I could talk to you, because I had the strangest dream that truly explained something that I know puzzles you as much as me. Is there a phone number where I could give you a ring?

Affectionately,
Claudia

Dear Jane,

How can you be back in Flanders so soon? I thought you'd stay in London for a while. I hate to think of you over there.

I'm sorry to hear your father's name was Albert, as I'm not fond of that name and so won't name my son Albert. But I had a wonderful idea and told the old dragon I would call our child Branston, in honor of his uncle. Well, she nearly had a fit! She said Bran could never be replaced. Such a tiresome woman. I was only trying to get along with her and felt my gesture was a kind one and should not have been thrown back in my face.

There's to be a memorial service for Bran after Roald comes home. I thought after Bran's body was brought home and buried in the family plot we wouldn't have to go through any more mourning rituals. The funeral was such a trial. I thought his mother was going to fling herself on the coffin. With so many of our brave boys buried in Flanders, I would have thought Bran would have preferred to stay there, too, with his compatriots, but his parents wouldn't hear of it.

You didn't ask about my dream! Perhaps you had the same one.

Much love, and do take care of yourself.
Claudia

Dear Jane,

The doctors removed Roald's bandages a few days ago. I wasn't there because I have to stay in bed until the baby is born. (My ankles and feet are swollen up like sausages, and my doctor mutters sinister warnings about toxemia.) I am sure I will explode long before the infant arrives.

When Ro's mater and pater came home from the hospital they were very quiet, very grave. I asked how Ro was, and his mother flew out of the room in tears. His father said (very tight-lipped), "As well as can be expected." What does that mean? Oh, Jane, I'm so afraid! What if Ro is monstrously disfigured? What shall I do? I don't want to see him—I don't want my baby to see him. Will I roast in hell for such feelings?

RSVP at once!

Love, C.

Dear Jane,

Your scolding letter was uncalled for. I certainly can't go anywhere just now, so I will have to be here when Ro comes home. They say he might be released from the hospital in a month or so.

I plucked up enough courage to ask how he looks. The pater says the doctors have done a remarkable job of reconstructing Ro's face. Apparently the surgeons are experimenting with new methods to restore some semblance of humanity to the features of men whose faces were destroyed by shrapnel or mustard gas. Dear God in heaven—if they had to reconstruct Ro's face . . . what does he look like now? Jane—he also lost one eye and will have a glass eye. It's all too horrible to contemplate. I can't help but think that perhaps Bran was better off than Ro. Isn't that too awful of me? But I dread having him come home.

Dear Jane,

Ro will be coming home on the 30th. I'm in an absolute panic! You must be here with me. I need you. Please come.

Jane, dear, dear Jane,

Please, please come! I can't face him without you. I know you're busy driving all the wounded men to hospital—the casualties are horrendous, aren't they? But I need you, too!

Jane, It's mean of you to ignore me. Roald is home. My worst nightmare is a reality. Is it possible that my baby will be marked due to the shock I've suffered, or is that an old wives' tale? I'm so dreadfully tired I think I might die. Oh, my poor baby, what will become of him? Will you swear to take care of him, Jane?

The last three letters all arrived together, too late for Jane to try to get to Willowford before Roald arrived. But she immediately requested leave, which was granted, and on a blustery autumn day she telephoned from the village station to let Claudia know she was on her way.

To Jane's dismay, a peevish voice informed her that Claudia had been admitted to the hospital that morning. Knowing that Claudia, like most women of her day, had planned to have her child at home, Jane felt great fear. Obviously if she required hospital care, something was wrong. Besides, the baby wasn't due for another two months.

"Which hospital?" Jane asked.

There was a pause. "I'm sorry, miss, but I'm not at liberty to say. Mrs. Kingsley is not allowed to have visitors, you see."

"I believe she would see me. Please—I came all the way from France to see her, at her request I might add."

"I'm sorry."

"Is her husband available? May I speak with him?"

The butler's voice expressed shock. "Mr. Roald is not able to come to the telephone."

"Sir Nigel, then, or Lady Kingsley?"

"None of the family are available, miss. Please excuse me now. Good day."

The line went dead.

Jane became aware that two other people were waiting to use the telephone. She left the booth and walked slowly out of the station. A taxi had just discharged its passengers at the entrance to the station, and on an impulse Jane asked the driver if he was available for hire.

"Where to, miss?"

"Rathbourne Abbey," Jane said.

* * *

Another ancient and unfamiliar butler responded to the abbey bell. Jane wondered fleetingly where all these aged servants had been hibernating awaiting the time when they would be needed to replace younger men claimed by the army.

"My name is Jane Weatherly. I'm not expected, but I wonder if by any chance Lord Marrick is in residence?"

"Lord Marrick is not receiving, miss. He returned from abroad just this morning."

"It's all right, Wilkerson." Marrick's voice echoed around the upper reaches of the gallery. "I'll see Miss Weatherly."

The butler stepped aside to allow her to enter.

Marrick waited at the top of the stairs, silhouetted against a blaze of sunlight spilling in through a tall window on the landing.

As she ascended the stairs and the man materialized within the silhouette, she was surprised by his appearance. Usually immaculately dressed and groomed, this morning Marrick wore a crumpled khaki jacket of the type worn in tropical climates. A kerchief was knotted loosely about his neck, and lightweight riding breeches were tucked into dusty boots. His black hair was tousled and badly in need of trimming. He even needed a shave.

Surely he had not been on an African safari, which was what his attire indicated! Jane's sense of outrage that he might have been off hunting big game while his countrymen suffered and died in Flanders fields momentarily eclipsed her concern about Claudia.

As she reached the top of the stairs she said stiffly, "Thank you for receiving me. I hoped you might have news about Claudia."

"Let's go into the morning room. Wilkerson, would you send up some tea and scones?"

"I'm sorry, milord, Cook was unable to obtain any sugar this week."

"Crumpets, then, or toast. Improvise, man. Come along, Jane."

She followed him along the gallery, past the long row of portraits. Those painted faces belonged to Claudia's ancestors, not Marrick's, and Jane wondered if Claudia had ever felt the connection of her bloodline, albeit from the wrong side of the blanket.

In the morning room Marrick pulled out a chair, and she sat down. Despite the sunshine, the room was cold, and the fire had not been lit. He took a chair opposite her.

After clearing her throat, Jane asked, "Did Claudia . . . Is she in labor?"

"No. From what I can gather—and you must understand that I have only just arrived home myself—her problems are not physical, other than the discomforts of advanced pregnancy. She's upset and, according to Lady Kingsley, a little irrational."

"Are you saying she's having a nervous breakdown?"

"Not at all. I interpreted it as a mild attack of hysteria. But we'll go and see for ourselves, as soon as we've had a bite to eat and I've changed clothes."

"Thank you, but I had a meal on the train."

"Ah, but I've traveled a great distance without food, so I hope you'll be patient for a few minutes while I have breakfast."

"I trust you enjoyed your holiday," Jane remarked with as much sarcasm as she could muster.

Amusement flickered in his dark eyes, but he answered in all seriousness, "Indeed, yes. My trip was full of unexpected pleasures."

The butler returned with a tray containing tea, toast, and a compote of dried fruits, which he placed on the sideboard. Marrick said, "We'll serve ourselves, Wilkerson, thank you."

He poured tea for both of them and passed her a cup, then spooned fruit into a crystal bowl. "Sure you won't change your mind?"

"Yes. Thank you. Lord Marrick . . . do you think it's possible Claudia's hysteria is due to her husband's disfigurement? How bad is he? Have you seen him?"

Marrick's brows knitted thoughtfully. "Yes, I've seen the poor devil. His features are unrecognizable, especially his mouth, which is twisted by scar tissue. When he speaks at all—which is rarely—it is with great difficulty. But I fear the injuries we can't see have ravaged him far worse."

"Shell shock?"

"I suppose that's as good a description as any. Young Kingsley was mutilated on the altar of war and lost a brother who was almost an extension of himself, and now he wonders who or what benefited from their sacrifices."

"Governments, politicians, aging field marshals yearning for the glory days of empire . . . the ruling classes," Jane said, her tone expressing the bitterness she felt. "Not to mention shirkers who stay home."

"Present company excepted, of course?" There was no censure in his tone, merely a deepening amusement.

"Of course," Jane said coolly, "since I understand you hardly ever stay at home."

"But you do feel I shirk my duty to king and country?"

"That's not for me to say."

"It has always fascinated me how much energy people expend worrying about how other people lead their lives. I'm occasionally guilty of it myself. For instance, I know of your fierce patriotism, but your contribution to the war effort consists of driving an ambulance. Now, if I were of an inquisitive nature, I'd ask myself why all of those months of nurses' training were being wasted, nurses being far more valuable than drivers."

Jane could not explain why she did not use her nursing skills, since she was no longer sure of her reasons. They had something to do with her feeling that driving the wounded seemed a more aggressive task than caring for them, but she couldn't explain even to herself why she deemed nursing to be passive, or why such thoughts made her ashamed, as though she were denying her womanhood. She decided her feelings were too complicated to discuss with him, or with anyone else, for that matter.

"You always manage to turn the conversation away from yourself, don't you, Lord Marrick?"

"Perhaps because the life of a shirker is so dull?" he suggested.

"You sound proud of it."

Their eyes met for a long moment, and Jane had the odd feeling that he was considering confiding in her his reasons for not going to war, but then he said abruptly, "If you'll excuse me I'll go and change."

Twenty minutes later, shaved, combed and clad in a dark

suit, he helped her into the passenger seat of his Bentley as she silently wondered how a civilian obtained petrol.

"I assume you know which hospital Claudia is in? The butler at Willowford wouldn't tell me when I called," she said as he slid into the driver's seat.

He hesitated for a second, then said shortly, "St. Agnes."

Jane knew the place, a private convalescent hospital popular with rich old men suffering from gout and maiden aunts too fond of elderberry wine. She had also heard sinister rumors that Saint Agnes was a haven for those afflicted with strange flights of fancy and lovesick daughters threatening either to enter a convent or to commit suicide. Jane couldn't see how Claudia's condition could possibly qualify her for a stay at St. Agnes.

The small convalescent hospital was set in parklike grounds abounding with evergreens, and the profusion of trees softened the lines of the ugly brick building that to Jane resembled a barracks. Surely Claudia must feel as if she were in prison.

Entering the lobby they were confronted by a stern-looking woman in nurse's uniform seated behind a high desk. She allowed her pince-nez to drop to the end of a black ribbon and fixed them with a ferocious stare. "May I help you?"

"We're here to see Mrs. Kingsley," Marrick said. "This is Miss Weatherly, and my name is Marrick."

"Visiting hours are at three o'clock." She raised her pince-nez again to scrutinize him. "That is, *approved* visitors. I trust you are on her list?"

"We will see Mrs. Kingsley *now*," Marrick snapped. "Which room is she in?"

"I really can't—"

"Either tell us her room number or be responsible for the fact that we disturbed all of your patients in our search for her."

The nurse glanced at the bell on her desk, then looked back into Marrick's imperious stare. "Mrs. Kingsley has requested complete rest. She does not want to see any visitors."

Marrick turned to Jane. "Let's start with that door over there."

Before they could move, the nurse said hastily, "She's in a

ground-floor suite. Number four. If you'll wait for a moment I'll have someone find out if she'll see you."

"Thank you, but we'll be sure to knock before entering. Come on, Jane."

As they left the lobby by way of heavy double doors and entered a long, narrow corridor, they heard muffled sobbing. The sound came from behind the first of several doors, which Jane saw was number two. Marrick quickened his pace, and Jane could hardly keep up with his long stride. At the third door, which was marked number four, they stopped. Marrick knocked and then, without waiting for a response, reached for the knob. The door was locked from the inside.

Marrick swore under his breath and called loudly, "Claudia? Are you in there?"

A white-coated orderly came running down the corridor just as Marrick was about to put his shoulder to the door. "I have a key," the orderly said breathlessly. "May I announce you?"

"Lord Marrick and Miss Weatherly."

The orderly opened the door a crack and said, "Mrs. Kingsley? Lord Marrick and Miss Weatherly are here and insist—"

"Jane?" Claudia's voice called. "Oh, come in!"

Claudia was propped up on a mound of pillows in a pleasantly furnished room. Although there were dark circles under her eyes, she did not look particularly ill. Jane embraced her as Marrick closed the door, leaving the orderly outside. He then approached the bed and stood staring at Claudia, who regarded him with wide eyes and a tremulous smile. "I didn't know you would be coming back so soon, Leith. You said you'd be gone for weeks."

"Does that mean you would have not admitted yourself to the hospital if I'd been here to question your reasons?"

"You admitted yourself?" Jane asked in surprise. She couldn't imagine anyone voluntarily spending time in a hospital.

"I needed the rest," Claudia answered defensively.

"But I'm told you never left your room at Willowford," Marrick said.

"I thought a change of surroundings would help." Claudia was obviously close to tears.

"Lord Marrick," Jane said quickly, "may I have a few minutes alone with Claudia?"

She thought for a second he might refuse, but he nodded and said, "I'll go for a walk around the grounds. I'll come back in half an hour."

When they were alone Jane said, "All right, Claudia, now you can tell me why you're hiding here."

"I'm not hiding—I needed the rest."

"Is someone making your life miserable at Willowford? In your letters you referred to Lady Kingsley as 'the old dragon.' Has she been unkind?"

Claudia's blue-violet eyes filled with tears. "She thinks I should take dinner with Roald in his room every night. She thinks I should read to him in the afternoons. *Jane, I can't stand to look at him!*"

Jane let out her breath slowly. "But you can't stay here forever. You're going to have to get used to the way he looks. Claudia, have some compassion for him. . . . Try to imagine how you would feel if you had gone through what he has."

"I would have killed myself," Claudia said vehemently.

Shocked, Jane snapped, "Don't you dare say that to him, do you hear me?"

Claudia clutched her hands. "Will you stay with me? We could ask Leith if we could go back to the abbey. It would be like it used to be, when we were children."

"I have two weeks' leave. I'll be happy to stay with you that long. But, Claudia, we can't go to the abbey, and we can't go back to being children. I think we should go to Willowford."

Claudia bit her lip. "Wait until you see Roald. You'll understand then how I feel."

Marrick drove them to a country inn for lunch, and while Jane and Claudia had Scotch eggs and barm cakes with thick slices of ham, he disappeared to call Willowford and make arrangements for their arrival. He had not made any comment about Claudia's sudden decision to go home, but had looked approvingly at Jane when she said she would be staying with her for a couple of weeks.

While he was making the telephone call, Claudia whispered,

"How did Leith know I was at St. Agnes? I only told Roald, and he promised not to tell anyone else."

Jane doubted that any secret was safe from Marrick, but she answered, "I don't know. Hush, here he comes."

"They're expecting you in an hour, and a room will be prepared for Jane," Marrick said, easing his tall frame into a chair. "Ah, fresh barm cakes and ham. How I miss good plain English food when I'm abroad."

There it was again, Jane thought, his careless reference to being abroad. Did he know how much it irritated people?

During lunch there was little conversation, and afterward he drove them to Willowford but refused Claudia's invitation to stay and visit, saying, "I'm rather tired, Claudia. I traveled all night. Jane will take care of you now."

Willowford's aging butler hobbled up from belowstairs as the two young women crossed the hall. "We've prepared the blue room for Miss Weatherly. Mr. Roald asks that you go to him as soon as you arrive, Mrs. Kingsley."

Claudia climbed the staircase with the slightly lumbering gait of a pregnant woman. She whispered to Jane, who remained protectively at her side, "Please come with me. I can't face him alone."

Jane nodded. She would have to see him sooner or later.

Claudia led the way to the end of the landing, knocked on the last door, and then opened it. She called out, "I'm home, darling," in a high brittle voice. "Jane is with me. She wanted to say hello. She came to see you while you were in the hospital, but perhaps you don't remember."

Jane steeled herself for her first glimpse of Claudia's husband, hoping her expression indicated sympathy without shock or revulsion.

At first she didn't see Roald's face, as he was seated in an armchair near the window, looking out over the rolling lawns of the estate. But she saw his empty right sleeve immediately.

Claudia didn't kiss her husband or even touch him. She lowered herself carefully into a chair slightly to one side of his.

Stepping forward, Jane looked into the wounded man's eyes. It was impossible to tell which eye was real; both were jade green, but the old sparkle was gone. She was aware of the disfigurement of his features, of his scarred and granulated flesh, but only vaguely, because she could not disconnect from his gaze, which seemed to be seeking something, perhaps the answer to an unanswerable question.

She mumbled something about being sorry he'd suffered so much and offered condolences on the loss of his brother.

His cruelly disfigured mouth moved slowly, painfully, as he formed the words of his response. "Thank you. I'm glad you're here. Claudia has been lonely."

At the sound of his voice, even distorted as it was by the reconstruction of his jaw and his difficulty moving his scarred lips, a drumming began in Jane's head. She wanted to run to him, to pull him into a fierce embrace, and swear to him that somehow, somewhere, he would be happy again. But of course she didn't; she didn't have that right.

She looked from him to Claudia and then back again. Was she the only one who was aware of the charade? Was it possible that no one in the family knew? Were they all too blinded with grief and pity to see the truth?

A red haze obscured Jane's vision; she felt dizzy with shock, relief, joy. Now she understood what that searching look had meant. Was she the only one who recognized that the man who had returned from that hell on the Somme to claim his dead brother's wife was Branston Kingsley?

❧ Twenty-one ❧

MIST SWIRLED along the riverbank, cloaking the willows in gray shrouds and silencing the chattering of the birds with the knowledge that winter was at hand. Her hands thrust into her coat pockets against the chill of the morning, Jane came to a halt as she realized she had walked beyond the boundaries of the estate and was probably now on Marrick's land.

She had spent a sleepless night, alternately convinced that Bran Kingsley was pretending to be Roald, then questioning her own sanity in believing such a thing. Yet deep in her heart there was no doubt. But why hadn't anyone else recognized his deception? Claudia, Jane thought, was probably so repulsed by his disfigurement that she never really looked at him. Perhaps his parents were so racked with grief over losing one son and having the other return with such hideous injuries that they simply accepted he was who he claimed to be.

The one piece of the puzzle Jane had no problem solving was Bran's reason for pretending to be his brother: Roald had married Claudia, the woman Bran loved.

A dog suddenly darted out of the mist and, as startled as she, began to bark furiously. Jane stood still. "It's all right, boy. I'm a friend." Recognizing the red setter as one of the stable dogs from Rathbourne Abbey, she crouched and held out her hand for him to sniff. He continued to bark, although he wagged his tail tentatively.

"What's all the barking about?" Marrick's voice floated out of the mist. A moment later she heard twigs snapping under his feet and he materialized out of the mist. "Jane! What are you doing here?"

She straightened up. "Just walking. I hadn't realized I'd come so far."

"I thought I was the only one foolhardy enough to walk in the fog. I usually take a morning ride, of course, but the mist is too thick today for the horses." He paused, staring at her with that peculiar intensity she had seen in his eyes on other occasions. "But you're not walking for pleasure, are you? Something is troubling you. Is it Claudia again?"

"No . . . no, she's fine," Jane said hesitantly. In that instant she made a decision: No one else must learn that Bran was alive and his brother dead. If it became known Claudia was a widow she would again have to contend not only with Marrick but also with Royce. If her brother learned Claudia was again free and now heiress to two fortunes, there was no telling what he might do. Besides, Bran loved Claudia and needed her.

"Everything is all right at Willowford, then?" Marrick persisted.

"Yes . . . Well, of course they're all under a tremendous strain, trying to cope with their grief."

"When Claudia's baby arrives perhaps it will help."

"I hope so."

"If it gets to be too much for you, come and visit me at the abbey. I'll be home for a few weeks. Bring Claudia, if she's up to it, but if not, come by yourself. I'd appreciate the company."

Jane blinked, recalling his busy social calendar before the war.

As if reading her thoughts, he shrugged and said, "I'm a pariah nowadays. Shunned. Sent to Coventry. Persona non grata."

"Oh," Jane said, the light dawning. He was no longer invited anywhere, and probably everyone refused his invitations because he was not in uniform. She couldn't resist remarking, "You must be very glad of Mrs. de Mora's company, then."

"Magdalena returned to Spain. She found wartime England too trying, especially since I am so seldom here."

Jane felt a glimmer of satisfaction that his exotically beautiful mistress had also deserted him. Still, to her surprise she felt sympathy for his loneliness. She had always been blessed—or sometimes cursed—by the ability to tune in to the emotions of others, and she could never remain unmoved by another's distress.

Perhaps sensing her sympathy, Marrick added, "I miss Claudia, too. Her presence lit up the dark corners of the abbey, although we never truly became companions."

"She was, and still is, a little afraid of you," Jane said. Something about the shrouding mist seemed to have weakened the barriers between them, inviting frankness.

"I can't imagine why. I indulged her every whim."

"Lord Marrick, you're one of those people who need only to walk into a room to command respect and a little fear from everyone present."

"But you've never been afraid of me, have you? Or, I suspect, of anyone else. I like the way you speak your mind. I would enjoy a leisurely conversation with you over dinner. Unless, of course, you also feel I should be shunned for not being in the trenches?"

"I'm sure you don't care one way or the other what I think," Jane replied.

"But I do. There are few people whose respect I would rather have."

Confused by his tone and unsure if he was again teasing her, she said, "I'll see if Claudia is up to coming to the abbey for dinner and let you know. Now I'd better go back; she'll be awake soon."

"I could drive you back, if you like."

"No, thank you. I'd rather walk."

"Jane . . ."

"Yes?"

"If you ever need anything . . . please come to me."

Surprised, she could only mumble, "Thank you."

The mist was beginning to dissipate, and she could now see his face clearly, his blacker-than-night hair and tropical tan making him seem foreign. But he wore an expression of complete sincerity that she found more disconcerting than any of the mocking glances he had given her in the past.

She turned to walk back the way she had come and heard him command the setter to stay.

As Jane anticipated, Claudia was aghast at the idea of having dinner with Marrick, and so Jane sent their regrets.

Several days dragged slowly by and Jane began to count the minutes until she could escape from the funereal gloom of Willowford and return to the trying, strenuous, but less complicated task of driving her ambulance. Claudia had again taken to her bed, "on doctor's orders," she claimed, but Jane doubted there was any real need for bedrest.

On the sixth day of her leave, Lady Kingsley approached Jane and said, "I wonder if you'd like to have dinner with us in the dining room tonight? Roald is going to come downstairs for the first time, and I thought it would be nice if we could make it as festive an occasion as possible." She paused, her eyes pleading. "Perhaps Claudia could make the effort, too? Will you talk to her, Jane? She seems to listen to you."

Appealing to Claudia's compassion for her husband had so far merely precipitated tears and protests that she didn't feel well enough to get out of bed, but Jane dutifully brought up the subject again. "Claudia, it's a special occasion for Bran—"

"*Bran*?" Claudia exclaimed. "You mean *Ro*! I say, do be careful not to make a slip like that in front of his mother."

Jane felt her cheeks flame. "Sorry, I meant Ro. Look, he's making an effort to resume a normal life. Don't disappoint him. You know it won't kill you to go down to dinner."

"Poor Ro." Claudia sighed. "I *do* feel sorry for him, honestly I do. But I get a sick feeling of horror every time I look at his poor face, and I'm afraid it will somehow do my baby some harm. Yes, I know that's an old wives' tale, but those things became old wives' tales because they have some basis in truth."

"It's nonsense, Claudia! Besides, I can't believe it's good for you to stay in bed all the time. You're getting that pasty, nunlike pallor again."

"The doctor said—"

"Oh, to hell with what the doctor said. At least come down for the soup course. Then if you feel ill, I'll personally escort you back up here."

That evening, to Jane's surprise, Claudia appeared just as the soup arrived. She had put on a loose white silk smock of the type worn by artists, with an outsize black bow at the throat, over a narrow black skirt, and she looked utterly lovely in a Bohemian, fragile sort of way. Her husband, who had been helped to his seat by his valet, now rose unsteadily and said, "Claudia . . . how beautiful . . . you are."

Claudia smiled vaguely and took the chair a footman pulled out for her. At the head of the table Sir Nigel nodded approvingly, but her mother-in-law's lips compressed in disapproval and Lady Alicia said, "We're glad you could join us, Claudia, and I do realize that your . . . delicate condition makes dressing difficult. However, we are in strict mourning. An all-black ensemble would have been appropriate."

Jane felt her hackles rise but tried to keep her tone civil as she said, "White is considered suitable mourning attire in some societies, Lady Kingsley. I remember when we were in America—"

"But we are not in America, Jane," Lady Alicia interrupted firmly. "In this family we will wear black, all black." She signaled the butler to begin serving, precluding further discussion of the matter.

After this strained beginning, the dinner conversation deteriorated even further. Jane realized that the Kingsleys were carefully avoiding mentioning the war, while Claudia seemed to be off on an astral plane, her enormous violet-blue eyes unfocused.

The tension at the table increased with the serving of each course, a watery broth followed by tiny portions of sole, followed by an almost meatless stew. Even in the mansions of the rich shortages were acute as the war dragged into its third year, but Jane wondered if the choice of menu had more to do with the fact that Bran had only one hand and anything that had to be cut up had been avoided.

Jane could see that Bran was miserably aware that his family felt uncomfortable eating with him. They were too solicitous, Jane thought, too apt to smile and utter some banality, too quick to summon a footman to help him.

Once he chided gently, "I'm really . . . getting rather adept . . . at eating with my left hand."

"Yes, of course, dear. You're doing splendidly," his mother said quickly.

"We're glad you were able to join us this evening, Roald," his father put in. "Nice to have you young ladies with us, too. Jane, I hope you won't run off too soon."

"I have another week's leave before I go back to . . ." Jane's voice trailed away as Alicia Kingsley shot her a panicked look that warned she was close to a taboo subject. Jane thought it ridiculous to pretend the war had not happened while Bran sat there with an empty right sleeve, his face a caricature of what it had once been. She was sure he felt the same way, as from time to time his fist clenched around his fork.

An awkward lull in the conversation developed as the footmen cleared the main course.

Lady Kingsley smiled brightly at everyone, obviously casting about desperately for some innocuous topic to introduce. She said, "Did you open your letter from America, Claudia? I believe one came for you today."

"Not yet. I'll read it later."

Jane tried to catch Claudia's eye, wondering if Frank Allegro had written her. It seemed unlikely that Mr Baron would have. But Claudia's gaze was fixed on some distant point, far beyond her immediate surroundings. Jane made a mental note to inquire later as to the identity of Claudia's American correspondent. Jane herself had kept up a sporadic correspondence with Frank, whose letters were filled with inquiries about Claudia's activities.

Lady Kingsley turned to her son. "Roald—"

"*Don't . . . call me . . . that*." The words were forced from between scarred lips.

A stunned silence fell around the dinner table. Sir Nigel's face turned a dull red, and he gave his son an angry look. Jane and Alicia Kingsley also stared at him, but Claudia continued to gaze straight ahead, although her expression was now alert.

His mother cleared her throat. "I'm sorry, dear. I must have misunderstood."

Jane felt herself tense with expectation. Was he going to admit to his masquerade?

But he said, "In future . . . I want to be called . . . by my first name."

"Blair?" his mother said, clearly mystified. "But you decided to use your middle name years ago, when you were just a little boy. You said it made you sound like a dashing cossack."

His scarred lips parted in a ghastly parody of a grin. "I left . . . the cossack . . . on the Somme."

No one spoke for a moment. Then Claudia said unexpectedly, "I think it's a jolly good idea. A new name, a new life." But she still didn't look at him.

"Very well," his mother said doubtfully. "We'll call you Blair." She dabbed the corner of her eye with her napkin. "Your father and I always liked the sound of our twins' names—Branston and Blair. They fit together so nicely. But you were adamant—"

"He wanted to be his own person," Sir Nigel said gruffly. "And so called himself Roald. But now Bran is gone . . ."

Lady Kingsley's face crumpled and she clapped her napkin over her mouth, gave a strangled gasp, and quickly left the room. Her husband rose instantly. "I shouldn't have mentioned your brother. Please, everyone, remain seated, finish your dinner. I'll go to her."

Bran-Roald-Blair said, to nobody in particular, "Perhaps I should have taken dinner in my room."

❦ Twenty-two ❧

AS PART of her duties as an ambulance driver, Jane was expected to administer first aid when necessary, but on days when the casualties were particularly heavy and the medical officers had their hands full at the clearing stations or the doctors were hard-pressed in the field hospitals, they soon learned that her skills went beyond those of most drivers. She was asked to sterilize and sort instruments, to hand them to the surgeons, to clean and dress wounds.

Sometimes the attractive young driver was merely requested to sit by the bedside of a dying man, hold his hand, and ease his passage to whatever lay beyond. She was calm and level-headed, needed little supervision or instruction, and even the most severely wounded men were soothed by her presence.

None of the doctors stopped to wonder where she had acquired her knowledge of nursing; they were too busy trying to save lives. But a day came when one of the medical officers observed her during a particularly difficult amputation and afterward said, "You didn't learn all that from a first-aid course or from driving an ambulance. Where did you study nursing?"

"In New York. But I didn't complete my training."

"Nevertheless, why in the name of all that's holy are you wasting your time driving an ambulance? You must see how much greater is our need for skilled nurses."

Before Jane realized what was happening, she had been assigned to a field hospital. She didn't want to be a nurse; she had discovered that she was unable to remain detached from the suffering of her patients. She felt their pain acutely and was appalled by the doctors' fumbling ministrations, which sometimes seemed to add to the suffering.

Since she had not completed her studies, officially she was classified as an auxiliary nurse, but on days when the casualties overwhelmed the hospital staff, there was little difference between her duties and those of the "proper" nurses.

The hospital was situated in a pleasant French village near an aerodrome, but not many of the patients were fliers, for pilots rarely survived being shot down. A few German pilots were brought in still clinging to life, but died within days. The burn victims suffered horribly. There were no enemy soldiers or allied soldiers, no friends or foes, in the hospital; the patients were all young wounded men who were far from home, lonely, and in need of care. The strain of taking care of them soon began to tell. Jane felt, despairingly, that those running the war seemed to feel that the side who sacrificed the most men would win.

She had decided to take her next leave when Claudia's baby was due, in January 1917, although, of course, those who counted nine months from her wedding night would expect it in March. A few days after Christmas, however, Jane received a telegram from Marrick: "Claudia's son born December 28. Both well. Regards, Marrick."

The baby was two months old when Jane arrived at Willowford on a freezing winter day. She was shown to Claudia's room and found her still in bed, although it was almost noon. Hugging Claudia, Jane remarked how well she looked, then asked, "Where is the baby? What have you named him?"

"Colin. He's in the nursery. Do you want to go and see him now—or you can see him when his nursemaid brings him to me for his afternoon feeding."

"Let's go and see him now," Jane said at once.

She waited while Claudia donned a pink satin dressing gown trimmed with swansdown, biting back a comment that surely it was time for Claudia to be up and about.

They walked the full length of the landing before coming to

the nursery, which adjoined the room occupied by the nurse-maid, a fresh-faced young girl who bobbed Claudia a curtsy.

"Marjorie, please don't do that," Claudia protested. "It really isn't necessary or even proper. We've come to see Colin. Is he awake?"

"I just got him down for his afternoon nap, madam."

"We'll just tiptoe in, then, and have a peep. You can go back to whatever you were doing. Come on, Jane."

They stepped into the nursery, with its cheerful yellow and white wallpaper and bright rugs. A large stuffed elephant stood in one corner of the room, a soulful clown seated on his back. There were shelves filled with colored wooden blocks and toy animals, a model train was set up, a miniature desk and chair at the ready.

Jane was so dazzled by the nursery that for a moment she didn't look at the sleeping infant in his old-fashioned wooden cradle. "Claudia," she whispered, delighted, "what a lovely room! Where did you get all these toys?"

"Oh . . . Blair did most of it."

For an instant Jane drew a blank, until she remembered that Bran now wished to be called by Roald's first name.

Claudia continued, "I told him Colin wouldn't be ready for trains and things for ages, but, well . . . I suppose it gave Blair something to do."

Jane looked down at the baby's tenderly curved cheek, the perfectly formed tiny hands, the mop of dark hair, and her heart turned over. Then she looked up at Claudia, her delight in her nephew's beauty checked by the realization that even at just two months old, he looked so much like Royce. How had Claudia explained that dark hair? The fair-haired Kingsleys and the platinum-haired Claudia surely had not produced that coloring.

Although she wanted to bend over and kiss the sleeping baby, to pick him up and hold him, Jane resisted the urge. "Let's go back to your room. I can see him again later."

Back in the bedroom, Claudia regarded Jane with obvious pride. "Isn't he beautiful? He's the absolute spirit and image of Royce. You haven't seen his eyes yet, but they're exactly like Royce's—that steely gray."

"He's certainly a lovely boy. But what do the Kingsleys think about having a dark-haired child?"

Claudia smiled conspiratorially. "That he's a throwback to one of my ancestors, of course. Dark eyes would have been more difficult to explain away."

"What about . . ." Jane managed to stop herself from saying "Bran." She had to think of him by his chosen name from now on. "Blair . . . how does he feel about the baby?"

"Adores him! But you'll see for yourself later. We'll go down to dinner. I usually have dinner with the family."

"Do you intend to stay on at Willowford now the baby's here?"

Claudia climbed back into bed and gestured for Jane to take a chair. "I'm really not up to running my own household yet. After all, I do have a weak heart, you know."

Jane looked her straight in the eye. "You look as healthy as a horse. That's just an excuse, isn't it? You don't want to be alone with Blair. Oh, Claudia, is that fair? How can you do this to him? He loves you so much."

"It's far more enjoyable to love someone than to be loved, you know," Claudia answered defensively. "He's as happy as anyone in his situation can be."

"But what about you? How do *you* feel about *him*?"

Claudia avoided her gaze. "The twins always loved me, no matter what I did. It's very nice to be loved unconditionally. But let's not talk about Blair now. Jane . . . I had my old dream again. About Royce."

She had told Jane of the dream she had while she was carrying Royce's baby, in which she saw him in a vast desertlike arena, surrounded by fierce warriors. She interpreted this to mean that Royce was in the army overseas, perhaps with General Allenby fighting the Turks.

"Because you dream something doesn't mean it's true," Jane said. "It just means you're thinking too much about him."

"You haven't heard from him, then?"

"No. And why would you imagine he's in the army? He pretended to have some dread disease that kept him a civilian."

Claudia sighed. "I can see it's no use talking to you. I wish you'd forgive him, Jane. He acted on a moment's weakness, and I'm sure he regretted it later."

"I don't want to talk about my brother. It makes me too angry."

"Then let me tell you about another dream I've been having. Three times now I've dreamed of a beautiful golden-haired woman and a little girl. They're both dressed in gauzy white gowns and have flowers in their hair and they're sitting together in a boat on a very large lake. Everything is tranquil and happy . . . but then all at once the skies grow dark and the water begins to churn and the boat is tossed about and they're so frightened. . . . Then the current catches the boat and they're rushed toward a bridge, but then all at once the boat is in the air, above the bridge . . . and then I wake up."

"Perhaps you're spending too much time sleeping," Jane said, then was immediately contrite. "I'm sorry, I didn't mean to sound callous. It's just that you worry about things like dreams, which seem so inconsequential when you consider what this war is doing to us. I'm sure your dream of the woman and child in the boat has something to do with the sinking of the *Lusitania*."

"N-no, I don't think it does. Janey, I think the woman in my dream is my ghost mother, and the little girl is me."

Jane was still trying to formulate an answer to this when there was a knock on the door and the nursemaid arrived with the baby for his afternoon feeding. Jane looked into Colin's big gray eyes framed by lustrous dark lashes and wordlessly held out her arms. She held the baby close, smelling the sweet, clean scent of him, feeling his silky hair against her cheek. His tiny fingers closed around her thumb, and he looked at her with her brother's eyes, but with none of Royce's guile or cunning. Over the top of the baby's head her eyes met Claudia's and it seemed to Jane that a silent pact was formed, although exactly what they were swearing to do was unclear.

It was a wrench for Jane to hand the baby over to Claudia. She did so reluctantly and said, "I'll go for a walk while you feed him."

"Oh, but it's so cold outside," Claudia protested as the baby nestled close to her breast.

"I'll bundle up. It seems I have a great need for fresh air lately. It has something to do with the stink of ether and carbolic soap and putrid flesh . . . Oh, sorry. I'll see you at dinner."

When she stepped out onto the terrace, however, she saw that snow had begun to fall. She stood for a few minutes as the white flakes cloaked the earth in silence and purity. The war seemed a long way away.

Her mind was filled with thoughts of the baby, of the miracle of the creation of life, when all she had experienced for so long was the destruction of life. She felt a sudden intense longing for a child of her own. If only Bran were not impersonating his brother, if only he had come back as himself, perhaps he would have come to realize that she could see beyond his scars. Perhaps he could have accepted her love. Oh, to be able to be with him, love him, have his child!

She was unsure how long she had stood daydreaming beside the stone balustrade of the terrace, watching the snowflakes drift by, enjoying the peacefulness of the white blanket settling softly on trees and lawns, when she felt someone place a fur coat about her shoulders. Her hand went automatically to feel the fur, and she looked over her shoulder in time to see Blair stepping hastily backward.

"I saw you from my window and thought you might be enjoying your solitude too much to notice how cold you were getting. Claudia never wears that coat, by the way."

His speech was less hesitant than before, but it broke her heart to see how he lowered his head and turned away from her as he spoke and how quickly he retreated after placing the coat on her shoulders, as if fearing she might be repulsed by being in close proximity.

"Thank you, you're very thoughtful. I *am* freezing, come to think of it. But the snow is so tranquil, so clean . . ."

"After the muck of war it's almost holy, isn't it?"

"Yes."

They were silent for a moment, each knowing the other had also witnessed the carnage of battle. Jane thought, His scars have faded quite a bit. Then she immediately wondered if it was possible she had unwittingly become inured to the ravages caused by bullets and shrapnel. Or perhaps she could see beyond the disfigurement to the man she loved. She said quickly, "Claudia is looking well, and I saw Colin. He . . . he's a beautiful baby."

Blair raised his head. "Isn't he a splendid little chap? I wish my brother could have lived to see him."

He really believes Roald was the baby's father, Jane realized, and that gives him another reason to masquerade as his twin. She wanted to tell him she knew and understood why he pretended to be Roald, but that he was making a terrible mistake. Instead she said, "You must miss him dreadfully."

"Yes. Sometimes I wish—"

She cut him short, fearing what he would say. "Time will help."

"Oh, please, Jane! Not that from you, too. I'd have expected more of you."

"Very well. More you shall have. First of all, you need to start making a new life for yourself and your family. You're not helpless or blind or paralyzed, like many of the men coming home are. You should be thinking about a home of your own and a career."

His voice was edged with bitterness as he replied, "Ah, yes, I understand there's a great demand for one-armed men with faces that frighten little children out of their wits."

Ignoring the sarcasm and self-pity, Jane said, "I'm quite sure baby Colin adores your face."

His tone softened. "He doesn't know any better."

Jane pressed her advantage. "Your father owns a newspaper and several magazines. Surely you could do something in publishing? You could type with one hand, hold a phone with one hand. There are so many wrongs in the world to be put right, starting with the war."

"You obviously haven't read any of my father's editorials lately. His paper doesn't print any criticism of the War Committee, and he doesn't even let his reporters mention any military or naval blunders. Offer him a feature story about some poor bastard being posthumously awarded a Victoria Cross and he'll splash it across the front page."

"All the more reason to get into the business and try to influence your father to change his policies. We're fighting a war of attrition; we need the voice of sanity to speak to the people." She paused and gave him an encouraging grin. "It would really help if women were able to vote."

"Good God, you're not a suffragette, too, are you?"

"I don't have time to chain myself to the railings at Ten Downing Street or march in parades but yes, I do firmly believe women should have the right to vote."

She realized Blair was no longer hanging his head; he looked her straight in the eye, his shoulders squared. "It would be a bloody disaster. Not all women are as intelligent as you, you know."

Jane flushed with pleasure. Ah, the power of even a minor compliment from a beloved man!

He went on, "They'd probably vote for a candidate because he had a nice smile or curly hair."

"What utter nonsense! Do men vote on that basis? Why should women? All right, if you don't want to work toward peace or toward votes for women, then there's the disgrace of child labor, conditions in the collieries—"

Blair held up his hand. "Whoa! I'm getting tired just listening to you. I'm afraid I don't have your passion, Jane. Come on, we'd better go inside before we're found out here frozen into statues."

Jane walked back to the house, although she would have preferred to stay out on the terrace with him, in the almost mysterious intimacy of a silent white world that seemed to belong to them alone.

Early in 1917 at long last America entered the war. Optimism ran high in England; now surely the balance of power would shift in favor of the Allies. The first American troops were sailing for France.

Jane, home on leave, was staying with Claudia when Marrick telephoned to tell them he had a visitor who was anxious to see her.

"Who is it?" Claudia asked.

"He's asked me not to tell you. He wants to surprise you. Seems a bit gauche to me, but—"

"Well, I can't come now. Jane is here."

"I'm sure he'd like to see Jane, too. Bring her along."

When Claudia hung up the receiver, she looked at Jane,

excitement on her lovely face. "We must go to the abbey right away. Someone is there who wants to see us—both of us! He asked Leith not to say who he is, as he wants to surprise us. Oh, Jane, that can only be Royce."

Jane sat quite still, afraid to speak for fear of unleashing a storm of rage. How could Royce still have Claudia under his spell after all this time?

Drawing a deep breath, Jane said, "First of all, I can't believe Royce would have the nerve to go to the abbey, and second, if he is there, surely you don't want to see him. I think you should call Lord Marrick back and tell him you're not going unless you know who the visitor is."

But Claudia was already on her feet, ringing for her maid, making plans. "Do you think it would be all right if I wore just a *little* jewelry? Or a lace jabot at the throat of my dress? Oh, how I hate wearing mourning! I wish I'd washed my hair! The baby can wear his little sailor suit—"

"You're surely not taking Colin?"

"Of course I am! He's Royce's son; he has a right—"

"My brother forfeited all of his rights!" Jane grabbed the phone and gave the operator the number of Rathbourne Abbey. Moments later Marrick was on the line.

"Lord Marrick, it's essential we know who we're coming to see. There's a certain person neither of us wishes to meet."

She listened silently to his response, then said quietly, "Thank you. We'll be there shortly."

To Claudia she said, "It isn't Royce. It's Frank Allegro. He joined the American army, and he's on his way to France."

"Oh," Claudia said, all of her joy evaporating. "I think I'm too tired to go."

"Nonsense. It's just for afternoon tea. Besides, it's the least you can do after all Frank did for us in America."

"Colin will be taking his afternoon nap."

"That didn't worry you when you thought Royce might be there. All right, let's go without the baby. Come on, Claudia, Frank's going to a hell you can't begin to imagine."

With much grumbling and protesting Claudia at last agreed, and an hour later they were shown into the drawing room at Rathbourne Abbey.

Frank, clad in the uniform of a sergeant in the United States

Infantry, swept Claudia into an embrace that was far too enthusiastic for propriety, swinging her right off her feet.

"You look great, Claudia!" he exclaimed. "Gee, I'm glad to see you looking so well." He set her down carefully and repeated the greeting to Jane, who as she was swung into Frank's arms caught a quick glimpse of Marrick in the background, glowering disapprovingly.

Frank seemed oblivious to his host's frosty demeanor. He thanked Jane for writing him, and Claudia, surprised, said, "I didn't know you two had been corresponding."

"Oh, yes. I know all about your marriage and your baby," Frank said. "I hoped you'd bring the little fella with you. But maybe I can wangle an invitation to meet your husband before I leave? I've got a room at the Hunter's Arms."

Claudia smiled vaguely and made a noncommittal reply. Everyone was seated, a maid brought a tea tray, and Marrick asked Jane to pour.

She and Frank kept the conversation bouncing back and forth, and she hoped he hadn't noticed that neither Claudia nor Marrick had much to say. Frank wanted to learn as much as Jane knew about conditions in France, and she filled him in briefly and then said, "But perhaps we'd better change the subject. Claudia and Lord Marrick don't care to discuss the war."

"On the contrary," Marrick said with studied casualness, "perhaps I should take this opportunity to tell you that I shall shortly be joining the Royal Flying Corps."

Frank immediately said, "Hey, that's great. Mr. Baron has told me about your flying prowess. He said he's seen you put a plane down in a jungle clearing no bigger than a blanket."

Claudia looked mildly surprised at Marrick's news, but made no comment.

Jane stared at him. "Why? I mean, what made you change your mind? We've been at war for over three years, and I thought you said you would never join up."

"I don't believe I said that, exactly, but to answer your question, I'm joining the Flying Corps at this point because now the war can be won, probably within the year. The United States will change the balance of power." He paused, regarding her with enigmatic dark eyes. "Or perhaps I'm just tired of being excluded from social events."

"Well, I can certainly understand that," Claudia said, to the amusement of Frank and to Jane's acute embarrassment. "Life is so impossibly dull at Willowford, because we're in mourning. Sometimes I think I shall go mad from boredom. How I long to have a party and burn every dreary black frock in my wardrobe."

"Ah, Claudia, you're such a child." Marrick sighed. "I was being facetious when I said I was tired of being ostracized. Actually I don't give a damn what people think of me." He turned to Frank. "Tell me more about my friend Baron. How is he bearing up to the United States being drawn into the war?"

Jane leaned back, only half listening to the ensuing conversation. Once again Marrick had surprised her. Just when it seemed she had him neatly fitted into one category he turned around and did the absolute last thing she would have expected him to do.

❦ Twenty-three ❧

August, 1918

A V-FORMATION of six Sopwith one-and-a-half strutters climbed into a rosy dawn sky, heading east.

In the pilot's seat of the last Sopwith in the starboard string, Leith Marrick glanced down at the shadows of the aircraft flitting across the plain below, felt the slight buffeting of the wings as his machine rose and fell in the air in the motion peculiar to this type of aircraft, and as the silver ribbon of a river came into view he allowed himself a moment of appreciation for his bird's-eye view of the lush French landscape.

At forty-two he was the oldest man in the squadron, but none of his fellow airmen joked about his age. He did not share in their camaraderie, join in their off-duty revelry, talk about himself, or form any close associations. When he was not actually flying, he withdrew to his quarters or set off on solitary excursions into the countryside. No one really knew Leith Marrick. Behind his back he had been dubbed the Lone Wolf.

Woolly puffs of charcoal smoke appeared in the wake of the Sopwiths as the German gunners opened up, and blossoms sprouted around the biplanes. His plane rocked violently as his engine cowling was struck and the fabric of his top wing was peppered with ragged holes.

Quickly he checked the controls. No serious damage had been done. Turning, he signaled to his observer in the rear seat, a quiet young man named McDowell, that all was well and they were proceeding.

Droning on, out of range of the guns, he wondered if any of his fellow airmen were aware that below them in the winter of 1711 Marlborough's troops had fought over distances that even from the air seemed daunting.

Sunlight glinted on the wings of the flight leader's aircraft as he dipped to signal that hostiles had been sighted.

A dot in the sky materialized into a DFW two-seater, the Maltese crosses on its wings and fuselage visible as it proceeded in the opposite direction. The reconnaissance plane had seen the British formation, but Marrick knew there was little likelihood of attack while they were outward bound. The Huns would await their return, when they would be dangerously short of petrol and the west wind would be in their faces.

They were now fifty miles behind enemy lines, their mission to confirm intelligence reports that the Germans were using an old French airship base at Maubeuge to house their zeppelins.

A plume of smoke moving through the town indicated a train, but the Sopwiths carried no bombs, which struck Marrick as a waste of a flight. They could have confirmed the intelligence about a large warehouse being built and then hit the enemy's supply lines. To Marrick, the most infuriating part of this conflict was the monumental waste—of men, of equipment, of time.

The Sopwiths broke formation to sweep the area in their search. Moments later Marrick spotted the huge airship sheds and began to descend. If the Germans had zeppelins there, he would see signs of activity even if the doors to the big sheds were closed.

He eased the stick forward, the aircraft's nose pointed earthward, and carefully scanned the area. A group of sailors were strolling along one of the lanes below. Their presence confirmed that naval zeppelins were here. Ships this far inland could only be airships.

He had just throttled back when the engine backfired. A flash of blue flame shot through the intakes on either side of his cockpit.

Damn. A valve had stuck. He opened the throttle again, and the Sopwith began to vibrate. Another backfire. He leveled out and banked around to head for home, hoping he could maintain altitude. Engine trouble this far behind the lines was cause for considerable concern.

The sound of the Clerget had changed from its normal buzzing to a clanking din, and Marrick had no doubt now that he had a sick engine on his hands.

Coaxing the plane forward, trying to maintain altitude, he knew he couldn't stay aloft much longer. The noise and vibration were growing worse, and he could smell the unmistakable odor of hot metal.

A loud crash and something tore through the starboard cowling and hurtled into the air. Simultaneously huge spurts of blue flame erupted from the intakes and the aircraft shuddered as the propeller jerked to a halt.

In the near silence that followed he contemplated the possibility of landing. Many wild stories circulated about how the Huns treated prisoners. He discounted most of them, but he absolutely could not take a chance of being interrogated. His activities prior to joining the Royal Flying Corps must never be divulged to the enemy, and although he believed himself to be a strongly determined man, he knew that even the staunchest patriot could be brought to breaking point. No, he would have to avoid capture at all costs.

A sighing of the wires warned him that the aircraft was about to stall, and he pushed the nose down again, then eased her level. Glancing at the altimeter, he saw they had less than three thousand feet. He could glide for a few miles, find a level spot to put her down.

How far had he coaxed her homeward? He'd been so preoccupied he wasn't sure where he was. There was no sign now of the rest of the formation. He turned and shouted to McDowell, "We're going down. Jettison the gun."

Nodding that he understood, the observer unlocked the Lewis gun from its ring and shoved it overboard. He then dumped the ammunition drums.

They were gliding now, with only the sound of the wind in the wires.

A small village appeared; they could almost reach out and touch the chimney tops. Beyond lay a pasture occupied by a few grazing cows.

The Sopwith touched down gently and rumbled to a halt. They were immediately surrounded by French farmers, all urging them to get up into the sky again before *les boches* arrived. While the observer tried to explain that was impossible, Marrick examined the engine. One cylinder was missing and the crankcase was badly fractured. An inlet valve was broken, a piston smashed.

Marrick pushed up his goggles and surveyed McDowell grimly. "It's hopeless. We'll have to burn her. Look, we don't have much time. I'm going to try to get to those woods before the Huns arrive. You can come if you wish, but we'd be better off to separate." He was already kicking holes in the fabric of the lower wings and fuselage.

"I'll stick with you, sir, if you don't mind. I don't speak the language," McDowell answered.

One of the farmers, realizing their intent, touched a match to the fabric in several places. Flames roared.

As the two airmen sprinted for the woods they heard the bullets from the belt of the fixed Vickers gun exploding, completing the destruction of the aircraft.

They were now on foot, miles behind enemy lines, wearing British uniforms.

They had evaded capture for three days, helped by French villagers who had exchanged their flying jackets and khaki uniforms for civilian clothes, fed them, and hidden them when the *boches* searched for the downed British airmen.

While taking shelter in a farmer's barn, Marrick, who spoke fluent French and German, translated for McDowell what their agitated host was telling him. "He says the boches have brought in Alsatian dogs to hunt for us and we must leave before dawn."

McDowell grimaced. "We can't outrun dogs. They're certain to pick up our scent and find us. Perhaps we should leave now. We don't want to get the farmer in trouble. Look, sir, it's hopeless. I'm surprised we haven't been caught before now. We're just too far from our own lines, and . . . well, no offense, sir, but you're not exactly a young man—"

He broke off, silenced by a warning glint in Marrick's dark eyes, reminding him that so far it had been the twenty-one-year-old McDowell who tended to lag behind in their mad dash across the French countryside.

Marrick studied the map he had transferred from his leather flight jacket to his borrowed coat. "We're less than five miles from an aerodrome. We could be there long before dawn."

McDowell gave him an incredulous stare. "A *German* aerodrome?"

"Of course a German aerodrome," Marrick snapped. "How better to make it back to our own lines than in a Hun aircraft?"

"You intend to *steal* one?" McDowell asked faintly.

Marrick gave him a frosty smile. "I doubt they'll offer to loan us one. You don't have to come. The farmer can get word to the Huns that you want to surrender to them. I expect you'll be treated reasonably decently. There's no shame involved, and it's always better to live to fight another day. The odds against my successfully getting aboard a plane, taking off, and arriving back at our own base in one piece are extremely high."

"Then why try it? Even if you escape the Huns, how will you get past our boys? One side or the other is bound to shoot you down."

"I have no choice. I can't be taken prisoner. I can't tell you more than that, but I would urge you to stay and turn yourself in."

McDowell was obviously wavering. He didn't want to be

considered cowardly, but what Marrick was proposing was foolhardy, insane. He'd never live to tell the tale.

"Good, it's settled, then." Marrick folded his map and pushed it into the inside pocket of his borrowed coat. "I'll explain to the farmer that he should send for the boches as soon as it's light. I'll leave immediately."

McDowell cleared his throat nervously. "Well . . . I think I'll go with you, sir."

The Fokkers were lined up in a neat row, silhouettes in the moonlight. But before Marrick and McDowell could approach the biplanes they would have to pass several hangars, and despite the hour there were German mechanics at work there.

Marrick kept his eye on the hangars as he quickly removed the uniform from the German sentry who lay unconscious at his feet. He handed the German uniform to McDowell, who donned each garment as he received it.

There were no clouds for cover, and Marrick knew that an early summer dawn would soon be gilding the rim of the earth. He looked toward the sentry patrolling the approaches to the hangars, then at McDowell, and nodded.

Silently they slipped through the sentries' gate, waited for the second sentry to turn so that his back was toward them, then raced across the airfield.

Marrick dealt with the second sentry as swiftly and noiselessly as the first, then dragged him into the shadow of the nearest hangar. McDowell briefly wondered where a member of the aristocracy had acquired such a lethal skill, but there was little time to speculate as Marrick donned the German uniform, then motioned that he was ready.

Calmly stepping out of the shadows, he began to speak to him in a low conversational voice in German, which McDowell didn't understand, but found strangely reassuring.

Marrick set a leisurely pace, and as they strolled he kept talking, even going so far as to chuckle a couple of times as if relating an amusing story. McDowell longed to break into a fast gallop but restrained himself. He avoided glancing toward the hangars.

Marrick walked slowly toward the last Fokker in the row. He appeared relaxed, unhurried.

McDowell felt the icy prickle of fear up his spine as one of the German mechanics suddenly left the hangar and ran toward them. Marrick stopped and looked back at the man, calling something to him in German.

A tumult of possibilities assaulted McDowell. Surely Marrick's English-accented German would give them away? Even if he had no accent, how could he explain what they were doing? Good Lord, he appeared to be barking *orders* at the German.

The moon was down now, but a silver dawn spilled across the field. McDowell stared in amazement as the German mechanic removed the chocks and stood at the ready in front of the propeller. Marrick climbed into the pilot's seat, and McDowell scrambled into the observer's seat.

McDowell was still holding his breath as they taxied along the strip and took off.

As they climbed into the rapidly lightening sky he called over the rush of air, "What did you tell him?"

Marrick glanced back at him. "That we were on a special mission."

"He believed you?"

"Not until I gave him a certain password used by German intelligence for such situations."

"What password? How did you know it?"

But McDowell didn't get an answer, as Marrick pretended not to hear. McDowell settled back to worry about what would happen when they crossed their own lines. By then the sun would be up and they would make an excellent target as they came in to land. Perhaps they could somehow signal the Allied gunners that they were not hostiles? But how? They were in a German aircraft and were wearing German uniforms. McDowell hoped Marrick had a plan.

They ran into antiaircraft gunfire shortly after crossing their own lines, and puffballs of smoke exploded dangerously close, but Marrick banked sharply and climbed into a stray cloud.

Minutes later an airfield appeared below. At the same time they were surrounded by smoke blossoms as the guns opened up.

Marrick went in low, barely skimming the treetops. McDowell closed his eyes and prayed as the first bullets ripped into the starboard wing and the airplane lurched. Something that felt like a red-hot nail grazed his forehead, and stars exploded in front of his eyes at the intensity of the pain.

Another explosion. Then his impressions became kaleidoscopic—flames engulfing the engine, the aircraft rocking violently as Marrick fought to control it, the ground rushing toward them.

McDowell's last conscious thought was *We're going to crash*.

❧ Twenty-four ❧

JANE HAD just come off duty and was wearily wending her way across the area used by arriving ambulances when she was spotted by a driver who knew her. "Jane! Wait a minute."

Turning, Jane recognized Penelope Tandy, a lanky Londoner with sharp features and piercing blue eyes that suggested one who was acutely aware of her surroundings. Jane knew that Penny Tandy was also noted for her incredible memory. She never forgot the slightest bit of information relayed to her.

"Hello, Penny. I suppose you've brought us another batch of patients?"

"You look absolutely buggered," Penny said sympathetically. "Just going off duty?"

Jane nodded. "I worked a double shift. We're shorthanded."

"Well, I won't keep you, but I thought you might like to know that I just brought in two Flying Corps blokes—alive, for a change. Would you believe it, they were shot down by our own guns! 'Course, they happened to be in a German aeroplane at the time. Seems they were shot down behind our lines, stole the Gerry aeroplane and flew it back. Naturally, our blokes didn't realize they were trying to land—thought they were going to shoot up our airfield. What a bloody irony—being shot down a second time by your own side."

"How badly hurt are they?"

"Not as bad as you'd think. The pilot managed to crash-land. Now, here's what I want to ask you. Don't I remember you telling me that your friend Claudia was the ward of Lord Marrick?"

"Yes." Jane recalled that Penny had taken on extra ambulance runs for her when she went home on leave. "Why?"

Penny's eyes glinted with satisfaction. "Thought I knew that name. Guess what? He's the pilot who flew the Gerry plane in."

Jane's head jerked up. "You're sure? Where is he now?"

"Being wheeled into the operating theater, I expect. They've got some broken bones to set. Oh, yes, and he's got a shoulder full of shrapnel."

A face floated into view. Wide-set gray eyes, filled with understanding and liquid with compassion, a tenderly curved mouth that he had often found himself studying with erotic interest, and burnished brown hair pulled smoothly back from a high forehead and topped by a starched cap materialized in his morphine-induced stupor. Was he dreaming that face? Surely it wasn't possible that of all the nurses in France Jane Weatherly was standing beside his bed?

Marrick felt a cool hand touch his brow, and a familiar voice asked, "Would you like some water?"

He tried to speak, but his lips seemed to be glued together. Gratefully he sipped the water she offered. Everything was coming into focus now. He was in a ward packed to overflowing with injured soldiers. There were even men lying on pallets on the floor. An unpleasant mingling of the odors of ether and disinfectant hung in the warm, still air, and several flies buzzed about his face. Jane brushed them away. He could see only one other nurse wending her way among the closely packed patients.

The water moistened his mouth sufficiently to allow him to speak. "Thank you, Jane. I thought at first I was dreaming you."

She smiled. How tired she looked. "I asked to be transferred to this ward when I heard they had brought you in. You crash-landed at our airfield."

"Of course," he said solemnly. "I chose it just to bedevil you." He glanced down at the casts on his left leg and left wrist, then at the bandages on his left shoulder. "I seem to have crash-landed on one side only. What's the damage?"

"Bullet wounds in your shoulder, a broken wrist, and . . . perhaps I'd better have the doctor explain about your leg."

"No—don't go. I'd rather hear it from you."

"Well . . . I'm not supposed to . . . but then, I'm not noted for following the rules around here. Your leg was crushed. The surgeons were going to amputate, but then somebody remembered that the French had captured a German surgeon who has been using silver wire to literally weave together crushed bones. They brought him from the camp where he'd been treating prisoners of war, and he set your leg. I expect the doctors will warn you not to get your hopes up, as you may still lose the leg, but you know how doctors are: They threaten you with the worst, and then you're grateful for the least."

"I don't remember any of this." The thought that he could have awakened to find his leg missing passed briefly through his mind.

Jane answered, "You had a concussion. You've been unconscious for the best part of two days."

"You took care of me?"

She nodded.

He gave a moment's consideration to all that her care had entailed and then remarked, "I suddenly feel rather decrepit."

Jane laughed softly. He'd forgotten how infectious her laughter was and how her gray eyes sparkled when she was amused. His shoulder ached abominably, and waves of post-operative nausea washed over him, but Jane's presence challenged him to put on an air of nonchalance.

"Oh, you're far from decrepit, Lord Marrick," she said.

"For a man of my age, you mean." Damn, why did he have to keep reminding her of his age? Or was he reminding himself?

"For *any* man. What you did was very brave—reckless, but brave."

"Jane . . . I hate to interrupt when you're complimenting me, but . . . do you think I could have a bedpan?"

Jane scrutinized the dressing on his shoulder. "I've heard about your exploits. They say in the few months you were flying you received two commendations and shot down a lot of Huns."

"Three, to be exact."

"But one was a German ace. I had no idea you were a hero."

"Don't gush, Jane," Marrick said sharply. "It's out of character."

"I was just trying to take your mind off what I'm doing to your poor shoulder."

"Only I can decide where my mind will wander. Just get on with it, will you?"

"What's it like—to fly?"

"Perhaps someday I'll take you up."

"I'd like that." She winced for him as she discovered the dressing was stuck to his wound.

"For God's sake, do it," he ordered. "Get it over with."

She picked gently at the edges of the bandages. "Tell me about your aerial duels."

"Dogfights. There's a lot of swooping and noise, and half the time we're shooting at one another instead of at the Huns. Still, it's better than being down below with the poor buggers who are up to their arses in mud in the trenches."

She ripped off his dressing in a single torturous motion. "Mind your language. You're not in your billet with the boys now."

He gave a ghost of a grin. "Sorry. My way of distracting myself." A single bead of sweat had formed on his upper lip.

He wished she did not have so many patients to care for, as it meant her stops at his bedside were of necessity infrequent and brief. He watched her as she moved among the wounded men, offering care and comfort, working long hours and often remaining after her shift ended in order to write a letter for a man who had lost his sight or the use of his hands.

Marrick felt a sense of pride in her, along with annoyance that she could not spend so much time with him as he wished. Telling himself that he was only one of many patients she had to care for did little to dispel his feeling of deprivation.

The longest periods she spent with him were when she changed the dressings on his shoulder, and despite the pain and discomfort of this procedure, he looked forward to it because she kept up a steady stream of reassuring, and distracting, conversation.

He had never known a woman quite like her, and he was constantly amazed at the wide range of her interests and knowledge. All at once it seemed that he had spent his life in one-way conversations with women or in flirtatious repartee that was enjoyable but left him wishing for more.

At first he balked when she came to give him a sponge bath. She pulled a screen around his bed, disappeared for a moment, and reappeared with a basin of warm water, soap, towel, and flannel.

"What do you think you're doing?" he asked, alarmed.

"I'm going to give you a nice sponge bath," she answered matter-of-factly.

"Oh, no you're not. Fetch a male nurse."

"We don't have any male nurses. They're all at the front."

"Then we'll dispense with the bath."

"Do you want to get bedsores? You know, you have to stop thinking of yourself as the lord of the manor and of me as the stable master's daughter. Here you're simply a wounded soldier and I'm a nurse, and that's the end of the argument."

"Very well. Do with me what you will." He decided she would be more embarrassed than he before she was finished. His injuries had not made him immune to the close proximity of an attractive young woman, nurse's uniform notwithstanding.

She worked quickly and efficiently, not conversing with him as she did when she changed his dressings. Her touch was gentle but firm as she thoroughly cleansed his uninjured foot and leg, his arm and hand, neck, shoulders, back. A folded towel remained discreetly over his lower torso, and when only that portion of his anatomy remained unwashed she paused, regarding him with a mischievous glint in her eye.

He stared back, unblinking, daring her. In that instant all the barriers that had previously separated them finally crumbled for good. He knew that hers had fallen as well as his. It was true: he was a just a wounded soldier and she a nurse. The balance of power had changed, just as it had between the warring enemies. She was in control now, and for the first time in his life, he felt powerless. But with a shock he realized that much more was happening here than appeared on the surface. An age-old gauntlet had been tossed down between them in the battle of the sexes, and it didn't matter that they were not only from different backgrounds but also from different generations. A magnetic field had sprung up between them and now charged the atmosphere with a tension that stunned him with its power.

Did Jane feel it, too? Surely she must!

Slowly she wrung out the flannel again and soaped it. Then with a careless shrug she placed it in his good right hand. "You can do the rest of yourself. Ring for me when you're finished."

As she disappeared around the screen, Marrick swore softly to himself.

It was after midnight and the ward was quiet except for one young Australian infantryman who groaned softly within his cocoon of bandages. He was a victim of that most barbarous of chemical weapons, mustard gas. Most of his body was covered with blisters, and the damage to his eyes and lungs was severe.

When Marrick could no longer bear to listen to the Australian's suffering, he rang for the night nurse and was surprised when Jane appeared at his bedside. "I thought you went off duty at eleven."

"I did. But a new batch of casualties came in and I was needed in the operating theater. What do you need?"

"Nothing for myself. I wondered if you could give the mustard gas patient some morphine."

"He had morphine just a little while ago. Perhaps he'll be able to sleep soon."

"How do you stand it—all this misery?"

"Not very well, I'm afraid."

"Then you don't intend to make a career of nursing?"

"No. I never want to see another hospital after the war ends."

"I'm surprised some dashing young officer hasn't spirited you away from all this. Every man in the ward is in love with you, you know."

In the night-darkened ward he couldn't see her expression because her face was in shadow, but her tone was teasing as she asked, "Including you, Lord Marrick?"

"Of course." Damn, he'd meant to sound much more flippant. To cover his embarrassment he added quickly, "Isn't it time you dropped the use of the title? You said yourself that here we're simply patient and nurse."

"If I dropped the 'lord,' you would be just Marrick," she answered innocently. "Is that what you're suggesting?"

"What else?"

He decided that he seemed to come off the worse in these exchanges because he was immobilized in bed and she was on her feet. He vowed that things would be different when he was up and about, which the doctor had promised he would be as soon as his wrist and shoulder mended sufficiently to allow him to use crutches.

A week later Jane arrived with a wheelchair. "How would you like to go for a walk? I can't conjure up a fogbank for us to walk in, but perhaps some balmy French sunshine would do?"

"I'd sell my soul to get out of here for a while. But will that old biddy of a ward sister let you waste your valuable time on one patient?"

Jane smiled. "It's my day off. Come on. I'll help you into the chair."

It was a warm September day, with a hint of autumn in the sprinkling of golden leaves in the trees. Jane pushed the wheelchair down the lane from the hospital, and they soon left the village behind and were surrounded by harvested fields.

"The wind's changed," Jane remarked, "or the artillery is taking a rest. We can't hear the guns. Had you noticed?"

The distant rumble of artillery fire had become so much a part of everyday existence that the silence did indeed feel unnatural. But Marrick had no wish to speak of anything connected with the war. He said, "I feel so euphoric at being outdoors with a pretty girl that nothing else registered."

He tried to turn his head to look back at her, but his shoulder protested, so he had to content himself with hearing her voice without seeing her expression.

"Have you heard from Claudia?" she asked.

"Yes, a short letter came a few days ago. Have you?"

"No. But I haven't had much time to write to her. How is she?"

"She sounded fit. Apparently she's considering defying the rules of mourning etiquette by going up to London for a few days during the coming season."

Jane gave a soft exclamation of dismay, the sound muted by the grinding of the wheelchair along the lane. "But what about Blair? He surely isn't going."

"That concerns you, doesn't it? I thought Branston was the brother you loved, not Roald who calls himself Blair." He hadn't meant to sound petulant, but feared he did. "Or is this merely a case of your empathy with suffering soldiers?"

"Claudia is treating Blair very badly. You must know that."

"Claudia treats everybody badly."

"That's not true!"

"Very well—she treats all *men* very badly. The Kingsley twins knew that and chased her anyway. Why do you waste your time worrying about Claudia's treatment of Blair when you can't change either of them?"

"Damn you, Marrick, after all you've had to put up with lately, I should think you'd be more sympathetic to Blair." They had reached a copse, and she pushed the chair into the shade, spinning it around with more force than necessary in order to glare at him.

He stared at her, taken aback by the ferocity of her response. Good God, he thought, she loves the other brother now! Marrick was surprised by a stab of regret that felt almost like jealousy, an emotion previously alien to him. To cover his confusion, he said, "I'm sorry for young Kingsley, but I don't think heavy doses of sympathy are what he needs."

"I agree," Jane said vehemently. "I told him the last time I saw him that he should find something interesting to do and move out of his parents' home."

"Offhand, I'd say what Blair and Claudia do is hardly any of your business."

She flushed. "You're quite right. But it's difficult to stand back and watch someone you care about make all the wrong decisions."

"You mean Claudia, of course?"

Her blush deepened, confirming his suspicions. He didn't hear her murmured response as he turned away, angry with himself for feeling jealous of a man so hideously scarred.

Sunlight still dappled the earth through the canopy of branches overhead and the breeze was mellow, but somehow the joy of the day had dissipated.

Jane had been tense all day without knowing quite why. Certainly the ward was no more chaotic than usual. The previous day she had taken Marrick out of the hospital, and it should have been a time to discuss what concerned them both—Claudia and Blair. Jane had planned the whole excursion with that in mind. She had even considered confiding in Marrick that "Blair" was in fact Bran. She hadn't expected Marrick's hostility or his not-so-subtle warning to mind her own business.

She avoided contact with Marrick as much as possible, which wasn't difficult, as a fresh batch of wounded had arrived. As she came to the end of her shift her feeling of impending doom increased.

The ward sister motioned her to come into her office, and as Jane entered she saw a khaki-clad figure sitting with his back to the door. There was something familiar about the set of his shoulders and the way his long legs sprawled in front of him. There were corporals' stripes on his sleeve.

Sister smiled brightly. "You have a visitor, Jane. He's been waiting patiently for you to come off duty."

The corporal slowly swiveled his chair to face her. "Hello, Janey," Royce said.

Jane felt the room spinning. Royce stood up and embraced her. He appeared to be healthy. "Had a hell of a time—oh, excuse me, Sister—finding you, Jane. It's taken me months."

Somehow Jane maintained her composure until they were able to politely leave the office. Like every other female on earth, the middle-aged nurse was enchanted by Royce's engaging smile and easy compliments.

The corridor outside was crowded with stretchers and gurneys as the staff moved patients and beds to accommodate new arrivals. Royce walked at her side, smiling and winking at the pretty nurses and occasionally offering a word of encouragement to a patient writhing in pain on a bloodstained gurney. Jane had forgotten how her brother seemed able to dispense charm to everyone in his path, no matter how trying the circumstances or surroundings.

Emerging into the late-afternoon sunlight, Royce slipped his arm around her shoulders, and said, "Well, Florence Nightingale, you're looking a bit pale and wan. Working you too hard, are they? Where are you billeted?"

"We're not going to my room, Royce," Jane replied. "There's a bench over there under that tree. We'll sit there and talk for a minute."

"Ooh, icy winds blowing. This doesn't sound promising. You still annoyed with me, love?"

"Did you expect me to welcome you with open arms after what you did to Claudia?"

"Hey, come on, look at me, fighting for king and country, one of the brave lads. You save all your patriotic spirit for the wounded, do you?"

Jane collapsed wearily onto the wooden bench. "I expect you joined up to get away from Edith." He didn't have to answer, she knew by his expression she had hit the nail on the head. "Where is she, by the way?"

He shrugged. "I've no idea. Last I saw her, she was in London, still dodging the long arm of the law."

"What do you want, Royce?"

"S'truth, you're a hard woman, Janey. I move heaven and earth to find my long-lost sister, and this is the greeting I get?"

"What do you want?"

He fished in his pocket and produced a gold cigarette case, extracted a cigarette, and tapped it against the case. "I was wondering . . . if Claudia had the kid."

"You stay away from Claudia, do you hear?"

He gave her a sly grin. "I *know* she had my kid and that she married Kingsley. His old man is even richer than Marrick,

Isn't he? Newspapers, magazines, and so on? I also know that Claudia's husband went home from the war with his face shot off. How about sounding Claudia out for me, find out if I can see her and the kid?"

Jane leapt to her feet, all fatigue forgotten. "Claudia never wants to see you again, and neither do I. Get out of our lives and stay out, or I'll—"

"You'll what, Janey?" His voice was soft, but his eyes emitted steel sparks that sent shards of ice into her very soul. She turned and ran as if all the hounds of hell were on her heels.

The German surgeon came to remove Marrick's cast and examine his leg. He was delighted when Marrick spoke to him in his own language, thanking him for saving his leg.

"What a terrible thing is this war," the doctor responded. "We will hope soon for peace. Yet, in the field of medicine at least, out of necessity we are learning new methods of repairing broken bodies"—he sighed—"even as the weapons manufacturers devise cunning new ways to destroy human beings."

Marrick considered the fact that he had been shot down by British antiaircraft gunners while flying a German plane, and then a German doctor had saved his crushed leg. The war made even less sense to him now than it had before, and he would have liked to ask the German how he viewed it, but the wounded men in nearby beds were becoming agitated by the sound of voices speaking in German, so Marrick merely nodded his agreement.

"Your own doctors will care for you now. Your injured leg is slightly shorter than the other one, but in time you should be able to walk without a limp. You might need a stick for a while, but I should think you'll be able to dispense with the crutches. I expect you'll be on your way home almost immediately. Ordinarily you would have been repatriated before now, but my British colleagues decided to keep you here until I could admire my handiwork."

"Going home . . ." Marrick repeated. His first thought was how much he would miss Jane; then he castigated himself for being an old fool.

Sometime after midnight he awakened and, since he knew Jane was on night duty, automatically glanced at the nurses' station. In the faint glow of the muted lamp he saw that her face was buried in her hands and her shoulders shook with silent sobs.

For one wild, improbable second as he was caught in that moment between sleep and wakefulness, he wondered if she could be saddened by the fact that he was leaving. He dismissed the idea instantly.

Sitting up, he reached for his crutches. He had not yet been provided with a walking stick and didn't trust his wired-together bones. As quietly as he could, he inched along the ward to the nurses' station.

Jane looked up as he reached her desk. "Marrick! For goodness' sake, why didn't you ring if you needed something?"

Her face was swollen and tearstained. He wished he could drop the damn crutches, vault over the desk, take her into his arms, and comfort her. "What's wrong?" he asked softly. "Why are you crying?"

She looked at him, something deeper than despair on her face. "The Aussie died. He was just a boy, younger than I am."

"Do you weep for every man who dies or just for the young ones?"

"I'm in no mood for your sarcasm," she said sharply.

"Sorry. Far be it from me to upset our angel of mercy."

"Now you're patronizing me, and I hate that even more than your stupid bantering."

Damn, why can I never say what I really mean? he thought. "I didn't intend to patronize you. I suppose like most males I feel helpless to deal with female tears. You know, you told me you became a nurse almost by accident, that you never had any intention of doing so. I want you to know that I understand how it is possible—perhaps, for some, inevitable—to perform some necessary task superbly . . . all the while hating it. But I'm not sure you can understand that yet; you're so very young."

"Why do you keep on reminding me of how young I am? Does it make you feel wiser, superior to me?"

"I'm not your enemy, Jane," he said quietly, "but lash out at me if it will make you feel better."

Jane sighed. "I'm not being very professional, am I?"

He leaned across the desk with his good arm and caught her hand in his. "Don't ever lose the ability to cry for your fellow humans, Jane. Don't become hardened, accustomed to all the horror. This war—all wars are completely useless. They prove nothing, solve nothing."

"Then why do we let them happen?"

"The hotheads drag those reluctant to participate in the madness into the mire with them. But the voices of reason must take their share of the responsibility for allowing it. Have you ever heard of a phalanx?"

"Wasn't that a formation of Greek infantry?"

"Not many women would have known that. Yes, several ranks of infantry armed with long spears rushed at the enemy in a solid block—an almost irresistible force. Philip of Macedon arranged his phalanx so that the spears of the fifth rank projected three feet in front of the first. Think what that meant: any warrior who decided that charging at the enemy was not a good idea would have been persuaded to keep going by the spears of his own comrades. I expect Philip ordered his generals to place the diehard warriors on the outside of the phalanx and the conscripted farmers in the middle. What I'm getting at is that some of us are trapped in the middle of a modern phalanx. Jane, why don't you go home? You've more than done your share."

He eased himself onto the edge of the desk, propped the crutches against it.

"I can't go home, not yet." She stood up and came around to him. "I'll help you back to bed. I'm sorry I awakened you."

"I'm sorry you lost a patient, but the poor devil is probably better off."

Her tears erupted again, although she fought valiantly to hold them back. Marrick, still leaning against the desk, reached out with his good arm and pulled her close to him. She didn't resist.

She laid her head on his chest, and he said quietly, "You've seen the shell-shocked men. Don't you think you might be experiencing a similar malady? You need to get away from the hospital."

Jane lifted her head to look at him and probably to protest, but her face was so close to his that he could feel her breath, smell the clean scent of her hair, and almost taste the tears that dampened her cheeks. His arm tightened around her, and the next second his mouth had found hers.

At first she tensed, and he might have stopped with a reassuring peck, but then her lips softened and parted slightly and he felt a wave of desire and need that blotted out everything but the sweetness of the kiss, the gentle pressure of her body against his, and the blinding realization that, like every other man in the ward, he had fallen in love with his nurse.

He wasn't sure how long they remained locked in that first heart-pounding embrace in the near-darkness of the ward. They were an island of two, bonded by the most elemental of human need—to feel wanted, loved.

Jane drew back first. "What are we doing?" she asked breathlessly. "Have we lost our minds?"

"I thought we were comforting each other."

She handed him his crutches. "I don't think you need my help to get back to bed. One of my lights is blinking."

"I believe several of mine are," Marrick said dryly, but she was already on her way to answer the call of another patient.

Early the next day, before Jane came on duty, he left the hospital to begin his journey home. He had time only to write a short note and leave it for her with the ward sister.

❧ Twenty-five ❧

AFTER KISSING Colin good night, Claudia tiptoed out of the nursery. She gasped as she almost collided with her mother-in-law.

On the dimly lit landing only Lady Alicia's pale face was visible; the rest of her, clad in somber, unrelieved black, vanished into shadow. "I didn't mean to startle you," she said, "but I knew you would disappear into your room if I didn't catch you now. Claudia, do you realize how much it hurts us to see you care so little about our terrible loss?"

Claudia's hand made a guilty flight to her throat, to a lacy beige jabot pinned in place with a cameo brooch. "I didn't think wearing a bit of lace was a crime. I *am* wearing a black dress because you asked me to, even though we've been in mourning for over a year now."

"Three years is the appropriate mourning period for a close family member. Surely you can restrain yourself that long, out of respect for your husband's brother? But it isn't only the jabot I'm referring to. I was appalled when you announced that you wish to go up to London . . . alone."

"I need some things for the baby—" Claudia began.

"If what you require isn't available in the village shops, then send an order to Harrods and have the items delivered."

"That isn't the same as shopping for them myself. In town, I mean."

"I must insist that you postpone such a trip."

"But this is so unreasonable! No one stays in mourning for more than a year. Why must you punish all of us because Bran was killed?"

She heard her mother-in-law's swiftly indrawn breath. "How could you understand our loss? You are an adventuress,

Claudia, who took advantage of a vulnerable boy. Do you think I don't know why you married my son? Do you think I don't know that you would have married the first man who was unfortunate enough to stumble across your path after you found out you were carrying an illegitimate child?"

Claudia leaned back weakly against the nursery door, terrified of what might come next. "Colin *is* Blair's child," she whispered.

"I doubt that very much. If my son had not returned so fearfully maimed, do you believe for an instant I would have allowed you to continue with this farce of a marriage?"

"Blair loves me," Claudia said, her voice shaking.

"Yes, he does, more's the pity. I can't understand why. You never spend any time with him. I doubt that he visits your bedroom. You'd better beware, Claudia. Refusal of conjugal rights is grounds for divorce."

"He would never divorce me. He loves me, he loves Colin. Please, can't we be friends, for his sake?"

There was a pause, and then Lady Alicia said, "While you reside under my roof, you will follow the rules of my household. We are in mourning. There will be no frivolous activities, and that includes shopping excursions that are conveniently timed for the London season. When we resume our social activities, your husband will accompany you. There's no more to be said on the matter."

She turned and walked away, leaving Claudia biting her lip in frustration.

Blair watched Claudia slide a pearl-tipped hatpin into the crown of her white felt hat, then pick up her handbag. She wore a deep blue dress with matching short jacket. When she turned from the mirror he immediately looked away, positioning his head so that the worst of his scars would be in the shadows.

She said, "I don't care what your mother says, I absolutely refuse to wear black another minute. If you came to chastise me, too, you'll be wasting your breath."

"You should wear whatever you choose, just as the mater can continue to wear mourning forever if she wishes. Personally I'm happy to see you wearing colors again."

He paused, summoning the strength to say what he had to say. "I came to ask you not to go to London by yourself."

"Oh, for goodness' sake! Not you, too. Blair, if I don't get out of this house I shall go mad."

"I . . . could go with you," he offered tentatively.

There was no disguising the dismay on her face. Her eyes widened in horror. "But . . . I thought . . ."

"Claudia, I just want to be with you," he said miserably. "I know I look as if I belong in a sideshow, but there must be plenty of men walking about the streets with war wounds as bad as mine. We just hired a new footman who was gassed. He blinks, and his face twitches all the time."

She didn't answer, lowering her eyes from his pleading gaze. He asked, "When are we going to resume marital relations, Claudia? It's been a year, and I'm as healed as I'll ever be. Oh, my darling, I want you so desperately. If you could just come close, touch me—"

A small scream escaped Claudia's lips. "I can't! Please don't ask me to. . . . I'm sorry. I don't want to hurt you, but I can't."

As Claudia fled from the room, he turned away, fighting to control his emotions.

"You're sure a sight for sore eyes. I was afraid you'd change your mind," Frank Allegro said to Claudia as she walked into the ladies' saloon at the Hunter's Arms. He stood up and pulled out a chair for her.

"You won't believe how I got here," Claudia said, indignation bringing a becoming flush to her cheeks. "I had to borrow a bicycle from one of the gardeners. My mother-in-law actually ordered the staff not to call for a taxi for me, and she's had the cars garaged for the duration. They sold all their horses at the outbreak of war or I might have come galloping up like Lady Godiva."

Frank's eyes widened hopefully. "Naked?"

"Oh, you know what I mean."

He pulled out a chair for her. "I could just as easily have picked you up at Willowford, but I guess that would have really caused an uproar with your mother-in-law."

She ignored the chair he held. "Can we get started for London right away?"

"Sit down for a minute, Claudia. Before I carry you off, I'd like to know the ground rules. What's this sudden desire to run off to London all about? Are you leaving home? Now, don't get me wrong. I'd be glad to take care of you permanently, but unfortunately I've only got a three-day pass and my C.O. sort of frowns on us taking women into the barracks. Besides, we sure couldn't leave your kid behind. So let's not go off half-cocked."

She giggled. "I'd almost forgotten how much I love your accent and way of putting things. Americans are so terribly irreverent. I think that's what I like best about you." There was an air of suppressed excitement about her; she seemed light-hearted, happy, and had never looked lovelier.

"Frank, I'm not leaving my husband, and my son is safely in the care of his nanny. I just need to escape from Kingsley prison for a couple of days, and since you said you could borrow a staff car, I thought it would give us an opportunity to spend a little time together. You do have the car, don't you?"

He nodded, grimacing slightly. Baron had been appalled when Frank joined the infantry as an enlisted man within hours after the United States declared war on Germany, and Frank suspected that the reason he had not yet seen any action at the front was due to Baron's pulling strings somewhere. Instead, Frank had been assigned to drive the staff car of a lieutenant colonel who was supposed to be coordinating the transshipment of ordnance arriving from America for the U.S. forces in France. Unfortunately, so far no materiel had arrived. American soldiers were still firing British guns and flying French aircraft. This left Frank's superior officer with very little to do except shuffle paper and Frank with even less to occupy his time. Repeated requests for a transfer to the front had been turned down.

"Okay, kid, let's go. I'm your driver, bodyguard, companion, and factotum for the next three days. Name your pleasure, and consider it a *fait accompli*."

Claudia's violet eyes lit up in anticipation as she considered the delights awaiting her in London. Her beauty took his breath away. Frank felt his blood churn. He stared at her, wanting her more than he had ever wanted anything in his life, yearning for her with a need that had been reborn the moment he saw her. He had tried to put her out of his mind, knowing from the start that the most he could hope for was that she would at least allow him to be her friend, although he suspected that to Claudia he was merely one of a legion of adoring idiots content to do her bidding.

She said eagerly, "I've been locked up at Willowford for so long I feel like a starving woman about to attend a banquet. I shall go shopping and have tea at the Savoy and go to a matinee and have dinner at a wonderful restaurant and go to the theater and then have supper and dance all night."

Frank rolled his eyes. "Don't I recall that when you indulged in that kind of frenetic activity in New York you got sick?"

"But I can only stay a couple of days, and, darling, life is so short! Once mustn't waste a moment." Her eyes clouded suddenly. "I shan't live to be old, you know. I must enjoy life while I can."

"Now you're getting morbid. Of course you'll live to be old. I can see you now, all bent over a cane, peering through pince-nez, and still surrounded by a bunch of old geezers madly in love with you."

She giggled, but then said firmly, "I shall die young, like my mother."

"Okay, have it your own way. Though it sounds kinda selfish to me. So let's get you to town and you can start killing yourself. What shall we do first?"

Claudia assumed a studiedly casual expression. "You won't have to worry about me once we get to London. I'm meeting a friend there."

He managed to keep his smile intact, but his heart dropped into his boots. "Oh? Which friend is that?"

She avoided meeting his eye. "Just a friend. You don't know him."

Something snapped, a single thread in the rope of restraint he kept tightly in place in regard to his feelings for Claudia. He'd reasoned that as long as he pursued her in a semicasual, half-joking way, he'd left himself an escape hatch to avoid humiliation. But now there was a great deal he wanted to express—anger and hurt and disappointment. Drawing a deep breath, he swallowed most of it. "You really take the cake, Claudia. You ignore all my calls, then suddenly ask me to drive you to London to meet another man. That's some nerve."

She regarded him in innocent surprise. "But I thought you'd enjoy the drive with me—that we could spend a little time together. You've been asking me to ever since you arrived in England."

"I was hoping you'd take pity on a lonely doughboy and invite him out to meet your husband and his family."

"I told you the Kingsleys don't entertain; they're still in mourning for my husband's brother."

"And you couldn't slip your husband out to meet me at the local pub?"

"Blair doesn't go out. I told you—he was horribly scarred in the war."

"Oh, what the hell. I didn't want to meet him anyway. I guess I'm mad because you're going to see another man and it isn't me. And don't insult my intelligence by telling me he's just a friend. You've got 'illicit romance' written all over you."

She had the grace to flush. Lowering her eyes she said, "Please don't make a scene. If you don't want to drive me to town, just say so. I can take the train, even though I detest traveling by rail; one gets so sooty. I just thought you'd be glad to spend a little time with me."

He rose abruptly. "Let's go. If I'm not going to get to spend my three-day pass with you, then I've got some phone calls to make in London. A couple of other ladies will be glad to keep me company."

On the drive to London Claudia kept up a barrage of inconsequential chatter, but Frank wasn't in the mood to be entertained by it. By the time they reached Victoria Station, the destination Claudia had requested, his anger had turned to icy resolve. He wouldn't allow her to make a fool of him again.

"You can drop me anywhere now," Claudia said, eyeing him nervously.

"You're meeting him under the clock, I take it?"

She didn't respond.

Frank parked the car and got out. Opening her door, he

offered his hand to help her. "I'm not going to leave you standing alone. I'll stay with you until he shows up."

"I'm . . . meeting his train," she offered tentatively. "You really don't have to—"

He took her arm. "Oh, but I do."

They waited in silence for a train coming from the south coast. Claudia clearly regretted her impulsive decision to ask him to drive her to town and several times suggested there was no need for him to stay with her. He took perverse pleasure in ignoring the requests.

The Dover train finally arrived and disgorged the usual crowd of servicemen and a few women in uniform. In this, the fourth year of the war, there were few able-bodied civilians to be seen, and Frank knew that many women, besides serving as nurses and ambulance drivers, also worked in munitions factories and other war-related industries.

Claudia caught Frank's arm and looked up at him beseechingly. "Please go now."

He scanned the platform speculatively. "Which one is he?"

There was no need for her to reply, as the next moment she was swept into the arms of a deeply tanned corporal. Frank stood back and watched the embrace, thinking it figured that her lover would be tall, dark, and handsome with that devil-may-care attitude women found so appealing. Frank didn't stop to consider that the description also could have been applied to himself. In fact, physically, he had a great deal in common with the corporal.

When their kiss lengthened to the point where Frank could no longer stand to watch, he said, "Hey, buddy, she's a married woman, you know."

Claudia pulled free and said breathlessly, "Royce, this is Frank Allegro. He worked for Mr. Baron in New York. You remember, I told you about him? He very kindly drove me up to London."

Keeping one arm casually around Claudia's shoulders, the corporal offered his hand to Frank. His smile seemed open, friendly, but there was a thinly veiled challenge in his eyes. "Royce Weatherly."

Frank ignored the outstretched hand. "I met your sister. You're nothing like her."

"You don't think so? Many people think we look a lot alike."

"Oh, sure, you *look* a little alike, but she radiates honesty and integrity."

Royce grinned and pulled Claudia's hand through his arm to lead her away. "Thanks for being Claudia's chauffeur."

"I feel more like her pimp."

Claudia gasped and for an instant Frank hoped Royce might pick up the gauntlet so he could have the pleasure of flattening him right there on the platform. But Royce merely shrugged and said to Claudia, "I'd heard that Americans were crude. Apparently it's true. But as he's a friend of yours, I'll consider the source and ignore that remark."

Frank clenched his fists and took a step toward him. Claudia cried, "Frank, if you don't leave us this minute, I shan't speak to you again as long as I live."

Blinking, Frank brought her back into focus. He stared at her. Was she really without guile? Could any woman be as unaware of the raging emotions she inspired in men as Claudia seemed to be? Had she honestly believed she could ask one man to drive her to London and turn her over to another without there being a fight over her? Was that, in fact, what she wanted?

A distant voice hammered at his brain, pointing out his own guilt. Hadn't he been ready to accept whatever part of herself Claudia offered, and her war-scarred husband be damned? What made him any better than this man who now watched him warily.

Wordlessly Frank turned and walked away.

That afternoon he sent a cablegram to Baron in New York: "Cut me loose or I won't be coming back to New York. Frank."

Baron didn't reply, but within a week Frank found himself on the front line, in the stinking muddy hell of the trenches.

❦ Twenty-six ❧

Hostilities will cease at 1100 hours today, November 11, 1918. Troops will stand fast on the line reached at that hour.

The message had gone out from Advanced GHQ at dawn, but it did not reach the hospital in the French countryside until several hours later. Jane merely nodded, acknowledging that she had heard, as one of the other nurses relayed the news.

There was little cause for celebration that four long years of war had come to an end, as the hospital was packed to overflowing with wounded men, and now another, equally deadly menace strained their resources and stamina to the breaking point. An influenza epidemic threatened to finish off those men who had survived the guns, bayonets, and poison gas of the enemy.

Moving on the leaden limbs of fatigue, Jane needed all of her strength to finish changing the dressings on the mangled arm of a boy who appeared to be no more than seventeen.

Gathering up the soiled bandages and a dish of instruments, she started back through the ward. Suddenly everything swam dizzily and she was forced to stop and grip the iron rail of the nearest bed. She had awakened that morning with a throbbing headache and a scratchy throat, and now she could no longer ignore the fever and chills she was experiencing.

"Weatherly?" The ward sister's voice penetrated a murky fogbank that seemed to surround her. "Are you ill?"

"Sister . . . I . . . I think I may be coming down with the flu."

During her illness, the first in her life, Jane frequently had fever dreams wherein she climbed a long stone stairway that ended at a brick wall. She would beat with her fists in desperation against the wall until at last it crumbled and a long bridge appeared, below which fog swirled and eddied like roiling gray surf. At the far end of the bridge a shadowy figure waited. Jane would start across the bridge toward the silhouetted figure, screaming in that silent way of dreaming, *No, no, no!*

She would awaken, drenched with perspiration, her lips still parted in the scream from her nightmare. She never knew who the silhouetted figure was, or even if it was a man or a woman.

During her convalescence, when it seemed that the slightest movement required a superhuman effort and she was convinced she would never feel strong again, she tried not to think about the dream, for fear of precipitating it.

Many times she had thought about the night before Marrick left the hospital. She assured herself that his kiss had been nothing more than an expression of gratitude or a gesture of comfort when he saw how distressed she was. Or perhaps he had simply succumbed to a moment's indulgence of that common malady, a patient's temporary infatuation with his nurse. . . . But still, Jane found it difficult to forget the pulsing energy of that kiss.

She had returned to duty the following evening to find him gone, repatriated to England. He'd left a note for her, as enigmatic as he was: "Please contact me when you get home. Marrick."

Why? she wondered. So that he could explain that in the highly charged arena of war male-female contacts should not be taken too seriously? No, she wouldn't demean herself by allowing him to do that. She would simply put the incident out of her mind. The war was now over, he was still the lord of the manor and she the stable master's daughter, and undoubtedly he would be embarrassed if she arrived on his doorstep. Besides, Jane had long ago given her heart to Bran Kingsley.

Her knowledge of what was happening to Claudia and the men in her life was sketchy. A couple of beflowered notes had arrived from Claudia, expressing her concern about Jane's illness and the hope for a swift recovery. Claudia mentioned that her father-in-law had come down with the flu also and had decided to remain in London rather than go home and infect the rest of the family. Jane took this to be a hint that she and her germs wouldn't be welcome at Willowford either.

Had Royce been in touch with Claudia? Even if he had, Claudia surely would have sent him packing. Jane dwelt on the problem of her brother only briefly, because she was simply too debilitated by her illness to concentrate on anything.

Then, on the day her fever finally broke, she awakened from a brief nap feeling mercifully cool, although frighteningly weak, to find a familiar face watching her. Frank Allegro sat beside her bed holding a large basket of fruit.

As her eyes fluttered open he smiled. "Hello, Jane. You look like death warmed over."

"Thanks," she croaked, her throat still raw. "You're supposed to cheer up a patient, you know. What are you doing in France? I thought you had a cushy assignment in England."

"I figured I'd better get over here and finish things. Army life isn't something I care to prolong. Been too busy to look you up before now. It's all over, you know. The armistice was signed November eleventh. I brought you some oranges." He placed the fruit basket on the bedside table.

"Bless you! I haven't had an orange for years. I suppose you'll be going home to America soon?"

"Well, this flu epidemic has created all sorts of complications. A lot of our boys are down with it, too. Guess it's worldwide. I decided to take my discharge here, so I could go back to England for a while, think things over."

Jane wished she could get rid of the fuzziness in her head. She had a vague feeling she was missing something important. She cleared her throat. "I expect a lot of demobilized servicemen will feel somewhat cut adrift now the war is over."

He shrugged noncommittally. "Have you heard from Claudia lately?"

"Wishes for a speedy recovery, no real news. Have you?"

He shook his head. "What about your brother? You heard from him?"

Jane blinked, feeling a throbbing begin behind one eye. "Royce? Why do you ask?"

"Claudia asked me to drive her to London just before I left for the front, and . . . well, she was going to meet him."

Jane felt as though a vise were squeezing her head. "Are you sure?"

"Yeah, I'm sure. I stayed with her until he arrived. Good-looking bastard. . . . Sorry, I forgot for a minute that he's your brother."

"Frank, if you came to see me to complain about Royce . . . I really have no control over him, or over Claudia."

"I know. I'm sorry. I shouldn't have brought up the subject. What are your plans for when you get out of the hospital?"

"A friend who lives in London has invited me to move in with her until I get a job." The prospect of starting civilian life in her present state of health had been so overwhelming that Jane had gratefully accepted Penny Tandy's offer.

Penny Tandy—a willowy six feet tall, with piercing blue eyes, mouse-brown hair, and a keen memory—also possessed a bawdy laugh that rang out when the ancient Humber, its rumble seat loaded with Jane's baggage, broke down only a mile from the railway station.

"I'll have it running in a jiff. Don't worry. Temperamental beast, miserable bloody machine." Penny jumped out and kicked a wheel, but laughed as she did so, obviously relishing the challenge of getting the engine going again. She raised the bonnet and disappeared from view.

"I'm impressed that you own a car, temperamental or not," Jane called to her.

"Oh, it isn't mine," Penny's disembodied voice responded, followed by several choice swear words, a snapping sound, a metallic ping, and another laugh.

Jane leaned back, the stress of her recent illness and the journey from France beginning to tell. Among the other ambulance drivers Penny had been known to be as good a mechanic as any of the men, and Jane had no doubt the Humber would soon be running again. Moments later Penny's oil-streaked but triumphant face appeared and she slammed down the bonnet.

They reached her mother's house in Hampstead late in the afternoon, and Penny led Jane into a tiny parlor to a comfortable chintz-covered sofa, ordered her to put her feet up, and went into the kitchen to make a pot of tea.

The afternoon was gray and drizzly. Penny stoked the fire with a mountain of coal. Jane sighed contentedly and sipped her tea. "You still haven't told me about your job," she reminded Penny.

· "It's sort of a long story, and I wanted you to be warm and comfy first." She dropped down onto the hearthrug, crossing her long legs. "I didn't feel like going back to being a shop assistant. I really enjoyed driving the ambulance, and you know I'm a bit of a mechanic as well. I just like being around cars and lorries, I suppose. Anyway, Mum and I were down at the corner pub one night and there's this funny little fat man—s'truth he looks like a roly-poly pudding—and he's spouting off about the plight of the working classes. You know, the usual tripe. Only there's something about him—he's got these burning eyes and a deep, musical voice—and, well, you could have heard a pin drop. He had everybody spellbound. The thing was, he really seemed to mean what he was saying. I think he could have led that lot out of the pub and captured the city."

Half asleep from the exertion of travel, Jane curled up on the sofa, content to listen without comment.

Penny continued, "Now, if you saw a picture of him, you'd think he was a clown—honestly, he's that funny-looking. I have to laugh every time I see him waddling along on his little short legs. . . ."

Her laugh rang out again, but just as quickly died, to be replaced by a misty-eyed reverence. "But when you get to know him . . . well, I've never known anybody like him. So it turns out he's running for a seat on the Labour ticket in some little country town and doesn't have a prayer of winning . . . and, well, he needs a driver. Now, he's got that ancient car that's gasping its last breath, and he's about as mechanical as a donkey and can't even drive to boot—the car was left to him in his uncle's will. So there you are."

Jane roused herself sufficiently to ask, "Where am I? Or rather, where are you?"

Piercing blue eyes sliced into her. "Haven't you been listening? I just told you. I'm Percy Templeton's driver, assistant, head cook and bottle washer. At least until the election. But you never know, he might just get in, because the Conservative member is an old dodderer. If we can get enough people to come to the meetings and hear Percy speak—"

"Percy Templeton?"

"Percival Reginald Templeton, esquire."

"Ah . . . he of the roly-poly build, burning gaze, melodious voice, and political aspirations?"

"Himself."

Jane badly wanted to drift off to sleep, but forced herself to concentrate. "So . . . what you're telling me is that you're working, and I suppose living, in a country town?"

"Upper Oakleigh."

Jane's eyes opened wide. "Why, that's not far from Willowford and the abbey."

Penny grinned. "Funny how things work out, isn't it? I hadn't even met Percy when I wrote and asked you to come. I've got to get back tonight, because we've only got days left before the election. But don't you worry, Mum will be home from work soon, and she'll take care of you."

Jane struggled to sit up straight. "Penny! I can't possibly impose on your mother! She doesn't even know me. Oh, I wish you'd let me know you weren't living here before I arrived."

Penny looked baffled by the objection. "But Mum won't mind, honestly. She'll be glad of your company, with me gone."

"No, Penny. I'd feel like a parasite. If you wouldn't mind dropping me off at a hotel on your way—"

Consternation creased Penny's sharp features. "Well, if you feel so strongly about it, how about coming to Upper Oakleigh with me? I've got a room we could share. You really ought to convalesce for a bit to get your strength back. You shouldn't be on your own. I'll be gone a lot, but at least I could bring in your food."

Jane accepted gratefully, although she was dismayed by the prospect of climbing back into the rattletrap Humber and facing another long drive.

After meeting Percival Reginald Templeton for the first time Jane never again noticed his rotund lack of stature, his comically cherubic face, or his short legs. Once she looked into his blazingly honest eyes and heard his resonant voice, outer appearances became meaningless. She was vaguely aware that his clothes were clean but well worn and he was careful with his money, that his accent was unabashedly north country, and that he exuded Old World courtesy, especially toward women. In his early fifties, he was a childless widower who had been in private practice as a solicitor in a small Lancashire town before the war and had spent the war years as an army defense counsel—or, as he put it, "trying my damnedest to keep a few poor sods from being court-martialed."

Before she knew what was happening, Jane was working as enthusiastically for his election as Penny, although neither of them would be able to vote. Women's suffrage had at last come about, but only women age thirty and over could vote.

Jane called Willowford shortly after moving in with Penny and, upon learning that Claudia was "indisposed," left word that she was living in Upper Oakleigh and gave Percy's phone number. He had taken a former greengrocer's shop as his campaign headquarters. Penny swore the place reeked of rotting cabbage no matter how much they scrubbed it.

There was no need to inquire as to what Lord Marrick had been doing since the war's end, as Penny quickly ferreted out every detail about the lives of all of the prominent families in the area and informed her that Marrick was abroad somewhere.

As the days passed, Jane's health improved and she announced that she would have to find gainful employment as her savings were depleted. "But I'll certainly continue to help you in any way I can in my spare time," she assured Percy.

"I wish I could afford to pay you, lass," he said regretfully. "But . . ."

"I know. But in any case, I can't go on crowding Penny out of her room. I must find a place of my own."

"Times are hard, lass. Too many men coming home from the war and not enough jobs to go around. A lot of people don't take kindly to women taking jobs they think should go to men. I hate to see you take a governess position or become a nurse-companion to some old lady." Percy's eyes blazed with an inner fire. "I wish you were old enough to get seriously into politics. You're bright and capable and educated and not some society debutante who doesn't know the difference between communism and socialism playing at doing good for the downtrodden working class."

"I'll keep that in mind for when I'm an old maid of thirty."

"An old maid? You? Never!" Percy responded gallantly.

She soon learned that his prediction about the growing number of unemployed was accurate, and after a fruitless search of Upper Oakleigh and neighboring towns, told Penny she would have to return to London to seek work immediately after the election.

"From what Percy says, it's no better there. Jane, stay on with us and we'll muddle through somehow."

Convinced that both Percy and Penny would shortly also be looking for jobs, Jane merely smiled.

But to everyone's surprise—including his, Jane suspected—Percy was elected by a narrow margin, to become the first Labour party MP ever to represent the district.

Elated, Percy told Jane, "Now you'll stay on and work with us."

In a state of postelection triumph, Jane telephoned Willowford once again. This time Claudia came on the line. "Jane? Oh, Janey, I'm so sorry I haven't been in touch. Sir Nigel passed away—complications from the flu. We've all been so ill with it. For a while it was touch and go with the baby, too."

Jane felt a chill. "But Colin's all right?"

"Yes, he's getting better."

"I'm so sorry to hear about Sir Nigel. Will you give my sympathy to Blair and his mother?"

"The old dragon has gone to a convalescent home in Cornwall for a couple of weeks, thank goodness, and she's talking about a long holiday in Spain. I'll give Blair your message. But you must come and see us at once."

Willowford had taken on an atmosphere of perpetual mourning and was beginning to look a little shabby. Carpets and paintings were badly in need of cleaning, the grounds untidy. The formerly charming house now seemed oppressive, unwelcoming. Jane saw at once that many rooms had been closed off and the household staff reduced to a minimum.

"The taxes are killing us," Claudia confided as she led Jane to her room. "Everything is in a turmoil since Sir Nigel died, and the rest of us were ill for so long that nothing seemed to matter. Sir Nigel's estate hasn't been settled yet; apparently some obscure legal problem has arisen because only one of the twins survived him. All the assets are tied up, and to add to the confusion, the executor of the will was killed in the war and the family solicitor died of old age! His junior partner is trying to sort things out. It's such a mess. I heard Mr. Babcock—he's the solicitor—tell Blair and Lady Alicia they'd have to sell off a big chunk of the publishing assets and that the newspaper isn't doing very well." She bit her lip. "Janey . . . if you talk to Royce, please don't tell him how bad things are here. I don't want him to know."

Jane felt her throat constrict. "I haven't seen my brother lately. But I take it you have?"

Claudia led the way into a bedroom and made straight for the window to pull back the curtains. The room smelled damp and musty, and there was a layer of dust on the furniture. She opened the window and then gestured vaguely around her. "I'll get a maid up here. I'm sure I told her to prepare this room for a guest."

"Don't worry about it. Claudia, what about Royce?"

"I only saw him once," she said defensively. "I came down with the flu right after that. He was on leave in London. Did you know he fought the Turks in Mesopotamia? So you see, my dream of seeing him in the desert was true."

Jane took off her hat and dropped it on the velvet bedspread, sending up a flurry of dust. "But you intend to see him again, don't you? No, don't look away from me and don't lie to me." Jane endeavored to maintain a conversational tone, knowing she'd learn more of what was going on if she controlled her temper.

"He's the father of my child," Claudia answered. "Yes. I'll see him again if I get a chance, and as soon as Colin is strong enough I'm going to take him to meet his father."

Jane swallowed hard. "What about Blair?"

"What about him?"

"You're deceiving him. Doesn't your conscience bother you?"

Even as she said it, Jane remembered that Blair was also deceiving Claudia by pretending to be her husband. What a tangled web they had woven, and who was to say which deception was crueler? Not for the first time, Jane wished she were not privy to the dramas Claudia created.

Claudia had remained at the window, looking down at the terrace. "Look, there they are now."

Jane moved to her side. On the terrace below the thin winter sunlight gilded Blair's fair hair as he bent over the small dark-haired toddler attempting to push a scooter across the flagstones. Every line of Blair's body, every gesture, expressed loving care for the child.

"Do you think I should tell him the truth?" Claudia asked.

"No," Jane said quickly. "Colin will give him the love you apparently can't offer. Don't deprive him of that."

Claudia didn't look convinced, but she didn't press the point.

Jane continued to watch the man and child on the terrace, feeling her heart swell to bursting with the dull ache of secret love. If only he were her husband, playing with their child. Ah, how unfair life was.

"Royce told me how cold you were to him when he saw you in France," Claudia remarked accusingly. "That was mean of you when he used up his leave to find you. He'd only just come back from Mesopotamia. But he said you'd come around. He decided to stay in the army, you know. I think the wandering life appeals to him, especially now the war's over. He's a warrant officer now."

Jane managed an acknowledging nod, feeing frustration at her powerlessness to prevent their perfidy.

"Come on." Claudia slipped her arm through Jane's. "Let's go downstairs and say hello to Blair and Colin while I get a maid up here."

They went downstairs and met Blair and Colin coming into the house. The toddler, pink-cheeked from the cold, laughed as he evaded Blair's attempts to remove his heavy coat and mittens. When Blair straightened up Jane saw that the passage of time had done little to minimize his cruel scars, and when he spoke she noticed that he was still able to move only one side of his mouth.

"Hello, Jane. Good to see you again." His speech was less hesitant than before, Jane decided. She shook his hand warmly.

"I was so sorry to hear about your father, Blair."

"We miss him dreadfully," he answered simply.

Claudia quickly excused herself to find the housekeeper.

Blair had succeeded in divesting Colin of his winter coat. "This is your auntie Jane, Colin. Give her a kiss."

For an instant the marble-floored hall spun out of focus, until Jane reminded herself that Blair believed he was merely giving her the courtesy title of "aunt." The little boy shyly offered his hand. "How do you do?"

Jane clasped the small fingers in hers, although she wanted to sweep him into her arms.

Blair said, "There's a fire in the drawing room. Let's get out of this drafty hall before we freeze."

The elegantly furnished drawing room was littered with toys. Blair picked up a large teddy bear to make room for Jane to sit down. "I don't believe in confining him to the nursery," he said by way of explanation.

"His nanny must love you for that," Jane remarked.

She thought Blair frowned, but with his distorted features it was hard to tell. He said, "He doesn't have a nanny at present. I caught her slapping him for not finishing his porridge and fired her on the spot."

"Good for you," Jane said. He sat down beside her on the sofa, and Colin began to play with brightly colored wooden blocks on the hearthrug. After a moment he brought them, one by one, and piled them onto Jane's lap.

My brother's son, she thought, born to my dearest friend. Pawn in a deadly game of deception? Oh, please God, not that.

❦ Twenty-seven ❧

"JANE . . . COULD YOU . . . could you come to Willow-ford?" Blair's anguished voice crackled over the telephone wire.

As she recognized the sound of desperation, every nerve in Jane's body tensed. "What is it? What's happened?"

"I'll . . . tell you when you get here." The line went dead.

Penny was packing Percy's files in preparation for their move back to London, where he was to take his seat in the House of Commons. "Something wrong?"

"I don't know. Blair Kingsley wants me to go to Willow-ford. He wouldn't say why."

Penny glanced at her sharply. "I don't like the sound of that. Shall I go with you?"

Jane was already reaching for her coat. "No, thanks. But could I borrow the Humber? I'll get there faster if I drive."

"Yes, of course. Percy's packing his personal effects at home, and I don't have to pick him up until tonight. Come on, I'll help you get the miserable machine started."

Out on the street Penny cranked the car while Jane sat at the wheel. The engine sputtered and died several times. Jane glanced at the bus shelter on the opposite side of the street. An old man and two women sat on the bench waiting for a bus that Jane knew was not due for another twenty minutes. She supposed if the car wouldn't start she could ride the bus to the outskirts of town and walk the rest of the way. Her slender resources wouldn't run to taking a taxi.

Penny flung several epithets at the Humber and jerked the crank around again. This time the engine caught. She waved Jane on her way.

As she pulled out into the middle of the street Jane again

glanced in the direction of the bus shelter. One of the women raised her head, and Jane almost swerved into oncoming traffic.

Surely she was mistaken!

Steering back to the left side of the road, she looked again, but now the end of the shelter blocked her view of the woman. Although the woman in the bus shelter wore horn-rimmed glasses and had black hair, Jane was convinced that she had just seen Royce's wife, Edith.

Reaching a corner, Jane made a U-turn and sped back.

When she reached the bus shelter she saw that only the man and an elderly woman remained. The bespectacled woman had gone. Had it been Edith? Had she recognized Jane? Had she, in fact, been observing her from across the street, rather than waiting for a bus? The abrupt disappearance seemed to indicate it was a distinct possibility.

Jane was tempted to cruise the adjacent streets to look for the woman but, weighing the urgency of Blair's request, instead turned around and drove out of town, toward Willowford.

As she passed the cottages on the outskirts of town and drove along the narrow lane winding toward Willowford, she considered possible reasons for Blair's urgent summons. Something had happened to Claudia? To Colin? To both of them? If that woman at the bus stop really was Edith, had Blair's call had something to do with her? Was Royce in the area, too?

Rathbourne Abbey came into view. Etched against a pale sky the tower and parapet walk rose above winter-bare trees. A picture of Marrick flashed into Jane's thoughts, and she dismissed it almost at once. Undoubtedly he was spending the winter in some more benign climate.

A little while later she parked the car in the driveway at Willowford and ran up the terrace steps.

The butler who responded to the doorbell wore a countenance as bleak as winter. "The master is in the east drawing room, miss."

"I know my way," Jane said. He made no attempt to accompany her.

She knocked on the drawing room door and pushed it open. An early winter twilight was falling, but the lamps had not been turned on. Blair sat in the shadows staring into the dying embers of the fire. He didn't look around, but said in a dull voice, "Come in, Jane. It was good of you to come right away."

Jane sat in one of the armchairs flanking the fireplace and waited.

"Claudia has left me," Blair said. His voice seemed to have a hollow echo.

"Has she taken Colin?" Jane asked.

His head jerked up, and he looked at her. "No. He's here. You don't sound surprised that Claudia left. Did she tell you what she planned to do?"

"No . . . but I knew she was unhappy. I can't believe she left without Colin."

Blair sighed. "He's the reason I asked you to come. I didn't know who else I could trust with him. Jane, I must go after Claudia and try to persuade her to come home. My mother is in a convalescent home, as you know, and I'd rather not ask her to come back until she's fully recovered from her illness. Would you . . . could you stay with Colin for a few days?"

"Yes, of course." Would I fly to the moon if you asked? Jane thought. "But . . ."

"You're wondering why I would trust Colin with you and no one else? Jane, I know Colin is your nephew. Claudia left me a note. It's over there on the desk, if you'd like to read it."

Jane switched on the desk lamp in order to read Claudia's note, written on her familiar flower-sprigged stationery.

Dear Blair,
    Please forgive me. I don't want to hurt you, but I can't stay with you any longer. I should have told you the truth long ago. Colin isn't your son. His father is Royce Weatherly, Jane's brother. I'm going to him now. I'll send for Colin as soon as we're settled. Blair, I'm sorry, I really am . . . but it's all been too much for me.
               As ever,
               Claudia

How typical of Claudia to assume that no matter what she did she would be forgiven and catered to, Jane thought. "I'll send for Colin later"—indeed!

Jane looked across the room at Blair's silhouette, cast in sharp relief in the firelight, at the dejected slump of his shoulders, the defeated droop of his head. "I'm so sorry," she said quietly. Still clutching the note, she went back to her chair and sat down. "I had no idea she was planning this. Please believe that."

"But you knew Colin was your nephew?"

"Yes."

"And were well aware she loved your brother—that she never loved me?"

"In her own way, I believe she does love you. You and your brother were always an essential part of her life, ever since she first came to the abbey as a little girl. You represent a carefree time of her life—indeed of life for everyone in England—that will never return."

He sighed deeply. "You always defend her. How I wish I had a friend like you. I love her, but I'm not so blind that I don't recognize that she walks all over those who care for her."

Jane said quickly, "No one truly knows another person. I think Claudia wants what she can't have. If she ever got Royce wholly and completely, I know she'd be disappointed. It wouldn't last."

"And I would take her back."

"Yes, I know."

"I wish she, or you, had at least been honest about Colin. Do you know how much I love that child?"

For the first time a note of self-pity had crept into his tone, and Jane was both disappointed and angered by it. "Oh, come on! Don't pretend you ever believed he was your son. I know better. You're as guilty of deception as Claudia was."

There was a long silence, broken when the clock on the mantelpiece chimed the hour. Jane waited. Would he deny it? What if she had been wrong? What if he really was Roald, not Bran?

At length he asked heavily, "How long have you known?"

Jane realized she had been holding her breath, and she let it out slowly. "From the beginning."

"How very observant you are. You must have noticed subtle

differences between Roald and me that others didn't. Not even my parents realized what I was doing."

"Or if they did, they decided to allow the masquerade to continue. Bran—"

"Please don't call me that. It's difficult to explain, but in becoming Blair I think I was trying to be both Roald and Bran. In a way, they both died on the Somme, you know." He paused. "At least you didn't tell Claudia. I'm grateful for that."

"You should tell her yourself."

"If I do, she'll never come back to me. And I'll lose my son, too. He *is* my son, you know. He's closer to me even than to Claudia, and has been since the moment he was born. If I can't persuade her to come home, I shall sue for custody of Colin."

"How can you threaten such a thing?" Jane asked indignantly. "For God's sake, be realistic. He isn't your son and *she isn't your wife!*"

"But no one knows that. If you tell her, I shall deny it, and there's no way for anyone to prove it. Jane, I lay beside my dead brother on the Somme for hours before the stretcher-bearers found me. I drifted in and out of consciousness, but oddly enough, there were moments of absolute clarity. I knew Roald was dead. The only way I could deal with that agony was to vow to live his life for him. I planned very carefully; I reviewed every possibility. I had to exchange anything that might identify us . . ."

Jane heard him give a strangled sob. "Not that there was much left of my brother to identify. His body was badly mangled. Since I could only use my left hand, it was difficult—but I believe concentrating on changing places with Roald kept me alive. I'd find myself blacking out—floating away to oblivion—and force myself back to the task at hand."

"There are ways to prove identity, Blair. Dental records, fingerprints . . . I'm sure the army has such files."

"Dental records?" He gave a mirthless laugh. "I lost all of my teeth and most of my face. I lost my right hand, and my left hand was burned."

Jane felt her heart melt with pity. "Oh, Blair, I don't mean to threaten you. I just feel the truth would set both you and Claudia free. But it has to be your decision."

"For now my only thought is to bring Claudia home. I can't decide anything until I see her again. Will you take care of Colin while I'm gone? Jane, I know you've been working for the little socialist, but he's going up to London and, well . . . if you'd stay, naturally I wouldn't let you suffer financially."

Shades of Marrick paying her to look after Claudia, Jane thought. Now history was repeating itself with Claudia's son. Recalling what Claudia had said about the state of the Kingsleys' finances, Jane wondered how Blair could afford to be so generous. Perhaps, as Claudia intimated, he simply ignored the problem. She said firmly, "I'm not going to become a paid nanny, Blair. But I will stay on as a friend. Do you have any idea where Claudia might have gone?"

He shook his head. "I was hoping you might have a clue."

Jane tried to recall Royce's visit to her. He had worn corporals' stripes, but she couldn't recall his insignia. What had Claudia told her about him?

"My brother stayed in the army. I believe he's a warrant officer now. I don't know his regiment, but they fought in Mesopotamia. Perhaps the army could help?"

"Yes. I'll use some of my father's old contacts."

At least Blair was about to leave the sanctuary of Willowford and go out to face the world, Jane thought, although she wished it could have been for a more positive reason.

He rose to his feet. "Let's go up and see if Colin is awake. His afternoon naps are getting shorter and shorter."

But the little boy was still asleep. They tiptoed into the nursery and stood looking down at him for a moment until, as if sensing their presence, he opened his eyes, smiled up at Blair, then rolled over and went back to sleep.

"You know, Jane, the first time I saw you and Colin together it occurred to me that he looked more like you than Claudia— that trusting look in his eyes, that smile, the dark hair, of course. Since I'd been with Claudia throughout her lying-in and had paced the floor the night he was born, I thought I was going off my rocker."

Blair gently stroked the child's cheek. "How could I have been so stupid as to question the irrefutable fact of motherhood, rather than the always questionable claim of fatherhood?"

◈ Twenty-eight ◈

As JANE WALKED through the chilly, sheet-shrouded rooms of Willowford the following morning, she was haunted by the echoes of remembered music and laughter. How long ago it seemed that she and Claudia had watched the Kingsley twins compete in the boat race on that lovely summer day.

She wandered into the ballroom, the hollow sound of her footsteps on the parquet bringing memories of girls in ball gowns spinning around the floor with handsome, carefree young men. So many of them had not returned from foreign battlefields. So many, like Bran, had come home with broken bodies and perhaps damaged minds, their lives forever changed.

Bran—or Blair, as he insisted on being called—had apologetically informed her that only Willowford's aging butler and an indifferent housekeeper remained on the staff. He put this down to the difficulty of finding servants, but Jane, recalling what Claudia had told her, thought the lack of staff and the dilapidated condition of the house and grounds were probably the result of financial problems. Certainly there were hoards of unemployed servicemen and munitions workers who could have filled the vacancies.

She walked back to the main hall and then went down to the kitchen. No one else was up yet, and Blair had left the previous evening after they spent a couple of hours with Colin.

As she filled a kettle to boil water for tea, Jane thought about her nephew. What a strangely old-fashioned little boy he was. Her father would have called him an old soul. Not yet three, Colin was so solemn, so thoughtful for a toddler, so watchful. He seemed to be seeking a clue from the adults around him as to how he should behave. He had listened attentively as Blair explained that, like his mother, he would have to leave for a while, but that Jane would take care of him.

Colin's lip had trembled. He'd looked at Blair imploringly. "Daddy not go. Please. Colin be a good boy."

Immediately Blair dropped to his knees and wrapped his arm around the child. "Just for a little while, Colin. I'll come back soon, I promise. And I'll phone you every day and bring you a present when I come back. I'm going to bring Mummy home."

As Colin wrapped his little arms tightly around Blair's neck and clung to him, Jane turned away to hide her tears. At the same time a troubling question surfaced: Was the child showing less interest in Claudia's return than distress at the prospect of losing Blair?

The kettle boiled and she made a pot of tea. A little while later the housekeeper, a sour-faced woman with thinning salt-and-pepper hair and a suspiciously red nose, came into the kitchen. She and the butler had been presented to Jane the previous evening, and Jane, knowing the nuances of staff hierarchy in a large estate, recognized immediately that both of them felt demeaned by the lack of underlings.

The housekeeper glared at Jane with malevolent satisfaction. "He's gone," she announced.

Believing she was referring to Blair, Jane said, "Yes, I know. It will be just for a few days."

"He's gone for good. Went to his sister's in Leeds. Packed up early this morning and left. Said to tell the master he won't be back."

"The butler has gone, you mean? Well, so be it. I doubt we'll need his services anyway. What about you, Mrs. Hibble? If you have any thoughts of leaving I'd appreciate knowing now."

The woman shrugged. "I'll see. I'm not making any promises."

Jane rose to her feet. "I'm going up to see if Colin is awake. You can get breakfast started and then clean the sink and drainboard and scrub the table. At least one room in the house should be fit to live in. We'll eat in here."

Mrs. Hibble's mouth dropped open in outrage as Jane swept past her.

Half an hour later Jane and Colin came down the stairs in time to see Mrs. Hibble, suitcases in hand, departing through the front door.

Jane looked down at the little boy. "Guess what? We're going to have this whole big house to ourselves until Daddy comes home. Won't that be fun? Come on, let's have breakfast and talk about what we're going to do today. Do you like eggs and bacon?"

Claudia awoke in a shabby room to find herself alone in the disarray of the bed, the memory of a night of lovemaking returning to momentarily distract her from the musty odor of the bed linen. A grimy window framed a row of chimney pots and gray slate rooftops, and below, hooves clattered and wheels ground the cobblestones of the small Lancashire town as a milk cart made its rounds. How dismal these northern mill towns were, how bone-chillingly cold and damp the climate— even worse than in the south. Claudia had been tempted to throw her sable coat on top of the worn quilt, but Royce had laughingly told her he'd soon warm her up.

Now he stood in the cramped space between the bed and scarred dresser, buttoning his uniform jacket.

He grinned at her. "Thought you were never going to wake up, love."

She stretched her arms above her head luxuriously. Last night she had felt alive again. Her body had tingled, vibrated with life. How handsome Royce had looked in the moonlight; how marvelous he looked now, freshly shaved and groomed, in his uniform. For a moment she lay in the warm cocoon of the bed, relishing his good looks. They had flung themselves at each other last night, coming together in a frenzy of carnal need that left neither time nor energy for anything else.

Royce turned back to the mirror above the dresser to comb his dark hair and put on his cap, and Claudia came out of her romantic haze. "You're not leaving?"

"Got to. I'm on duty today. But I'll be back tonight."

Claudia sat up, clutching a blanket to her naked breasts to ward off the damp chill of the room. "Royce, you can't leave me here! What shall I do all day? Besides, we haven't talked about our plans."

"Why don't you spend the day looking for a nice house for us? The sooner we get out of this place the better. There's an estate agent's office on High Street. It's just around the corner; you can walk there. Look, love, no time for conversation now. I've got to go. I'll see you tonight."

"But what if I need to talk to you before then?"

"Look, pet, you can't talk to a soldier on duty, y'know. Come on, give me a kiss and I'll be on my way. Don't forget this is a bed-and-breakfast place. Have a good meal before you go."

"I brought a picture of Colin—" she began, reaching for her handbag, carelessly dropped beside the bed the previous night.

"No time now. See you tonight." He kissed her mouth and was gone.

Claudia shivered, still half asleep, her mind not yet functioning properly. Royce had not mentioned Edith or her whereabouts, and that was frightening. Claudia now knew that Edith had refused to give Royce a divorce and that she was somewhere in England, not back in the Irish prison as Claudia had believed. Royce had explained that Edith was violently jealous and that he had left to protect Claudia from her. Edith had also managed to abscond with Claudia's trust fund. Claudia still wasn't sure how she had accomplished that, but certainly Royce didn't have the money. If he had, he wouldn't have stayed in the army. It would be a challenge to live on a warrant officer's pay, but Claudia was prepared to make sacrifices. She wished she had been wide awake enough to ask how much rent they could afford to pay for a house. She would just have to look at modest houses. The main thing was to find a place quickly, so that they could send for Colin. Perhaps she could manage with just a nanny for the child, a cook, and a daily cleaning woman, in order to eliminate the necessity for servants' quarters.

After slipping out of bed, Claudia dressed hurriedly in the unheated room. She and Royce were together again, and that was all that really mattered. Her love for him was irrevocable, eternal. He was a part of her very being. She could no more live without him than she could exist without the veins that carried her lifeblood, the lungs that drew in life-sustaining oxygen.

Her trunk had been put into the boxroom. Before leaving, she went there, unlocked the trunk, and took out a leather case.

A little later she asked the proprietor of the bed-and-breakfast house to call a taxi.

She told the driver, "Take me to the nearest pawnshop. I shall need you to wait for me."

The pawnbroker looked at the perfectly matched pearls of the necklace lying in its bed of velvet in the leather case. He frowned. "Five quid."

Claudia gasped. "You're joking!"

"Six. Take it or leave it." He glanced at the small diamond brooch pinned to a silk scarf draped over the collar of her fur coat. "Throw in the brooch and I'll make it ten guineas."

Her gloved fingers moved defensively to the brooch. "But the pearls are worth hundreds of pounds, and this brooch is an antique. I couldn't part with it."

"How about the coat, then? You want to pop it?"

She clutched her sable as if afraid he might remove it forcibly. "No! Absolutely not. My husband gave me this coat the day we were married. Besides, I'd freeze without it. Please, won't you give me a reasonable amount for the pearls?"

He turned his back on her and began dusting a shelf behind the counter.

The taxi driver was waiting outside. Royce had not given her any money, and she had used most of her cash to travel north. If she found a house, she would probably have to pay the rent in advance. What a bother it was to have to deal with such matters. She said in a low voice, "I'll leave the pearls with you."

As she watched him count out the pound notes, Claudia was glad that she had had the foresight not only to bring her jewelry with her but also to slip into her trunk one or two small pieces of jade from the Willowford collection. She reasoned that her dowry had more than paid for them.

The estate agent she went to next was an older man with a florid complexion and deep-set, rather sly eyes that quickly took in her fur coat, the diamond brooch, and her upper-class accent. "Some young officer at the army base is a lucky man. Or maybe you're the daughter of the C.O.?"

"My husband is a warrant officer." In her own mind, Royce *was* her husband, her only true husband.

The estate agent's eager smile faded. "A warrant officer? You should be looking at army housing, then, unless you've got a private income?"

"We . . . we would prefer to rent a house. We don't have a private income. I thought perhaps a modest little place . . . as long as the rent isn't too high."

"Modest, is it?" His sly eyes flickered over her again. "Listen, lass, why don't you phone Daddy and see if he'll help with the rent. You're not going to get much on a warrant officer's pay."

"If you would just show me what you have . . ."

He went to his desk and scribbled an address on a slip of paper. "I've got an appointment, so you'll have to go on your own. It's a cottage not far from the base. An old lady owns it, but she's in a nursing home. Needs a bit of repair."

The taxi driver dropped her on a country lane, and she was grateful that at least she wouldn't have to live in one of those dreadful terraced houses with common walls and front doors spaced only inches apart.

As she trudged through a quagmire toward a whitewashed wall and glimpsed the house through a tangle of overgrown brambles, Claudia's spirits fell. "Needs a bit of repair" indeed! The cottage was so tumbledown it surely had been vacant for years—broken windows, a door hanging on rusted hinges, part of the roof open to the sky. One glance into the litter-strewn interior confirmed her worst fears. The place was in ruins, uninhabitable. What a cruel joke. Tears sprang to Claudia's eyes. The estate agent had surely sent her here to get rid of her.

When Royce at last arrived at the guesthouse that evening Claudia huddled under the blankets in bed, still wearing her fur coat. "Oh, Royce, I thought you'd never come! I'm so c-c-cold."

He tossed his cap on the dresser, kicked off his boots, and, grinning, started to unbutton his jacket. "We'll soon warm you up, love."

"Royce, no! Please, we must talk. I've had a perfectly dreadful day."

"Me too, pet. Let's have a bit of comforting, and then we'll go out for supper and talk to our hearts' content."

"Royce, darling . . . no . . . please wait . . . ooh!"

Warm lips covered her mouth; warm hands cupped her face, then slid downward, taking her fur with them. By the time he had removed her dress she was already writhing in an agony of need. She still shivered, but with the promise of passion.

Laughing softly, fully aware of his power over her, he rolled onto his back, pulling her with him, then jerked the blanket up over her. She slid down onto him with a soft sigh, feeling him grow inside her, probing all of her secret places. She murmured, "Oh, how I love you! How I worship you!" Then as her excitement grew, she was incapable of speech or rational thought. The icy chill of the room was banished, lost in the fire created by the friction of flesh, the joining of mouths, the feverish exploration of tongues and fingertips.

The winter twilight was brief, and darkness fell. The mournful moan of the wind under the eaves and a sudden patter of rain against the window intruded. Royce sat up, bundling the blankets around her. "It's started to rain again. You stay here. I'll go and get us something to eat."

Alone again in the awful little room, she felt bereft. She began to shiver violently and pulled her fur coat up over her.

Half an hour later he returned, bringing with him the appetizing aroma of fish and chips. He discarded his uniform again while she unwrapped the newspaper and, starving, began to devour the food.

"Now, let's see that photo of the little lad and tell me about your house hunting," Royce said, climbing back into bed with her and helping himself to fish fried in a golden batter that crunched deliciously as he bit into it.

"Colin's photo is over there on the dresser—I propped it up against the lamp, but you knocked it over when you threw your cap."

Royce glanced in the direction of the dresser. "I'll go look in a minute—I've got grease all over my hands."

"I have to ask a rather awkward question of you, darling," Claudia said tentatively, knowing they had to talk now while they were eating or she'd lose another opportunity. "You see, when I went to the estate agent, he seemed to think a warrant officer couldn't afford to rent a house. I was wondering . . . well, how much *can* we afford to pay?"

He looked down at her, his gray eyes suddenly curiously blank, like mirrors reflecting nothing, then drawled lazily, "Why, that's up to you, pet. How fancy do you want to get? There's some nice houses on the outskirts of town that would be handy to the barracks."

She choked down what felt like a fish bone. "I don't understand. What do you mean, it's up to me?"

"You're the rich half of this duet. The agent was right: A warrant officer's pay isn't much. That's something else I wanted to talk to you about. I've come up through the ranks as far as I can go. I want to buy a commission. You'd rather be an officer's wife wouldn't you?"

"But—isn't a warrant officer an officer?"

"A noncommissioned officer. Next rung up is a lieutenant. But to become a commissioned officer I've got to have a private income, the pay doesn't cover all the expenses. That's where you come in, my love."

Claudia's appetite vanished abruptly. She lay back on her pillow. "Oh," she said.

Royce finished the fish and leapt out of bed. "Now, where's that son of mine?"

He picked up the photo and a smile spread across his handsome features. He whistled softly. "S'truth! He's the spittin' image of me."

"The spirit and image," Claudia corrected softly, almost to herself. Her thoughts flew wildly in several different directions as she sought solutions. Royce had expected she would still have a personal income even after liquidating her trust fund. Of course Leith was wealthy and she had married into a wealthy family. But Leith no longer gave her an allowance, and the Kingsleys' fortunes were on the wane.

Some sixth sense warned her that it would be better, for the time being, not to divulge these facts to her lover.

Royce put the silver-framed photograph of his son back on the dresser. "Now, tell me about the house hunting. You find us a place?"

"Well . . . I did look at one, but it wasn't suitable. The estate agent is going to take me out again tomorrow."

As Royce came back to the bed and gathered her into his arms, Claudia decided that she would pawn the rest of her jewels and the jade pieces. Surely that would bring in enough to pay the rent for a month or two. She would tell the agent that her father would be helping out with their finances. Regretfully, she decided to leave Colin with Blair for the time being, until something could be done about living expenses. Perhaps there was a way to recover her trust fund from Edith?

Sighing, Claudia nestled closer to Royce. Having to cope with money matters was frightening, but she was prepared to do absolutely anything to be with her love.

❦ Twenty-nine ❧

BLAIR MADE his daily telephone call promptly at nine on the fifth day after leaving Jane in charge of Colin. She waited anxiously for him to conclude his conversation with the little boy. At length Colin said, "Come home soon, Daddy. Bye."

Jane gently took the receiver from him. "Blair? How are you? Any news?"

"No. I swear the army is deliberately trying to throw me off the scent. Either that or they're all blithering idiots. Today I'm going to try to get hold of a retired general who was a close friend of Father. He's my last hope. I've drawn a blank everywhere else. What about you? Sounds as if you're coping very well. I suppose you heard Colin telling me about your cricket match? I'm glad your weather has been better than ours."

Jane decided not to explain that the cricket game had been played in the great unused cavern of the Willowford ballroom.

"You don't think you'll be coming home within the next day or two, then?"

"No." There was a pause. "Everything's all right, isn't it? Do you need anything?"

She was tempted to tell him that there had been no delivery of coal and, despite lighting only one fire in the kitchen and another in the nursery, they would soon be without fuel to heat the house. The butcher had stopped deliveries, and so had the grocer. All of the merchants complained about long-overdue bills. Fortunately the pantry was well stocked with tinned and dried food, flour, and tea. But living at Willowford was like being in a fortress under siege.

"We're fine," she said brightly, "but Colin is counting the minutes until you come home."

"Good, good. I'll give you a ring tomorrow."

Jane hung up the phone and looked down at Colin, who regarded her hopefully. "Daddy's not coming today. But soon. Let's bundle you up warmly and go for a walk. We need some fresh air."

It was also a way to conserve coal. She wouldn't light a fire in the nursery until they returned. Besides, although she put on a brave face for the child, Jane found the empty rooms eerie. Curiously, the house seemed smaller now that it was deserted. She supposed the continual parade of family members and servants going about their daily routine had somehow expanded the house, giving it the movement and life that it now lacked.

As she crouched down to button Colin's coat she looked into his trusting gaze and impulsively wrapped her arms around him. "You're an absolutely splendid little boy," she said, unconsciously repeating Blair's praise. "I'm so proud of you."

Colin shyly returned her hug, then gave her a smile that tugged at her heartstrings.

The morning was bright and clear, but a silver sheen of frost glistened on the trees and lawn, and icicles hung from window ledges and eaves. They set off down the driveway, and Jane paused to gently brush away the frost from a tiny green shoot.

"Look, Colin—a snowdrop. That means spring will be here soon."

He nodded solemnly. Never having dealt with a child

before, Jane wondered if she was being ridiculous in speaking of such things. How could a child of less than three make the connection between a snowdrop and spring? He didn't yet comprehend the days of the week. Still, she'd fallen into the habit of holding conversations with him almost constantly. It was a way to dispel the silence of the deserted house.

They went out through the ornate wrought-iron gates and walked down the lane toward Rathbourne Abbey. The other direction led to the river and the woods, and Jane told herself that the surface of the lane would make for easier walking, but as the abbey came into view above the hawthorn hedge bordering the lane, she was gripped by a nostalgic sadness for times that were lost and could never be recaptured. The stable master's cottage at Rathbourne Abbey had been her home, and she'd spent many happy hours there with her father and Royce, and, of course, with Claudia, whom Jane had always regarded as the sister she had never had. But overshadowing all the other memories was the enigmatic presence of Marrick. She remembered the field hospital in France and the brief interlude when the chasm between their stations in life, even their different generations, had been bridged. A vague longing stirred, somewhere deep inside some long unused chamber of her heart, a yearning that slipped away, elusive as a spring zephyr, without defining itself.

"Car coming," Colin said, solicitously tugging on her hand to pull her to the side of the lane.

A moment later an open roadster came around the bend in the lane and stopped before the gates of the abbey. Marrick was at the wheel, the backseat was piled high with luggage, and a beautiful dark-haired woman sat in the passenger seat. Jane recognized her at once. Magdalena de Mora, Marrick's former and obviously present mistress, had changed little in the past five years. Jane felt a stab of acute resentment. Magdalena had fled to a safe haven during the war. How could Marrick take her back? Even he had eventually taken up the colors.

They were too close to avoid being seen. Marrick jumped out of the car and waved as they approached.

"Jane! How are you? Where did you spring from?" He extended his hand, but when Jane attempted a handshake she found instead he clasped her hand in a warm grip and did not lct go. His dark eyes probed hers, as though searching for something. "It's so good to see you again. I've never thanked you for all your care and patience. I know what a difficult case I was."

"I was just doing my job," Jane muttered, reading into his words the hidden message that what had passed between a wounded aviator and his nurse should be discounted as wartime folly. Undoubtedly that intense look he gave her was also due to his fear that she might have misinterpreted his attentions.

Aware also of Magadlena's cool appraisal, Jane eased her hand out of Marrick's grip and turned to acknowledge the presence of his mistress. "Good morning, Mrs. de Mora."

"You remember Jane Weatherly, don't you, Magda?" Marrick said, and she responded with a nod.

He looked down at Colin, who stood close to Jane, holding her hand. "And who have we here?"

"This is Colin Kingsley," Jane said.

"Claudia's son," Marrick said. It was not a question.

"I'm surprised you didn't recognize him," Jane said.

"I haven't seen anything of Claudia or her family for quite some time. I take it you're staying with them?"

Jane thought of the chilly and vacant rooms of Willowford and murmured noncommittally. Obviously Marrick had just returned from abroad—nobody in England sported a tropical tan at this time of year—and he would learn soon enough of the drama unfolding at Willowford. She certainly wasn't about to tell him, in front of his mistress, that Claudia had run off with Royce.

"We mustn't delay you," Jane said. "Come on, Colin. Good day, Lord Marrick, Mrs. de Mora."

They walked on down the lane and a moment later heard the engine of Marrick's car roar to life.

Jane had put Colin to bed and was sitting in the kitchen, staring at the formidable stack of letters that had been delivered that day and which undoubtedly were mostly bills, when the front doorbell chimed.

Marrick stood on the threshold.

Standing aside to allow him to enter, she said, "I wasn't

expecting anyone. I'm afraid the fires aren't lit, except for one in the kitchen."

He walked into the hall. "Then let's repair to the kitchen."

"I . . . I'm not sure that's a good idea."

"Jane, let's not play games. I've been informed that Sir Nigel is dead, Alicia is recovering from the flu at a convalescent home, the servants have left, and young Kingsley and Claudia have run off and left you in charge of the boy and the house. I'm here to offer whatever help you need."

She hesitated for a second and he added, "Come on, don't be too proud to let someone else share the burden. You can't handle this situation alone."

He was right, of course, and Jane felt a sense of relief just having him here. She led the way to the kitchen and reached for the coal scuttle to bank the fire. He took it away from her. "Why don't you find a bottle of sherry? We'll talk over a glass of wine. It will warm the cockles and help you relax. You're obviously as tense as a bowstring."

"I have no idea where the key to the wine cellar is," Jane answered. "I'll make some cocoa."

Minutes later they huddled close to the fire, chilled hands cupped around mugs of steaming cocoa. Jane reflected briefly on the incongruity of the lord of the manor and the stable master's daughter warming themselves at the kitchen hearth. Perhaps Percy Templeton was right in saying that the war had already blurred the lines of class distinction and it was only a matter of time before the entire class system crumbled. Marrick's inherited seat in the House of Lords certainly had less clout than Percy's elected place in the House of Commons. But in Marrick's imposing presence it was difficult to remain convinced of that.

"You'd better tell me everything," Marrick said. "Where are Blair and Claudia?"

Jane told him only that Claudia had left, apparently for good, and Blair had gone to try to find her. Marrick was silent for a while. Then he said, "First of all, Blair should come home. He isn't going to do any good running around looking for her. Secondly, like it or not, he's the head of the family, and he'd better stop feeling sorry for himself and see if he can salvage something out of the ruins. In the meantime, you and the boy shall come back to the abbey with me. You can't stay here all alone."

"Oh, we can't leave . . ." Jane faltered. "Well, at least not until Blair phones tomorrow and I talk to him. Don't blame him too much. He doesn't know the butler and housekeeper left. He relied on them to run the house and pay the bills; he has no idea how bad things are here. Besides, I don't think it would be a good idea for me to take Colin to the abbey. I mean . . . well, isn't Mrs. de Mora in residence?" Jane felt her cheeks flame with embarrassment and hoped he would think it was just the glow of the firelight.

"Actually, Magdalena had to return to town." Marrick paused. "You don't approve of my . . . friendship with her, do you?"

Jane didn't reply.

He leaned back in his chair, the firelight playing over his features making him look more than ever like a satyr. At length he said, "I've observed the institution of marriage carefully over the years, and I long ago came to the conclusion that most marriages quickly become arenas in which two people have unlimited opportunities to savage each other with impunity. On the other hand, a relationship such as I have with Magdalena, wherein we can both come and go as we please, seems less taxing."

"Yet you wanted to marry Claudia."

A black eyebrow arched. "I was *willing* to marry Claudia. There is a difference, both in semantics and cause and effect. Since you are her confidante, I'm sure she told you my reasons for suggesting we marry. Besides, at the moment I'm not discussing Claudia and myself, I'm explaining why Magdalena and I decided to forgo matrimony."

"Why?" Jane asked. "I mean, why explain that to me, of all people?"

A smile played across his mouth. "Damned if I know."

Jane relaxed slightly. "I still don't think it would be a good idea for me to take Colin away from Willowford. But when Blair calls I will tell him that the last of the servants have gone."

"What about Claudia? Have you any idea where she might have gone?"

Jane shook her head.

Marrick's dark eyes were filled with anger. "I didn't think even she would abandon her own child."

"She hasn't abandoned Colin," Jane said quickly. "She said in her note she would be sending for him."

Marrick gave an exasperated sigh. "You don't recognize that you are as much under Claudia's spell as any hapless male who stumbles across her path, do you? You always make excuses for her, rationalize her behavior, cater to her moods and whims and hypochondria."

"But you were the one who suggested I do all of those things," Jane exclaimed indignantly. "You *paid* me to protect her from the results of her actions."

"She was still a child then. I was wrong, of course. But I can't go back into the past and change anything. I no longer enable her to run roughshod over everyone. Can you say the same?"

Jane was silent, thinking about Claudia. How did anyone chastise a zephyr or stand firm against a will-o'-the-wisp? Claudia simply wasn't like ordinary mortals and could not be dealt with in the same manner. She certainly didn't intend to hurt people, there was no malice to her actions, she was not deliberately cruel. A little selfish, perhaps, but who with her breathtaking beauty would not be?

Marrick said suddenly, "Sometimes I wonder if Claudia was born missing some essential component of feeling—pity, empathy for those who love her. In fact, she seems to resent their adoration and find ways to punish them for it."

"Perhaps because she feels unworthy of such devotion," Jane suggested slowly, and the thought was a revelation, because it occurred to her that the only person who treated Claudia abominably—Royce—was the one Claudia apparently loved obsessively.

"Jane." Marrick's voice, low and resonant, interrupted her reverie. "You love what you know of Claudia—her beauty, her sudden laughter, her capacity for enjoyment, even her inexplicable melancholia. But there are unplumbed depths of Claudia, a dark, destructive substructure to her personality that, when it collapses, will drag you down with her if you're not careful."

"Did you ever consider that she might simply be what the

circumstances of her life have made her? Didn't she ever tell you any of the horror stories about the Abelard women who took care of her before she came to you? And what about her life at the abbey? She was raised like some fairy princess locked away in a castle, never allowed to associate with ordinary people, never having the guidance of a mother figure—"

Marrick interrupted her with an explosive laugh. "Just listen to yourself! You're completely blind when it comes to Claudia, aren't you? Tell me, where was *your* mother figure?"

"I had teachers—friends at school."

"Claudia had you." Marrick slammed his cocoa mug down on the hearth and stood up. "Why do we always end up discussing Claudia? That isn't why I came."

"If Claudia hadn't left Blair, neither of us would be here."

"Call me tomorrow morning after you've spoken to Blair. In the meantime, I'll send a couple of the abbey staff over here to help out. Don't bother to see me out. Stay here by the fire."

He had reached the kitchen door in a few long strides when Jane called after him. "Wait!"

Instantly he turned, his expression suddenly eager, hopeful. "Yes?"

"I just want to . . . thank you . . . for coming over."

She had risen to her feet, but stood motionless, a strange feeling of loss creeping through her. He nodded and opened the door to leave, allowing an icy draft to sweep into the room.

Even after the door had closed firmly behind him, Jane remained where she stood, bewildered by a powerful emotion that gripped her. *She had not wanted him to leave.*

❖ Thirty ❖

JANE STRODE purposefully across the lawn to where Blair and Colin were playing cricket. Clear spring sunshine and fluffy white clouds scudding across the panorama of blue sky promised an end to winter. A week had passed since Blair had returned to Willowford, without Claudia.

Colin's little arm made a slow circle, and he bowled the ball toward Blair, who stood with the bat at the ready before an improvised wicket. At the last second Blair moved slightly and allowed the ball to crash into the wicket.

"Bravo! You bowled me out!" Blair cried, and Colin jumped up and down, clapping his hands in glee.

Watching, Jane forced herself to harden her heart. She could no longer allow herself to be beguiled by them. "Colin," she called. "It's time for lunch. Go and wash your hands. Daddy will be along in a minute." To Blair she added, "I have to talk to you."

"Run along, Colin," Blair said, ruffling the boy's dark hair.

"From the look on your face," Blair said as Colin sprinted toward the house, "I'd say something is wrong."

"You're drifting," Jane said, "letting everything slide."

"When Claudia comes home—"

"No!" Jane's voice was almost a scream. "I don't want to hear 'when Claudia comes home' or 'when she calls' or 'when she writes' or anything else about Claudia. Some decisions can't wait for Claudia. Do you realize we've had three of Lord Marrick's servants here for a week now? Have you even looked at the pile of bills I put on the study desk? Blair, if you can't afford to keep Willowford going, perhaps you should find a smaller house."

He looked aghast. "But I *have* to keep Willowford going.

It's been in our family for generations—far longer, I might add, than Marrick has had the abbey. Don't worry, I'll manage somehow. Jane, I'm grateful to you for staying on and running the house, and I do hope you won't desert us until . . . just yet."

Until Claudia comes home, Jane thought, but at least he had stopped himself from saying it. "Blair, it's time to have a meeting with your solicitor about settling the estate or at least releasing enough money to keep things going. I took it upon myself to phone Percy—Percy Templeton, the MP my friend works for; he was a solicitor before the war, you know—and he suggested a complete review of the current status of your assets."

Jane didn't add that Percy felt something was exceedingly fishy about the handling of Sir Nigel's will. Percy had said bluntly, "A grieving widow secluded in a nursing home and a shell-shocked war veteran would be easy prey for an unscrupulous lawyer. I'd have an independent audit done. Young Kingsley probably doesn't know what to look for. I expect that, like many sons of wealthy families, all he knows is a hedonistic style of living."

"You can't put it off any longer, Blair," Jane said.

He sighed. "I suppose you're right."

"While you're in London, you should go to the newspaper offices, too. Look into your father's business. Find out what's going on there."

"Jane . . . I . . . well, I suppose I should tell you the truth. When I went to town to try to track down Claudia, I . . . I spent most of my time in a hotel room making phone calls. I thought I could accept that people would look at me with horror. I had steeled myself for it. I'd even convinced myself that there would be other men as scarred as I walking about the streets . . . but of course there weren't—at least, not on the streets of the West End."

Jane bit her lip. "Blair, your scars aren't so bad, honestly. You're too sensitive."

"My first day in town an old lady took one look at me and burst into tears. When I went into the hotel dining room a couple at the next table got up and left their food untouched. And the remarks I overheard . . . Well, I'll spare you. My experiences made me even more grateful that you look at me without wincing, Jane. You're a true friend. I don't know what I would have done without you. I do hope you'll stay on. As soon as summer arrives I'm sure the mater will come home and relieve you of the burden."

She was tempted to seize his shoulders and shake him. "For God's sake, Blair, will you please wake up? Waiting for Claudia, waiting for your mother—you're not a little boy any longer. You have to act now or you'll lose everything. Will you go to London? Look, I've got an idea. Let me go with you—and Colin, too. You won't feel so alone."

He had a habit of hanging his head, looking away, even when he spoke to her. But now he looked directly at her. "Would you? You don't object to being seen with me?"

Oh, Bran, I would be proud, her heart whispered. Aloud she said, "I'll pick up a railway timetable right away."

Claudia slowly took off her sable coat and draped it over the counter. She shivered and wrapped her arms closely around her body, although she had worn a wool suit under the fur.

The pawnbroker said, "Oh, don't look so woebegone. It's spring. You won't be needing it till next winter." He pulled the fur over to his side of the counter.

Claudia watched as he counted out the bank notes. There would be enough to pay their outstanding bills and next week's rent. Then what? Royce believed she had unlimited funds and never asked where the money came from. He squandered his army pay on expensive champagne and drinks for his fellow NCOs at the pub, and he had a taste for exotic food—out-of-season fruits, imported cheese, even caviar and pâté de foie gras. He did bring bouquets of hothouse flowers and boxes of chocolates for her, but she would much rather have had the money to pay bills. He used his army pay as pin money, for nonessential luxuries. Whenever she tried to talk to him about living expenses they invariably ended up in bed, and then nothing serious was discussed. All of her jewelry, all of the Willowford jade, was now in the possession of the pawnbroker.

She gave one last regretful glance at her beautiful sable. Was she destined forever to sacrifice her sables? Her first had gone down with the *Lusitania*, and this one—her wedding gift from Blair, who was called Roald at that time—would now languish amid all the other forlorn mementos of hard times that had bought their former owners a moment's respite from pennilessness.

Shivering in the thin spring sunshine, she began the long walk back to the house they had taken on the outskirts of town. En route she would stop at the butcher shop and buy a small joint of beef for dinner. The woman she had hired as cook-housekeeper had been grumbling that she didn't know how to prepare some of the food Royce brought home. Claudia sighed, remembering that she owed the woman two weeks' wages. But a cook-housekeeper was a necessity, not an extravagance, Claudia reasoned, since she certainly didn't know how to cook and take care of a house.

A group of small boys came bounding toward her, kicking a ball between them, which one of them scooped up in order to let her pass. She blinked back a tear. The youngest boy had dark, wavy hair and fair skin, big dove-gray eyes, and a rather solemn expression. He reminded her of Colin.

Royce had explained that until he received his new orders, due any day, it would be better to leave Colin at Willowford. When she tried to press him to send for their son, Royce had become withdrawn. When she begged to be allowed at least to telephone Colin, Royce had lost his temper. "Damn it, I can't be bothered with a kid under my feet just now, Claudia. Just let well enough alone until it's more convenient."

She loved her child and missed him desperately, but she could not give up the father for the sake of the son. She rationalized that sons were temporary attachments at best; few remained with aging parents, and those who did, like Blair, were less than men. So, although she missed Colin and longed to see him, she never considered returning to Willowford to be with him or defying Royce by telephoning him. Her goal, as she saw it, was to persuade Royce to agree that their son must come to live with them. But how to accomplish that, for the present at least, was beyond her.

Besides, she had too many other things to worry about, for in addition to their money problems, Claudia lived in fear that the violently jealous Edith might suddenly appear on the scene.

This fear also reinforced her decision to leave her son with Blair. She would just try to keep going until Royce got his new orders. She hoped fervently that they would be for a warm climate somewhere. Royce himself was hoping for India. He'd been there briefly and loved the country. Yes, that was it; they simply had to be sent abroad. Then Colin would have to go with them and they'd be safe from Edith.

Blair, Colin, and Jane stayed in London at a mews house that belonged to the Kingsleys, situated close to the Fleet Street newspaper offices.

At first Blair was uncomfortable demanding explanations from the solicitor and investigating the current state of his father's business, but, prodded by Jane, he did so.

Although he was convinced his scarred features were the reason for his reticence, Jane pointed out, "You were brought up to be a gentleman, never to raise your voice or make a scene. But that isn't the way you get things done in the business world. Your father knew that. Your war wounds aren't going to be a hindrance to you, Blair, but your attitude is. Your father knew when to be a gentleman and when to be a businessman."

"I'm afraid I'm not the man my father was."

"Of course you are. Blair, if you'd like, I'll ask Percy to look over any documents you don't understand. We can trust him."

"Thank you. I'd appreciate his help."

There was much hedging on the part of the family solicitor until Blair mentioned that Percival Templeton, MP, wanted to look into the matter of his father's estate. After that, events moved rapidly toward a conclusion. It turned out that certain funds had been transferred to the solicitor's account—"to cover expenses," he claimed—and the rest of the inheritance had somehow been stalled in probate court. Percy quickly had the proceedings moving again, and the solicitor made restitution to avoid prosecution. However, Percy privately told Jane that the Kingsleys, like many other aristocratic families, might find themselves impoverished in the postwar period unless Blair was able to salvage his father's publishing companies.

At Jane's urging, Blair then went to his father's office and began the laborious and frustrating task of resurrecting what had once been one of the city's leading newspapers. After the first agonizing days of forcing himself to face the staff, he found that he was too busy to concern himself with other people's reactions to his scars.

For Jane, the days were happy and productive. She enjoyed living in the small house, caring for Colin, cooking dinner for all of them, and, especially, the quiet evenings when Blair came home and relayed all that had happened during the day and listened carefully to her opinions.

She almost felt she was directing the paper herself, since Blair adopted many of her suggestions, especially with regard to the editorial pages. "Your father was so biased in favor of the conservative viewpoint that he lost a lot of readers. You have to be more objective," she told him. "The country is going to see some major changes in the next few years, and your newspaper can't ignore them. I know you find it hard to believe, but the Labour party will run the country eventually."

Blair had given her the funny little half smile that was the best his poor scarred mouth could manage and replied, "I expect you feel we should give more space to editorials complaining that we're moving too slowly in regard to the emancipation of women, too, don't you?"

Jane grinned. "Of course."

"Your friend Percy and his stalwart assistant Penny have succeeded in turning you into quite a political creature, haven't they?"

"Actually I was interested in politics long before I met them," Jane responded thoughtfully, allowing the memory of Royce and Edith to intrude for a moment. She quickly dismissed the image. Everything was going too well at present to dwell on the past.

Jane was guiltily aware that her castle was built on quicksand, but for a little while at least she could pretend Blair was her husband and Colin her son. She dared not imagine how bereft she would feel when she was inevitably forced to separate from them.

There were children in the house next door, and Colin had playmates for the first time. He no longer cried for his mother, and as the days went by, Claudia's absence became less of a strain on all of them. Jane knew that Blair was still looking for Claudia, but he didn't mention her.

Shortly after they arrived in London, Penny Tandy called to see her. Jane's eyes widened as she took in Penny's appearance. She was clad in one of the new short, shapeless dresses recently introduced into postwar England by young women. Jane had never seen so much exposed flesh, both arms and legs. There was no hint in the cylindrical frock that Penny had breasts, waist, or hips. Even more shocking, she had cut her long hair into an extremely short, masculine-looking bob.

Her bawdy laughter filling the small entry hall of the mews house, Penny spun in a circle so that Jane could admire her. "What do you think?"

"Dear heaven, what have you done to yourself?" Jane asked. "You look like a twelve-year-old."

"That's the whole idea, ducks," Penny said. "A new age is dawning, and women—young women, emancipated women— are going to have a say in what goes on in the world. We can't be hindered by flowing skirts and corsets we can't breathe in and hair that takes four hours to dry. We've more important things to do. The old styles are for matrons, so our clothes create the illusion of youth for them, too, as long as they've got a modern attitude."

"Let's go into the parlor and I'll make a pot of tea," Jane said. "I need a cuppa to help me cope with this."

"Where's the nipper?" Penny asked, looking around.

"Colin was invited to a birthday party for the little boy next door. He loves having other children to play with."

"Doesn't miss his mother, then?"

"Well, yes, of course. But it helps that he isn't isolated at Willowford, forever watching for her to come home."

Penny glanced at Jane shrewdly. "I expect it helps his dad, having you here to wait on him hand and foot, too."

Jane replied defensively, "You're a fine one to talk. Last time I saw you and Percy together, you were doing more for him than I do for Blair. If you're so emancipated, why are you still Percy's bond servant?"

To Jane's surprise, Penny colored deeply. "I'm . . . more than that to him."

"Oh," Jane said faintly. "I'm sorry. . . . I didn't know."

"I'd die for him," Penny said passionately, "You don't know how I love that little man! He held back at first, because of the difference in our ages, but now he wants to marry me. He might have asked me out of guilty conscience, because we've been sleeping together. I know he's worried about what his constituents think—he's thirty years older than I am. What do you think?"

"Do you *want* to marry him?"

"Oh, yes. But I don't want to ruin his political career."

"Never mind him. What about you? Are you willing to be with an elderly man while you're still in your prime? Aren't you embarrassed about being mistaken for his daughter? What about children? He probably won't live long enough to bring up a family, and you'll be left struggling on your own."

"I've thought about all of that, and the answer is yes. No matter what happens, I want to be Percy's wife."

"Then marry him," Jane said simply, "and to hell with what anybody else thinks."

As summer approached, Blair began to worry about Willowford, now in the custody of part-time caretakers. "I really should go down there and hire gardeners and servants. I'd like to open the house again so we could go down on weekends and you and Colin could spend the summer there. Perhaps we could go next weekend?"

He seemed to take it for granted that Jane would be a part of his plans, and she disregarded a distant warning voice that asked when she would start thinking about her own future.

"If you like, I could go to Willowford tomorrow and start interviewing servants," she suggested. "Then you can look them over when you arrive. It would save time."

"That's a splendid idea." His cruelly scarred mouth curved almost into a smile. "What would I do without you?" he asked for the hundredth time.

They had just finished dinner, and Jane stood up to clear the table. "I'll do the dishes and then start packing."

Blair rose, too, and reached across the table to pick up one of the serving dishes. As he did, his hand brushed hers and he said quickly, "Sorry. I'm not as dexterous with my left hand as

I used to be with my right. I do wish you had hired a housekeeper. I hate to see you doing everything for us."

Almost undone by his touch, Jane felt herself flush. "Oh, I knew we would only be staying here for a short time. It wasn't worth it. Please, Blair, put the dishes down. I'll have them done in a jiffy."

The following morning he accompanied Jane and Colin to the railway station, and as the conductor began slamming doors and blowing his whistle, Blair hugged the child and kissed his cheek, then turned to Jane.

She wasn't sure what happened next. Did she take a step toward him or he toward her? Her arms went around his neck, his arm around her waist. Impulsively, she leaned closer and kissed his cheek. His arm tightened; she felt him tense. He whispered, "Oh, Jane . . ."

There was a burst of steam from the train, and the conductor lifted Colin aboard. Jane stumbled up the steps after him. She stared at Blair as the train began to move, watching until he was out of sight, unsure exactly what had just happened.

❧ Thirty-one ❧

ROYCE WEATHERLY was better educated and better informed than most of his army peers, and he had a fairly clear picture of the world problems left unsolved at the end of the Great War.

His own abrupt enlistment had been the result of Edith again going on a jealous rampage and attempting to choke a young neighbor she had caught with him in flagrante delicto.

Fearing either that Edith would be caught and arrested and drag him to prison with her, or that she might decide to whack him over the head while he slept in punishment for his infidelity, Royce had joined up and quickly found himself on his way to India. His elation that he was to be spared the possibility of trench fighting in Flanders was short-lived. Before he had time to enjoy the privileges of the white soldier in the Indian army, waited on by subservient Hindus, Royce had found himself a part of Major General Stanley Maude's second British-Indian invasion of Mesopotamia, marching across scorching desert sands to capture Baghdad and bring down the Ottoman Empire.

The question now, Royce knew, was how that victory would be maintained. He didn't believe, as some of his superior officers did, that the Arab world would become a version of British India, perhaps even a dominion of the Crown rather than a colony. Oh, T. E. Lawrence and other British military men had raised an Arab legion to fight the Turks in Transjordan all right, but Royce knew from personal experience that other Arabs, especially those in Baghdad, had remained loyal to the Turks to the very last. Besides, they were nomads who simply didn't recognize national boundaries and therefore would be difficult to contain within borders that were invisible in the desert sands.

Even though high-flown talk of liberation and freedom was blown about on desert winds, the postwar reality was direct rule from Britain and British India, and a bloody Arab uprising was in the making. Royce was enough a student of history, particularly military history, to realize that a swift and efficient offensive leading to victory was less a chore to the common soldier than becoming a part of a long-drawn-out occupation wherein he would have to act as policeman.

Seeing the handwriting on the wall, Royce began to suspect that his regiment's peacetime orders, rather than involving a cushy billet in India, might mean a return to the arid sands of Mesopotamia. Since there was a surfeit of second lieutenants in his regiment, he stood a good chance of being transferred back to the Indian army if he received a commission. In either eventuality, he had no intention of remaining a noncommissioned officer, and that was where Claudia Kingsley fitted into the picture. Her money could buy him his commission and provide the ongoing private income he would need as an officer.

The trouble was, she was vague to the point of stupidity about her financial resources. As Lord Marrick's ward and

Kingsley's wife, she had to have thousands of pounds at her disposal. All he'd got out of her so far was one measly trust fund—he grinned to himself as he recalled the spree he and Edith had gone on with that.

With time growing short before his regiment received new orders, he decided he couldn't wait any longer. He'd have it out with Claudia, get her to put his name on her bank accounts. On his way home he stopped at a florist's shop to buy a spring bouquet of narcissi and daffodils.

As he reached their house he saw her waiting for him at the parlor window, and he felt a surge of pride in her beauty. With the delectable Claudia on his arm, he was the envy of every man in the regiment. She was the perfect foil for his own good looks, and he relished the way people gaped at them in awe. More than that, her obvious breeding and aristocratic demeanor would be an asset to an ambitious young officer.

He supposed he was fond of her, in a way. He certainly lusted after her constantly, and with the possible exception of Edith, she was the best lover he'd ever had. Royce envisioned the two of them in India, surrounded by servants, enjoying every privilege of the raj.

Claudia opened the door before he reached it and hurled herself into his arms, almost crushing the flowers. He slipped his arm around her waist and lifted her into the air to press a long kiss on her sweet mouth.

Breathlessly she whispered in his ear, "Do you want to go upstairs?"

Placing her on her feet, he looked toward the kitchen and sniffed appreciatively. "Something smells good. I hope it's beef and Yorkshire pud. Let's go into the parlor and whet our appetites with a drink. We need to have a serious talk, pet. I've got to get my hands on some cash."

A few miles down the river from Upper Oakleigh, the bustling market town of Beddington boasted one of the finest public libraries in the county. The library had been run by three quietly efficient young women under the direction of the head librarian, a bristly spinster named Miss Wilson. On a bleak winter morning some months earlier, one of her employees had abruptly terminated her employment, and to Miss Wilson's relief and surprise, a fully qualified librarian with excellent references from two libraries in Ireland and one in Yorkshire had immediately appeared on the scene to fill the gap.

Miss Yardley was dark-haired, bespectacled, well spoken, and inclined toward rather shapeless garments—perhaps to disguise her less-than-ladylike curves. She kept strictly to herself, and not by word or deed did she raise the slightest suspicion that she had not spent her entire life in the hushed world of dusty books and well-thumbed magazines.

Yet Miss Wilson felt uneasy in the presence of Edith Yardley. She exuded a flinty coldness, a clinical detachment, that held everyone at bay. With a glance from her green eyes, she could cause a personal question to die on the lips of the asker or forestall an invitation to have lunch with one of the other librarians. Her time away from the library, she made very clear, was her own.

When Miss Wilson assigned to Miss Yardley the task of conducting the Saturday-morning children's story hour, she was astounded to see the circle of usually unruly youngsters huddle together in petrified silence as Miss Yardley read from Dickens's *Great Expectations*.

Dickens could be very frightening, the head librarian reasoned, especially the scene where the escaped convict Magwitch suddenly rears up over Pip on the moors, but Miss Yardley's reading, although low and well modulated, carried an inexplicable ring of authenticity. Indeed, it almost seemed as if Miss Yardley *became* the convict. The children fled immediately the story hour ended, and only two of them returned the following Saturday, dragged in by their mothers. Miss Wilson didn't ask Edith Yardley to conduct the story hour again.

The head librarian did, however, write to all three libraries where Miss Yardley had previously been employed, asking for confirmation of her references. As the weeks slipped by, she wondered why no response to her inquiries arrived.

Edith could feel Miss Wilson's beady eyes on her as she pushed the cart down the aisle, pausing to return books to their assigned spaces. The old witch was suspicious of her, she was sure, asking not-so-subtle questions and making remarks designed to draw out facts about her private life. If only she knew!

Miss Wilson had also tried to verify her references. Two letters had been returned to the library, marked "undeliverable" by the Dublin post office. Naturally they were, since no such libraries existed. Edith had intercepted and destroyed the returned inquiries. The third library would send word that Edith Yardley had been a reliable employee before leaving to get married, and if and when Miss Wilson questioned her about this, Edith would explain that she had been jilted at the altar, perhaps eliciting sympathy from one old maid to another.

Edith bore absolutely no resemblance to the real Edith Yardley, a slender little mouse she had met during a period when she had been forced to lie low. Books had been her sole companions at that time, and she had visited the library in the dark of winter, just before closing. Hearing one of the other librarians address someone as "Edith" she had almost jumped out of her skin. When, a week or so later, Edith Yardley left the library to be married to a man who intended to emigrate to Australia, Edith Weatherly saw an opportunity to assume both a new identity and a respectable profession.

Unfortunately, the real Edith Yardley had apparently only worked at that particular library for a few months, so Edith created the two mythical Irish libraries to fill in the blanks in her employment history, hoping only the last place of employment would be checked.

She had been a fugitive too long to become complacent, and she knew that Miss Wilson's watchful eyes and the small town gossipmongers were a lethal combination. But she simply had to hang around and keep her eye on her sister-in-law. Jane was Edith's only hope of finding Royce.

Royce had warned her to stay away from his sister, saying that she might well notify the police if she spotted her. Jane had never liked her, Edith was well aware of that, and for the time being at least she decided against a direct confrontation. But Edith knew that the only person on earth whom Royce truly cared about was his sister. He wouldn't stay away from her forever. Sooner or later he'd show up on Jane's doorstep, and when he did, Edith would be ready for him.

It had been easy to keep an eye on Jane when she was

working for the MP, although Jane had almost caught her that time she'd been sitting in the bus shelter, but since Jane had moved to Willowford surveillance of the sprawling estate was nearly impossible. All Edith could do was to walk up and down the lane, watching the comings and goings through the ornate wrought-iron gates.

Sliding a book back onto the shelf in front of her, Edith glanced at the clock on the wall. Almost time to go home, and since it was Saturday, she'd have the afternoon off. On her last trip out to Willowford she'd passed a pair of tweedy types clumping through a meadow in their brogues and carrying butterfly nets. With the arrival of spring no doubt the butterfly hunters would be out in full force. Who would notice one more?

Clad in sensible shoes, a baggy skirt, and a nondescript cardigan, a felt hat jammed down on her head, and carrying a brand-new butterfly net, Edith spent the afternoon prowling about the meadows and fields adjacent to Willowford, seeking without success a peephole in the stout walls, beyond which a thick hedge and densely planted trees further protected the estate from prying eyes.

The weather had turned unseasonably warm, and tired and irritable, she flopped down on a grassy bank beneath a towering oak tree. Pinpricks of light stabbed her left eye, and a dull throbbing had begun somewhere deep inside her head. The greasy fish and chips she'd hastily consumed on the way there churned miserably in her stomach.

Anger began to build, welling up until she felt ready to choke on it. Damn them. Damn all of them. It wasn't fair that everyone else had it so bloody easy, everything handed to them on a plate, while she, who deserved as much as anybody, received nothing but hard knocks.

Royce. It was all Royce's fault. Everything she'd done, she'd done for him, trying to keep him with her, desperately needing his love, giving him all she had to give. Only it was never enough. He had an appetite for life's luxuries that she had never been able to satisfy. Lord almighty! The things she had done to keep him. And was he grateful? No, not him.

Where the hell was he?

He'd simply dropped off the face of the earth.

If it hadn't been for the fact that he'd gone to great lengths to avoid being called up for military service, she might have suspected that he'd escaped into the army. But he'd sworn never to fight in the trenches. Besides, the war was over now. Even if by some quirk of fate the army had got him, he'd be home now. She never considered that he might have been killed, for the simple reason that a devil like Royce would never have been so foolish as to die in such a gallant way.

Her headache was driving her mad. Pressing her fingers to the sledgehammer pounding her brow just above her left eye, she leaned back against the rough bark of the oak.

She heard it then. The soft murmur of water flowing over smooth stones. Ah, to wet her handkerchief and lay it over her eyes. That would help.

Pulling herself to her feet, she looked around. She couldn't see the stream, but she felt sure that it wasn't too far. Perhaps through that copse of beech and willow over there.

Picking her way carefully to avoid a patch of nettles, she almost stumbled into a swiftly flowing stream. She was about to soak her handkerchief when she realized that the narrow stream widened beyond the copse, joining the broad expanse of the river.

Slowly Edith straightened up, gazing at the landscape on the far side of the river. Rolling lawns, shrubberies, flower beds, and a gazebo led the eye from the riverbank to the great house beyond. *Willowford!* The stout garden walls kept out the world on all sides except for this stretch of the river.

She smiled grimly. Did they really think that expanse of gently flowing water would keep out intruders? Why, she could probably wade across at the narrowest point. Certainly she could swim, if necessary.

As she watched, a small boy came running from the house, pursued by a flustered young woman wearing a white apron and mobcap. She was calling to him, "Colin! Come back, you naughty little boy."

The drumming in Edith's head suddenly became deafening. She blinked, swaying drunkenly on her feet, as a searing wave of white-hot rage rushed through her, possessing her completely.

The child—a dark-haired, fair-skinned boy with long legs,

who moved almost too gracefully for a boy—had skidded to a stop on the opposite bank. She could see his face clearly now—the pure gray eyes, with no trace of blue or green, the high forehead, the cheeky cleft in the chin, the nose, those cheekbones!

She knew beyond a shadow of doubt that she was looking at Royce's son. He was a perfect miniature of his father.

Edith stuffed her fist into her mouth to keep from shrieking her pain and rage for all the world to hear.

❦ Thirty-two ❧

LADY ALICIA KINGSLEY, fully recovered from her illness, returned to Willowford to find the house again running smoothly under the direction of Jane Weatherly.

The matriarch of the Kingsley family took a refreshing bath and a nap and then summoned her son to the solarium to inquire about Jane's position in the household.

The French windows were open to take advantage of balmy breezes bearing the scent of roses. Sunlight filtering through the elms outside formed a golden path connecting them to the garden, and perhaps for the first time since he and Roald had so blithely set off to war Blair felt a small measure of contentment. He hoped his mother's reaction to Jane's presence was not going to shatter that seedling sense of peace.

"Is Jane our housekeeper?" she asked. "Or Colin's nanny?"

"Well, yes . . . and no," Blair answered. "Mother, I'm not sure I can explain properly."

"Why don't you try, dear?"

He studied her expression, trying not to be too obvious about it, attempting to determine whether she intended to continue treating him like a helpless invalid—her only response to him since he returned from the Somme.

"I was sinking, Mother. After Claudia left I honestly didn't know which way to turn. I was in the grip of a terrible lethargy. And . . . well, Jane jolted me out of it."

"Aren't you giving her more credit than is due, dear? I'm so proud of how you've taken over and put us back on an even keel." His mother had come from a long line of seafarers, her father having held a senior position at the Admiralty, and she still sprinkled her conversation liberally with nautical terms. She went on, "Why, when I stopped off to visit friends in London you were the talk of the town. Everyone marveled at how you'd taken over the helm and pulled the business up out of the doldrums and how clever it was of you to find out that the young solicitor was embezzling from us. Why, I—"

"Mother," Blair interrupted, "will you please listen to me? I couldn't have done any of it without Jane's help. I couldn't go on if she weren't here."

"What . . . are you trying to tell me, Blair?"

He hesitated. "I'd hoped not to have this conversation with you right away. I'd much prefer that you spend some time in Jane's company and get to know her better."

The expression on his mother's face at this suggestion, Blair decided, would have stopped a clock. Casting about desperately for a way to delay the inevitable, he asked, "Could you simply accept for now that Jane is indispensable, to me and to Colin, and let it go at that?"

Alicia cleared her throat. "Darling, you do realize that you are rather susceptible to . . . I mean, well, you must have been devastated when Claudia ran off, although frankly I feel you're better off without her. Now, please don't misunderstand. I think Jane Weatherly is a fine young woman. But we must keep in mind that her father was stable master at Rathbourne Abbey, and her brother was a chauffeur there. . . . She isn't of our class, Blair. You will remember that, and ignore any romantic overtures she makes?"

He made a small unintelligible sound. "I think it's interesting that you point out what you perceive to be Jane's shortcomings while ignoring the fact that as a married man I'm the one who should be aware of propriety in my association with her."

His mother flushed, and he pressed his advantage. "Not to

mention that any man as monstrously disfigured as I am surely wouldn't presume to expect an attractive young woman to —as you put it—make romantic overtures."

"Darling, with Claudia out of the picture you will be besieged by eager young women. Are you forgetting? You are master of Willowford, head of a publishing empire."

Blair gave a short laugh. "Perhaps I should further define that for you, Mother. I'm behind with the taxes, and the house needs extensive repairs. Nothing was done for the four years of the war. On the surface—mainly thanks to Jane—everything looks fine. But there are no foundations beneath us, either here at Willowford or in our business. They rotted away due to the war and neglect. I shall have to suspend publication of the magazines shortly, and at the paper we're barely keeping our heads above water." Damn, he was beginning to sound like her.

Alicia's gaze drifted away. "Can you smell the roses? They're really lovely this year, despite the fact that the gardeners didn't prune them properly last autumn." She fingered a jet button on her black gown and added vaguely, "I really should go and see if my maid has finished unpacking my trunk. Then I'd like some tea. Will you join me, dear?"

He sighed. "Yes, of course, Mother."

As he opened the door for her, she whispered, "All I ask is that you don't make the same mistake twice. The Claudia liaison was a dreadful mistake; to become involved with Jane Weatherly would be an even greater error because she's so clever, whereas Claudia was merely conniving."

Jane was well aware that Lady Kingsley took great pains to treat her like a favored employee, with the same privileges wealthy families usually bestowed on governesses, but firmly drew the line at accepting her as a family friend. In discussing the situation with Penny Tandy, Jane confessed that she'd had to bite her tongue more than once when facing the lady of the manor.

"Why do you stay, Jane?" Penny asked bluntly. "From what I can see, all the benefits go to the Kingsleys. I can't for the life of me see what you're getting out of the arrangement."

They had met at a tea shop in Upper Oakleigh, as Penny had

come to Percy's district to take care of some business for him. Jane poured milk into her tea and answered, "I know I should be moving on, thinking about the future, but I love being with Colin, and . . . well, he needs me."

"What about Blair?" Penny asked shrewdly. "He needs you, too, doesn't he? Come on, Jane, bare your soul. You love both of them."

Jane sighed and sipped her tea.

Penny leaned forward. "You're going to be hurt, Jane. I can feel it in my bones. Now that the old lady is back, why don't you come to London with me? I know Percy could find you a good position. He says you're the most intelligent woman he's ever met." Penny grimaced. " 'Course, he doesn't know what a fool you are when it comes to love."

"Tell me about *your* love life, Penny," Jane said pointedly.

Penny's eyes twinkled. "I'm still mad about the little man."

A week later Jane was delighted to receive an invitation to the wedding of Penelope Tandy and Percival Reginald Templeton, MP.

On that same day Frank Allegro called. As it happened, Jane was in the study when the telephone rang, and it was she who picked it up. Recognizing his voice immediately, she said, "Frank! How are you? *Where* are you? I wondered what had happened to you. I thought you intended to stay in England after the war ended."

"I did stay for a couple of weeks, but then I got word from New York that Baron was ill, so I went home. But I'm back over here now. I'm calling from London."

The usual lilt was missing from his voice. "Something's wrong, Frank. Are you all right?"

"I'm okay. Baron had leukemia, Jane. He died a month ago. It's hell how much I miss him."

"Oh, Frank, I'm so sorry. Why didn't you let us know?"

"Marrick knew. He came to see Baron a few days before he died and stayed for the funeral."

"He didn't let us know. I would have written at least."

There was a moment's pause. "Is Claudia there?"

"Marrick didn't tell you? Claudia . . . left. We don't know where she is."

Jane heard a muttered curse on the other end of the line.

"But you know who she's with, I'm sure." Jane didn't respond. He asked, "Forgive my curiosity, but what are you doing there?"

"Helping to take care of Colin, Claudia's son."

"She didn't take the kid with her?" There was revulsion in his voice.

"She left word that she would send for him as soon as she's settled. Frank, I can't discuss this with you, especially on the phone."

"That's okay, Jane. I get the picture. I'll be visiting Marrick at the abbey one of these days. I'll see you then."

Jane was putting on her hat when she became aware of the scrutiny of a pair of wide gray eyes. Colin peered around the doorway of her room, his expression worried.

"Hello, there!" Jane said, smiling. "I thought you were with your grandmother."

"Grandmuvver sleeping now." He wrung his hands in a gesture of helplessness. "Jane not go 'way! Please! Colin be good boy."

"Oh, Colin, sweetheart!" Jane immediately bent to put her arms around the little boy. "I'm not leaving for good, honestly. I'm going to visit a friend for a couple of days. I'll be back on Monday. That's just two bedtimes away."

But his unbelieving eyes filled with tears. Jane felt her own throat constrict. Damn Claudia for her heartlessness. Naturally Colin lived in fear that he would again be abandoned. Hadn't his grandfather vanished? Then his grandmother had disappeared for months, and a succession of nannies had come and gone. His beloved father now spent more time in London than at home. But the most shattering blow of all was his mother's defection. There had not been a single word from Claudia.

Gently brushing a tear from the child's silken cheek, Jane said brightly, "Your grandmother is here now, and you have a wonderful new nanny. They'll take good care of you, and I'll be back before you can blink an eye."

His little fingers burrowed into hers, gripping with surprising tenacity. "Take Colin, too."

"I can't, my darling. You see, I'm going to a wedding. My friend is getting married, and it's an event just for grown-ups.

Tell you what, how would you like me to bring you a piece of wedding cake? You can put it under your pillow when you go to bed and make a wish."

He was momentarily distracted. "Make crumbs."

Jane chuckled. "We'll put it in a paper bag, but in any case, most wedding cakes I've encountered are encased in icing as hard as iron, and there's so much fruit in the cake they don't fall into crumbs too easily."

Colin listened intently, frowning in concentration, trying to understand.

"Come on," Jane said, standing up. "You can walk downstairs with me and we'll find your grandmother."

They found Alicia in the library, interviewing a new parlormaid. When Jane attempted to explain that the little boy was feeling lonely, Alicia was obviously annoyed. "Can't you see that I'm busy? Take Colin to his nanny."

Although she was running late and her train would probably leave without her, Jane accompanied the child back upstairs. She turned him over to his nanny with the promise that she'd telephone before he went to bed that evening.

She was lucky: The train arrived at Upper Oakleigh late, and she reached the station in time. As she journeyed toward London she worried about how attached Colin was becoming to her, especially since she had immediately sensed Lady Kingsley's hostility toward her. The key to the situation, of course, was Blair. Would he stand up to his mother?

As the train entered the outskirts of the city Jane's spirits lifted. It was such a happy occasion, the wedding of Penny and Percy—she stifled a giggle; they sounded like a music hall act. Not only that, but the three of them had jointly managed to persuade Blair to stay in town and attend. He had been grateful for Percy's help with his father's will. For the first time, she and Blair would be away from the responsibilities of Willowford—and together.

The brief wedding ceremony was conducted at the Registry Office, as Percy wanted to keep the event as quiet as possible. He was still worried about taking a young bride. Penny looked radiant in a pale pink dress and matching jacket. She carried a small bunch of violets and lilies of the valley. Percy, in his usual business suit, looked proudly shy. Only a few guests went to the Registry Office, and Blair was not among them.

A reception had been arranged at a West End hotel, and Jane found the banquet room so packed with well-wishers that it was not until the breakfast was served that she found Blair, who was seated next to her. As usual, he looked ill at ease.

"Why didn't you come for the ceremony?" Jane whispered as she took her place at the table.

"I was afraid the press might be there, although I took care not to mention it to our own reporters." Seeing Jane's blank expression, he added, "I didn't think any wedding photos should be blighted by having my gargoyle of a face among the guests."

"Oh, Blair!" Had Percy's best man not risen to propose a toast at that precise moment, Jane would again have chastised Blair for his obsession with his scarred face. It almost seemed that he deliberately called attention to his disfigurement. Although Jane loved him as much as ever, she found herself becoming increasingly impatient with his self-pitying attitude.

When the meal ended and everyone began to drift from the table to the dance floor, Jane found herself surrounded by former ambulance drivers and nurses she had known during the war. By the time she had exchanged reminiscences of Penny's daredevil driving and legendary mechanical skills, Blair had disappeared.

The music had begun and couples were dancing. Penny had changed into a short fringed dress and a beaded headband and was trying to drag her reticent bridegroom onto the floor. Jane made excuses to several unattached male guests who asked her to dance and went in search of Blair.

She found him hiding in an alcove, hunched down on a high-backed chair. He gave her an apologetic look. "I shouldn't have come. I don't belong at social events. To tell you the truth, I came only because I wanted to see you away from Willowford."

"Then let's leave," Jane suggested. "It's a lovely evening. We could go for a stroll in the park."

"Can we do that? Leave now, I mean."

"Of course. We stayed for the wedding breakfast and all the

toasts. Our social obligations are finished. Besides, Penny will probably dance until dawn."

"On her wedding night?" Blair asked incredulously.

Jane laughed. "*Especially* on her wedding night." Even as she spoke, Penny's bawdy laugh rang out somewhere on the dance floor. Penny loved parties, loved to dance, and Jane knew that Percy was no eager bridegroom impatient to consummate his marriage to a virgin bride. In fact Penny had confided that she'd kept him in bed all morning to keep him from succumbing to pre-wedding jitters. "Come on, we'll slip out the side door, so we don't start a general exodus."

Still basking in the romance and excitement of the wedding, Jane was scarcely aware that she had slipped her arm through Blair's as they walked across the street to the park. She breathed deeply of the balmy summer air and smiled happily as the moon rose above the tree tops.

Blair stopped suddenly. "Listen!"

Somewhere in the distance a nightingale had begun his sad, sweet song. Spellbound, they fell silent in order to savor the sound.

Jane moved closer to Blair and, still caught in a romantic haze, embraced him. His arm went around her, pulling her close and she wrapped her arms around him, only momentarily aware of his empty right sleeve. She laid her head on his shoulder and felt the drumming of her heart.

"Jane," he whispered, "you are very dear to me."

"I've cared for you since we were children, Blair, you must know that." Her voice trembled with the love she felt for this man. "These past weeks have been the happiest of my life. I wish I could stay with you and Colin forever."

"Do you mean it?" There was urgency in his tone now. "Oh, do you really mean it?"

"Yes," she breathed. Their mouths were almost touching.

"I want you to stay, Jane, very much."

Her lips brushed his and she felt the warm rush of his breath as he kissed her lightly, tentatively, almost apologetically. Puzzled by his reticence, since she had made the first overture, she tried to press her mouth closer. But he drew back and she realized that he was self-conscious about his reconstructed lips. Having been a nurse, she was aware of the many painful operations, including skin grafts, he had endured as the surgeons rebuilt his mouth and jaw, and it broke her heart that he should be afraid to kiss her for fear of disgusting her.

Jane placed her hands on either side of his face, pulled him close, and kissed his mouth with all the pent-up ardor of the years she had loved him, needed him, wanted him. In that moment he was transformed in her mind into the young god he had once been, handsome, perfect. That was how she would always see him, but how could she convince him of that without drawing attention to his scars?

She became aware that he was not responding. Slowly she disengaged her mouth, although she stayed close to him. "Blair . . ."

"Jane, bless you," he said, his voice ragged with emotion. "You've just given me a gift more priceless than you know. But you don't have to kiss me out of pity."

"Oh, my God, Blair, how can you think that? It isn't pity I feel for you. I love you. I've loved you for a long time."

He drew a deep breath. "I hadn't dared to hope . . . But, Jane, we must talk about the future. There's so much to be settled. I feel in all conscience I must confess to Claudia that I deceived her. I must let her know she is not my wife. Yet how do I do that when I don't know where she is?"

"I've been thinking about that," Jane answered. Sensing his discomfort at the pressure of her fingers on his face, she dropped her hands to his shoulders. "You're in the newspaper business, Blair. You must know the name of every leading paper in the country. Couldn't you place one of those adverts . . . you know, the 'Come home, all is forgiven' type?"

"Yes . . . of course. Why didn't I think of that?"

A park policeman strolled by and murmured, " 'Evening."

Embarrassed, Blair stepped away from her. "Jane, could we go back to the hotel? I . . . I feel the need to shut out the rest of the world and be truly alone with you."

"Let's *run*!" Jane exclaimed and seized his hand.

Laughing, they ran back to the park gates, darted around the diminishing pedestrian traffic on the street, and covered the distance to their hotel in record time.

Breathless, Blair approached the desk to pick up his key. As the night clerk handed it to him he also gave him a folded sheet of hotel notepaper. "There was a telephone call for you, sir. I took a message."

Jane whispered, "Don't open it. The paper can get along without you for one evening, surely."

But Blair was already reading the note. His gaze met Jane's, and even before he spoke she could see that the hope burning brightly was not for her, not for a life they might have made together.

He said slowly, "It's from Marrick. Claudia is at the abbey."

❦ Thirty-three ❧

USING THE HOTEL DESK telephone, Blair called the railway station to inquire if there would be a northbound midnight train that would stop at Upper Oakleigh. There was a pause; then he said into the mouthpiece, "No, I don't think we'll need sleepers. Would you reserve two seats in first class for us, please?"

Jane said quickly, "I think you should go alone, Blair. I'll take a train in the morning."

He avoided looking at her. She squeezed his arm gently. "This is between the two of you. Good night. I'll see you sometime tomorrow afternoon."

As she walked unsteadily across the lobby she heard him cancel the second seat and wondered, with a desolate sense of loss, if he had even noticed that she was no longer with him.

She didn't sleep that night. She was tormented by the memory of holding him, kissing him, feeling free at last to tell him all that was in her heart. How close they had drawn together, not just this evening but during all of these past weeks. Blair was beginning to care for her, she was sure of it, but gentleman that he was, he couldn't declare his love until he had ended his masquerade as Claudia's husband.

If only Claudia had stayed away a little longer, long enough for Blair to send word to her that she was a widow, not a wife. But she was back, and what would that mean to Blair? It wasn't hard for Jane to understand why Claudia had gone to Rathbourne Abbey rather than to her own home. She hadn't wanted to face Alicia at Willowford.

Would Blair go home before going to the abbey? Would he take Colin with him? Perhaps, Jane thought, it would have been better if she'd traveled with Blair on the midnight train. The child needed to be protected from any drama Claudia might bring with her.

Jane rose before dawn and arrived at the station long before the first train was due to leave for Upper Oakleigh.

She arrived at Willowford just after noon. Colin was sitting on the terrace steps, watching the driveway. He ran to her and flung himself into her arms before she had paid the taxi driver. "Auntie Jane! Mummy was on the phone. Grandmuvver says we can't see her, and Daddy not stay with Colin."

"Mummy is at the abbey, Colin. She's not far away. I'm sure Daddy will take you to see her soon." She took the little boy by the hand. "Come on, let's go and talk to your grandmother."

Alicia sat behind the desk in her late husband's study, a frail, shrunken figure clad in somber black and almost engulfed by the enormous leather chair. Red-rimmed eyes looked dully at Jane as she entered the room.

There was a moment's silence, and then Alicia said, "I worried that he was getting too fond of you, Jane. We always worry about the wrong things. Have you ever noticed that?"

"Yes," Jane answered quietly. "Is Blair at the abbey?"

"He came to see Colin for a few minutes after breakfast, then went back."

"Why didn't he take Colin with him?"

"All I know is that Claudia has returned and we're immediately thrown into a turmoil. Blair asked me to keep the child here for the time being. He said he needed time to discuss the situation with Claudia."

Colin's small hand gripped Jane's more tightly. She stifled

the unpleasant thought that perhaps Blair was using Claudia's son as a bargaining tool. "But Colin knows his mother is back. I think it's cruel to keep them apart. I'll take him there myself."

"Do you think that's wise? Apparently Claudia is ill."

"Unless she has some highly contagious disease, which I doubt, then yes, I do think he should see her. Come on, Colin, let's go and wash your face and put on your jacket."

They were shown into the library at the abbey and were joined almost immediately by Marrick and a uniformed nurse.

Marrick gave Jane one of his penetrating stares as he introduced the nurse and then instructed her to take the boy to his mother's room.

When they were alone Jane asked, "How ill is she? Is it her heart?"

Marrick made a derisive sound. "She looked healthy enough when she arrived. I believe she's suffering from an attack of guilty conscience for all the heartbreak she's caused. Taking to her bed is a ploy to escape retribution."

"But the nurse . . . ?"

"Blair sent for her early this morning."

"He's with her now, I suppose?"

Marrick looked at her sharply. "What did you expect?"

"I don't understand your question."

"Oh, yes, you do. Well, never mind. Have you had lunch?" She shook her head.

"Neither have I. Come on. We'll have a bite to eat while you're waiting your turn to pay homage to the enchanted princess."

"I'd rather do without, if you're going to be sarcastic and overbearing."

"Then I'll endeavor to restrain myself." He gestured for her to precede him through the door.

As they made their way to the dining room, Jane could not help noticing the difference between Willowford and the abbey. Marrick's fine old house gleamed with a patina of expensive care; nothing at Rathbourne Abbey had been allowed to decay or crumble.

The dining room shutters were open, and the sunlight

spilling into the room found not a trace of dust on the handsomely carved furniture or a faded spot on the priceless tapestries. The carpet had no tread paths. The table was already set for lunch, and there were two places.

Fresh garden salad and cold chicken were served on delicate china, a light white wine was poured into cut-crystal glasses, the bread had been baked less than an hour earlier. Despite her anxiety, Jane found she was ravenously hungry and fell upon the food with more enthusiasm than she intended.

When a footman arrived with tea in a silver pot and a delectable array of petits fours Jane looked up to meet Marrick's amused dark eyes. "What a pleasure it is to see a woman enjoy her food." There was no sarcasm in his tone.

Jane slid a silver server under a tiny chocolate-iced cake and transferred it to her plate. "I didn't have time to eat breakfast before I left London. How did you know we were there, by the way?"

"I phoned Willowford shortly after Claudia arrived. Lady Kingsley told me you and her son were spending the weekend in town. She made it sound almost as though you and Blair had run off together."

"Percy Templeton helped Blair settle his father's estate, and Penny is a dear friend of mine. We went to their wedding."

"No need to explain to me."

"Please . . . tell me what's going on with Claudia. Is she back for good?"

He shrugged. "There's no such thing as 'for good' with Claudia. Let's just say she's back for now and giving a fair performance at being repentant, contrite, and eager to resume her former position as Kingsley's wife."

Jane laid down her cake fork, her appetite vanishing. She stared morosely at her plate.

Marrick leaned forward. "The man she ran off with, Jane . . . who was he? No, don't pretend you don't know."

"Does it matter now? He obviously abandoned her or she wouldn't have come back."

"*Who was it?*"

"My brother, Royce."

"Ah, now I begin to understand your own feelings of guilt and responsibility. But you must realize that even if you had not brought Royce into her life, Claudia would have found some other conscienceless cad to treat her badly. It's in her nature."

Jane rose to her feet. "I need some fresh air. Do you mind if I go for a walk on the grounds?"

"By all means. May I accompany you?"

"If you wish."

They didn't speak as Jane set a brisk pace across the lawns, through the rose garden, circling the stable yard. At length, slightly out of breath, she stopped and looked back at the abbey.

From where they stood the tower and parapet walk were etched against the sky, darkly forbidding. The flagged courtyard below looked like a gray river spanned by a tall bridge.

At her side Marrick followed the direction of her gaze and said dryly, "When I first heard that story about the lovesick nun flinging herself into the arms of her lover and killing both of them, I was skeptical. Oh, I didn't doubt that some foolish young couple had attempted such a feat, only that the fall would actually have killed them both. If he hadn't caught her and she'd struck the ground she could have been badly hurt, but—"

Jane wheeled around to face him, her eyes blazing. "Stop it! Just shut up! I don't want to hear your morbid theories. I don't care about some long-ago nun, I don't care about your damn monstrosity of a house. It's a relic of another age and so are you."

She was screaming like a fishwife, tears streaming down her cheeks, her clenched fists raised. Before she knew what was happening, Marrick grabbed her and pulled her into his arms, holding her so tightly she could hardly breathe.

"You little fool," he said softly as she stopped struggling. "He isn't worth this much anguish. Can't you see that he'll never be free of Claudia? All she'll ever have to do is to snap her fingers and he'll crawl back to her like a whipped dog licking the boot of the master who kicked him. For your own sanity, Jane, give up on both of them."

Pulling free of his embrace, she brushed her fist across her eyes. "I'm sorry. I don't know what came over me. You've been kind to me and I had no right to be so rude to you."

A hint of a smile curved the corners of his mouth, and she couldn't tell if it expressed irony or sadness. He shrugged. "But you're quite right. The abbey and I *are* relics."

"I didn't mean—"

"Oh, yes you did. Before we go back to the house, there's something I want to ask you. I assume you won't be staying at Willowford under the circumstances?"

She shook her head.

"If you don't have anything better to do, I'd like to offer you a position."

"I don't think—"

"Please, hear me out. I'm not going to ask you to be a watchdog again. I need to have the abbey library cataloged. It's quite a task and will probably take several weeks. The job is yours if you want it. You'd have a breathing spell before deciding on your future, and I'd be relieved of the anxiety inherent in the hiring of a stranger."

Jane chewed her lower lip thoughtfully. "I do need a job and a place to stay. But I don't need charity. If you're creating this position just to accommodate me . . ."

"Not at all. In addition to the library, I shall need an inventory of the paintings and tapestries and various other items. You see, I'm considering disposing of Rathbourne Abbey, lock, stock, and barrel."

She turned to look at him. It seemed unthinkable that the abbey would continue to exist without Lord Marrick. In her mind one was an extension of the other.

"But . . . why? I mean, why would you give up your home? It isn't because . . ." She broke off, cheeks flaming. How could she even imagine he'd make a spur-of-the-moment decision based on her taunts?

"It seems the proper time, that's all. I spend very little time here, after all. Once I thought I was the custodian of Claudia's inheritance, but now . . . well, Claudia and I had a long talk last night. It seems she has always hated the abbey and would never live here."

After clearing her throat, Jane asked, "When would you want me to start?"

"The Kingsleys will be returning to Willowford today. I

suggest you go over and pick up your things and come back right away."

"I . . . hope it will work out, between Claudia and Blair. For Colin's sake. He's suffered so much."

A mask came down over Marrick's face. "He's your nephew, of course. I knew from the start he wasn't a Kingsley. Poor little chap, he'll need a stalwart aunt to help him deal with the rest of his family. Shall we go back to the house? I expect you'll also want to tell Claudia and Blair of your decision."

As they walked back toward the abbey it occurred to Jane that once again Marrick had come to her rescue, giving her a graceful way to extricate herself from a difficult situation.

Blair and Colin were waiting for them when they entered the house. Blair, despite his obvious fatigue, looked happier than Jane had seen him since his return from the war. The little boy was dancing with joy. Seeing Jane, he burst out, "Mummy's coming home with us, Jane."

Jane ruffled the child's soft dark hair absently, her eyes fixed on Blair. "Yes, I know, dear. You and Daddy must be very happy."

Blair said awkwardly, "Perhaps we could talk later, Jane? Claudia is eager to see you. She asks that you go right up."

She nodded, knowing—as undoubtedly he did—that they would not talk later. There was nothing to be said. She bent to take Colin's hands in hers. "I shall be staying here at the abbey for a time, Colin. But I want you to ask your nanny to phone me if you need me for anything. Will you remember that?"

The little boy's face fell. "No! Jane come home, too!"

Blair said, "Yes, of course. I'm sure Claudia—"

"Lord Marrick has offered me a job cataloging his library, and I've taken it. I'll explain to Claudia." She blinked, shutting out the relief on Blair's face and the bright glint of tears in Colin's eyes, and ran up the stairs.

Claudia was in bed. She looked relaxed and, as Marrick had said, perfectly healthy. She wore a lacy shell-pink bed jacket, which was open to reveal a white satin nightgown. Her hair was a pale halo around her exquisite features. Jane would not have been surprised to see gossamer wings protruding from Claudia's narrow shoulders. She gave a radiant smile as Jane entered the room. "Dear Jane! I'm so glad to see you."

Jane didn't approach the bed. She stood several feet away, feeling like a lackey in the presence of the princess. An angry coil of hurt and resentment twisted her insides, but it was mostly directed at herself and her own weakness, and at Blair. Finding fault with Claudia for behaving in character was akin to blaming the wind for blowing.

At length Jane said, "You don't look very ill, Claudia."

"I'm feeling much better now."

"Since you managed to persuade Blair to forgive you and take you back, you mean?"

Claudia's smile faded. "Please don't be cross with me."

"Just answer one question, Claudia—no, I'm not going to ask you where you've been or with whom; I can use my imagination about that. But tell me—and be honest, please—do you really and truly intend to be a good wife to Blair and a good mother to Colin?"

Tears shone brightly in Claudia's eyes. "Of course I do! How could you ask such a thing?"

"All right. I'll say no more. I'm going back to Willowford to pick up my things. I've accepted another position."

"Oh, please don't go! I want to show you how grateful I am to you for taking care of Blair and Colin for me. You're a true friend."

Jane looked away quickly, her conscience stabbing her. Hadn't she tried to steal Blair's affections in Claudia's absence? Not exactly the action of a true friend. "I have to work for a living, you know."

Claudia sighed. "Where will you be working?"

"Here at the abbey. Cataloging the library. Apparently Marrick is considering selling. Didn't he tell you?"

The sunlight shifted suddenly as the curtains on the open window fluttered in an errant breeze. Jane was momentarily blinded, but she had the distinct impression that a greedy gleam had flickered in Claudia's violet eyes at the news of the possible sale of the estate.

Claudia's voice was a contented purr. "Then you'll be close by. I'm so glad."

❧ Thirty-four ❧

THE BEDROOM was in complete darkness. Claudia gritted her teeth and tried to conjure up a vision of Royce. If only it were her beloved who was easing himself into bed with her.

A sob caught in her throat, and Blair, mistaking the sound for the anticipation of passion, whispered, "Ah, Claudia, I love you so much. I'm the happiest man alive. These past days have been a dream come true."

He pressed his mouth to hers, and for an instant she fought the urge to scream her distaste. But she forced herself to relax and ignore the stump where his arm should have been, and the feel of granulated skin rubbing against her face. Sometimes his false teeth shifted horribly as he attempted to kiss her. Having to submit to the lust of a man she didn't love would have been bad enough, but lying in an intimate embrace with this ruined shell of a man was a nightmare.

Since their return to Willowford Blair had been like a raving idiot, dragging her off to their room at every opportunity and keeping her up all night with his obscene demands. As if he expected to make up for all of her previous neglect instantly. Or was it, she wondered, that he didn't expect her to stay?

Claudia squeezed her eyes tightly shut, despite the fact that the room was dark, as Blair wrapped his arm around her and pulled her on top of him. That arm was so strong, as though the strength of his entire body were concentrated in it. Sometimes she had nightmares in which his disembodied arm arose out of the darkness like a blind serpent that searched for her.

Tears scalded her eyes. She felt cold, so cold! But she willed herself not to shiver for fear of precipitating further indignities. She lay very, very still and hoped it would soon be over. Think of something else, she told herself. Think of Royce.

At last Blair climaxed. He murmured to her of his love and devotion, but she wasn't listening. She whispered impatiently, "Darling . . . I hate to bring this up now, but . . ."

"What is it, my dearest? Tell me, please."

"Well . . . I ran up some awful debts while I was gone, and my allowance just won't cover them. I hate to owe people. . . . I was wondering . . ."

"Tell me how much you need, and you shall have it."

"There's something else, Blair. I want to tell you about Rathbourne Abbey. You see, it's really mine. Marrick admitted that much to me long ago. I need your help in claiming my inheritance."

"Anything at all . . . I'm your slave, Claudia. You know that."

Was he listening to her? His voice was still thick with passion. He pressed kisses to her hair, forehead, and eyelids as he spoke. "Ah, my dearest darling, these past days have been heaven for me. Are you happy, too? Please tell me you are."

"Yes, I'm happy, too." She stroked his chest absently, as though petting an anxious spaniel. "I'm . . . I'm mad about you, Blair. Why . . . I don't even notice what the war did to you anymore. You certainly . . . didn't lose any of your manly vigor, my darling."

A long sigh of contentment slipped away from him.

Claudia tried to ease away from him, but he held her fast as he became aroused again.

Oh, Royce, please, please, come back for me soon.

Jane waited in vain for an invitation to visit the Kingsleys, but none came. It was as if she had never been a part of their lives. Claudia had come home, and they needed no one else. Jane threw herself into the task of cataloging Marrick's vast library and tried to ignore the hurt, which became easier to bear as the days slipped by.

Marrick often dropped in while she was working, and their association gradually returned to what it had been during their time together in France during the war. Jane didn't try to analyze it too deeply; she was simply aware that a friendly camaraderie had developed and they were at ease with each other.

As midsummer approached, the grounds of the abbey acquired the lush growth of the season. Mellow sunshine dappled the ancient walls, and the rose garden bloomed in all its glory. How peaceful it was, how serene. Jane felt a contentment in her surroundings that helped compensate in a small measure for her sadness about the loss of her personal relationships. It seemed that not only were Colin and Blair gone from her life, but so, too, were her closest women friends, Claudia and Penny. Penny was so busy with her husband and his work that she rarely had time for Jane, who occasionally wondered if she didn't miss Claudia and Penny even more than she missed Blair.

Almost unconsciously, and without realizing he was filling the void, Jane drew closer to Marrick.

Frequently he invited her to have lunch or dinner with him, and he had not departed on any of his mysterious trips abroad since her arrival, so that when he told her he was expecting a visitor and would not see much of her for a few days, she felt slighted, although she knew it was not her place to be included in his social life. She hoped fervently the visitor would not prove to be Magdalena de Mora.

Jane was taking an early-evening walk through the grounds, wondering, not for the first time, how Marrick could bear to give up all this beauty, when a big black Daimler pulled up in front of the house. Since she was out of sight, hidden from view by an arch of rambling roses that led to the rose garden, she stopped to observe the arrival.

The man who emerged from the car had light blond hair, held himself rigidly erect, and marched rather than walked. Jane recognized him instantly: Karl Bruner, who had visited Marrick so long ago, just before the war.

Jane was shocked. Why, Bruner was the enemy . . . or had been, not so long ago. What was he doing here? All the old suspicions about Marrick's loyalties and wartime activities flared again briefly, but she quickly extinguished them. She had grown to like Marrick too much to believe ill of him.

The following day as Jane was at work in the library she noticed that two volumes of a set of works by an obscure nine-teenth-century author were missing. At the same time she recalled seeing two leather-bound books on a table in the portrait gallery.

Marrick had probably been reading them and put them there to return to the library. Feeling the need to stretch her cramped muscles, she decided to go and get the missing volumes.

She heard Marrick and Bruner talking as she approached the study on her way to the gallery, and she quickened her pace. Long ago she'd overheard a conversation between those two concerning Marrick's intentions toward Claudia, and Jane regretted that inadvertent eavesdropping. But before she could make good her escape, the study door opened.

Marrick appeared, but as he was looking back over his shoulder he didn't see her. "Damn it, Karl. I've told you that I've had enough. I'm getting too bloody old for cloak-and-dagger activities. Tell them I'm not available. Tell them to get some other fool to do their dirty work. I've done my share."

Behind him Bruner said something in German. Marrick answered in English. "I'm still a patriot. I served my country well, and you know it. I'm simply tired of dealing with . . ." He broke off as he caught sight of Jane.

His eyes narrowed. "Do you need something, Jane?"

"I . . . thought I saw a couple of books in the portrait gallery. Excuse me." She flew past him.

She spent the remainder of the day thinking about that revealing snatch of conversation. Marrick had been a spy—surely his reference to cloak-and-dagger work could not mean anything else. That explained his long absences and his reluctance to join the Flying Corps. But he had joined up eventually—in the eleventh hour of the war—and undoubtedly had done so to facilitate his clandestine work for the Germans. Now it became clear how he had managed to escape from behind enemy lines in one of their own aircraft. Why hadn't anyone suspected that he was a German spy? How had he managed to get away with it?

Jane was too angry to work. She paced about the library trying to decide what to do. The war was over, but that didn't alter the fact that Marrick was a traitor and should be punished for his crimes. How many had died because of the intelligence he had gathered? She would have to tell someone. He would have to be brought to justice. Still she paced and seethed and took no action, although several times she reached for the telephone.

Late that night Jane was forced to admit to herself that another feeling was overriding her anger at Marrick's perfidy—overwhelming disappointment. She had admired him so! How could she have felt any warmth toward a man who had betrayed his country? Why, a traitor had no morals whatsoever; he was the lowest creature that slithered through the slime. Probably he was now planning to return to Germany. That was undoubtedly the reason he intended to sell the estate.

She wavered back and forth, wanting him punished, wanting it not to be true.

Early the following morning, long before the servants began to stir, Jane rose and left the house. She walked all the way to the village to use the post office telephone. She called Percy Templeton and asked if she could see him immediately, then bought a ticket to London. Before departing on the first train, she called Marrick's butler and told him she was taking a day off.

Percy Templeton looked older, more tired. He ushered her into his office, shuffling with a weary step. But that fierce determination still blazed in his eyes.

"Thank you for seeing me right away, Percy," Jane said.

"You made the matter sound extremely urgent. What is it, Jane?"

She told him of the conversation she'd overheard and of Karl Bruner's visit to the abbey just before the war started. She reminded him of Marrick's amazing escape from behind enemy lines, how he'd flown out in a German plane. "He was educated at Heidelberg; he had close German friends. Don't you see, Percy? It all fits."

Percy drummed his fingers on his desktop, pursing his lips in silent concentration. "I'll grant you that it sounds highly suspicious. I'll make some discreet inquiries, see what I can find out. You say the German's name is Karl Bruner?"

Jane nodded.

"I'll check on both of them. Meantime, you should return to the abbey and get on with the cataloging job. Don't say anything to anybody about this. Just go about your business as usual until you hear from me."

"I'll take the next train back. I want to keep an eye on Marrick and Bruner. Will you say hello to Penny for me? How is she, by the way?"

He rolled his eyes. "Far too energetic for an old man, but I'm not complaining. I'd ask you to join us for dinner, but Penny took her mother down to Brighton for the day and I'm not sure how late it will be when they get back."

"That's all right. You weren't expecting me, and I really do want to get back."

Jane returned to the abbey and again immersed herself in her work. Marrick did not put in an appearance, and upon inquiring, she learned that Bruner had departed and Marrick had gone "up north" for a few days. She was glad she would not have to face him, since she felt certain she would not be able to keep from accusing him and possibly flying at him with fingernails and teeth.

A few days later when a maid brought her a sandwich for lunch, she decided it was too beautiful a day to remain indoors.

She walked toward the river, savoring the springy feel of the turf beneath her feet and the sweet, clean scent of a breeze that rustled through the trees. At length she found herself on the grassy bank that had been their favorite spot when she and Claudia were children. How many times they had sat here and confided all their hopes and dreams—yes, and all their fears and dreads—to each other. Was that why Claudia was so important to her? Jane wondered. Was that why she found it impossible to rid herself of a constant nagging concern for her well-being? Was it simply because they had been so close for all those years that in some vicarious way Jane suffered Claudia's woes and enjoyed her pleasures? The thought was too complex, and she relinquished it. Why, she was beginning to analyze herself just as Marrick had attempted to do.

How delicious a cheese and watercress sandwich tasted out here in the fresh air! She was glad she hadn't remained in the library. She had just finished eating when she heard the thunder of hooves on the turf. She shaded her eyes with her hand, and a thrill rippled slowly up her spine.

The rider coming out of the sun surely rode from the

long-ago past. She was transported back to that summer day of 1914 when she and Claudia had sat in that same spot and Bran Kingsley had come galloping over to invite them to the regatta.

The sunlight blazed on his fair hair, forming a golden halo, and although his face was in shadow, the proud way he held his head, the set of his shoulders, the easy way he handled his mount so that he and the horse became one, a fluid flowing of muscle and bone and pure energy . . . "Bran," Jane breathed softly, restored to all his former perfect wholeness.

But when he drew close, she could see that only one hand held the reins; the empty right sleeve of his white shirt was tucked into his belt. He turned his head, revealing the cruel legacy of war. No, not Bran but Blair, who in attempting to live his brother's life as well as his own had become neither of them.

Still, Jane felt her spirits lift at the sight of him. He carried himself with his old easy grace and self-confidence, even a hint of boyish pride. His scars were still there, his arm was missing, he was older, wiser, infinitely sadder, and yet within a matter of days he had been transformed from the beaten shell of a man who had come home from the war into a man with a purpose in life, a reason to live.

Claudia did this for him, Jane thought. Oh, I got him to come out of that dark place he was in and face the world again, but she gilded it with sunlight for him. If I gave him back his humanity, Claudia gave him back his manhood.

The realization should have brought with it a sense of defeat, but Jane felt too much compassion for him not to be glad he had found himself.

"Hello, Jane," he called as he approached. "Hope I'm not disturbing you. The butler told me you were here." He dismounted and stood stroking the silky muzzle of his horse, a chestnut mare with a white star on her forehead. Jane's practiced eye recognized the animal's breeding and, knowing the Willowford stable had long ago been sold, wondered where he had acquired such an expensive mount.

Seeing her eyeing the mare, Blair said, "Isn't she a beauty? Claudia gave her to me . . . as an anniversary gift."

Some hitherto unknown demon answered for Jane. "Oh? The anniversary of her marriage to your brother, you mean?"

He cleared his throat awkwardly. "Jane, I should have came to see you before this, I know. It was unforgivable of me to simply let you walk out after all you've done for us."

"I take it you've come to tell me that you intend to continue the masquerade?"

"I can't give her up, Jane. I love her more than life. I . . . I hoped to make you understand that, in a way, I love you, too. You're a dear friend, and I hope—"

Jane interrupted savagely. "Oh, spare me the balm for my wounded pride! I'm not going to tell Claudia of your deception, or anyone else for that matter. So don't bother buttering me up. It's not necessary."

"I'm quite sincere, Jane. I know you must feel that we used you. You're such a tower of strength that everyone leans on you. We love you and admire you for your strength, for that utter purity of spirit you possess, and we couldn't bear to lose your friendship. Colin adores you, too, you know. Please, could you find it in your heart to forgive us for not being as strong as you are? Don't turn your back on us. All of us—Claudia and Colin and I—want you to be a part of our happiness. Oh, Jane, we're a family at last. I feel as if I've just emerged from a long, dark tunnel. I don't even care anymore that I have only one arm and the face of a gargoyle. The most beautiful woman on earth loves me . . . *me*, Jane . . . not my brother."

"I'm glad for you, Blair." Her voice seemed to be echoing back to her from some deep, unfathomable cavern. She wanted him to leave, to simply go and let the waves of desolation wash over her.

But he had to twist the knife in the wound still further. "Jane, I owe it all to you. That night in London, after the wedding, when we walked in the park and you kissed me on the mouth . . . If it hadn't been for your generous, loving spirit, I would never have had the nerve to take Claudia in my arms and make love to her. And when I did . . . well, we both knew then that the days of heartache were over for us."

Jane was sure her face had congealed into a frozen mask. "I'm happy for all of you, really. I'll be going back to London soon, and I would like to see Colin before I go."

"We'd like you to come to see all of us," Blair replied, "as often as you like. How about dinner tonight?"

"I'm rather busy today," Jane said.

"Tomorrow, then? About eight?"

Jane nodded and he mounted again. She watched him ride away, then walked back to the house, feeling very alone.

As she entered the main hall on her way to the library she met the butler. "Ah, there you are, Miss Weatherly. Did Mr. Kingsley find you all right? There was a telephone call for you, also, but the gentleman didn't have time to hold on while I brought you to the phone."

"Did he say who was calling?"

"Oh, yes, miss. It was Mr. Templeton, the MP. He said he'd be coming to Upper Oakleigh tomorrow to meet with some of his constituents and asks that you meet him at his office. He said he has some rather important news to give you."

❧ Thirty-five ❧

PERCY TEMPLETON, Jane decided, looked positively gray around the gills. She'd have to have a word with Penny and tell her not to run the poor old chap ragged.

As he pulled out a chair for her, however, Jane noticed that in addition to looking incredibly tired, Percy also wore an expression not unlike that of a cat that had caught a gigantic mouse.

Resigned to hearing her worst suspicions about Marrick confirmed, she asked, "You have news about Marrick's wartime activities?"

"Indeed I do. Now, Jane, I pulled several strings to get this information, and I must ask you to keep it strictly confidential."

"I won't breathe a word to anyone. Was he a spy?"

"He was." Percy's cherubic countenance broke into a wide, impish grin. "But not, as you supposed, for the kaiser. He was a British agent."

Jane felt her mouth drop open. "But . . . what about Bruner?"

"You were correct that Lord Marrick formed several close friendships during his undergraduate days, especially at Heidelberg, and that he had kept in touch with them over the years. Karl Bruner was an emissary of the late Archduke Ferdinand, who had planned to bring his wife to visit England just before their assassination. Bruner approached Marrick to ask if they could stay at the abbey, but of course the visit never took place. After they were murdered, Bruner told Marrick he would work for British Intelligence if Marrick would make the contact for him. Further, there were other Germans who had no love of the kaiser and his cronies and who could also be recruited to work for the Allies. Marrick took this information to an old army friend, and although Marrick apparently wanted to join the Flying Corps, he was persuaded that with his contacts he would be more valuable as an agent."

Trying to digest this startling news, Jane was primarily aware of a vast sense of relief. But she also recalled how Marrick had been ostracized for remaining a civilian, even receiving that ultimate symbol of cowardice, a white feather. She felt a wave of shame for doubting him, followed by a surge of intense admiration.

Percy went on, "You must understand there was a great deal of reticence about telling me *anything* about Marrick's wartime activities. I do know that he spent some time in the Middle East. Since Marrick owned a plantation in Africa and was an experienced aviator able to land and take off in difficult terrain, he flew key people to remote desert battlefields."

"But what about this current visit of Bruner? It sounded as though he wanted Marrick to continue spying. But we're no longer at war with Germany."

Percy smiled. "You think governments don't spy on one another in peacetime? Intelligence-gathering goes on all the time, my dear. There are those among us who don't believe we've just won the war to end all wars. They fear the Germans were too badly humiliated by the armistice not to become aggressive at some future time."

"Marrick joined the Flying Corps during the last months of the war," Jane observed thoughtfully. "Do you think that by that time he wanted to declare his true colors to all the people who shunned him for not being in uniform?"

"From what I've heard of Marrick, he doesn't give a damn what people think of him. No, I expect by then he was simply sick and tired of secret operations and wanted to test his flying skills against those of the German aces."

"I heard him tell Bruner he didn't want to go back to cloak-and-dagger work. But you know, Percy, I wonder what he does intend to do after he sells the abbey and its holdings."

Percy's eyes glinted with amusement. "Why don't you ask him? I should think he'd be flattered by your interest."

Jane looked away. "You must think I'm an awful busy-body."

"Not at all. Your interest in Lord Marrick reminds me of my wife's interest in me when we first met, and my own reaction to her interest. I was aware that I enjoyed her company, but I couldn't believe a young, attractive woman would ever regard me as anything but a fatherly mentor. Penny eventually made me see the light."

"But that was a different situation entirely. Please don't misinterpret my asking you about Marrick. I did so only because I suspected he was a traitor."

Percy leaned forward. "No need to rationalize your feelings for him for my benefit. I'm gently trying to point out to you, Jane, that if you care about the man, it might be up to you to make the first move."

Jane was so shocked by his assumption that she was momentarily at a loss for words. Was that what Percy thought? That she was interested in Marrick because she was in love with him? But that was absurd. She loved Blair . . . didn't she? Of course she did. She merely admired Marrick's bravery and self-assurance. He needed no one but himself. But she disliked many of his traits—his arrogance and domineering attitude not least among them. "You've really got the wrong idea about Marrick and me," she said at length.

"Of course," Percy murmured, but his irritating little smile of amused disbelief lingered.

As her taxi drove past the gates of Willowford Jane glanced at her watch. She'd barely have time to change her clothes and hurry over for her dinner engagement. She hoped Colin would still be up. She had missed the little boy so much and was eager to see him again.

She had paid the taxi driver at the entrance to the abbey and was about to climb the long flight of steps leading to the living quarters when a prickly sensation told her that something was amiss.

Turning, she looked toward the tower and its connecting parapet walk. A solitary figure stood halfway between the tower and the house, leaning over the stone balustrade. Claudia! What on earth was she doing up there . . . ?

Jane set off running, driven by a nameless fear, racing into the abbey, up the stairs, and along the endless corridors, wending her way upward to the great studded door that led to the parapet walk.

Her feet seemed leaden, her breath wheezed in her chest, and her heart thudded. She felt as if she were moving in the slow stupor of a dream. Indeed, had she not dreamed this very scene? Only in her dream she had not recognized the person who was about to jump from the parapet walk, and had known only that she would not reach that lonely figure in time.

There was no reason for Claudia to be here, at least none except for that one dread possibility. As Jane struggled to open the heavy door all she could think of was that Claudia had always been fascinated by the story of the nun who flung herself to her death from the parapet walk. Was she despondent because she had again been abandoned by Royce? Jane had no doubt that this had happened, or Claudia would never have returned.

Wrenching open the door, Jane mouthed the words, *Claudia, Claudia, oh, please don't do it*!

A gust of wind caught Jane as she stepped out onto the narrow walk high above the gray ribbon of the paved path that led to the garden. Breathless, she walked unsteadily toward Claudia, who appeared to be mesmerized by the ground below and did not turn to look at her until she was close enough to hear her footsteps. Then she raised her head and, seeing Jane, smiled.

"Oh, Jane, there you are at last! I was afraid you'd decided to stay in town and we'd get a phone call of excuses." She turned her back to the balustrade and leaned against it, the rising wind whipping her pale hair about her face.

"Do . . . be careful." Jane's mouth was so dry her voice was barely audible. "That balustrade is . . . awfully low. You could tumble over."

Claudia glanced downward and said in an unconcerned tone, "The nuns' walk isn't nearly as high up as we imagined it was when we were children, though, is it? Have you noticed that when you grow up everything seems to shrink in some way?"

"That depends on how you look at it. Claudia, what are you doing here? I was planning to come to dinner at Willowford, honestly."

Large blue-violet eyes didn't quite meet her gaze. "Well, that's the reason I came. . . . Jane, would you mind awfully if we postponed our dinner engagement?"

"Of course not. But you could have phoned to cancel. . . . There's more to it, isn't there?"

"I . . . told Blair you weren't feeling well and that I was coming over to spend the evening here at the abbey with you. If he should ever ask . . ."

Jane could hear the wind gusting around the courtyard, sounding like a giant's labored breathing. Or was she hearing her own blood pounding in her ears? "And do you in fact intend to spend the evening with me?"

Claudia looked at her feet. "Well . . . no . . ." She looked up imploringly. "I just need a little time away from them—Blair and Colin. They . . . cling to me. Sometimes I feel I can't breathe, that they're suffocating me."

"You're going to meet Royce, aren't you?"

"No!"

"Don't lie to me, Claudia. I can stand anything but a lie."

"I'm not lying, Jane. I truly want to be alone for just a couple of hours. I shan't leave the abbey. I thought I might go down to the nuns' warming room and just sit quietly by myself for a little while."

Jane scrutinized that lovely face to try to find evidence that would confirm her suspicions. But although Claudia's cheeks were pink and her eyes bright, perhaps that was only because of the wind. "But you were always terrified of the nuns' quarters."

"As I said . . . when one is a child everything seems larger, more threatening. Now I long for the solitude of the quarters."

"Claudia . . . will you swear to me that you won't leave the abbey?"

"Oh, yes! I swear by all that's holy—why, I'd even swear on my ghost mother's grave, if I knew where it was—that I will not leave the abbey tonight until I go home to Willowford."

There was no doubt that she meant it; she looked into Jane's eyes and spoke with such conviction that Jane could not doubt her. Still, Jane could not get rid of a nagging worm of worry. "What about Marrick? Does he know you're here? How will you explain to him this sudden desire to sit alone in the nuns' quarters?"

"He's gone out for the evening. I had afternoon tea with him, and he said he was going to drive out to the aerodrome to look at a new aeroplane he's thinking of buying when he sells the abbey. Did he tell you he has a prospective buyer? I couldn't believe anyone would want this drafty old mausoleum, but apparently some rich foreigner wants to convert it into a hotel. Can you imagine such a thing? Marrick says pretty soon all the stately old homes will be given up, because people can't afford to live in them any longer, what with the taxes and cost of upkeep. So you see, Jane, you were right when you said that the age of the common man is dawning. Soon everyone will live in little houses all shoulder to shoulder with their neighbors. Does that make you glad? I hate the idea; it's like being on an anthill."

"But you still have Willowford," Jane pointed out. "Blair told me he would never give up his ancestral home. So you won't have to worry about finding yourself on an anthill, will you? Come on, let's get off the parapet. It's beginning to give me the creeps, and you're shivering."

"I left my coat inside. I'll put it on before I go down to the quarters."

* * *

Claudia shivered in the dank chill of the nuns' quarters, jumping at every flitting shadow. She cried out as a drifting cobweb brushed across her face and caught her hair.

She called out softly, "Royce? Are you here?"

For answer his arms went around her and he pushed away her hair with his mouth and pressed a warm kiss to the nape of her neck. Claudia turned to face him and threw her arms around his neck. "Oh, my darling, I've missed you so!"

He swung her up into his arms and carried her over to the great urn set upon its stone pedestal, behind which he had already laid a blanket on the floor. As he eased her down onto the blanket he chuckled. "Just like old times, pet. Remember?"

"Darling, I hate this dreadful place. Couldn't we go somewhere else?"

But he was too busy with buttons and hooks to reply. He slipped his hand inside her blouse and fondled her breast, kissed her eyes shut and reached under her skirt to find her trembling need.

She surrendered to his passion, as she always did, powerless to resist that primitive urge to be a part of him, joined so completely that his sensation, his pleasure, became hers. What magic they created! A symphony of erotic delights that rose to an incredible crescendo. She could no longer feel the hard floor under the thin blanket or the cold chill of the air on her bare flesh. She was spiraling upward to mingle with comets that exploded in the black velvet canopy of the heavens.

After they climaxed—simultaneously, as they always did—Royce wrapped the blanket around her and held her. "Now, my love," he said, "let's get down to brass tacks. First of all, you're now looking at second lieutenant Weatherly."

"You got the money, then? You *were* careful about how you cashed the check?"

"Of course I was. But, Claudia, pet, we need a letter of credit and a lot more cash than you sent."

She squirmed uneasily. "I told Blair I'd run up huge debts, but he didn't have any more money available. He said he'd go to London and transfer funds from the business accounts. But he keeps putting it off. Oh, Royce, he's driving me insane! He follows me constantly, and . . . well, he doesn't want to leave me; he wants me to go to London with him. He says he'll have to stay there for several days to take care of business. I don't want to be with him. I want to be with you." She began to shiver again.

"There, there, calm down. I've got a fourteen-day embarkation leave. I'll run up to London and be close by."

"Embarkation . . . you got your orders?"

His teeth flashed in a brilliant smile. "India, love! Just as we hoped. You'll be a memsahib, with a flock of servants at your beck and call."

She nestled closer. "I shan't ever be cold again! I'll never have to spend another winter here. Oh, I can't wait to get away. I can't wait to end the deception and lying. I even lied to Jane. I swore I wasn't going to meet you tonight."

"That's my girl. Don't think of it as lying, pet. Think of it as telling people what they want to hear."

"I wish you'd let me tell her what we're planning to do. She's your sister and my best friend. We have to make her understand we can't live without each other."

"All in good time, sweet. What about Marrick? Did you talk to him about your inheritance?"

"I didn't have to. He's decided to sell the abbey and most of the land that goes with it. He told me that when the sale is complete he intends to place the bulk of the proceeds in a trust for me. He said there would be some conditions, but that I would receive far more than my father turned over to him for my care. Royce, it will be a great deal of money . . . but we can't possibly get any of it before we leave."

He nibbled her ear. "No matter, love. As long as it will come to us. You're sure it will? No matter what? Maybe you should stay close by until it's all settled? To take care of our interests."

"No!" Claudia clung to him. "No, you can't leave me here. I'll die. I swear I'll die if you do."

He kissed away her fears, stroked her body, soothed her in the way only he could. "All right, sweet, let's make our plans. Is your passport up to date? First thing is to get passage booked for you and the boy. We'll find a ship for you in London while your husband is taking care of his business."

"But why can't we sail with you?"

"Now, pet, be sensible! I'll be in the hold of some old rust bucket transporting troops. You and the lad will have a nice stateroom."

"You still haven't met Colin," Claudia said. "I do hope you'll like each other."

" 'Course we will. We're blood-related, aren't we? Come on, sweet, give me a kiss and a bit more comfort before I leave you."

But a strange numbness seemed to be creeping over her. For a second she could neither speak nor move. She lay rigid in his arms, as though turned to stone.

Alarmed, Royce asked, "What's wrong? For Christ's sake, Claudia, what is it? Are you ill?" He shook her slightly, and all the air rushed from her lungs.

She gasped. "I . . . I'm all right. I just had the eeriest feeling . . ."

"Someone walked on your grave?"

"Royce . . . did I ever tell you about my ghost mother?"

❦ Thirty-six ❧

EDITH LEANED on the library counter, oblivious of the nervous boy waiting to hand her his book, her opaque amber-green eyes narrowed in concentration.

Her patient vigilance had at last provided all the answers. The little boy she had seen at Willowford was Colin Kingsley. Ha! Kingsley indeed! She knew better than that, but evidently the Kingsleys didn't. His mother was the former Claudia Abelard of Rathbourne Abbey, who was now married to a hideously maimed man who thought the child was his.

How neatly all the pieces clicked together! Royce had been a chauffeur at the abbey, and Royce had once romanced

Claudia. Only he hadn't told Edith that he'd fathered a child with her. Edith needed no further proof that the boy was Royce's son; he was almost an exact replica of his father.

The postmistress at Upper Oakleigh had proved to be a valuable source of gossip, and Edith had visited the post office frequently, pretending she was expecting a poste restante letter. From the postmistress Edith had learned an interesting tidbit: Claudia had left her husband and son for a time, but had now returned. Rumor had it that she had a fancy man, an army bloke.

So Royce had joined the army, after all. Claudia had apparently run off with him for a time and then returned. No doubt because she needed more cash from the family coffers. So, despite his denials, Royce had gone back to Claudia— more than once—even after the bastard swore to Edith that he wouldn't. That was why she hadn't seen him for so long. No doubt he'd go back to the rich girl again, first chance he got.

The more Edith thought about it, the more convinced she became that either Royce would come to see Claudia or that she would go to him. But she couldn't watch their movements every minute, meeting every arriving train, hanging around Willowford. She needed someone to help her. But who? A Willowford servant? The stationmaster or a railway porter? Even if they saw him, how would they get word to her in time for her to intercept him?

As Edith stamped the library book of the waiting youth, a solution to the problem hit her. She slammed the book down on the counter so hard the kid jumped. She could hardly keep from laughing aloud at her own cleverness. She'd been approaching the problem from the wrong angle. She didn't have to go to Royce—all she had to do was make him come to her.

What more compelling reason to give him than to come and get his son?

Jane was convinced that Marrick would look into her eyes and know instantly that she had been guilty of spying on him. On the morning following Claudia's visit to the abbey, which was also the day after Percy's startling disclosure about Marrick's wartime activities, Jane went down to the kitchen and asked Cook if she might have some tea and toast to take to the library.

"You're not eating in the breakfast room, miss?"

"I'm a little behind with my work," Jane explained. "I'd like to get an early start." In truth, she didn't want to face Marrick with the memory fresh in her mind of her meeting with Percy.

Half an hour later she was seated at the library desk nibbling toast and cataloging the works of eighteenth-century poets when the butler told her there was a telephone call for her. She went out into the hall to the telephone table.

"Jane?" Claudia, who never arose at this early hour, sounded alert and happy. Evidently her solitary meditation had done her good. "Blair and I are taking an early train to London. We're staying for a few days, and . . . well, Colin has been asking for you. He'll be perfectly all right with his grandmother and his nanny while we're away, but . . . would you be an angel and come over and have tea with him this afternoon? He's quite upset that Blair and I are leaving and . . . you will? Oh, bless you. About four? I'll tell his nanny to have him ready."

After replacing the receiver, Jane went back into the library.

Before she began to work again, Marrick arrived. He glanced at her breakfast tray. "Shall we also chain you to the desk?"

"I . . . took some time off yesterday and felt I should make it up." She didn't meet his eye.

"Ah, I feared you were offended by Herr Bruner's presence. We did sign an armistice, you know. He's gone, by the way. As far as your taking time off is concerned, please don't feel you have to make it up. I'm not a slave driver. Take all the time you need. I missed your company at breakfast this morning."

"I . . . er . . . also need some time off this afternoon. I'd really feel better making it up."

"Another visit to your mysterious friend?" He affected a casual attitude, but she knew he was watching her closely. She almost told him that her recent meetings had been with Percy Templeton, but decided the less said about that the better.

"Actually, I'm having tea with Colin. Claudia and Blair are going up to London."

Marrick considered this for a moment and then said, "Why don't you invite him to come here for tea? I believe I have something a small boy might like. It might help to distract him from his parents' departure."

He left without giving her a chance to demur.

Colin's nanny agreed immediately to bring her charge to the abbey when Jane called to inquire, and so at half past three that afternoon she cleared her desk and went to await Colin's arrival in the great Gothic hall through which one entered the living quarters of the abbey.

She sat in one of the carved wooden chairs that lined the walls between niches occupied by terra-cotta statues, now aware that the statues, which were alive with movement, were pure rococo rather than Gothic. It had been impossible to spend time poring over the countless volumes in the library without learning a great deal about Rathbourne Abbey. She had been fascinated to learn that apparently Marrick was only the latest in the succession of crooks, rogues, and adventurers who had owned the abbey over the centuries.

It seemed paradoxical that a convent and church built to house the gentlest of people had become home to so many less than godly men. One former owner had been beheaded for plotting against the Crown; another had made a fortune cheating the Mint by clipping the edges of coins and resmelting the clippings; yet another had supplied mercenaries to various potentates in remote corners of the world, enthusiastically leading his soldiers of fortune into battle. Finally, there was Leith Marrick, whose own catalog of exploits she was only now beginning to uncover. How interesting it would be to spend one's life with such a man, she thought idly, never knowing what new secret about his past one would turn up.

She remembered then, with a pang of regret, that Marrick was about to pass the abbey along to yet another owner. She wondered who it would be and if, when her work here was finished, she would ever see these rooms again.

The doorbell clanged then, and the butler hurried into the hall to respond. He didn't see Jane at first and gave her a startled glance just before he opened the door.

Colin raced ahead of his nanny and smothered Jane with hugs and kisses. Minutes later Marrick arrived, dressed casually in riding breeches, boots, and an open-necked shirt. He suggested to the butler that Colin's nanny might like some refreshments and then turned to Jane and Colin.

"Come on, you two, let's not waste a minute." He ruffled Colin's dark hair. "I have a surprise for you, young man."

Jane felt almost as eager as Colin, who pranced ahead as Marrick led them outside, through the rose garden, then the kitchen garden, in the direction of the stables. She glanced questioningly at Marrick, but he smiled enigmatically and didn't explain.

For Jane it was a journey into her own childhood—the familiar cobblestones of the stable yard underfoot, the distinctive scent of hay and warm animal flesh, the clattering of hooves and the excited barking of the dogs at their approach, sights and sounds and smells that played on her senses, evoking feelings that recalled carefree summer days when, in innocent childhood, the world and all of its people were good and pure and evil was only an imaginary witch in a storybook.

Marrick opened the stable door and gestured for them to enter the first stall. As their eyes became accustomed to the dim light, Colin clapped his hands gleefully and Jane caught her breath in delight.

Nine pairs of soft brown eyes looked up at them. Lying in the hay was Marrick's favorite red setter with eight beautiful puppies. Two of the puppies jumped up to lick Colin; another tugged at his shoelaces. The rest of the litter joined the fray, pulling the little boy down. Colin laughed and rolled in the hay with fat puppies exuberantly crawling all over him.

Jane turned to look at Marrick, who smiled broadly. "Is there any more appealing sight?"

She shook her head. "How old are they?"

"Eight weeks. I thought the lad might like to choose one to take home with him. Every boy should have his own dog."

Colin's head appeared above a squirming sea of red fur. "Oh, can I? Please, may I have one?"

"Perhaps we should ask your mother and father—" Jane began, but the child's lip trembled and Marrick said, "Nonsense. How could they refuse? You pick out your favorite, Colin, and we'll take him with us on our picnic."

"Picnic? I . . . er . . . dressed for afternoon tea," Jane said.

"I thought we might ride over to the meadow on the far side of the woods. Two horses are saddled and ready. The boy can ride with me, and I'll have one of the grooms bring the puppy and the hamper Cook packed for us."

Jane looked down at the simple summer frock she was wearing, but he quickly forestalled her objection. "There are some riding togs waiting for you in the stable master's cottage."

Assuming she would be borrowing riding clothes from the current stable master's wife, she left Colin playing with the puppies and walked to the whitewashed cottage that stood beyond an archway of rambling roses. How long ago it seemed that she had been a schoolgirl, running up the crazy-paving pathway to the front door, calling to her father that she was home. Memories rushed back—her father smoking his pipe in his favorite armchair, Royce sprawled on the sofa plucking at his ukelele.

The stable master's wife was expecting her. She was considerably shorter and plumper than Jane, whose first thought was to hope she had a daughter closer to her size. "The master said you'd be coming, Miss Weatherly. I've laid out your things in the back bedroom."

Jane's old room. Her eyes blurred with tears as she closed the door and stood looking at the marble-topped washstand, the rag rug beside the plain four-poster with its patchwork quilt. The furniture was older, more worn, and the rug and quilt had not been there when the Weatherlys were in residence, but still the years fell away and the child she had been returned. What promise the future had held then! How infinite the possibilities! But never in her wildest imaginings had she foreseen that she would one day form a friendship with the master of Rathbourne Abbey, that she would be standing here about to don riding clothes . . .

As her gaze focused on the clothes spread on the foot of the bed, she was jarred back to the present. Why, they looked brand-new, and they appeared to be her exact size. Picking up a linen shirt, she fingered the material appreciatively. The breeches were tailored to perfection, and she saw a pair of polished riding boots on the floor. She knew before she examined them that they would be her size.

Jane sat down weakly on the bed. There was no doubt now that the items had been purchased specifically for her. Surely Marrick had not gone to so much trouble in order to ride with her? How had he known her sizes?

Something was protruding from the pocket of the shirt. A folded sheet of paper. She recognized Claudia's handwriting.

Dear Jane,

    Just a little gift from Colin (he helped me choose the boots, honestly) to thank you for taking care of him while I was away. We do hope you like them. You used to love to ride in the old days, and now that you're back home we thought you might like to do so again.

Much love,
Colin and Claudia

Jane bit her lip. She had always refused Claudia's expensive gifts. How cunning of her to say this was a present from Colin, which Jane could not possibly refuse.

The clothes fitted perfectly. Jane regarded herself in the dressing table mirror with a pleased smile. Even she had to admit that she cut a fine figure. She almost looked as if she belonged in the company of the lord of the manor.

When she emerged from the cottage and walked across the stable yard, Marrick's gaze was openly admiring, but he made no comment. She went straight to Colin, who held the smallest puppy of the litter in his arms. "Thank you very much for all these wonderful presents, Colin. The boots are so comfortable."

The little boy flushed with pleasure. "Mummy helped me."

Jane kissed his cheek. "I'm very grateful to both of you."

A groom stood nearby, holding the reins of their mounts, and when Marrick was in the saddle the groom lifted Colin up in front of him and took the puppy. "Meet us near the biggest oak in the north meadow," Marrick instructed the groom, who then turned to help Jane.

It had been too long since she'd been in the saddle on a fine horse, feeling the power of the animal, the rush of the wind.

She couldn't resist breaking into a gallop, giving her horse his head. Marrick's pace, of necessity, was slower, since he had Colin and the puppy in front of him. He and the child dismounted in the meadow, but Jane kept going, reluctant to end the ride.

At length she returned to where Marrick sat on the grass beside a picnic hamper. Colin and the puppy played nearby.

"You're an excellent horsewoman, Jane," Marrick remarked.

"I'm out of practice."

"You hate compliments, don't you?"

"I suppose I feel undeserving."

He looked at her shrewdly. "You've always felt eclipsed by Claudia's beauty, haven't you? You shouldn't. Few mortal women are cursed with Claudia's physical beauty. But you have the ultimate gift—true beauty of the mind and soul. I've never known anyone quite as selfless as you, Jane. I must confess that at times I find it irritating. I want to shake you and tell you that it wouldn't hurt for you to take a little, instead of constantly giving."

Jane laughed, in spite of her embarrassment. "I'm taking today, am I not? Lovely clothes from Claudia, time off from you. And I hope there's something good to eat in that hamper. The ride has really given me an appetite."

He opened the wicker hamper and produced two vacuum bottles of tea, one of milk, and a package of sandwiches. Jane helped him spread a checkered cloth on the grass and then unpacked almond tarts and chocolate biscuits. There was even a ham bone, almost as large as the puppy, for the setter to gnaw on while they ate.

Colin, more at ease than Jane had ever seen him, kept up a steady stream of chatter. Marrick, considering he was a childless bachelor, seemed to be able to draw the child out of his shell, and Jane realized after a while that he listened carefully to what the little boy said and commented appropriately, in effect treating the boy with the same courtesy he would have afforded an adult. Little wonder Colin obviously was enjoying himself tremendously.

After they finished their tea, Marrick further surprised them by producing a kite, which they flew over the meadow. There was also a ball hidden in the hamper. The three of them tossed it back and forth, and the puppy chased it, skidding on the grass and falling in an undignified heap, to Colin's great amusement.

At length both the child and the puppy were worn out and flopped, panting, on the grass. As if by magic, the groom appeared to take them home.

Jane reluctantly started to mount her own horse, sorry the afternoon interlude was over, but Marrick said, "Don't go yet, Jane. I want to talk to you. Colin will be safely delivered to his nanny, and she can take him home to Willowford."

They watched the groom ride away, the puppy inside his jacket and Colin in front of him. Jane said, "He had a wonderful time. Thank you. How do you know so much about little boys?"

"Believe it or not," Marrick answered gravely, "I was once a little boy myself."

Jane laughed.

"Do I seem so ancient to you, Jane? Come on, now, answer honestly."

"Only when you remind me of your venerable age, which you do frequently."

"Your friends Percy Templeton and his wife are a May-December couple, aren't they? Are they happy, do you think?"

"Oh, yes," Jane replied.

"So you believe it's possible for two people of different generations to love each other?"

"It depends on the people, of course, but yes, it's possible. Penny and Percy can't be the only exceptions to the rule."

She sighed and lay back on the soft grass, her mood suddenly sweetly sad. Such a lovely afternoon, and yet there was something lacking, something she needed to make it perfect. The mention of Percy and Penny's love affair, perhaps, had brought it on. As the sunlight mellowed to that rich golden glow that signaled the end of the day, Jane yearned for a lover's arms to enfold her. She wanted to make love to a man. In her secret dreams her fantasy lover had always been Bran Kingsley, but she was not thinking of Bran today.

Turning her head, she looked up at Marrick, who sat with one elbow on his knee, absently chewing a blade of grass. His face was in silhouette as he stared across the rolling meadow, now being claimed by soft shadows. Her gaze drifted to his broad shoulders and muscled arms, noted his long legs, the way his torso tapered to narrow waist and hips. He had the body of a young man, and with his face in silhouette the tiny wrinkles around his eyes and the faint creases on his forehead were not visible.

Although she tried to pull her gaze away, she could not. She felt a warmth seeping through her, a melting, yielding languor. For one wildly improbable second she wanted him to turn to her and kiss her as he had once, in France.

As if in response to her thought, he suddenly looked down at her. Disconcerted, she said quickly, "You wanted to talk to me about something?" She sat up, tried to look businesslike.

When he didn't answer for a moment, she babbled on, "I'm sure you want to know how I'm coming along with the work. . . ."

"No, Jane, I really don't. I'm sure, with your usual. efficiency, you'll complete the work in record time. And what shall I do then to keep you nearby?"

She didn't answer for fear of saying the wrong thing. In her heart she wanted this conversation to proceed, to lead them . . . somewhere . . . where? She found it difficult to breathe, and a pulse hammered her temple. To cover her inner turmoil, she made a pretext of replacing the picnic items in the hamper.

Marrick leaned over and caught her wrist to stop her, and the shock of his touch was instant, electric. "Must you forever clear up, tidy up, pick up the debris left by other people? You know, I actually believed you might learn a slightly more hedonistic way of living from young Kingsley. But instead you eagerly put your nose to the grindstone there, too. In fact by your sheer energy and determination you got him going again. You make it very difficult for a man to take care of you, Jane."

She didn't look at him. "If you're telling me that he took Claudia back and let me go because I goaded him into facing his problems, that's unfair."

"Ah, so you did goad him into resuming living?"

Jane wrenched free of his grasp and leapt to her feet.

"Dammit, you're not going to spoil a perfect day by giving me that old lecture about Bran."

"*Bran?*"

"I meant Blair." She ran to her horse and climbed into the saddle, feeling disappointed, deprived. Although she urged her mount forward at a fast canter, Marrick quickly caught up with her.

They rode in silence, circling the far perimeter of the grounds, lost in thought, together, yet separated by an ever-widening chasm of their own making.

As the sun began its descent down the darkening sky, they rode back toward the abbey and, as if by unspoken agreement, dismounted to lead their horses along the riverbank. Across the soft blue sheen of the water, framed by a filigree of willow and beech, they could see the abbey basking in mellow golden light. How beautiful it was, how tranquil.

"Won't you miss all this?" Jane asked softly.

"Yes, I suppose I will have moments of regret. But you see, it was never truly mine. I hoped that one day Claudia would live here and that her children and her children's children would make the abbey their home. Since she's chosen instead to live at Willowford, I shall give her the means to do so."

"You're selling the estate so she can have the money?" Jane blurted out. "But you can't do that! Why, she'll—"

"Fritter away her fortune? Give the money to your brother, who will undoubtedly abscond with it?" Marrick smiled grimly. "I think not. Claudia will not have control of her assets."

The remaining warmth of the afternoon, already tainted by their earlier flare-up, now completely dissipated for Jane. "Do you think it's fair to put her completely under the control of her husband? If you give her inheritance to Blair, she'll—"

"Never be able to leave him?" Marrick finished for her, his voice harsh. "Is that what you want, Jane? For Claudia to run off again so that you can take care of Blair and the boy? Is that what you perceive to be your role in life? For God's sake, woman, wake up! If Claudia were to leave him a hundred times, he'd still love her, he'd still take her back. And what would happen to you? How many times do you think you could stand the heartbreak?"

"You're so wrong, Marrick, so bloody wrong! I would never go back to Blair. Oh, I care about Colin, but I'd never go back to Blair. I don't love him. I'm beginning to wonder if I ever did. The Kingsley twins were the fairy-tale princes of my childhood. They seemed to have been blessed by the gods with everything—looks, money, family. . . . They lived a life I could only imagine. Do you know what I used to long for when I was a child? To live in a house that we *owned*. To have a tiny piece of land that belonged to us, so that we'd never have to move. To have a sense of permanence and tradition and all the things the Kingsleys—and you—took for granted. Only nothing is permanent, is it? Now Willowford is on shaky ground, and I don't see how even Claudia's money can save it, and you're giving up the abbey. There's no such thing as forever, is there? Everything that happens in our lives is just a prelude to what comes next, and what comes to all of us in the end is that we go on to glory, and it doesn't matter whether we're rich or poor, or live in a palace or a stable master's cottage. It only matters how we connect with other people along the way."

She stopped speaking and stared at Marrick, all at once aware that his usual unreadable mask had been replaced by an expression of raw emotion. He seized her by the shoulders and held her, his dark eyes burning into her.

"Do you mean it? That you're at last over your infatuation for Kingsley?"

"Yes, yes!" Her voice was sharp, as she was assailed by a battery of bewildering thoughts and feelings. Somewhere inside her the echo of her earlier yearning made itself heard. How could she have been so blind as to have failed to see that the man she most admired, the man she had grown to love, was the man who was at this minute standing in front of her?

She felt dizzy with the impact of the realization. How many times had he been the rock she had leaned upon? How many gestures, small as well as large, had endeared him to her? She wanted to cry out, I love *you*, Marrick. I've loved you without daring to admit it, even to myself, because there are too many reasons we can never be together. My feelings for you run so deep that even I could not bring them to the surface and see them for what they really are.

His voice softened. "Jane, don't you know how much I care

for you? I want to be with you all the time. I miss you when I don't see you; my world lights up when I do. I've fought my feelings for you ever since you came home from university that summer of 1914. I told myself I was too old for you, that you couldn't budge beyond the class lines you'd drawn between us. But you know, the human heart doesn't recognize the barriers we build. Then there was that brief idyll in France when the barriers were down. Ever since then I've looked for some sign that you might be able to care for me, but I never saw one."

"I thought it was just a nurse-and-patient interlude," Jane said. "I was afraid that if I came to see you after we got home, you'd be embarrassed, that you wouldn't want to be reminded of that time."

He rolled his eyes. "Why do we persist in attempting to read the minds and motives of others? Why do we thwart our desires by pretending we don't care? Ah, Jane, the foolishness of the human heart! You know, I even brought Magdalena back here, although our affair ended years ago, hoping to create some spark of interest in you. I wanted you to see me as an ordinary man, in just as much need of a woman's love as any other. But to you I was the old man who owned the abbey. I imagined you and Claudia giggling about me behind my back, looking upon me as the ogre, the taskmaster. Is it any wonder I hid my feelings for you? I'm old enough to be your father, and I thought I would go to my grave without telling you I love you. But then, this afternoon, for a little while you looked at me in a way that made my blood churn. Jane, tell me it wasn't my imagination. Tell me I'm not making a complete fool of myself telling you all this."

She caught her breath, unable to speak for the waves of love and longing washing over her. As though directed by some inner force she was powerless to control, she stood silently holding the reins of her horse waiting for him to come to her.

He swept her up into his arms and carried her away from the riverbank to a grassy hollow surrounded by willows whose trailing leafy arms created a rustling curtain to conceal them, and there he laid her down.

She looked up into his eyes, all at once feeling shy. "I don't know why I didn't recognize . . . that what I mistook for respect, admiration, envy even . . . had grown into something much, much more. I could love you, Marrick. I think I could love you as much as any woman has ever loved a man."

Their lips met then in a kiss that drove all other thoughts away. Her lips parted, and she eagerly returned his kiss, feeling acute sensory awareness flow through her body. Were those barely audible sounds coming from her? Why could she not keep still?

This was not like the kisses and clumsy caresses of the students with whom she had been briefly infatuated— disappointingly mundane, adolescently selfish, easily forgotten. This was the kiss of a man practiced in the art of lovemaking, mature enough to defer his own pleasure in order to bring a woman to the same peak of desire.

She felt herself melting, drifting toward some dazzling revelation that, although shrouded in mystery, was within her grasp.

He held her tightly at first. Then, feeling her yield, he relaxed his grip and stroked her throat, allowed his hand to drift to her breast and remain there. For a moment his mouth lingered against hers, and then, sensing her surrender, he drew away.

Jane was breathing raggedly, her heart pounding against his.

Raising his head to look at her, he said softly, "I want you desperately, Jane. I'd like to make love to you here and now. But I love you enough to curb my desire and wait until we're man and wife. Will you marry me?"

She was deeply touched. Inexplicably, tears sprang to her eyes. She felt bereft, denied the ultimate bonding, yet grateful to him for his strength and solicitude. She would have given herself to him there and then with no thought for the future, but he had—oh, so tactfully—shown her that there was no hurry, that she would be happier in a traditional union. She was not Magdalena, or even Claudia. She was Jane, who would have acted impulsively this evening and regretted it, perhaps even been ashamed tomorrow. How very astute, how wonderfully caring, he was to recognize that.

"Jane?" he prompted.

"Yes," she whispered. "Yes, I'll marry you."

Her arms crept around his neck, and her eyes closed as their lips met in a kiss that was filled with promise. She gave herself up to the pleasure and comfort of his sheltering arms, feeling a sweet lethargy like slow-flowing honey move along her veins.

They lay entwined, speaking softly of the future, touching tentatively, kissing passionately, but always he kept his passion tethered. "I'd like to take you to Africa," he said. "Will you come?"

"Oh, yes!"

"After we dispose of the abbey we'll be free to travel wherever we please. We'll decide where we want to live, and I'll build you a house."

"You have a definite buyer for the abbey, then?"

"Frank Allegro."

"*Frank*! I can't believe it. He's the last person I'd have expected to buy it."

"He inherited the bulk of Baron's fortune, which was formidable. I'm not sure exactly what his reason is for wanting the abbey, but I suspect it has something to do with Claudia. Perhaps he thinks she'll want to go home someday. He spoke of turning the living quarters into a hotel, which I'm sure would delight the Kingsleys! I can see Alicia now, having a purple fit. But Frank has the experience and knowledge of running hotels in America, and the abbey gobbles up money for taxes and maintenance at a fearful rate, so it probably isn't a bad idea."

"I can't see Frank living here permanently. He's too fond of his beloved New York."

"He wouldn't have to. Transatlantic crossings are becoming so rapid, and before long there'll be regular flights to New York. He'll be able to divide his time between his American hotels and the abbey."

"Still, I feel a little sad for him if he's doing this to be near Claudia. She doesn't care for him."

He kissed the tip of her nose lightly. "Let's be selfish for now, shall we, and rejoice in our own happiness? Ah, Jane, how can I express my joy and pride in you, my delight and amazement that you will be my wife."

When twilight brought deepening shadows and a cool evening breeze he rose and took her hand to pull her to her feet. "Come on. Let's go back to the house and make plans."

They rode back to the abbey, and as they entered the stable yard a groom came running toward them.

"Lord Marrick, sir, they've been looking for you all over. You're wanted at the house right away, sir."

Jane had to run to keep up with Marrick's long stride. A cold knot of dread formed in her throat. *Please, don't let Claudia spoil things for us, not now when everything is going so well.*

The butler stood in the hall, and when he spoke it seemed to Jane his voice was grinding like tumbrels. "It's young master Colin Kingsley, sir. They called from Willowford. It seems he and his nanny didn't return after their outing with you today. They sent a servant to look for them, and she found a setter puppy playing with the child's cap on the lane between Willowford and the abbey."

❧ Thirty-seven ❧

"HE CAN'T BE far away," Marrick said. "There hasn't been time to take him far. The police will throw a cordon around the area and check every train and bus; they'll stop every car."

"I should have stayed with him," Jane said, the sharp edge of fear in her voice.

"His nanny was with him. She's a local girl, with excellent references. Jane, stop looking for a way to blame yourself. Probably the whole thing is some sort of misunderstanding on the part of the nanny and they'll turn up any minute."

"I can't stay here doing nothing. I'm going to search for him myself."

She turned to leave, but Marrick caught her by the arm. "Wait a minute. There's something else we have to consider. Do you think his father has him?"

"Royce? No. He's in the army. How could he care for a little boy?"

"Perhaps he simply wanted to meet his son and intercepted them between here and Willowford."

"Royce hasn't shown any interest in seeing him up until now, has he? Oh, God, I keep imagining what Colin's going through, how terrified he must be. He's so little!" She pulled free and ran for the door.

Before she opened it Marrick was at her side. "You won't cover much ground on foot. Come on, we'll take one of the cars."

They spent almost the entire night searching, but when the dawn broke there was still no sign of the child or his nanny.

Marrick and Jane pulled up in front of the abbey and sat for a moment in silent exhaustion. Then Marrick said, "There have been cases where nannies became excessively attached to their charges, even to the point of running off with them. Try not to worry, Jane. I'm sure the police will have some news for us soon."

Jane had never felt so helpless, so paralyzed with fear and yet unable to do anything to alleviate it. She buried her face in her hands and wept.

So far, so good, Edith thought, settling back into the taxi seat and kicking off her shoes. Things weren't going as she'd originally planned, but maybe this was even better. Royce's bastard sat shivering with terror between her and the nanny.

"I should've gone and got him a change of clothes," the nanny said. "And I don't like the idea of leaving the puppy on the road like that; he could get run over."

"We had to leave right away, Gladys. There wasn't a minute to lose. Somebody will find the puppy later and we'll buy new clothes for the boy in town," Edith said. "I told you, his mother is very ill and we've got to get him to her as fast as we can. You don't think we'd take a taxi all the way to London if it wasn't an emergency, do you?"

Gladys didn't look convinced. A country girl of no more than seventeen, she was kind and loving, but in Edith's opinion, a bit on the dim-witted side. Gladys slipped her arm around the boy and pulled him close to her side.

She was probably having second thoughts about going off with a stranger, Edith decided, but it was too late for that now.

Everything had fallen neatly into place. The postmistress's remark that Blair and Claudia Kingsley had gone up to London had sent Edith hurrying out to Willowford, intending to slip across the river, get into the house, and grab the child. They'd be on a bus to Beddington before anybody missed him, and from there they could hop a train to London.

But she had to pass the abbey gates on the way and it was then she saw the nanny and her charge walking up the driveway, undoubtedly going to visit Claudia's guardian. Edith could scarcely believe her good luck. All she had to do was to wait for them to come out and intercept them on the usually deserted lane on their way home to Willowford.

She raced back to the village and hired a taxi. She had the driver wait halfway between Willowford and the abbey. The two great estates were pie-slice shaped, coming together where a curving lane bordered by a high hawthorn hedge wound between the two entry gates.

When Gladys and the boy reappeared, Edith told them Claudia had been taken ill and they must go to London right away. She added that she had been sent by Mr. Kingsley and that Lady Kingsley had already left in their private car to be at her daughter-in-law's side. Gladys was still trying to grasp the situation when Edith pushed her and the boy into the taxi.

Now as they sped through the rapidly advancing evening shadows Edith had two problems to solve. First, she had no idea where in London Claudia and her husband were staying. Since she'd have to get a message to Royce via Claudia, this information was crucial. Not only that, but she'd ordered the driver to go to the city, and any minute now he'd be asking for a specific address. Added to that, Edith's meager funds would not run to long-distance taxi fare.

The gray wig she was wearing was a little tight, and she surreptitiously tugged it into place, then made a pretense of rummaging in her handbag. "Oh, good heavens, I seem to have misplaced Mr. Kingsley's London address, and that's where you're supposed to go, Gladys, while I take the boy to the hospital. Let's see, now, which hotel were they staying at?"

In the diminishing light she saw Gladys give her a puzzled

look. "They weren't at a hotel, mum. They always go to the town house."

"Oh, that must be the address they gave me. I'm from the hospital, you see. In an emergency like this everybody gets a bit muddled up, don't they, dear?"

Gladys nodded, reassured by Edith's self-deprecating tone.

"Now this is what we're going to do," Edith continued. "The taxi driver will drop me and the boy off at the hospital and take you on to Mr. Kingsley's place. Better give him the address now."

As the nanny leaned forward to speak to the driver, Edith's forefinger moved to Colin's brow and her pointed nail traced a sharp path to his ear. He stared at her with wide, terrified eyes. Edith gave him a sly smile. She would have liked to strangle the little bastard, but she needed him alive and well. At least for the time being.

She made a mental note of the Kingsleys' London address and decided on a suitable hospital where Claudia was supposed to be. When the driver dropped her and the kid off at the hospital she would tell him Mr. Kingsley would pay his bill when he delivered the nanny to their house.

Edith sighed contentedly, well pleased with herself. She couldn't wait to see Royce. Wouldn't he be surprised at her changed appearance! These past weeks of waiting had given her time to slim down. If he liked scrawny women like Claudia Kingsley, then that's what he'd get. When Edith divested herself of the loose old-lady clothes she was wearing, removed the gray wig and donned a blond one (Claudia was fair-haired, wasn't she?), why, she'd look like Claudia's sister.

❧ Thirty-eight ❧

CLAUDIA AWAKENED to hear Blair's voice, sounding agitated, speaking to someone downstairs in the hall. She slipped on her dressing gown and went to the top of the stairs.

Colin's nanny cowered near the vestibule door, her face crumpling into tears. Blair was reaching for the telephone. Claudia stumbled down the stairs. "What is it? What happened? Something happened to Colin! Oh, dear God! What? *What*?"

Gladys whimpered, "She said you were very ill in hospital, ma'am. She said she was taking Colin to see you."

"Who said? Who took Colin?" Claudia grabbed the girl's shoulders and shook her.

Behind her, Blair spoke to someone on the telephone. "Will you please make a thorough search? The boy has dark hair and light gray eyes. He's not quite three years old. Gladys, what was he wearing? What did the woman look like?"

"C-Colin had on n-navy shorts and a white shirt and a little Fair Isle p-pullover," Gladys stammered through her sobs. "The woman was older, on the plump side, with gray hair and thick glasses. She was wearing a b-black two-piece costume."

Claudia clutched her throat. "Are you saying my son was . . . *kidnapped*?"

She slid to the floor in a dead faint.

The sedative the doctor had given her made her feel as though she were floating in a viscous cloud, groping her way toward dimly seen people surrounding her. She struggled to understand what the earnest-faced policeman was saying to her.

"Do you understand, Mrs. Kingsley? This may be the

woman who has your son. Agree to anything she wants, but tell her you must be assured that the boy is all right. Try to keep her on the phone as long as you can."

Something cold and hard was placed in Claudia's hand, and she realized she was supposed to speak to someone on the telephone.

"This . . . is Mrs. Kingsley." The words seemed to rumble slowly from a deep pit within her.

"*Claudia* Kingsley?" an unfamiliar female voice asked.

"Yes. Do you have my son? Is he all right? Please . . . don't harm him."

"You tell his Dad to come for him."

"Yes, yes, of course my husband will come—"

"Not your husband, Claudia. The kid's father."

Claudia's hand remained frozen to the telephone receiver, but she could not speak.

"You still there?" the woman's voice hissed.

"Y-yes. Who—who are you?"

A sound something like a snort crackled over the wire. "Use your imagination, ducks. Now listen, you get a message to the kid's father to meet me in the usual place tomorrow night at ten."

"Will you let me speak to my son—"

But the line had gone dead.

Claudia leaned back weakly, the phone slipping from her hand. A babble of voices broke out around her. Blair's hand clasped her shoulder reassuringly, and he bent close to her ear to whisper, "Do you know how to reach him?"

Claudia nodded. "How . . . how did you . . . ?"

"I was close enough to hear what she said. Claudia, we can't keep any secrets now. We must tell the police everything."

Royce was furious. "How the hell could you have let this happen?"

"I told you," Claudia said, "she somehow found out that Colin was your son and went to Willowford and persuaded his nanny to bring him to London. Then they vanished. Please, darling, there's no time for explanations or recriminations. You must go and get Colin back. You have to be there in less than an hour. I've been trying to get hold of you all day . . . but the hotel said you hadn't arrived yet, and I knew your leave had started so I didn't call the barracks. Royce, I've been out of my mind with worry. Do you know where she wants you to meet her? Can you be there in time?"

"Dammit, I don't want to see Edith—not tonight or ever."

A chill crept along Claudia's veins. She clutched the back of a chair to steady herself, the hotel room slowly revolving before her blurred vision. The effects of the sedative had not completely worn off. She had a nagging headache, and her stomach was upset. Somehow Royce did not cut quite his usual dashing figure. How could he not be frantic with worry? How could he think of himself at such a time?

"Please, Royce, we have to get Colin back. Nothing else matters. You must go to her at once."

He shrugged. "It'll only take me ten minutes to get to Euston Station. What did you find out about your inheritance? Marrick sell the abbey yet? Did your husband give you any cash?"

Claudia decided he must be thinking about ransom money, since any other possibility was too horrible to consider. She replied, "Both Blair and Leith have said they will put up the ransom money, but as to how long it will take to get it, that will depend on how much she asks for."

Hysteria gripped her again, and she fought to control it. "Try to persuade her to accept a reasonable amount, Royce. We can't leave our son with a woman like that for another minute."

He gave her a speculative look. "She won't have the kid with her, you know. She wouldn't take him to a public place. Knowing her and how crafty she is, she'll be watching to see if I'm alone before she shows herself, so don't get any ideas about having the police follow me."

"She's an escaped felon, Royce, who is now also guilty of kidnapping. . . . We must do everything possible to put her back behind bars. But we can't risk our son's life. . . . Oh, I don't know what to do. The police do want to follow you. I'm supposed to let them know where you're going."

He frowned. "So the police and your husband and the whole damn world know about us now, do they?"

Claudia bit her lip. "We have to get Colin away from her. I couldn't worry about anything else."

"What did he say—your husband?"

"That we must get Colin back unharmed and nothing else is important," Claudia whispered, her answer barely audible. "Blair loves me; he'll forgive me for deceiving him. And he loves Colin, too. He's been a father to him since the day he was born." *More of a father than you have ever been.* She lowered her eyes, afraid he would see the accusation there. "Please go now, Royce. I'm afraid you'll miss her. I'll stay here. You can call and let me know how much she wants, and I'll bring the money to you. Oh, do please try to get her to release Colin to you!"

Royce buttoned his uniform jacket. "Don't call the police. Let somebody else catch her. You don't know Edith. If we put her back in prison we've no guarantee she'll stay there. She escaped once, don't forget. We'd have to look over our shoulders all our lives. Swear to me, Claudia, that there'll be no policemen breathing down my neck."

She said stiffly, "I promise not to tell the police where you're going. But they might be watching for you to leave the hotel and follow you anyway."

"I'll slip out through the kitchen. Stay by the phone and I'll give you a ring as soon as I can."

He kissed her, but for once she felt no response. His lips might have belonged to an impudent stranger.

Claudia left the room only seconds after he did. She ran down the hall and tapped lightly on the last door. It was opened instantly. "You swear you won't tell the police?"

"Have I ever broken my word to you?"

"No." Claudia drew a deep breath. "He just left—for Euston Station."

"Go back to your room and wait. Try to remain calm."

Marrick reached out and touched her cheek lightly with one finger. "Don't worry. I've had a great deal of experience in subterfuge. I spent three of the four war years engaging in it."

Royce paced nervously under the clock at Euston Station. It was nearly a quarter past ten. Damn stupid idea to meet here. Could Edith have meant somewhere else? No. This was where they always met in the old days if they got separated for some reason.

A pair of young tarts strolled by and gave him inviting smiles. He wasn't in the mood to respond. An old man wearing plus fours and a battered felt hunting hat sat on a formidable stack of luggage nearby, and a station employee in a dark blue uniform and peaked cap was polishing a ticket window in a lackadaisical fashion.

Someone tapped Royce on the arm and he jumped. He looked down at a grinning newspaper boy. "Paper, mister?"

"No, I don't want—" he broke off as he looked down at the paper the boy was offering. Handwritten above the front-page headline were the words "Taxi at gate."

He grabbed the paper, thrust a coin into the boy's hand, and raced out of the station.

The door of the waiting cab opened before he reached it, and the second he was inside it moved swiftly out into traffic. He turned to look at the blond woman wearing a green dress. For a split second he didn't recognize her. Then she gave him a sultry smile that didn't quite reach her eyes, and he suppressed a shiver.

"Hello, Edie. What the hell have you done with the kid and what makes you think he's mine?"

Marrick tossed the railway porter's cap on the seat beside him as he pressed the accelerator to the floor and steered around a lumbering charabanc bus to catch up with the taxi Royce Weatherly had just entered.

Framed by the taxi's rear window, he could see Royce and a blond woman. They appeared to be arguing. Still, Marrick wasn't yet convinced that Weatherly was not an accessory to the kidnapping.

They passed Marble Arch, made several unnecessary turns, wandered around Westminster for a while. The woman looked back frequently, but Marrick's borrowed Morris did not appear to worry her. Eventually the taxi set off on a direct route that led to a modest hotel near Piccadilly Circus.

Marrick parked the Morris two blocks away and remained inside the car as Royce and the woman left the taxi and went into the hotel. As soon as they were out of sight he put on the porter's cap again, picked up a leather valise, and followed.

The reception clerk looked up as he approached the desk and, seeing his uniform, gave him a disdainful stare.

" 'Scuse me, guv," Marrick said in his best Cockney accent, "the lady wot just arrived—she left 'er bag behind." He waved the valise. "Wot's 'er room number?"

"Leave the bag here," the clerk said. "I'll see she gets it."

"Oh, nah you don't. I'll give it to 'er meself and get the reward, ta very much. Didn't I follow 'er all the way from the ruddy station wiv it?" He leaned over the counter, his expression ferociously indignant.

The diminutive clerk backed away nervously. "Very well. She's in room two-oh-three. But you'll have to use the stairs; the lift isn't working."

Marrick took the stairs two at a time.

The door marked 203 opened easily when he slipped his penknife into the lock. He pushed open the door.

He saw Colin immediately; he was gagged and tied to the bed. Royce was bending over the child, speaking to him. The blond woman stood in the middle of the room watching, and she spun around as Marrick burst into the room.

Ignoring Royce, Marrick dived for the woman, grabbing her arms and pinning them behind her back. She struggled violently and was stronger than he expected. She almost wrenched free before he subdued her.

Keeping her face down on the floor with his knee in her back, Marrick reached into his pocket and pulled out a pair of handcuffs. He snapped them on the woman.

She shrieked, "Bash him, Royce! Knock him out!"

Marrick fixed Royce with an unblinking stare. "You'd better think carefully before you do anything foolish."

Weatherly remained frozen. He looked from the woman on the floor to Marrick.

Marrick snapped, "Remove the child's gag, for God's sake, and untie him. Then call the police."

His former chauffeur avoided looking at the woman and remained oblivious to her shrill barrage of curses as he pulled the gag from the boy's mouth. Marrick said quietly, "It's all right, Colin. You're going home to your mother and father now. Don't be afraid. It's all over."

Colin nodded. When Royce untied him, the little boy crawled to Marrick's side and clung to him.

❧ Thirty-nine ❧

MARRICK RAN up the abbey steps in a state of high anticipation. He was minutes away from sweeping Jane into his arms again and oh, how he longed to hold her! He didn't care that he was behaving like a schoolboy. He was in love with a woman and wanted the whole world to know she returned his love. He was also not averse to having Jane heap praise upon him for bringing little Colin safely home. Ah, life was very, very good!

"Where is Miss Weatherly?" He handed the butler his coat and valise.

"She's in the rose garden, milord, but I believe you should know—"

"Whatever it is, it can wait."

Jane was standing in the middle of the rose garden, and he slowed his pace in order to catch his breath and savor the sight of her. The clear morning sunlight burnished her hair, finding golden glints among the mahogany waves, and a slight breeze blew her simple cotton frock back against her womanly curves. As he watched, she bent to inhale the fragrance of one of the blossoms, and he was tempted to compare her loveliness to that of the rose. But a rose's beauty concealed thorns. Jane, he decided, was a heather-covered hillside, or a grassy meadow— simple, natural, unspoiled, with no hidden hazard. He felt his heart swell with love for her.

Claudia would have called Jane from London to tell her that Colin was safe, that her brother had apparently returned to his regiment, and, not least, that Edith Weatherly was back in custody. When Jane turned and saw him, her lovely gray eyes would light up with gratitude and admiration and he'd feel like a hero.

As he started toward her he didn't see the errant rose bramble that trailed across his path, and it slashed his forearm, drawing blood. He wiped away the red streak as Jane looked up and saw him approaching.

There was no gratitude or gladness in her expression. Her large gray eyes were haunted, dark circles under them testifying to a night without sleep. She seemed to recoil at the sight of him.

His eager pace faltered. Surely she must have heard that Colin was safe? As he drew near he could see that her face was tear-streaked. She didn't move toward him. He stopped, feeling an invisible barricade go up between them. "Jane . . . what is it? What's wrong?"

"Percy . . ." she said, her voice cracking. She cleared her throat. "Percy Templeton. Penny phoned early this morning."

"Something happened to him?"

"A sudden heart attack. He died in Penny's arms. . . . Oh, God, Marrick, they were making love!"

Marrick stifled his first impulse, which was to rush to her side to hold her and comfort her, because she had folded her arms across her chest in a gesture clearly intended to keep him at bay.

"I'm very sorry, Jane." He paused, not wanting to comment on the circumstances of the MP's death, puzzled that Jane was so shattered by the news. He would have expected her to be saddened, to feel grief at the loss of a friend and sympathy for Penny, but Jane wore the look of one whose whole world had come to an end. He added lamely, "You'll want to go to Penny, of course. I'll drive you up to London."

"No," Jane said quickly. "Thank you, but I'll take the train. I'd rather be on my own." She bit her lip, staring at him with eyes that filled with tears again. "Marrick . . . I won't be coming back."

"I see."

He didn't see, of course. He needed answers to questions he couldn't ask: What has this to do with us? Why have you changed your mind about marrying me? Was it something I did, or didn't do, or just that you decided we're wrong for each other?

"I've almost completed the library catalog," Jane went on. "You won't have any trouble finishing it up. I've packed my things. I'll take the twelve o'clock train. I've ordered a taxi."

Marrick forced himself to speak. "Jane, could we sit down and talk before you go storming out of my life forever?"

She turned her head slightly, so that their eyes no longer met. "I'm sorry. I . . . just don't think that we . . . that you and I . . ."

"Don't you think you're feeling a little emotional just now, and perhaps this isn't the time to make sweeping decisions?"

"Please don't let's drag this out. It's difficult enough as it is. I've thought it over carefully. A quick break will be painful, but if we delay, it will be worse, because we'll have to tear apart."

Perplexed, he took a step closer to her. "That doesn't sound like a change of heart, Jane. It sounds more like an intellectual decision. Sensible Jane wanting to do what's best and right and proper instead of following her heart for once. What are you afraid of? What's this all about?"

"Let's just say that I was swept away for a moment, and so were you. Don't make me say things I'll regret later. Just accept that I'm leaving, and I don't think we should see each other again. It would be a mistake for us to marry. When you have time to think about it, you'll see what I mean."

"You sound as if you rehearsed that speech. Jane, perhaps this isn't the time to discuss any of this. Why not go and spend some time with Penny and then we'll talk."

"No. I want to end it now, before it's really begun."

He studied a perfect tea rose on a nearby bush. "You know, the members of certain primitive tribes mutilate themselves when someone close to them dies. But Percy Templeton was not really that close to you, so I'm bewildered that his death seems to have precipitated this panicked need in you to run away from me."

"It hasn't anything to do with Percy. I just . . . did a lot of thinking about us and decided we were both carried away and didn't really stop to consider exactly what we were doing."

"If you leave now," he said slowly, "we'll never have a

chance to find out if it could have worked out. You know, Jane, we always think our opportunities will be unlimited, that if we carelessly pass this one by, there will be plenty of others. But life—fate—isn't that accommodating. Sometimes we don't recognize the landmark moments that come along when, if we fail to seize the opportunity, it will never present itself again."

Jane raised her head to look at him. "Good-bye, Marrick. I'm so glad you returned Colin to his mother. Please don't be too hard on Claudia." She turned and ran from him.

He didn't follow. For several minutes he remained among the roses, noting a patch of powdery mildew on one and several rose hips on another. He would have to get after the gardeners to do some serious pruning before he turned the abbey over to Frank Allegro, who was a former denizen of a stone and concrete world and would know little about flower gardens.

A summer rain threatened to drench the army of mourners who came to the cemetery to pay their last respects to Percy Templeton.

Jane stood behind Penny and her mother, who huddled together before the flower-bedecked coffin and cast occasional anxious glances toward the storm clouds rapidly darkening the sky.

As the minister began to speak, his opening words were lost in a long rumble of thunder, and the heavens opened. Raindrops the size of florins fell, crushing the delicate flowers, splashing onto faces already damp with tears.

Penny's mother unfurled an umbrella, and they disappeared under it. Several other mourners also had umbrellas. Some ran for the long line of waiting cars and carriages as lightning ripped the sky and thunder exploded overhead. A few, including Jane, remained standing while the minister hastily concluded the service.

Percy would have loved the sheer drama of his funeral, Jane thought, and he would have been surprised by the number of people who had jammed the tiny church and spilled out into the street to follow his hearse, despite the inclement weather.

She hadn't yet had an opportunity to speak with Penny

alone, as Penny had been busy arranging the funeral. But her grief was obvious. It was evident in her quick, nervous movements, in her swollen eyes, in the hollow echoes of her voice, and above all in her pain-racked expression. Jane realized that Penny kept going at a frenetic pace so that she would not have time to dwell on her loss, but ultimately she'd have to slow down and face it, and what would happen to her then?

Jane drove Percy's old car in the funeral recession, with two of Penny's friends wedged in beside her and the rain slashing in through the open sides. By the time they reached Penny's mews house they were drenched to the skin. They joined the somber line of mourners moving into the cheerful living room where a fire blazed in the grate and Penny and her mother rushed around serving port wine and sandwiches and seed cake.

Penny paused long enough to whisper in Jane's ear. "Percy's relatives will be leaving today. I'll have a room for you tonight, so don't go back to the hotel. We'll get your things tomorrow. Go on up to my room and find some dry clothes."

Long after midnight Jane and Penny sprawled on the hearthrug before the dying embers of the fire, drinking the last of the port.

"Are we getting maudlin?" Penny asked.

"No," Jane answered. "But we might be getting a little tipsy."

"You haven't said I told you so. I appreciate that."

"Why would I say that to you?"

"Because you warned me what might happen if I married a man so much older than me."

Jane was silent.

Penny jabbed her with a sharp fingernail. "Don't fall asleep. I don't want to be alone tonight."

"I'm not asleep. I was . . . thinking about May-December romances."

"Mine or yours?"

Jane turned to look into Penny's red-rimmed eyes. "Oh, Penny." She sighed deeply. "I told Marrick it was over before I left the abbey. I'm not going back."

"Why, for God's sake?"

"Because I love him too much to . . . I love him too much."

"Why, you silly goose, you're afraid he'll drop dead on you

like Percy did to me. But Marrick isn't Percy. S'truth, my Percy was years older than Marrick in the first place, and in the second he wasn't in such good health, and he drove himself unmercifully. He had a bad heart; the doctor warned him not to work such long hours, not to take on so many of other people's burdens. Percy wouldn't listen. He said there was too much to do and too little time to do it. That people were starving and living in misery and out of work or working sixteen-hour days under conditions that were dangerous and appalling, and poor little children spent every hour God sent working in factories and mills, and there was just too bloody much of a gap between the rich and the poor in this country."

Out of breath, Penny paused. She drained her wineglass, and when she spoke again it was with the exaggerated dignity of one becoming aware of the effect of the wine. "Anyway . . . why don't you go and use the phone in Percy's study to give Marrick a ring and tell him you didn't mean it?"

"But I did mean it, Penny. Oh, I'll admit it frightened me to realize that if I married him he'd undoubtedly die before I do. But there's more to it than that. When Royce's wife kidnapped Colin, I knew there was no hope for Marrick and me. I'm Royce's sister, and I'm the one who brought Royce and Claudia together. I never told you, but I saw Edith in Upper Oakleigh when you and Percy and I were working on his campaign. I should have done something then—told the police, found Royce and made him do something. But I didn't. If anything had happened to Colin, I couldn't have lived with myself."

"For pity's sake, Jane, you're the giddy limit, you really are. You can't be responsible for Royce and Edith—or Claudia, for that matter. It doesn't make sense for you to punish yourself—and Marrick—for something that wasn't your fault."

"Perhaps it was the fact that Colin was kidnapped by Edith and then, right on top of that, Percy dropped dead. . . . Oh, forgive me, Penny, I didn't mean to sound so insensitive. I've had too much wine. But anyway, it just seemed that all the signs were telling me that I should leave Marrick before I bring any more tragedy to two families."

"You'll think better of it when everything calms down again, and it will. Ever since I've known you, Marrick has been the most important man in your life, although you were too busy feeling sorry for the Kingsley twins to realize it. What are you going to do in the meantime?"

"What I should have done ages ago. I'll get a job. What about you, Penny? You won't curl up in this house and spend all your time grieving, will you? You need to keep busy, you know."

Penny leaned forward and seized Jane's hands. "The morning after Percy died, before the news was out, a woman phoned to ask for his help. Her husband had been horribly injured at a factory where he worked, and the owner refused to pay for the doctor and hospital. An hour later there was another call—an old man being evicted from a house he thought he owned."

In the firelight her eyes had a fierce gleam that reminded Jane, unnervingly, of Percy's burning gaze. Penny said, "I'm going to continue Percy's work, Jane. I'm going to run for his seat."

Jane blinked. "Penny, you're not even old enough to vote!"

An impish smile appeared briefly on Penny's thin features. "I will be next month. I've got my thirtieth birthday coming up. Stay and help me, Jane, the way you helped Percy get elected. While we were married I learned an awful lot about politics, and I've met all the people who'll help me continue his work."

"Penny, it wasn't long ago that women didn't have the vote; women under thirty still don't. What do you think your chances will be? I'd hate to see you get hurt."

"Don't you want to see the women's voting age lowered to the same as a man's? An end to child labor? God, there's so much to be done!"

"You sound just like him, Penny," Jane said softly. "How can I refuse?"

She filled their glasses again and raised hers in a toast. "Let's drink to Penelope Templeton, MP."

The two glasses clinked together.

Penny took a sip of port and regarded Jane over the rim of her glass. "You know what my mum always says? She says that somewhere in the worst things that happen to us we'll find a gift, something good to help us overcome the bad. Don't be sad for me that I lost Percy. Be glad that I had him for as long as I did. Besides, he left me a legacy that's going to get me through the rest of my life." She giggled self-consciously. "Now I *know* I'm getting maudlin."

Jane gazed into the fireplace. The last embers glowed briefly and then died, but she didn't see them. She saw only the image of a beloved face. Ah, Marrick, my love, she thought longingly, how am I going to face the rest of my life without you? Despite all of her rationalizations—to him, to Penny, even to herself—her reason for leaving him was primitive, visceral. In her secret heart she concealed the fear that if she married Marrick she would kill him. Hadn't Percy died while making love to Penny?

❦ Forty ❧

"CLAUDIA?" Blair's voice, tentative, pleading, came through the closed bedroom door. "Please don't shut us out. . . . Colin needs you. I need you. Let me in, please."

"Go away. I'm ill. I must rest." Claudia turned over and buried her face in her pillow.

She drifted in and out of troubled sleep. The first few days after Colin was restored to her had been joyous, filled with hugs and kisses and the enormous relief of a tragedy averted. Blair had not mentioned Royce's part in Colin's rescue, nor had Marrick, who had rushed home to the abbey. Claudia had waited for some word from Royce, expecting every hour to hear from him. But she had not. She tried calling the hotel, then the barracks, where a disinterested clerk informed her that Second Lieutenant Weatherly and his records were no longer available there.

Blair had felt that Colin should go home to Willowford, to familiar surroundings, to help heal the wound left by the abduction, and so they had returned

Lady Kingsley refused to speak to Claudia. If their paths crossed, Blair's mother simply turned her back. She did not join them for meals. Blair made excuses for her. "She was shocked to find out that Colin was Weatherly's son. Please try to understand, Claudia. Mother is afraid of a scandal erupting. Oh, I know Marrick managed to keep the whole thing quiet, but . . . well, *I* know it's all over between you and Weatherly, but she . . ."

Feeling trapped and helpless, Claudia tried to call Jane, but learned she was staying in London with the widow of the MP who had died. In desperation, Claudia asked to speak to Marrick. The butler's voice, faintly scornful, informed her, "His lordship is not in residence, madam. He's abroad. We're closing the house to await the arrival of the new master after the legal proceedings transferring the estate are concluded."

They had all deserted her, Claudia decided—Royce, Jane, Leith—leaving her at the mercy of Blair and his mother, who would surely punish her for loving Royce, bearing his son. Claudia locked herself in her room and refused to come out.

The Harley Street doctor had given her a prescription for the sedative she'd taken during Colin's kidnapping, and she had sent her maid to the village chemist's shop to have it made up. The drug kept her from feeling too much pain; in fact it kept her from feeling much of anything, especially her need for Royce, who had again slipped away from her.

Claudia lived in a fog, her days blending, merging, flowing forward with little to distinguish one from another. The first time Blair came to her room with the intention of sleeping with her, she fled to the nursery and spent the night curled up in the window seat. Colin and his setter puppy crawled into her lap and slept contentedly. The following day she had a bed put into Colin's room and informed Blair that she would be sleeping there henceforth as she feared Colin might be kidnapped again. It was certainly true that the little boy had become fearful and withdrawn and suffered constant nightmares, which abated slightly after his mother began to sleep in his room.

Someone was shaking her arm and patting her cheek. She struggled to the surface of consciousness, feeling like a swimmer trapped in quicksand.

"Please, madam, wake up. Lady Kingsley says you must come down to the drawing room. There's someone here to see you." The anxious face of her maid materialized above her.

"I'm not receiving . . ." Claudia began. Lights flashed behind her eyes, her head throbbed.

"Her ladyship says you must come down or she'll send him up. Please, ma'am, let me help you get dressed."

"Who . . . who is it?"

"An American gentleman, ma'am. A Mr. Allegro."

Claudia sat up, groaning with the effort. "Frank? What's he doing here?"

"I'm sure I don't know, ma'am," her maid answered primly.

Dressing was such an effort that Claudia was exhausted by the time she was ready to leave the sanctuary of her room. She avoided looking at herself in her dressing table mirror.

Blair was in the drawing room with Frank, who leapt to his feet as Claudia arrived. She was painfully aware of the shocked look on his face as his gaze scanned her ravaged face.

"Claudia! I'm sorry—I had no idea you were so ill, or I'd have put off calling on you. But your husband said you'd see me and, well, it is kind of important. Here, let's get you into a chair."

Blair moved to her side also, and they practically carried her to a chair, sat her down, and placed a footstool under her feet.

When she was seated, Blair said stiffly, "Perhaps Mr. Allegro would prefer to discuss the matter with you alone—it's about your inheritance, Claudia." He paused. "Unless, of course, you'd like me to remain."

"Please leave us, Blair," Claudia said. She tried to clear her mind, to rid herself of the strangling fog that obscured her thinking. She had to pay careful attention if Frank's visit concerned her inheritance, as Royce would need all the details. But what could Frank possibly know about her inheritance? Besides, Royce had again abandoned her. She blinked, her thoughts spiraling away into a crazy kaleidoscope again.

She heard the drawing room door click shut and then felt Frank's finger under her chin. He tipped her face upward, pulled down her lower eyelids and peered into her eyes.

"What have you taken, Claudia? No, don't deny it. Your pupils are as big as bowling balls."

"Just a sedative the doctor gave me. . . . Oh, Frank, I've had such an awful time."

"Yeah, I heard. But drugging yourself stupid isn't going to help. You've got to pull yourself together, Claudia, for your son's sake. Hell, for your own sake, too."

"Why are you here, Frank?"

"Marrick didn't tell you?"

"He went back to Africa rather abruptly. We—we haven't exactly been close lately. I rarely see him. But he sold the abbey, you know."

"I know. He sold it to me."

"What? But . . ."

"He set up a hefty trust fund for you, Claudia. That's why I'm here. He wanted someone of his choosing to administer your trust. He selected me."

"You! I don't understand. Why you?"

"I guess because he figured I had so much money of my own I wouldn't be likely to steal any of yours. Besides which, as the new owner of Rathbourne Abbey I'd be close by to keep an eye on you."

"You're rich, Frank?"

"Filthy rich, sweetheart. Baron left everything to me, and it was more even than I imagined."

"Am I rich, too? Leith said when the abbey was sold the proceeds would be mine. How soon can I get my money?"

"You'll have a modest monthly allowance starting immediately. If you want to make a large purchase—say a car or a horse or a sable coat—you'll submit an invoice to me. If it isn't too outrageous, I'll okay it and pay for it."

Claudia was indignant. "But that isn't fair! It's my money, isn't it?"

"Uh-huh. But Marrick wants to make sure you won't hand over your money to . . . Well, let's just say, he wants you protected from fortune hunters."

"If you're implying that my husband would—"

"You know who I'm talking about. Did you think Marrick didn't know you'd given away every penny you could get your pretty little hands on?"

"It's none of his business, what I do with my money, and it's none of yours. Frank, you have to *do* something. . . . I need my inheritance. I have to get away from here. I can't begin to tell you what living in this house is like."

"Do you want to come home to the abbey? I'll take you and the boy now if you say the word."

"Will you give me my inheritance if I do?"

"Hell, no. What do you take me for? A complete fool? Besides, even if I wanted to, I couldn't."

"Then there's nothing further to discuss, is there?"

He shrugged. "Let me know how you want to handle your allowance from the trust fund. And, Claudia, get off that sedative while you still can. You'll addle your brain with it if you're not careful. Believe me, I've seen it happen."

❧ Forty-one ❧

THE FIRST DAYS were filled with the agony of regret, the fierce pain of longing, and there were many times when Jane reached for the telephone or started to write a letter to Marrick. She always managed to stop herself in time. Nor did she contact Claudia and Blair, although she sent picture postcards to Colin regularly.

She stayed with Penny, helping her sort out Percy's affairs, and when Penny began a determined effort to run for the seat in the House of Commons left vacant by Percy's death, Jane dutifully accompanied her on her campaign rounds. But Jane quickly realized that she had no real interest in a political career.

"I'm just not cut out for it," she told Penny after a particularly irritating interview with a Labour party organizer. "I can't stand all the maneuvering for position and toadying to people I'd rather belt in the chops then ask for favors. And frankly, I wouldn't be able to handle hecklers at meetings the way you do. To tell the truth, Penny, I'd rather scrub floors than have anything to do with politics."

Penny laughed. "I can't say I'm surprised. I've seen the look on your face at meetings. But listen, you stay with me as long as you like."

A few days after this conversation took place Jane was leaving the grocer's shop during a heavy rainstorm when a wet and bedraggled urchin, a little girl of about ten, darted into the street near her just as a coal cart lumbered out of the misty rain.

Everything happened so quickly that Jane wasn't sure whether the horse pulling the coal cart slid on the rain-slippery cobblestones or the child fell. The horse's hoof struck the little girl with a sickening thud, and she rolled into the gutter. The driver of the coal cart either didn't see what had happened or didn't care, and the cart trundled on by, leaving the child where she lay.

Jane ran to the little girl, gathered her into her arms and carried her back into the grocer's shop. She was unconscious, a trickle of blood from her matted fair hair running down her sunken cheek.

Feeling for a pulse, Jane called to the grocer, "We must get her to a doctor right away. Her skull may be fractured."

The man avoided meeting her eye. "I'm not sending for a doctor. Who'll pay him? That nipper's been living on her own on the street for weeks. We've chased her from our rubbish bins nearly every day. You'd better take her to the charity ward."

Before Jane could give him a piece of her mind, the little girl stirred and her eyes flickered open. "Please, miss . . ." Her voice was barely audible. "Me baby sister . . . in the parish 'ome, Daisy Macklefield. I'm all she's got. . . . I've got to see to 'er. Don't take me to no hospital. Please . . . Daisy needs me."

Soft brown eyes rolled upward and she lay limp in Jane's arms.

"Get me a cab," Jane snapped at the grocer. "Hurry."

That evening when Penny arrived home she found Jane sitting at the dining room table, staring morosely at a rain-ruined loaf of bread and a soggy bag of flour. She seemed transfixed and didn't look up when Penny entered the room.

"Looks like you got caught in the downpour, ducks," Penny remarked cheerfully. "Maybe we should throw that out before it makes a nasty mark on the veneer?" She picked up the wet groceries, but Jane still didn't respond.

Penny bent to look closer into her friend's eyes. "Hey, what's wrong?"

Jane jumped, as though just realizing she was there. "A little girl died in my arms this afternoon."

"Oh, my God, what happened?"

Jane told her. "She died a few minutes after I got her into the cab. Penny, right up to the end she was worrying about her baby sister, in a parish home. I went there . . ." She was so overcome with emotion that her voice broke.

Penny pulled a chair close and sat down. She handed Jane her handkerchief. "Did you find her baby sister?"

Jane dabbed the tears away and nodded. "Little Daisy Macklefield is nearly a year old, but looks about three months. She's got a fearful rash, and I think she might have croup."

"They're orphans, I suppose?"

"According to the matron at the home, their mother died trying to get rid of another baby four months ago. The father disappeared after she died. Daisy's sister, the little girl who was killed today—Lord, I don't even know her name—was put in the workhouse because she was thirteen years old, although you'd never have guessed it, and she ran away. She'd been sneaking into the home to see her sister." Jane stopped to blow her nose.

Penny patted her shoulder sympathetically.

"Oh, God, Penny, the babies in the home . . . the babies are in cots, all jammed together in a bare ward, sometimes two or more to a cot. One nurse goes around every four hours to feed them. She props bottles up for them, and if they lose the bottle . . ." She choked up again.

"If I get elected, I'm going to do something about the orphanages and workhouses, Jane, I swear it."

Jane shook Penny's hand from her shoulder. "I don't want to hear a politician's promises, damn it. Those babies won't live long enough for you to get elected and do something for them.

They lie there in their own urine and excrement for hours on end with nobody to pick them up and comfort them."

Penny bit her lip. "Jane, I've seen the parish homes. I've been to the workhouse and seen those gray-faced men and women. I'll never forget when I was a little girl they came and took away an old man who lived next door to us. My mum took me to the workhouse to see him. There was this long, scrubbed wood table, and down the middle was a row of salt cellars, and mum said the only seasoning they got was salt. They put in on their porridge for breakfast and on whatever they had for dinner. When they brought out our old neighbor he hung his head in shame and wouldn't look at us. He'd worked hard all of his life, and I couldn't understand what he'd done to be put in the workhouse. My mum said he didn't have enough money to pay for rent. Honest to God, Jane, my heart bleeds for the poor old souls and the poor little orphan babies, so I do understand how you feel. And if you want to add to your indignation, go and look at how some of our crippled war heroes are warehoused."

Jane brushed her fist across her eyes angrily. "While I was at the parish home a couple came. They weren't *sure* they wanted to adopt a baby, but were *considering* it. They strolled through the ward, looking at the babies . . . as if they were in a meat market selecting a joint of beef!"

"I know. But there's too many babies and not enough people who want to adopt them. You can't let yourself dwell on what you saw today, because there's not much you can do about it."

"Oh, no? I volunteered to work at the home. They haven't the money for wages for another paid employee, and I'm not sure yet what I'm going to live on when my savings run out, but I held little Daisy in my arms and I've got to do something."

Penny sighed deeply. "Oh, Jane, you'll break your heart."

❦ Forty-two ❧

NEVER A DAY passed that Jane did not think of Marrick. His face floated into her mind in every still moment and haunted her dreams. His dark eyes met hers every night before she fell asleep and greeted her every dawn when she forced her weary limbs to obey her mind's command that another day's hard work must begin.

She had spent only a couple of weeks at the parish home when Penny came to see her, following her on her rounds as she went from one baby to the next, changing wet nappies, holding a fretful infant for a few minutes. There weren't enough hours in the day to do all that needed to be done.

Unable to compete with one squalling baby, Penny picked him up, held him to her shoulder, and patted his back as she trailed along behind Jane. "Are you listening to me, Jane? I said I found a paying job for you. It's an orphanage, but it's run by the Sisters of Mercy and they've got a Lady Bountiful organizing their charity drives so they can afford a nurse. I told them about you. I bent the truth a bit and sort of intimated that you were Roman Catholic."

"Penny, you really are turning into a politician, aren't you? I hope you didn't intimate that I'm a fully qualified nurse, too."

"I told the reverend mother about your wartime service and that you're currently working here with the babies. Anything else she assumed . . . well, that was up to her."

They had reached Daisy's cot, and Jane picked up the baby. She rocked the tiny girl back and forth tenderly.

Watching, Penny commented, "No need to ask which one this is. Oh, Janey, you should have kids of your own. I never saw anybody more cut out to be a mother. Are you sure all this isn't a substitute for what you really want? For instance, a husband and family? Look, if you're going to moon about Marrick for the rest of your life you'll never meet anybody else. Now, I've met this nice bloke, and he has a friend—"

"Penny!" Jane was shocked. "I can't believe you're seeing somebody else so soon. Percy is hardly cold in his grave."

Penny shrugged. "But I'm not, am I? All right, if you must turn yourself into an old maid, so be it. Will you come and talk to the reverend mother?"

"Yes, of course. I need a paying job. Do you think they'd let me take Daisy with me? I wish I could adopt her, but I'd need a husband for that."

Penny rolled her eyes. "Maybe we could say you were related to her. Let's talk to the reverend mother first, shall we?"

❦ Forty-three ❧

FRANK ALLEGRO had just completed yet another transatlantic crossing and was sorting through accumulated letters and bills awaiting him at Rathbourne Abbey when he found Jane's letter. The return address was that of a Sisters of Mercy foundling home in London's East End.

Dear Frank,

This is a begging letter, so if you aren't feeling generous, now is the time to burn this before I succeed in making you feel guilty.

Marrick told me that as Baron's heir you inherited a fortune. But it's not your money I'm after (although the sisters wouldn't turn down any donations). I understand that you are now the owner of Rathbourne Abbey. Frank, there are children here who have never been out of the city. Oh, I know we could take them to the park, but that's not the same as seeing a cornfield or cows grazing or a sheepdog rounding up the flock . . . well, you know what I mean. I'd like to bring a small group—no more than six—of the older children, and I wondered if I could persuade you to let us camp out, just for one night, on abbey land. If you could donate a little food from your kitchen, too . . .

I wouldn't have the nerve to ask you except for the fact that I think maybe you of all people will understand that a kind gesture to these children now might make all the difference to their future. But, Frank, if this is too much of an imposition, I'll understand. If you do agree, I'll make sure they stay well out of sight. I thought perhaps the woods along the river would be a good spot. We've had a couple of tents given to us, which is what gave me the idea.

Fondest regards,
Jane

"You haven't changed a thing," Jane said as she and Frank walked through the abbey. "I thought you were going to turn it into a hotel."

"I was. But then I moved in and . . . I dunno, it seemed like sacrilege. I am thinking of opening it up to the public, though, maybe a couple of days a month. Do you think I could persuade Claudia to act as tour guide, since she knows the place so well?"

Jane gave him an incredulous sideways glance. "You're joking—about Claudia, I mean."

He pushed open the drawing room door and stood aside to let her enter. "I've ordered some tea and scones sent up. No, I'm not joking. I'm trying to find a way to get her to start living again. From what I gather, she's taken to her bed again, playing the invalid. She hasn't returned any of my calls since I got back. I'll be honest with you, Jane, I figured if I let you bring your orphans here maybe you could get Claudia to come visit us. You will be going to see her, won't you?"

"I have to supervise the children," Jane said. "I did hope to see Colin, if his nanny could bring him over, but I certainly can't take six children from the worst slums of London over to Willowford. And I really should get back to them, in case they're making a nuisance of themselves belowstairs. . . ."

"Oh, sit down and have tea with me. We've got a cook who'd put most sergeant majors to shame when it comes to keeping order. Your young hooligans will be fine."

"They're not hooligans! They've never seen a country estate and have no idea how to behave, that's all."

A maid entered the room carrying a tea tray, and when she left, Frank said, "I've been gone for about six weeks. I come back to find you up to your ears in orphans, Marrick flying all over Africa like a madman, and Claudia still sequestered like a nun. . . . What the hell is going on here?"

Jane's hand shook slightly at the mention of Marrick, rattling the fragile china cup against the saucer as she was about to pass it to him—a fact that wasn't lost on Frank. "Ah, I struck a nerve," he said. "You know, I always wondered about you and Marrick. You're both extremely attractive people, and yet neither of you are married."

"One could say the same thing about you, Frank."

"But it's no secret that I'm carrying a torch for Claudia." He leaned forward. "Shall we talk about unrequited love? Believe me, it's no fun. If I could quit I would. But some sixth sense tells me if I hang around long enough . . ."

"It won't happen, Frank. Stop expecting it to." Jane gave an exasperated sigh.

He didn't look convinced. "That was pretty cunning, the way you sidestepped my question about you and Marrick."

Jane sipped her tea and didn't respond.

"I had a phone put in here." He gestured toward a small table beside the sofa.

"How convenient. I suppose you'll fill the abbey with lifts and dumbwaiters, too? My first impression that you hadn't changed anything wasn't quite accurate, I see."

"Jane . . . will you call her?"

"I'd rather not. Frank, we—Claudia and I—drifted apart. You know about my brother, and you know that his wife kidnapped Colin, so I won't go into detail. I just feel that it's time for me to make as graceful an exit from Claudia's life as possible. In fact, I was going to ask if you'd call Colin's nanny for me—"

They stared at each other for a moment; then both smiled ruefully. Jane murmured, "We're a fine pair, aren't we?"

"We're overwhelmed by our surroundings, I guess," Frank said. "We simply don't belong here. I mean, come on! We weren't born with silver spoons in our mouths, either of us. Yet here we are, and I have a feeling we'll endure, while those ethereal creatures who created this highly exclusive way of life will eventually fade away into the mist. So why the hell are we in awe of them?" He reached over and picked up the phone, winking at her as he asked the operator to connect him to Willowford's number.

"This is Mr. Allegro," he said a moment later, "of Rathbourne Abbey. May I speak with Mrs. Claudia Kingsley, please?"

Jane watched his confident expression change to one of disappointment. Then he said, "Okay, how about Lady Kingsley?" After another pause he snapped, "All right, all right! Put Colin's nanny—Gladys, isn't it? Put her on the phone."

Seconds later he tossed the earphone down without bothering to connect it to the speaker and gave her an exasperated look. "Even the blasted butler can make me feel inferior! I'm rich enough to buy and sell the pack of them, and yet . . . Well, anyway, Claudia isn't home. I guess that's a good sign. At least she's out and about. The boy and his nanny had to go to the dentist. We'll try again later."

Jane stood up. "I'm going back to the children. Frank . . ."

"Yes?"

"Thank you for letting them come. They have so little. Their lives are so bleak. If you have time, come and meet them. It might make you feel less envious of the Kingsleys and Marricks of the world and appreciate what you have."

Frank gave a sheepish grin. "Bull's-eye! Come on, let's take them to the stables. Marrick's horses are still here until he decides what he's going to do with them."

Jane and Frank sat on a low stone wall watching a groom lead one of the gentler mares around the stable yard, to the delight of the two boys on her back. The other children clustered about a half-grown foal, stroking his muzzle, offering him the sugar cubes Frank had provided. From time to time, all of the children glanced warily in Frank's direction, as if expecting at any second to be banished back to the foundling home.

"That anxious look they give tears at my heart," Jane murmured to Frank. "See how their shoulders are always hunched, as though they're wincing, flinching away from life. The sisters treat them kindly, but heaven knows what horrors are locked away in their memories."

"So you did what you swore you'd never do—you went back to nursing. Is taking care of children easier than nursing wounded soldiers?"

"It's different. Perhaps it makes more sense to me. There's a baby girl I'm particularly fond of. . . . I wish I could have brought her with me, but I need all my wits about me to watch these six."

"You should have children of your own, Jane."

"That's what my friend Penny is always telling me, despite the fact that she hasn't any children of her own—and neither, for that matter, do you. So you both have a lot of cheek to bring up the subject."

"Sorry, didn't mean to offend. Your work is important to you, and I had no right to assume you'd rather be doing something else."

Jane bit her lip. "Oh, there are a lot of things I'd rather be doing. The work is hard and often thankless and frustrating. These six children I brought to the country are fairly healthy, and I'm sure it seems to you that I'm little more than a nanny. But drop in on me at midnight some time when I'm trying to feed six babies simultaneously or quiet down a dozen terrified toddlers."

He listened quietly but she felt his sympathy and understanding and after a moment she went on, "I can't begin to describe the helplessness of watching a little pigeon-chest rise and fall as a poor mite fights to breathe, knowing there's very little I can do beyond rocking and comforting and trying to get a spoonful of gruel into her. . . ."

"You're speaking about the little girl you mentioned. The one you're particularly fond of?"

Jane nodded. "Daisy has asthma. I'm worried about how she'll stand the cold weather when it comes. I wish I could get her out of the home; the wards are so damp and drafty. I'd adopt her if I could, but of course, I can't because I'm not married. Oh, God, Frank, I never really wanted to be a nurse. I just sort of stumbled into it."

"You think I wanted to be a hotelier? Hell, I wanted to play the piano in a smoky dive and have a different chorus girl on my arm every night. Maybe some power beyond our understanding decides what we're best suited for. What do you think?"

" 'More things in heaven and earth, Horatio . . .' " Jane quoted softly. Feeling suddenly sad, she abruptly asked, "How long will you be staying at the abbey?"

"A week or two, probably. Then back to New York."

"If you're in London, come and visit the foundling home. I'm afraid I've made it sound too grim and depicted myself as a martyr, which is far from the case. I think if you come and see me in my natural habitat you'll understand the rewards I receive for the work I do."

He looked at her shrewdly. "And I imagine you're kept so busy you don't have time to brood on how the adults in your life have let you down."

Jane turned away. "The children must be getting hungry. Is it all right for us to have a picnic on the south lawn?"

Later that day Jane stood in the deepening twilight looking toward Rathbourne Abbey, no longer resisting the memories of Marrick that flooded back. She gave herself up to them, feeling the bittersweet pleasure of reliving every moment they had spent together, every word they had ever exchanged. Soon the sadness would become unbearable, but for a little while her mind didn't distinguish between past reality and present need.

Someone called her name softly and she turned to see a shadowy figure approaching along the riverbank. "Jane, it's me, Frank."

"Ssh! The children are asleep."

He emerged from the shadows, and she saw his expression

was tense. "Bad news, I'm afraid. It's about your sister-in-law, Edith."

Jane stood still, her blood slowly turning to ice.

Frank continued in a low voice. "Apparently they kept her in this country to face kidnapping charges, but decided the murder and escape charges in Ireland should take precedence. Anyway, as they were transferring her to the Dublin boat she apparently got away somehow."

"Are you saying she's at large? Here, in England?"

He nodded. "The police are calling those people she might possibly go to for help. The nuns at the home told them you were staying here. I imagine they've contacted Willowford, too. Jane, you can stay here, if you wish, until she's caught."

"No . . . no, I must take the children back to London. Daisy—the baby girl I told you about—gets fretful if she doesn't see me. Besides, there's not much chance Edith will come looking for me. If she goes to anybody, it will be Royce."

"She kidnapped little Colin," Frank said grimly. "She wouldn't try to hurt Claudia, would she?"

Jane shivered. "I believe there's not much that Edith is incapable of doing. Who can tell what goes on in that warped mind of hers?"

❧ Forty-four ❧

SOMEONE WAS POUNDING on her bedroom door. Claudia rose slowly to the surface of consciousness, struggling from the depths of drugged sleep.

"Do you hear me? Open this door or I shall have it broken down." Alicia Kingsley's voice, shrill with anger, assaulted her senses.

The room swam as Claudia slid out of bed and made her way

unsteadily toward the door. Late-afternoon sunlight slanting into the room suggested that she must have slept away most of the day. She still spent her nights sleeping in the nursery with Colin and couldn't remember returning to her own room or locking the door. Judging by the state of the room, her maid hadn't been able to get in either.

"I'm coming," Claudia called, pulling on her dressing gown.

Alicia pushed past her into the room the second the door opened, leaving a footman, who had evidently been doing the pounding, standing outside. Claudia closed the door and turned to face her mother-in-law.

"What a fright you look, Claudia," Alicia said, raking her with a glance that made Claudia's soul shrivel. "When did you last bathe or wash your hair? Look at this room. It's a disgrace. The staff informed me that you keep the door locked and they can't get in to clean. Well, young woman, this is all going to change. Now. Today. We've had quite enough of your nonsense."

Claudia swallowed a dry lump in her throat and sat down on her dresser stool, pushing aside an array of underwear and stockings. She winced as her finger connected with the lethal point of a five-inch hatpin, evidently left there when she removed her hat after returning from London. She licked away the drop of blood and said, "I haven't felt well lately. I'm sorry."

"The chemist's shop called to say they could not fill your prescription again; the doctor refused to authorize it. You are not ill, Claudia; you are simply lazy."

Claudia lowered her eyes, trying to ignore the squeezing sensation in her head and the ominous flashing lights behind one eye. If Alicia only knew, there was a duplicate prescription at every chemist's shop in Oakleigh, Beddington, and several other nearby towns.

"However, since you insist that you are ill and behave in a completely irrational manner, we must assume that your illness is of the mind rather than the body," Alicia continued, "and so we are delivering you today into the care of a psychiatrist at the St. Agnes Convalescent Home."

"No! No, I don't want to go there!" Panic gripped Claudia. She couldn't leave Willowford. How would Royce know where or how to find her? "Blair . . . where is Blair? He won't force me to go, and no one else has the power to commit me."

Alicia's lips compressed. "My son is in London, attending to the family business. If you refuse to go to St. Agnes willingly, I shall send for attendants and have you put into a straitjacket and taken there forcibly. I shall tell them you have threatened to harm yourself. Believe me, after one look at you and at this room they will not hesitate to act. We do not need a husband's permission to deal with a dangerous situation."

There was no doubt she meant what she said. Staring wide-eyed at her mother-in-law, Claudia whispered, "Colin . . . I can't leave Colin. Please don't make me."

"The child will be far better off without you, Claudia. What kind of an example do you think you're setting for him? I've tried to persuade Blair to send your son to his natural father, but Blair has some misguided sense of duty toward you and the boy. Now there's nothing further to be said. I'll send your maid to help you dress and pack."

Claudia tried to grope her way through the fog of her mind. What to do? *What to do?* "Please . . . if you commit me . . . they'll never let me leave."

"You should have thought of that when you turned my son out of your bed and refused to be a wife."

Oh, God, Claudia thought, how much does the old witch know? She wished she could remember the events of the past weeks, but everything was blurred, indistinct. All she really had been aware of was waiting each day for some word from Royce.

"Could you . . ." Claudia cleared her throat. "Would you let me see my doctor in London? I could take a train up there today and—"

"And go to my son's office to persuade him to intercede for you? No, I think not. You will go into St. Agnes today."

Alicia went to the bellpull and tugged. Evidently Claudia's maid had been standing by, as she came into the room immediately.

"See that she looks decent—the burgundy travel suit, I believe—and pack only an overnight bag. We'll send a trunk later. Call me as soon as you're ready. I'll be in the study. I shall accompany her to St. Agnes."

Claudia noted that her mother-in-law avoided using her name. "She" and "her" might have referred to an ailing cat being sent to be put to sleep.

Alicia picked her way carefully around the debris scattered across the floor, her black gown swishing with a snakelike hiss as she made her way from the room. Claudia remembered vaguely that she had been searching for her pills and had tossed the contents of her dresser onto the floor in her haste to find them.

"Ma'am? I said I've drawn your bath." Her maid's anxious voice broke through the fog. "And I brought up a pot of coffee for you to drink."

Claudia blinked, unsure how much time had passed. This was happening frequently lately—the little lapses of memory, the realization that time had passed and she had no idea where or what she had been doing, or even thinking.

She felt her maid's hands grasp hers to help her to her feet.

The warm bath and scalding coffee helped. She sat at her dressing table as her maid gently eased a brush through her tangled hair. Looking up at the girl's reflection, Claudia said, "Will you help me? I must go to London to my husband."

"Ma'am . . . couldn't you give him a ring on the phone?"

"No. Lady Kingsley won't let me. I must get out of the house without being seen. I could slip down to the kitchen through the servants' quarters and leave by the tradesmen's entrance. But you must promise not to go near Lady Kingsley until after I'm gone."

"Oh, ma'am, I daren't. I'd be dismissed."

"You can tell her that I said I had to go to my husband's room to get something—that I tricked you."

Claudia turned and clutched the girl's hand. "Please! You've done so much for me. Do this one last thing. If you don't, I shan't ever see you, or my son, again. She'll make sure of that. She's going to commit me; I'll be locked up at St. Agnes. You know that's where people like Lady Kingsley hide anyone who is an embarrassment to them." Tears trembled on the brink and then slipped down her cheeks.

"Oh, don't cry, ma'am. It'll be all right. I'll help you."

* * *

Claudia's sense of relief as she settled into a deserted first-class compartment on the London-bound train was fleeting, due to her physical miseries. Every nerve in her body twitched and writhed. She couldn't sit still. Her head throbbed, and blinding lights stabbed her eyes like rapiers. Perspiration lay in clammy pools all over her body, and her tongue seemed to fill her mouth like a sponge. She desperately needed to take one of her pills, but didn't dare risk falling asleep.

She unpinned her hat and placed it carefully in the overhead rack, then, since she was alone, unfastened the top buttons of her blouse, which seemed to be choking her.

Listening to the wheels grinding their repetitive melody on the steel track, Claudia willed herself to keep control until the journey ended.

Someone had left a magazine in the compartment, and she picked it up, hoping that it would help her think of something other than her terrible, gnawing need for one of her pills.

Flipping through the glossy pages she noted the photographs of society matrons and newly presented debutantes, the chatty articles about their lives, the gossipy pieces about who was visiting whom and for what event. Her eyes refused to focus on the print and so she merely glanced at the photos and read the captions. Some were of handsome young couples caught off guard, above sly hints that their "friendship" might possibly blossom into love and marriage.

Suddenly Claudia felt a jolt like an electric shock pass through her. Her hands gripped the magazine so tightly she tore the page loose from its binding.

Smiling up at her from a magazine page was the familiar face of Royce Weatherly. She stared at those finely hewn features, the familiar cleft in the chin, the sensual mouth, the eyes that regarded the world with a buccaneer's gleam of appraisal, and even though there was no doubt that she was looking at Royce, for one second she hoped beyond hope that she was mistaken—because his arm was draped carelessly around the shoulders of an attractive young debutante. The caption beneath the photograph read: "Miss Alexandria Prendegast attending the Debutantes' Charity Ball with Lieutenant Royce Weatherly (see details page 27)."

Claudia scrabbled through the magazine to find the article. The words blurred and ran together: "Miss Prendegast is the only daughter of the brewery king . . . her mother's family in banking . . . constant companions . . . engagement expected to be announced."

Blinking rapidly, Claudia attempted to read it all again and, more important, to understand it. Royce had said he was going to India. That was weeks ago, wasn't it? Why was he still here? But, of course, he'd lied to her. She hadn't been able to get the money he needed fast enough, so he'd turned to someone who could. Claudia knew of the Prendegasts, who managed to get their name in print constantly. They were nouveaux riches and quite common. Why, Alexandria couldn't be a day over eighteen, a blank-faced young hussy with the too-full lips and slightly prominent teeth that some people found attractive.

The article went on to say that her "brewery king" father would be the host of a party on the twenty-first of the month, at which time an announcement of the couple's engagement would probably be made.

What date was it today? Claudia couldn't remember. She signaled to a porter passing along the corridor outside her compartment. "What is the date today, please?"

"The twentieth, miss."

"Thank you." She leaned back weakly against the starched antimacassar on her seat and read the article again. The party was to take place in the banquet room of a West End hotel and would no doubt be one of those flashy affairs so beloved of people with too much money and too little taste. The guests would have overnight accommodations at the same hotel.

Claudia's pain was unbearable. For several minutes she was too numbed by it to think.

Then gradually the hurt gave way to anger. How dare some common little tart imagine she could waltz along and steal her beloved? Royce was hers, her true love, her only love. Alexandria Prendegast was trying to buy him with her father's beer money and her grandfather's bank, and Royce, who always needed money, had been dazzled by the great gobs of wealth dangled before his nose. But Royce didn't love that vacant little minx who, like most middle-class girls, had undoubtedly been terrified into preserving her virginity until her wedding night. How could he? He needed a woman's love. How often he had told her that he was amazed and bewitched by the fact that his Dresden doll—he often called her that, saying she was so delicate, so exquisite—who appeared to be such a perfect lady in the drawing room, had proved to be more than his match in the bedroom. No, Royce had simply forgotten his Claudia and how perfectly suited they were. Besides, their last meeting had been under strained circumstances, when Edith kidnapped Colin—

Edith! The name rang a clarion bell in Claudia's mind. *Edith was still legally married to Royce.*

She sat bolt upright, the miseries of her aching limbs and pounding headache momentarily forgotten. What would stupid little Alexandria and her family think about the fact that Royce was married to a murderess and kidnapper?

But she couldn't tell them. All of Claudia's breath left her body; she felt as if she were slowly deflating like a leaky balloon. She couldn't treat Royce as badly as he'd treated her; she loved him too much, needed him so desperately. Her body screamed for the release of his lovemaking. She wanted him inside her with a longing that transcended reason. But no matter what, she could not betray him.

Tears came, splashing down onto the magazine picture she still clutched to her breast. It had been so long since she lay in Royce's arms, so long since she had looked into his eyes, kissed his lips . . .

Of course! That was the problem. The business with Edith had temporarily obscured their love, and they had been separated by circumstances beyond their control. She hadn't waited for him in London after Marrick found and returned Colin. She'd gone running back to Willowford with her husband. But Royce had wanted her to go to India with him, hadn't he? Heaven only knew what he'd had to do to get his orders changed. Royce probably thought she blamed *him* for Edith's actions!

Relief washed over Claudia. Now she understood! After Marrick brought Colin to her there was no opportunity for her to see Royce. Foolishly she'd expected him to get in touch with her, but how could he? Blair and Colin hadn't let her out of their sight.

Oh, poor, dear Royce, how he must have suffered! When she returned to Willowford, Royce probably thought she was finished with him. Certainly she had been cold to him, but that was only because Edith had Colin. In his misery over losing his one true love he had turned to Alexandria—but he was merely trying to forget Claudia. She knew this with certainty.

She smiled to herself. All she had to do was tell him she was still his and would be until the day she died. Not only that, but she now had the trust fund Marrick had set up for her—there had to be a way to gain control of it from Frank Allegro.

The solution to her dilemma was so simple, so beautiful! And hadn't fate stepped in to show her the way? She had time to go to the hotel and talk to Royce before the party. His engagement to Alexandria need never be announced, and Claudia would never have to return to Willowford or, worse— she shuddered—be committed to St. Agnes.

Royce would be so happy to see her! They would fling themselves into each other's arms, and after all the misunderstandings were ironed out, they would make love, sweet, sweet love.

The train was now passing the familiar landmarks on the outskirts of London. Claudia forgot the miseries of her body in joyous anticipation of her reunion with Royce.

She took a taxi from the station to the hotel where the engagement party was to take place and, on a whim, registered under the name of Edith Weatherly. She rationalized that the Prendegasts had probably booked a number of rooms for their guests and she was more likely to be accommodated in one of them if she appeared to be related to Royce. Another thought lingered in the back of her mind—that perhaps Royce would see her registration and come to her. There was, after all, a great deal of shock value to the name Edith Weatherly.

That evening Claudia dined at the hotel, hoping to see Royce, but the dining room was almost deserted. She picked at the food, lingered over a glass of wine as she watched the doors for a glimpse of him, then finally returned to her room. She took several of her pills and fell into a deep sleep.

The next morning, groggy and unsure where she was when she awoke in the strange bed, she took two more pills and slept until noon. Although awake, she lay in bed for a long time attempting to summon the strength to get up.

Bathing and dressing required an effort, and by the time she went down to the lobby the afternoon was well advanced. She walked straight to the desk. The clerk, who had just come on duty, remembered her from the previous evening. "Good afternoon, Miss Weatherly."

She noticed he stared at her hair, and she had the uneasy feeling he was not admiring the color, but rather was taken aback by how unkempt it was. She'd have to do something about it before she met Royce. "Has Lieutenant Weatherly arrived yet?"

He glanced at the register. "Why, yes, miss, your brother arrived about an hour ago. He's in room one-oh-seven."

My *brother*, Claudia thought, amused.

"Is the dining room open yet?" she asked, feeling her stomach grumble and remembering she hadn't eaten since the previous evening.

"Not yet, madam, but afternoon tea is being served in the mezzanine, or you could order a tray sent to your room. Perhaps you'd like to have it sent to your brother's room?"

"No, no, thank you. I must give him time to unpack."

She felt giddy, light-headed, and not yet ready to face Royce. She ordered ham sandwiches and a pot of tea to be sent to her room, forced herself to eat, then took a hot bath and put on her most delicate satin underwear, frowning at the way the garments hung loose. She hadn't been aware that her slender body was becoming gaunt.

Sitting at the dressing table she picked up a hairbrush, wishing her maid were there to do something with her hair. No matter how she brushed and combed, it still resembled a tangle of pale straw.

After several unsuccessful attempts to tame her hair, she gave up and put on her hat, wishing she had worn a more becoming one. In her haste to leave Willowford she had donned a plain felt with a little eye veil, but fortunately she had secured it with a handsome pearl and diamanté hatpin, which added a little decoration.

Her maid had packed an ecru blouse with an outsize bow at the throat, which helped soften the man-tailored travel suit of dark burgundy that Alicia Kingsley had ordered her to wear for her banishment to St. Agnes Convalescent Home.

Surveying herself in the mirror, Claudia decided that perhaps the suit and hat were appropriate attire, as it would appear that she had just arrived. She wasn't sure why she didn't want Royce to know she had waited all night and all day for him, but thought perhaps it had something to do with not wanting to appear desperate.

She was sorry now that she had taken so many of her pills, as she felt disoriented, not completely in control of her faculties, rather like a sleepwalker. Still, as she made her way to Royce's room, her anticipation of seeing him again brought an inner rush of excitement.

She knocked on the door to 107. There was no response for several seconds. Then the door opened and a red-faced maid carrying a bundle of linens appeared, sidestepped around Claudia, and fled down the corridor.

"Who is it?" Royce's voice called from inside the room.

Claudia went into the room and closed the door.

Royce lay on the rumpled bed, his lower body covered by a sheet, his chest bare. He had been about to light a cigarette, but seeing her, he slowly placed his lighter and unlit cigarette on the bedside table, never taking his eyes off her.

"Well, well . . . Claudia. You're the last person I expected to walk in on me."

She didn't speak, for the simple reason that waves of nausea were washing over her. The ham sandwiches sat uncomfortably in her stomach and the tea had done little for her pounding headache, but more than that, she recognized that sated look on his face for what it was.

Royce cleared his throat. "You look ill, Claudia. Are you all right?" There was no welcome in his expression, no joy in his tone. Her own happy anticipation dissipated rapidly.

"Do you care? I haven't heard a word from you for weeks. I didn't even know you were still in England."

His jaw moved slightly. "I thought I'd better lie low until I was sure Edie was safe behind bars."

But you were there when she was arrested, Claudia thought. The drumming in her head had begun again. She walked across he room toward him. He didn't move. As she drew close, the unmistakable smell of recent sex assailed her.

Royce surreptitiously pulled the sheet a little higher. "Look, Claudia, I can't talk to you now. I'm glad the boy is safe and your husband is taking care of you. I'll be going to India soon. I . . ." His voice trailed away, and a wary look crept into his gray eyes.

Claudia realized that she was breathing rapidly, panting almost, and her heart was a trapped bird in its cage of ribs trying to break free.

Royce asked, "What have you done to yourself?"

She stood beside the bed, looking down at him. "Are you going to marry Alexandria Prendegast?"

"Well . . . I'm not sure. There's the problem of Edith, of course."

"Oh, yes, there's always that excuse."

"You look bloody awful, Claudia, and you sound strange. Maybe you need to see a doctor."

The fog that crept toward her was red today, and the squeezing sensation in her head had returned. When she spoke her voice sounded shrill. "You made promises to me, Royce. I loved you. I gave you all I had to give. Why wasn't it enough?"

"Don't get hysterical, Claudia. For God's sake, pull yourself together and get out of here before somebody sees you."

"How could you turn to someone else so soon? How can you forget all we meant to each other?"

His look was contemptuous now. "Christ, did you look in a mirror before you came? You look a fright, Claudia. Your face is like a death mask, and you're bony as a skeleton. Hell, I've seen better hair on bacon. If you were trying to disguise it you'd have done better to put your hat on straight."

Her hand automatically went to her hat, her fingers grazing the pearl and diamanté baubles decorating her hatpin. Royce was still speaking, saying horrible things about her ravaged looks, taunting her with vile promises to send her an invitation to his wedding, to name his first daughter after her, to send Edith to see her. He swore he had never loved her, he'd only loved her money, but she'd been too damn miserly with it and too generous with her body. How could he ever trust a woman who gave herself so easily? If she submitted to him, probably she submitted to others—not like Alexandria, who was still a virgin.

Claudia wished she could close her ears, wished she could make him stop. But he went on, stabbing her with his words, torturing her until she was sure she would die from it.

"Get away from me, Claudia. Leave me alone. We're finished, do you hear me? You're not going to jeopardize my chances with Alexandria. I'll see you in hell first."

His words echoed around the hollow chambers of her mind, reverberating, deafening her, pulsing like a wound pumping blood until she could not bear the pain of hearing any more. She had to make the sound of his voice stop.

She gave a small cry, like that of a trapped animal, and the next second the five-inch hatpin was in her hand. She plunged it into his heart, driving it in until only the topmost pearl was visible above the red surge.

His eyes widened, as if in surprise, and he stared at her, but he didn't move.

Claudia turned and stumbled blindly from the room.

❧ Forty-five ❧

THE KINGSLEYS' London mews house was no longer the welcoming sanctuary from the day's labors that it had been when Jane and Colin stayed there, Blair thought as he entered the living room and switched on a lamp. His daily cleaning woman had laid a fire in the grate before leaving, and he lit it, hoping to dispel the gloom of a heavy rainstorm lashing the city.

His evenings in town were lonely, and he usually brought work home with him, but this evening he was in the grip of deep melancholy and had no desire to pore over yet another financial statement. The accountants were correct in their assessment of the situation. The simple fact of the matter was that the business could no longer support the upkeep of a country estate the size of Willowford. He was going to have to either sell it, turn it over to the National Trust, or withdraw to a small suite of family rooms and open the rest of the house for paid public tours, as many other owners of country homes were doing. But the idea of gawking tourists tramping through his home was abhorrent to him.

He added more coal to the sputtering fire and rubbed his shoulder. Damp weather caused the stump to ache, and tonight the phantom pain in his missing arm had returned. How he longed to go home to Willowford, to play with Colin, to make love to Claudia . . .

Ah, Claudia, he thought, please be well soon. His mother wanted to have a psychiatrist examine Claudia, but he had opposed the idea. Claudia was sensitive, fragile, and she had endured a mother's worst nightmare when Colin was kidnapped. In Blair's mind she merely needed time to recover. If only she would agree to live here in town with him, but she became hysterical if he suggested it.

The fire began to warm him, and he leaned back in his chair and dozed. In his dreams his twin still lived, and it seemed that sometimes he was Ro and sometimes himself. But never, thank God, was he Blair, who was faced with problems he could not solve. Only Claudia and Colin's presence in his life made the burden bearable.

Bran and Ro were skimming downriver in their shells, neck and neck, oars dipping in perfect unison. How the water shimmered in the sunlight! Ro was going to win. Jane was on the riverbank, jumping up and down and shouting encouragement. Dear Jane, what a good friend she was to all of them.

The ringing of the doorbell shattered the dream and brought him abruptly to consciousness. He rarely had visitors at the mews house, and the insistent ringing of the bell indicated his unexpected visitor bore an urgent message. He hurried to the front door.

Windswept rain gusted into the vestibule as he opened the door, and at the same time Claudia collapsed against him, sobbing. He pushed the door shut and wrapped his arm around her.

"Claudia! Where on earth did you spring from? Darling, it's all right, I've got you. I'm so happy to see you. I've missed you so. Don't cry, you're safe. Come on, let's get you in by the fire."

He almost had to lift her off her feet to get her to move, but managed to lead her into a fireside chair. He looked anxiously into her face. "Darling, what happened to you? What are you doing here? Why didn't you let me know you were coming?"

Her burgundy suit was soaked with rain, which helped disguise the darkening stains on the jacket. She had lost her hat, and her wet hair straggled about her shoulders in pale wisps. He pulled off her sodden shoes and massaged her feet. When she still didn't speak he asked, "Is everything all right at Willowford?"

Her blue-violet eyes, huge in her pinched face, stared at him uncomprehendingly. He peeled off her wet jacket, wondering about the dark stain the rain had not completely washed away. As he began to unbutton her blouse he realized that her skin felt excessively warm and yet she was shivering uncontrollably. He touched her forehead and confirmed his suspicion.

"Claudia . . . I'm going to leave you for a moment to get a dressing gown and blanket for you. You feel a little feverish; you may be coming down with a cold. Don't worry, I'm going to take care of you. I love you so much, Claudia. I'll always take care of you."

When he returned a few minutes later, she was sound asleep. He looked down at her, feeling such a wave of love and tenderness for her that he didn't at first notice she had curled into a tight ball and her thumb was in her mouth.

He wrapped the blanket around her and sat beside her, watching her sleep. After a moment her thumb slipped away from her mouth, and glancing at her fingers, he noticed that her nails were tipped with scarlet crescents . . . that looked very much like blood.

Paperboys were shouting the news of her brother's death as Jane herded her charges from the railway station. "Children, wait a minute," she said, her heart lurching. She signaled to the newsboy and bought a paper.

"Fiancé of Brewery Heiress Murdered," the headline screamed. Beneath it was a subhead: "Hatpin in the Heart Wielded by Jealous Wife, an Escaped Murderess and Kidnapper."

Jane scanned the article quickly, keeping one eye on the children to be sure they didn't stray. Edith had been caught lurking near the Prendegasts' town house a couple of hours after Royce's body was discovered in a room at the hotel where a party was to take place at which his engagement to Alexandria Prendegast would be announced. Edith was wearing a blond wig when she was caught. The hotel confirmed that a woman with untidy blond hair, which certainly could have been a wig, had taken a room the night before the murder, registering as Edith Weatherly and claiming to be Royce Weatherly's sister.

Royce's handsome face flashed into Jane's mind. Dead, she thought. He's dead. I'll never see him again. He'll never hurt Claudia again.

Several emotions assailed her. Disbelief, sadness, anger, a heart-stopping panic. Then all of these faded before an overwhelming sense of guilt. She should have done something, anything, to prevent this tragedy.

"Miss Weatherly," one of the older boys called, "Albert has to go to the lav."

Jane folded the paper and tucked it under her arm, then went to take care of the children.

A police constable awaited her arrival at the orphanage, and as one of the sisters led the children away, he said gruffly, "I see you've already seen the paper. I'm sorry for your loss, Miss Weatherly. We don't like to intrude in this time of grief, but there'll be a few questions. If you wouldn't mind coming down to the station with me?"

"Yes, of course."

"Just routine, won't take long, but you're his only relative, I understand." He coughed discreetly. "Except for the . . . ah . . . accused."

"There's no doubt that his wife did it, then?"

"Oh, no, miss. No doubt whatsoever. Well, she'd killed before, hadn't she? A very violent woman."

"The paper said she used a hatpin. . . . It seems such a puny weapon."

"Well, miss, you'll be given a copy of the coroner's report. It's full of medical terms—ventricular tachycardia and pericardial tamponade, I believe it was. The detective inspector said what it boils down to is that a five-inch steel pin in exactly the right spot is what did it. If it had lodged in a slightly different position he might have survived."

Jane made no comment. Royce shouldn't have been so foolish as to allow the Prendegasts to announce an engagement party. He must have known it would send Edith into a jealous frenzy. But then, he had believed she was safely in custody. How could he have anticipated—how could anyone have anticipated—that she would escape again? There was a terrible inevitability to the tragedy of Royce and Edith.

❧ Forty-six ❧

SNOW FLURRIES whirled from the winter sky as Jane paid the taxi driver in front of the Kingsleys' mews house. Strange, she thought, but she felt no pang of regret for the happy hours she'd spent here with Blair and Colin. Time and tide had carried her far beyond those days.

Blair opened the door and took her coat and hat. He ushered her into the sitting room. "Thank you for coming, Jane. I need to talk to you privately before you go up to see Claudia."

"How is she?"

"Well . . . everyone but me thinks she's doing much better. Here, sit down for a minute and let me explain."

Jane took the chair he offered, still wondering what she was doing here. Did Blair expect her to comfort Claudia? Or worse, nurse her through yet another psychosomatic illness? Jane had cared for too many desperately ill and dying children to feel the concern for a pampered rich friend that had once dominated her life. Besides, it was time for Claudia to put the past behind her and tell herself, as Jane had, that they had both lost Royce a long time before Edith plunged a hatpin into his heart.

Blair said, "I suppose Claudia's malaise began when Colin was kidnapped. She became withdrawn, wouldn't eat, started taking a sedative that made her lethargic. Mother wanted to take her to St. Agnes so that a psychiatrist could help her. I was against it, but apparently Claudia began acting irrationally one day while I was in town and Mother insisted she be examined by a doctor. Claudia became distraught and, terrified that she was to be committed, came to London to me."

He paused. "When she arrived here she was quite ill. She'd caught a bad cold. Almost immediately there was the shock of hearing about your brother's death, which seemed to push her toward the brink of a breakdown. She began acting childlike, and frankly I feared a doctor might indeed tell me she'd lost her mind. So I kept her here in London and took care of her myself. When she began to improve I sent for Colin and his nanny to come for short visits, and that seemed to help. But then Edith was convicted of your brother's murder, and instead of feeling relieved that the woman would no longer pose a threat to us, Claudia suffered a relapse. She's slipped into a melancholy state that deeply disturbs me."

"Perhaps you should reconsider your mother's suggestion about having a psychiatrist talk to her?" Jane suggested. "I know most people believe there's some sort of stigma attached to mental illness, but—"

"Jane," he interrupted swiftly, "if you would just try to find out what is troubling her. I feel you might learn more than a stranger. If, after talking with her, you still recommend psychiatric care, then I'll see to it. Please—I'm at my wit's end to know what to do to help her. She speaks of you constantly; she respects you more than anyone else on earth. If anyone can bring her out of her depression, I believe you can."

"Blair, I'll talk to her, but I'm not making any promises."

He breathed a sigh of relief. "Good, good. She's expecting you. She's in the front bedroom." He hesitated. "Jane, I should warn you . . . she speaks of death and oblivion, of suicide as a merciful release."

Jane digested this silently for a moment, then went up to Claudia's room.

For a moment Jane stood in the semidark room staring at the stick-thin figure in the bed, at her shrunken features and wispy hair that in the flickering firelight looked almost white. Only those large blue-violet eyes were familiar. "Hello, Claudia," she said softly.

"Oh, Jane!" Claudia's lip trembled, and tears brimmed over and slipped down her hollow cheeks. "I'm so glad you came. . . . I've wanted to talk to you for ages, but Blair has kept me a prisoner here. He wants me all to himself and won't let anyone else near me. I begged him to send for you, but he wouldn't."

"I'm here now, Claudia, and Blair sent for me. He told me Colin has been to see you, too."

"Only for an hour or so, and Blair stayed with us the whole time. And you wouldn't be here if I hadn't threatened to kill myself."

Jane said carefully, "Then you weren't really thinking of suicide?"

Claudia dabbed her eyes with a lace-edged handkerchief. "You should have let me drown when the *Lusitania* was sunk."

"Sometimes I wish I had," Jane said matter-of-factly.

Claudia gave a tremulous smile. "You're quite awful, you know. I think that's why I love you."

Jane pulled a chair close to the bed and sat down. "What are we going to do with you, Claudia?"

She rose up from her mound of pillows, her eyes bright with tears. "Take me home. I must go home. Blair says I'm better off here, but I must . . . go . . . home."

"Claudia, you know that Blair is going to turn Willowford over to the National Trust, don't you? Even if you went back there, I don't know how long you could stay."

"I don't want to go to Willowford. I want to go home—to Rathbourne Abbey."

Jane was taken aback. "To the abbey? But why? You've hated the abbey ever since you first arrived there. Besides, Marrick sold it to Frank Allegro."

"I know that. Frank controls my trust fund. Blair dislikes him because he thinks Frank's in love with me. He refuses to let me talk to Frank or go near the abbey. But I must go home, I must!"

"Why, Claudia? What's behind this compelling urge to go back to a place you claimed to hate?"

Claudia twisted her handkerchief. "I can't explain. . . . I just feel that I'll be able to find the answer there."

"The answer to what?"

"To the riddle of Royce and me. I never told you . . . but we used to meet, sometimes in the summerhouse, sometimes in the nuns' warming room. I need to go back there, Jane."

Jane picked up Claudia's hand and held it. "Don't let Royce haunt all the rest of your days, Claudia. He's dead, gone, and so is all the pain he caused you. Put it behind you. Don't perpetuate it by returning to places you once went to with him. I've grieved for him, too, in spite of all he did, and when the sadness gets to be too much I remind myself that he was a conscienceless cad and the world is better off without him—and so should you."

"You don't understand, Jane. I . . . I died with him. I feel . . . nothing. When Colin was here . . . he looked so much like Royce that I could do nothing but weep. Did Blair tell you that?"

Jane shook her head. "Listen to me, Claudia. You're too wrapped up with yourself and your own grief. If you'd get out and do something for somebody else for a change you wouldn't have time to brood. Come and spend an hour with me at the children's home, and I guarantee your own problems will seem so trivial you'll be ashamed of yourself. Look, I have to go. We're shorthanded, and Daisy . . . but you don't know Daisy, do you? She's a baby girl I'm especially fond of, and she's been ill."

She stood up. "Please think about what I said. Put Royce out of your mind and get busy doing something for others. You could start with your husband and son. If you need to talk to me, make the effort to come and see me for a change. Sometimes I feel my whole life has been punctuated by visits to your bedside. I don't mean to sound unsympathetic, Claudia . . . but most of your woes you bring on yourself."

Claudia regarded her sadly. "I wish you could understand . . . Jane, please, before you go, ask Blair to let me go home to the abbey for a while. Just for a few days."

"You're a grown woman, Claudia. Get up out of the damn bed, get dressed, and go to the abbey if that's what you want."

Claudia began to cry again, and Jane said hastily, "All right, I'll talk to him."

She went down the stairs, feeling frustration and a measure of guilt. Had she been too hard on Claudia?

Blair awaited her in the sitting room. He presided over a brandy decanter, but Jane said, "I can't stay, Blair. All I could get out of Claudia is that she wants to go to the abbey for a while."

"But Frank Allegro is back in New York and the abbey is temporarily closed. I told Claudia that. He left a caretaker in charge. She can't stay there."

"Couldn't you take her for a brief visit, then? Frank wouldn't mind, I'm sure."

Blair was silent, considering. "We'd have to stay at Willowford, at least overnight, and for all intents and purposes Willowford is no longer ours. Mother and Colin and his nanny are still there with a housekeeper, occupying a couple of rooms on the second floor, but they're preparing to move into a small country house. Well, yes, I suppose Claudia could visit the abbey if she has her heart set on it."

"Probably a few hours in the abbey in winter will be all it takes to send her back here. Claudia is always cold, under the best of circumstances, and if the abbey has been closed for a while, it will be as chilly as a tomb."

How beautiful the snow was, Claudia thought. Strange that always before she had been repelled by the coldness of it and had never noticed how the sunlight glittered on the pure white drifts that blanketed the lawns or how proudly the trees wore their opaline mantles.

She felt a tremendous sense of peace and tranquillity as she inhaled the frosty air. Her feet sank silently into the soft snow, and it was like walking on goose down. Ahead the tower and parapet walk lay golden in the winter sun, standing watchfully beside the abbey as they had for centuries. There was comfort in the knowledge that man's creations endured beyond the puny limits of his life span.

The tower door yielded reluctantly to her straining hands, and she was too winded by the effort for a minute to climb the stone stairs. Pausing to catch her breath, she reassured herself that all was in order.

She had spent a pleasant hour with Colin, assured him that she loved him, and given him a miniature of herself encased in a gold watch fob. "When you're old enough to wear a pocket watch, my darling," she had told him, "you'll be able to pop it open and see that I am always with you. Now this is our little secret. We'll hide your watch fob under your toys, and we won't tell Daddy or Gladys about it."

Lady Kingsley had been icily polite, but Claudia had overheard her asking Blair how long it would be before Colin moved into the mews house. Blair had answered that he intended for Colin to return to London with them in a few days.

Claudia had walked slowly through the abbey, then donned the sable coat she had bought with Marrick's allowance before leaving London, and gone down to the nuns' quarters. Royce's presence was everywhere. His clear gray eyes followed her accusingly as she strolled through the warming room, and his breath felt cold upon her cheek as she stood next to the great urn.

She had to go to him. She had to tell him she was sorry for what she had done. She had to spend eternity with her beloved.

When her breathing returned to normal, Claudia climbed the stone staircase to the top of the tower. The decision she had made was the right one. She had weighed all of the options and decided that this was best not only for her but for everyone else as well. It was true that Edith was paying for her crime, but then, Edith had already committed murder. Nothing would be gained by confessing that she, and not Edith, had killed Royce. How could Colin live with the knowledge that his mother had killed his father? Yet Claudia knew she had to be punished. She had spent many hours in a state of mystical communication

with her own dead mother, her ghost mother, and they had
agreed this was the answer.

As she stepped out onto the parapet walk Claudia felt a sense
of happy anticipation. Why, not only would she be reunited
with Royce, but also, at long last, she would meet her ghost
mother!

The bitingly cold air almost took her breath away. She had
to hurry, before Blair came looking for her.

Halfway along the walk she stopped and climbed up onto the
stone balustrade, swaying as the wind caught her coat and
dress.

For a moment she looked at the white world below, so pure,
so innocent under its blanket of sparkling snow, like a great
ivory cathedral beckoning her to come to her reward.

Then she stepped daintily into the pristine air and for a few
seconds flew like an angel.

❦ Forty-seven ❧

JANE WAS DOWN on her hands and knees coaxing Daisy to take
her first tentative steps when one of the sisters came looking
for her.

"Nurse Weatherly? You have a visitor. A Mr. Kingsley.
He's waiting in the common room."

Sweeping Daisy up into her arms, Jane made her way to
the common room. Today was her day off, and she hoped
Blair had not come with another summons to Claudia's
sickbed.

He stood rigidly erect, hat in hand, and his poor scarred face
looked gray. She knew at once that something was terribly
wrong. "Blair . . . it must be bad news to bring you here. It
isn't Colin, is it?"

"Colin's fine. I'm afraid it's Claudia." There was no doubt from Blair's stricken demeanor that, whatever had happened to Claudia, this time it was no ordinary bout of hypochondria. Jane thought, panicked, Claudia's dead and we didn't believe she was really ill.

"Please sit down, Jane."

Daisy's tiny arms fastened themselves securely around Jane's neck, and she pressed the baby close, the sweet warmth of her little body a connection to life and hope, an antidote to whatever horror was about to be relayed.

"I had no idea what she intended to do. No one could have foreseen . . . You must tell yourself that, Jane, or you'll go out of your mind, as I almost have," Blair choked out the words. "I believed enough time had gone by that she had accepted Royce's death. I mean, one would have thought that if she was going to do something like this she would have done it immediately afterward, not now—"

"Blair, for God's sake! What happened to her?"

"We went to the abbey, and she went out along the parapet walk—"

"Oh, dear God!" Jane breathed. "She didn't jump?"

Blair nodded, a single tear rolling slowly down his cheek.

Daisy tugged on a fistful of Jane's hair, but she didn't feel it. "Is she . . . dead?"

"No, she's alive. The doctors say her back is broken, that she'll never walk again."

"Oh, poor Claudia," Jane whispered. "Poor, poor Claudia."

"We haven't told her yet that she won't walk again, but I think she knows. Oddly enough, she seems calmer now, more in control of her emotions, than she was before. She said something to me that broke my heart. She said, 'Ah, so this is to be my punishment.' I suppose she was referring to her deception when she married Ro while carrying your brother's child."

"Will you ever tell her that Ro was killed on the Somme, that you are not her husband?"

"No, I don't think so. There's no point, is there? I shall devote the rest of my life to taking care of her."

"I should have realized what she was going to do when she

said she wanted to go to the abbey," Jane said raggedly. "She was always morbidly fascinated by the story of the nun who jumped from the parapet walk."

"Jane, you couldn't possibly have anticipated this; no one could have. Please don't blame yourself. I was there with her, and yet I couldn't prevent it."

"What about Colin? How is he taking this? Is he all right?"

"He's been a little brick. We told him his mother fell accidentally. Outside of the family and Frank and you, no one will be told she tried to commit suicide."

"Frank? He was at the abbey? I thought he was in New York."

"He arrived—shortly before I found her lying in the snow."

"If Claudia's up to it, I'd like to visit her," Jane said.

"I'm sure she'd like that."

"Which hospital is she in?"

"Well . . . as a matter of fact she isn't in hospital; she's still at the abbey. It was rather a coincidence, really, that Frank Allegro arrived when he did. He brought in a whole team of doctors and nurses and turned a portion of one floor of the abbey into a miniature orthopedic ward. She seems content to stay there, and he's generously allowed Mother and Colin and me to move in with her. Frank has to be in America much of the time, and he insists we make the abbey our home for as long as we wish. He's a very decent sort, isn't he? Generous to a fault."

"Yes, he is."

"I must be getting back. Come and see us whenever you can." Blair started for the door, then turned and looked back at her. "By the way, Lord Marrick is on his way home from Africa. Claudia wanted to see him—to make her peace with him, I believe."

So nothing had changed, Jane thought. Months of building a life centered on work that she found fulfilling, on giving all of her love and affection to the children and, above all, to little Daisy, had been to no avail. If the mere mention of his name could evoke a yearning so powerful that she was almost paralyzed by it, what would happen if she actually saw him again?

No, she couldn't let herself slip back to where she had been before, in that state of hopeless, helpless love for him. If she did, all of the painful healing of the past months would have been for nothing. She must not see him. Hadn't he made it very clear that there would be no other opportunities for them to come together? Their time had passed; it couldn't be retrieved. He was returning to England to see Claudia, not her.

Jane decided to go to see Claudia immediately, before Marrick arrived.

The reverend mother was sympathetic when she explained, and the following day Jane caught a train to Upper Oakleigh.

Claudia was in her old room, but the doorway had been widened to accommodate a wheelchair. A uniformed nurse occupied the room next door, and as Jane was ushered into Claudia's room she saw that a hospital bed and other equipment had been installed. The room was filled with hothouse flowers.

"Hello, my dear friend," Claudia said from the bed. "So sweet of you to come. You look well, and so pretty and pink-cheeked. Is it frightfully cold out?"

Jane blinked. Could this serene and composed young woman be the neurotic Claudia of old? Surely she had indeed died when she jumped from the parapet walk, to be replaced by this changeling. Jane kissed her cool cheek, noting that her pale hair, restored to its former glossy state, was now cut in one of the new short styles, which emphasized her fragile features and made her eyes look larger than ever. Claudia looked rested, tranquil, beautiful.

"I suppose I should ask how you are," Jane said, handing her a ribbon-tied box. "But you look so well it seems unnecessary."

"A present! How lovely!" Claudia untied the pink ribbon. Inside the box was a satin and lace sachet, delicately embroidered and filled with dried lavender. "Oh, Jane, it's beautiful, thank you."

"I wish I could tell you I made it for you myself, but I frankly don't have the time. One of the novices made it." She glanced about the room. "It looks as though Frank and Blair have provided everything you could possibly need."

"Yes," Claudia said softly. "It's strange, isn't it, how things worked out? Did Blair tell you he's selling the newspaper and the mews house? Frank offered him the position of estate steward here at the abbey, and Blair accepted. So we'll be staying. Blair was never really happy having to face people in town, you know. We'll both be able to shut out the world again and live in blissful seclusion."

"Estate steward?" Jane's heart sank for Blair. But of course he would want to spend all of his time with Claudia.

Claudia merely smiled. "Are you going to chastise me for what I did?"

"No. But I am going to ask why."

"I had to. I couldn't live with my conscience. I had to be punished, but I couldn't punish the innocent along with me—Colin, Blair. I do realize that now—that I was seeking punishment. For a time I thought I wanted to join him, but I don't feel that way anymore."

"What on earth are you talking about, Claudia?"

"Didn't you know? Couldn't you guess? It was I who killed your brother. Now I am paying for my crime, gladly, willingly. My punishment is fitting, just."

Jane sank into the nearest chair, all of her relief at Claudia's progress evaporating. So it was all an illusion, after all. She had retreated into fantasy. "Claudia . . . I know Royce's murder was a shock to you. But you didn't kill him. Edith did."

Claudia regarded her with forbearance. "Don't worry, I shan't admit my guilt to anyone but you. But I owe you the truth. You know, when I came to my senses and realized I wasn't dead after all, at first I was beside myself. I swore I'd find a way to kill myself. But then I realized that a swift oblivion would have been too easy for me and too difficult for everyone else. I shan't ever leave this bed, you know. Oh, perhaps eventually I'll be able to move about in a wheel-chair, but I'll never walk again. They've been careful not to tell me, but I knew right away what my punishment was to be. Oddly enough, knowing that I shall be helpless for the rest of my life brought me a strange sort of comfort. Oh, Janey, don't look at me like that! I'm not mad, honestly."

Jane swallowed hard. There was no doubting Claudia's sincerity. She really believed she had killed Royce. Perhaps, Jane thought, it was her way of dealing with his murder . . . and with her own attempted suicide.

"Claudia . . . swear to me you won't tell any of this to anybody but me?"

"Of course—I just told you that, didn't I? But I had to confess to *you*; you're my best friend, and you were his sister, his only blood relation."

Jane was in a silent battle with herself. Should she tell Blair of Claudia's grisly flight of fancy and suggest psychiatric help, or would it be better to leave Claudia alone and allow her to deal with her grief in a way that obviously was working?

"I must rest now, Janey. I tire so easily, and I want to be alert when Colin comes to have tea with me. I'll see you at dinner, yes?"

"No, I must get back to town. Daisy needs me. . . . Did I tell you about Daisy?" Jane asked distractedly.

Claudia closed her eyes, her face serenely lovely. "You must bring her to see me. On your way out, would you tell Blair he may come and read to me while I fall asleep? You know, I think he's secretly relieved that I can't ever run away from him again. . . ."

The winter was a hard one, and there was an epidemic of colds and bronchitis among the children. Hot water pipes in the high-ceilinged dormitories did little to dispel the damp chill, and the sisters had lost their angel of mercy, who had gone to live abroad, leaving a severe gap in their charitable contributions. Blankets were wearing thin; warm clothing and shoes for the older children were difficult to come by. The younger ones wore outgrown clothing.

In spite of all the shortages, Daisy was thriving. Jane would wrap an enormous shawl around her body, forming a sling in which to carry Daisy, so that the baby girl could be warm and close as she went on her rounds.

On a bitter-cold February morning Jane finished checking on

the babies and went to the common room to have a warming cup of tea. She sat at the scrubbed wooden table with Daisy on her lap, ignoring a mug of tea as she dangled a homemade rag doll before the baby's delighted gaze.

"Hello, Jane," a deeply resonant voice said behind her. She turned slowly. Marrick stood in the doorway.

Her first thought was that he looked exactly the same. His tropical tan, impeccably tailored suit and overcoat, the fine kid gloves he held, all spoke of health and wealth and were in such sharp contrast to the appearance of everyone around her that Jane was astonished to find that she was not bowled over by his sudden appearance. Instead, all of her old class resentment came rushing back. Picking up Daisy, Jane stood up to face him. "Has something happened to Claudia?"

"No, she's still reigning supreme over her subjects at the abbey."

"Then I hope you came to make a charitable contribution."

"I came to see you, but I'll pay for the privilege if I have to. Tell me what's needed here, and then tell me what you need personally."

"We need blankets, clothes, shoes, and more cots. As for me"—she looked enviously at the fur-lined kid gloves he held—"I've got chilblains on both hands."

Marrick chuckled and tossed his gloves on the table. "They're yours. The other items will be here tomorrow. Now put that child down and let me take you out to lunch. No, don't argue. I've already spoken to the reverend mother, and she's assigned one of the novices to take your place for an hour or two."

"I'd sell my soul for a nice hot sit-down lunch," Jane said, "but couldn't we take Daisy with us?"

"No," Marrick said firmly. "I don't want you distracted. We have important matters to discuss."

There had been a time when Jane would have been embarrassed, shamed even, by her threadbare coat and battered hat, but as she was seated at a table at the Savoy she felt a certain perverse satisfaction at the way well-dressed diners averted their eyes. Marrick, however, appeared to be oblivious to this, and to the disdainful look on the face of a hovering waiter.

Jane was so hungry she fell upon the bread before the rest of their order arrived. Marrick watched, his dark eyes twinkling as they had in countless dreams.

"What are you grinning at?" Jane demanded. "I've been up since five this morning, and I'm starving." She peered into the empty bread basket. "Could we get some more, do you think?"

Marrick managed to summon a waiter by merely raising an eyebrow. He reached across the table and picked up her hand, gently rubbing the frostbitten joints. "Don't fill up on bread. The roast beef will be here any minute."

She withdrew her hand, suddenly seeing the chilblains and calluses through his eyes. "I didn't expect to see you again."

"Nor I you. But here we are."

"Why did you come?"

"I suppose to satisfy my curiosity about how you're faring— no, more than that, to find out why you insist upon doing penance. Have you converted to Catholicism, by the way?"

"No. Well . . . the nuns sort of took me to be Roman Catholic. But I'm not doing penance. I get as much from taking care of the children as I give."

"So this work you're doing has nothing to do with any feelings of guilt about Claudia?"

Jane sighed. "You've been talking to Blair, and he told you that I suggested he take Claudia to the abbey. And you think I feel guilty because she . . . fell from the parapet walk."

"She didn't fall; she jumped."

"How did you know?"

"There was no reason for her to go up there on a freezing cold day unless she had decided to make her grand gesture. Jane, I told her many times—every time she mentioned the story of the nun who supposedly killed herself by jumping from the parapet walk—that a fall of that distance probably wouldn't kill anyone. I believe I told you the same thing. Claudia wanted what she now has—everyone dancing attendance on her, everyone sympathizing with her, doting on her, and expecting nothing from her in return. What we have is a classic case of the tyranny of the weak."

Jane stared at him. "She paid a terrible price for what you

call her grand gesture." Still, as she reflected on his words, an almost imperceptible burden seemed to be lifted from her shoulders.

The food arrived, but Marrick didn't seem interested in it. He waited until she had eaten and then said quietly, "I was hoping you'd feel the same sense of time lost and opportunity wasted as I do, that the realization that we could have been together all these months would be the stimulus you need to admit that you care for me as much as I care for you."

"I do care for you," Jane said. "More than you know. I went away because I was frightened. I thought I would lose you, so I made damn sure I did. There, make sense of that if you can. Why are we humans such idiots, Marrick?"

"My given name is Leith. Will you ever call me that, do you think?"

"Probably not. You see, everything's changed now. There's my work, the children, Daisy. I'd never desert them."

He leaned forward. "The reverend mother told me that her chief charity organizer has abandoned the home. Who do you suppose was more important to the children—a woman who provided the wherewithal to buy food and clothes or a skivvy who changes nappies and scrubs floors?"

Jane jumped to her feet and flung down her napkin.

"Jane, wait! I haven't finished what I was going to say. Damn, I always choose the wrong approach with you—"

But Jane was already running for the door.

Jane awakened the following morning to the sound of strange male voices, the thumping of furniture and boxes, the clatter of heavy boots on the bare wood stairway of the home.

She scrambled out of bed, pulled on her dressing gown, and hurried out onto the landing, almost colliding with a beaming reverend mother who was directing an army of deliverymen. "Take the cots into the ward on your left. The blankets and bedding can go into the storeroom for the time being. No, don't bring the clothes boxes up; we need to sort through them. Ah, good morning, Jane. 'Tis a fine brisk morning, is it not?"

"I must have overslept. I'm sorry."

"We let you sleep in, dear. Sister Vida turned off your alarm clock and took care of the babies."

"But why? And what's all this?" Jane gestured toward the boxes being borne past her.

"All donated by your friend Lord Marrick, God bless him. Oh, yes—and there's something for you and Daisy in the common room. No, no, my good man, don't leave that here on the landing; it belongs in the storeroom."

Jane dressed hurriedly and went down the stairs in a daze, dodging a seemingly endless parade of deliverymen.

The first thing she saw upon entering the common room was a huge bouquet of hothouse roses surrounded by a dozen smaller pots of blooming bulbs—hyacinth, narcissus, crocus—creating a splash of color on the bare wooden table. Two parcels, one large and one small, lay on a nearby chair. The smaller was labeled "Jane Weatherly." Jane tore open the larger box marked "Daisy Macklefield."

The first yielded a warm woolen coat with matching leggings and bonnet for Daisy, along with three dresses, shoes, a beautiful goose-down comforter, and an enormous teddy bear. Turning to the second parcel, Jane unwrapped a pair of ladies' gloves and a jar of chilblain ointment. She grinned.

As the day wore on, the donations continued to arrive. Boxes and boxes of food, toys and games, even a carpet for the common room, and almost every hour, more flowers for Jane. But no word from Marrick.

That evening Jane was again summoned to the common room, now warmed by a blazing fire on the hearth, thanks to a generous delivery of coal. Marrick sat at the modest wooden table, now groaning under the weight of bowls of out-of-season fruit, cheeses, fruitcakes, and a steaming tureen. He lifted the lid of the latter, and the aroma of beef stew drifted appealingly into the room.

"Will you join me for dinner, Jane? The chef at my club felt that a hearty stew would be suitable for the children."

Jane took the chair he held for her. "Isn't all this a bit much, even for you?"

"Not if it got your attention."

"It got the attention of the entire parish."

"Perhaps you'd be good enough to serve the stew while I finish what I tried to say yesterday?"

Jane picked up the silver ladle, her mouth watering.

Marrick continued, "In my clumsy fashion yesterday, I was attempting to point out that there are other ways to help your orphans besides doing menial work."

"There's no such thing as menial work," Jane interrupted, "if it makes a child's life bearable. But in any case, I'm here as a nurse, to take care of the children who are ill. Only there's so much to do for all of them . . ."

"I understand perfectly. I also spoke with the reverend mother, who told me of your attachment to little Daisy. What I wanted to suggest to you is that the orphanage desperately needs to replace its former patroness. As Lady Marrick you would be able to fill that vacancy nicely—and as a married woman you could, if you wished, adopt Daisy. You could even, if you insisted, spend some time here nursing the sick children. Naturally I will expect a great deal of your time and attention myself, and your companionship on my excursions to warmer climes. Frankly, although I love my country dearly, the winter climate does chill old bones. . . . Oh, excuse me, I didn't intend to call attention to my advancing years, since my age seems to be your only reason for refusing me. But as you can see, I have deteriorated hardly at all since our last meeting."

Jane slowly put down the ladle, some of the warm glow she had been feeling fading. There was a dismaying hint of a suggestion of love for sale in this proposal, an undercurrent that whispered, "If you marry me you'll be rich," that sullied what should have been beautiful.

Angry, she rose to her feet. "Are you saying that all of your gifts were simply a scheme to make me feel grateful to you? That you were trying to *buy* me?"

One black eyebrow arched. "With a pair of gloves and a jar of chilblain ointment?"

"Dammit, Marrick, you know what I mean. You did all of this as a show of your wealth. You don't give a damn about the children."

He was on his feet, too, and he caught her wrist in a painfully tight grip. "I care about *you*. I care about you as I've never cared about anything else since the day I was born. My God, Jane, I got rid of everything—the abbey, the coffee plantation in Kenya, all my foreign investments. I wanted a fresh start, a new life, with you. I thought if I severed all ties to the past we could build a new life together, that you would dismantle all the barriers you'd erected between us and accept me simply as a man who loves you, who wants to spend the rest of his life with you."

Jane stared at him. The mocking, arrogant lord of the manor was gone, and she wondered if he had ever existed outside of her own imagination. What she witnessed now was the naked need of a man for a woman, a love that remained as steadfast as the man himself, and she felt overwhelming tenderness and a powerful urge to nurture that love. She had suppressed her own love for him for so long that now it seemed to flow from her in an unquenchable tide. For a moment she was so overcome she could not speak.

Marrick's fingers curled around hers and drew her hand to his heart. "I was not, as you put it, making a show of my wealth with the gifts to the orphanage. I was courting you, trying to get your attention, striving to prove my love. If this was the wrong method, and if I said all the wrong things, at least give me credit for honorable motives, if misguided actions. Jane, you'll never know how many times I've cursed the stupid pride that made me say things to you that were no more than a safety net against rejection. If I was sarcastic or flippant, you see, I was leaving a back door open through which I could escape if you turned me down."

"Marrick, I—"

"Before you say a word, Jane, I must caution you that I intend to do everything in my power to persuade you to be my wife. I won't give up. I'll never give up. I love you too much."

She placed one finger against his lips. "Don't ever stop. Don't ever give up."

He caught his breath. "Do you mean it?"

"I love you with all my heart. I want to be your wife."

His hand went to the back of her head to pull her face close to his, and their lips met in a long kiss. Then he wrapped his arms around her and she pressed closer, feeling his strength, the comforting bulwark of his body, but above all the soaring passion his nearness aroused in her.

She whispered, "Oh, Leith, my darling, I love you, but I'm

so afraid. . . . We argue so much, our views on so many things are poles apart, and I don't think I'll ever be able to change, and I'm sure you won't. What sort of a married life will we have?"

He laughed softly. "An exciting one that I can't wait to begin." Holding her away from him, he said, "Put on your coat and hat and don't forget your gloves. I'll have to use my own ring, and even then it will be a job getting it on past your chilblains. We'll get you your own ring later."

"What are you talking about?"

"About going straight down to the Registry Office and getting married."

"Now?"

"Now. I have a special license in my pocket, and I won't be put off another minute. You might change your mind again."

Jane smiled happily. "I won't change my mind. I believe there may be a law against refusing to let dreams come true."

The implication of his statement struck her then, and she jerked away from his seeking lips. "You already have a license? You were damn sure of yourself, weren't you? You might as well know right now that I won't stand for you telling me what to do or when to do it."

"But, my dearest darling, there will be times—now, for instance—when I feel my decision is in your best interests—"

They both began to speak at once just as, somewhere beyond the Spartan room in which they stood, the chapel bells called the sisters to prayer, and the sound seemed to be a gentle rebuke.

They stopped speaking and stared at each other. Marrick murmured, "Shall we make a special effort not to argue until after the ceremony?"

"Which will take place tomorrow, after I've bought a new dress."

"Today, Jane. We'll buy a dress on the way."

"You really are the most insufferable, domineering, arrogant—"

"And you, my dear, are the most stubborn, infuriatingly opinionated—"

How insignificant their argument seemed when, hours later, they closed their bedroom door on the rest of the world and

Jane lay in her husband's arms for the first time, feeling fulfilled in a way she could never have imagined. With his mouth close to hers and their hearts beating in unison, if she felt a fleeting regret, it was only that they had waited so long for this moment.

KATHERINE SINCLAIR

JOURNEYS OF THE HEART

Intelligent and passionate, two young women share hopes and desires far beyond the restrictions of remote turn-of-the-century Cornwall.

From the moment Joanna confides to her lifelong friend Megan that she is pregnant by her brother-in-law, both girls are flung on a tide of misunderstanding and danger that will tear them apart and send them headlong into the unknown, guided only by the dreams they once shared.

Joanna – is saved from certain death by the care of a man whose dark secrets match her own. He will come to rely all too heavily on her undiscovered strengths.

Megan – when her dream of becoming a doctor is snatched away, it seems, for ever, she finds herself at the mercy of the one man more dangerous to her than anything else.

HODDER AND STOUGHTON PAPERBACKS

KATHERINE SINCLAIR

FAR HORIZONS

A glorious journey to the ends of the earth, where every woman's dreams come true.

They were three very different women, each searching for happiness in the changing world of the nineteenth century.

Bethany, unjustly sentenced and transported to Australia, forced to leave her baby daughter in England.

Mary, trapped in a loveless marriage, seeing hope and desire in the eyes of her husband's business partner.

Alison, hidden away with Bethany's child and a broken heart, dreaming of independence in a man's world.

Three women, clinging to their dreams of love and freedom. Women determined never to surrender.

HODDER AND STOUGHTON PAPERBACKS

SARA FITZGERALD

RUMOURS

Aurore Callaghan knew how damaging words could be. She wasn't ever going to let anything hurt her that much again.

A successful lawyer now, she had waited years to find out who had tried to destroy her. At last she had discovered the truth – and she was determined that justice would be hers.

For the sake of Robert and the life they could have had together. For the child she never really knew. But most of all for the guileless young woman who disappeared in a sea of scandal half a lifetime ago.

But if revenge is sweet, how much sweeter still to find again the happiness that was so cruelly snatched away?

HODDER AND STOUGHTON PAPERBACKS